TWILIGHT PATROL

Laurence Raphael Brothers

Alban Lake Publishing

Twilight Patrol
Laurence Raphael Brothers

Twilight Patrol is a work of fiction. Names, characters, places, and incidents are products of the author's imagination. Any resemblance to actual events or persons, living or dead, is entirely coincidental.

Story copyrights owned by Laurence Raphael Brothers
Cover illustration by Clarissa C. S. Ryan

First Printing
September 2019

Alban Lake Publishing
P.O. Box 141
Colo, Iowa 50056-0141 USA
e-mail: albanlake@yahoo.com

Visit www.albanlakepublishing.com for online science fiction, fantasy, horror, scifaiku, and more. Stop by our online bookstore at www.irbstore.co for novels, magazines, anthologies, and collections. Support the small, independent press and your First Amendment rights.

For my mother, my first reader, and my father, who inspired my love of books and of writing, with all my love.

CHAPTER 1
INTRODUCTION

20 December 1917. Droglandt Field, Flanders.

Harry Tregeseal finished the inspection of his DH.5 biplane in the cockpit. He left the Vickers machine gun for last. The blued steel fixed his attention like the gaze of a snake. In a few minutes this weapon might be the difference between life and death, for him or for some enemy pilot. He'd fired hundreds of rounds in training without much thought, but here at the western front the gun gained an awful significance that he'd never considered before. Harry had spent his first week as a commissioned officer in the Royal Flying Corps without a single encounter with the enemy, and the prospect of entering combat for the first time was dominating his every waking moment.

"Lieutenant Tregeseal! Ready to go?" Harry looked up to see his flight commander, Captain Fish, standing beside his machine.

"Yes, sir!" He still felt a little strange about sirring his superior officers, as if he was an actor playing a part.

"Good job. Just follow my lead and stay in formation and you can't go wrong."

♍   ♍   ♍

Harry had both hands on the control stick as he struggled to control the DH.5. The hammering roar of his engine, the violent shaking of the airframe, and the frigid blast of the prop wash made it hard for Harry to concentrate on the enemy, three German Albatros D.III fighters cruising a mile below. The black crosses on their sky-blue wings stood out clearly against the brownish blur of the ground.

Around him five other white-painted British biplanes in a chevron formation were poised for the attack. They were flying 8,000 feet above the German lines east of Ypres, their mission to protect a flight of observers taking photographs of German artillery positions behind the lines. The Germans had spotted the observers but had failed to notice their protectors, who had been cruising above a thin layer of clouds. Harry's was the last machine on the right side of the reversed V. Captain Fish, in the lead position, banked his DH.5 hard over and dove sharply toward the Germans. The other British pilots followed instantly, and Harry swore as he found himself alone in the sky for a few frozen seconds before he was able to copy the maneuver.

The control stick shuddered in Harry's hands as he forced his biplane down into a dive. The airspeed indicator on his wooden dashboard swung past a hundred miles an hour. Harry's machine was shaking badly at well over its rated top speed and still he couldn't keep up with the other five pilots of C Flight, 32 Squadron, all of whom were veteran flyers.

The Germans had failed to notice the British patrol dipping below the clouds a mile above their heads, and now C Flight was in perfect position for a surprise attack. Except for Harry who was trailing several hundred yards behind trying to master not only his controls but his compunction. This wasn't what he'd imagined combat would be like.

The rest of C Flight was already lining up their shots, waiting for Captain Fish to open fire. There: a line of tracers from the captain's biplane, almost immediately duplicated by the other attackers. Harry was at long range himself now, but he had to hold off firing because from his trailing position he was afraid of hitting his comrades.

The center German's tail assembly was riddled in the first moments of the attack, and then as the streams of bullets traversed his fuselage black smoke started to billow from his engine. The enemy biplane nosed down into a steep dive. Harry guessed the German pilot had been shot dead in the air because he made no attempt at evasion.

With no easy way to communicate the pilots of C Flight had to make their own targeting decisions. Two followed Captain Fish in shooting at the Albatros in the middle of the group, and another two fired at the enemy on the left. Tracers converged, and Harry saw a flash from the nose of the German biplane. The Albatros fuel tank must have ruptured because a moment later a sheet of flame erupted from around the engine, washing over the cockpit and setting the upper wing plane ablaze. Even in the heat of the action Harry felt a twisting in his gut at what the enemy pilot must be going through if he was still alive.

The remaining German flyer broke hard right when he noticed the British pilots shooting at his comrades. The other DH.5 pilots had already committed to their attacks, so the final Albatros was left for Harry. He had the advantage of a tailing position, but the speed of his dive and the fragility of his biplane meant that he couldn't turn nearly as sharply as the Albatros.

The world spun crazily sideways as Harry banked, and then he pulled back on the stick as hard as he dared, feeling the vibrating protest of the aileron cables communicated through the stick to his hands. In another few seconds the German would cut the corner of his right turn too sharply to follow. Harry pressed his thumb down on the trigger button and the Vickers gun rattled, shell casings spewing off to the side. The line of tracers from the gun skewed crazily past the enemy biplane. He might have scored a few hits, but they didn't have any visible effect. Now the shots were in front, now below, and now the enemy was past him to the right: the chance was over. Harry's dive carried him rapidly below and beyond the German. Breath-ing a prayer that his wings would hold up under the strain, he pulled back on the stick to soar into a zoom climb.

If the German wanted to engage, this would have been the time. But the Albatros pilot continued his hard-right turn, heading east toward safety. With the superior power and mane-uverability of the Albatros the German would certainly have gotten away, but as Harry watched over his shoulder some crucial spar must have snapped. The entire right upper wing plane of the Albatros collapsed, breaking away from the fuse-lage. The enemy biplane flipped over and fell sideways and down, and Harry lost sight of it for a few seconds. Then, bank-ing steeply for a better view below, he saw the broken Albatros half-spiraling and half-tumbling downward, completely out of control.

The rest of the afternoon patrol was uneventful after Harry finally managed to re-join C Flight's formation. He didn't have his full attention on his flying. Harry kept replaying in his head what he imagined to be the fate of the enemy pilot he'd shot at. The German must have died with his hands on his controls, but with his wings coming apart around him there would be no way to pull out of the spin. Finally, the better part of an agonizing fifteen or twenty seconds later, a hard crash into the unfor-giving earth.

The poor bastard, Harry thought. One way or another he'd just killed the man, either by shooting away a strut or by forcing him into a maneuver that revealed some defect in the German's rigging. It was the same as if he'd just walked up to the pilot and shot him in the head with a pistol. The whole thing made him sick to think about it, now that he'd participated in the carnage.

Harry only came back to himself climbing down from the cockpit back at 32 Squadron's home aerodrome, Droglandt Field, a converted farm not far west of Ypres. In retrospect he was pleased with himself for managing a good landing without much conscious thought. He found it difficult enough to land cleanly at the best of times.

Droglandt Field had the benefit of a few permanent stone and timber buildings formerly part of the farm, but otherwise it was the usual Royal Flying Corps western front airfield, with two big canvas-clad A-frame hangars to keep the aeroplanes out of the weather, an array of half-cylinder Nissen huts for housing, and a cluster of flimsy canvas-roofed wooden structures used for storage and for overflow quarters for some of the unluckier enlisted men.

Just now the field was also home to a flock of forlorn-looking hooded crows that must have been displaced from some other customary winter haven by the fighting. If they were expecting to find much at Droglandt their hopes had been dashed, as apart from a little grass and some tenacious fast-growing brambles the farm's crops had been cut back years ago to make the airfield's landing surface. A few of the men had been feeding the crows scraps and a plaintive cawing could often be heard from here and there around the aerodrome.

The other pilots of C Flight were already standing in a cluster around Captain Fish when Harry clambered down from his cockpit on the field by the hangar. The flight commander left the other men and walked over to Harry, holding out his hand. Harry shook it numbly.

"Not bad," said Fish. "Perhaps next time we'll do that on purpose."

"Sir?"

"Leave someone behind on the dive, don't you know? To clean up."

Harry flushed. "I'm sorry. I should have been in formation."

"Not to worry," said Fish, smiling. "Happens to everyone at first. I take it you shot down your man though. Just as well you came in late. We would never have been able to re-engage after that godawful dive."

"I think he just broke a strut on his own," said Harry. "He was turning very hard when it happened, and my last shot at him was a good ten seconds before that."

"Well, none of the rest of us saw it. We were too busy hoping our bl—hoping our blessed wings wouldn't snap off recovering from the dive. I think we're the last squadron at the front flying these DH.5 death-traps. But if the observers saw your man go down, it'll be a solo kill for you so long as you're sure you got a few shots in. Otherwise, too bad."

The idea of being credited for a kill was appalling now,

though for the last week Harry had been hungry for his first combat action.

"Frankly sir," said Harry, "I'd just as soon not count it for myself, unless you think it's good for the squadron. I was out of position, and if I did get a few shots in, they just went through his fabric."

Captain Fish squinted at him for a moment. Harry wondered what he was seeing in his face.

"He would have shot you down if he had the chance, you know," said the captain. "And if we hadn't been there, they would have gotten some of our observers, more than likely."

Christ, thought Harry, he'd stepped in it now. The captain thought he was a coward.

"Yes, sir," said Harry, fumbling for what he thought the proper response should be. "I know it, and you're quite right. I'd shoot at him again, and I'll aim better next time, too. It's just... I hate to claim credit for a mistake."

"Don't worry about that," said Captain Fish, and Harry almost sighed in relief. He wasn't being blamed for that last remark. *Next time keep your mouth shut, you fool*, he thought.

"Just be greedy like the rest of us," said the captain. "Who knows but you might have nicked a strut or cut a cable with one of your shots, and that's why he folded up."

Harry nodded, and Fish patted him on the shoulder. "This was your first real action, wasn't it? Take some time for yourself, now. We've got nothing scheduled till afternoon tomorrow. Looks like B Flight has managed something particularly fine, so we'll be having a spot of entertainment after dinner."

The other pilots of C Flight offered Harry handshakes and smiles, and at last he turned away to go through his post-flight inspection with the sense of having dodged a bullet.

Harry had flown a dozen uneventful patrols and escort jobs in his first days with 32 Squadron. He'd wondered how he'd react to actual combat, what he'd think of it. Now he had his answer: sick at heart. At least he hadn't funked out in the air. He'd got his wind up after the fact. He remembered thinking that Lady Macbeth's horror at imagining a bloodstain on her hand was silly when first he read the play in school, but now he understood her feelings all too well.

Harry heard a few words of congratulation during dinner, but most of the evening passed for him in gloomy introspection. He was only roused from his self-involvement by a general call to celebration later that night that brought all the pilots together.

♍   ♍   ♍

The pilots' club-room hut was sharp-edged, glittering, and loud with the revelry of a binge night. As a newcomer to the squadron Harry was on the fringe of the party, but he wasn't too upset as they had broken out the good champagne and he had a mild, pleasant buzz. Also to the good, the pilots' chatter had been distracting him from the black mood he'd been in since returning from the afternoon patrol.

The pilots of B and C Flights were celebrating the fifth victory of Lieutenant Tyrrell of B Flight (A Flight was scheduled for dawn patrol and had retired after just a few drinks). The achievement no longer merited a line in the London Gazette as it would have two years before, but it was a good excuse for a night of drinking.

The new ace recounted the course of his dogfight once again, moving his hands around to indicate the positions of the aeroplanes.

"Ha ha, well done, very well done indeed." Captain Pearson, commander of B Flight, poured yet another glass of Veuve Clicquot (that was what the label said it was, anyway) and slid it to Tyrrell across the makeshift bar.

Tyrrell nodded and downed the drink in a gulp. He turned pale and staggered, putting his hand down heavily on the bar to steady himself.

Captain Pearson noticed Tyrrell's pallor. He slapped Tyrrell on the back and said "Well, well, old man! Perhaps we've had enough jollity for the evening, eh? Tomorrow's a new day, so I've heard."

Tyrrell gulped and visibly mastered himself. "Y-yes. One drink too many for me, I'm afraid. I must thank you all for this pleasant evening, however. Carry on, chaps, and I'll see you in the morning."

Pearson said "Enough fun for me tonight as well. Goodnight all." He put a hand casually on Tyrrell's shoulder, and began unobtrusively helping him out of the club room. The two were almost out of the room, with the remaining pilots starting a new round of drink-pouring and chatter, when the door opened.

"It's the major," someone said, and the talking stopped. Everyone turned to the door.

From what little Harry had seen of his squadron commander, Major John Russell was a capable officer. Knowing that his presence would be a constraint on a binge night the major had retired early after toasting the new ace. It was a surprise to see him return so close to midnight.

Even more surprising though was the person for whom he held the door. "A WAAC?", Harry heard someone say, "Up here near the front?"

She was slender and very tall, in a tan trench-coat, her hair pinned up under a demure but non-uniform cloche. For a woman to appear at a forward airfield at all was unprecedented, much less at the pilots' club so late at night.

Pearson stopped short when the door opened, and taken by surprise Tyrrell almost stumbled into the woman. He halted just in time, however, and stood there swaying, helplessly goggling at the unexpected female presence.

"Ah, Major, sir, what's going on?" Pearson pulled Tyrrell back and to the side, clearing the way, but Major Russell didn't reply.

The woman stepped forward into the room, scanning the assembled pilots who as a group were frozen in place in astonishment. From somewhere in the crowd a low whistle sounded, which she ignored. No doubt that was the American volunteer, Harry thought. The Yank would probably regret it the next day when the major was done with him. But what was she doing there? To his enormous surprise her gaze stopped on Harry, and she was looking him in the eyes.

"That's him, isn't it?" She pointed at Harry, speaking with a mild Scots accent.

"Indeed it is," said the major. "Lieutenant Tregeseal. My office. Now, if you please."

"Yes, sir. Of course." Harry stumbled into motion. He couldn't imagine what was going on. He hadn't said anything to anyone about how badly he was feeling about his part in today's action. Surely it wasn't obvious, was it?

"Er, Major, sir?" Captain Fish stood up from his seat at the bar.

"Yes, Will?"

"Should I..." Fish gestured uncertainly. "Is it something to do with C Flight?"

"Oh, nothing to worry about," said Major Russell. "We may have a special assignment for Tregeseal, here. I'll let you know about it tomorrow, if it turns out that way."

The sounds of revelry, somewhat muted now, resumed behind him as Harry emerged into the chill December air. A light layer of frost covered the ground here at Droglandt. When the wind was right you could smell traces of mustard gas still, months after Passchendaele, the pungent odor rolling in off the battlefield a few miles away. The brief walk to Major Russell's fieldstone administrative building served to clear Harry's head, though in truth he hadn't been drinking that much—well, not as much as Tyrrell, anyway.

He observed the Scotswoman covertly as she strode briskly in front of him at Major Russell's side. She didn't seem to be in uniform under the coat. Perhaps she wasn't a WAAC after all? But what else could she be? Surely not a war correspondent.

Major Russell unlocked the admin building and ushered them into his office, pulling the cord to turn on the unhooded bulb that hung above his desk. The building was cold at night with no fire in the hearth.

"I'd offer drinks," said Major Russell, "but I imagine the lieutenant here has already drunk his fill, and Miss Sheehy has already declined to partake."

"Yes," she said. "There's little enough time as it is. Now then, Lieutenant, are you ready to travel? How long will it take you to prepare?"

"Not long," he said, stammering slightly. "Fifteen minutes if it's urgent. But sir, ma'am, what's going on? Am I being relieved of duty here?"

"Frankly," said the major, "I don't know myself. No need to know, you understand? This is highly secret. Miss Sheehy has approval all the way from Brigade and is carrying orders from London."

"I see," said Harry slowly, "but why me, all the way out here on the front? Miss Sheehy, is it possible you've confused me with some other officer? I'm only just out of flight school, and I don't understand why anyone would want me for—for a secret mission."

She looked at him steadily for a moment before answering. "I don't think a mistake is possible," she said, "but I suppose it's just as well to be sure."

Miss Sheehy rustled a sheaf of papers out of an inner lapel pocket in her coat and flipped through them for a few seconds before finding the page. "You are Harry Tregeseal, of Tregeseal in Cornwall are you not? Of the Dancing Stones?"

"Yes, ma'am," said Harry. "But of course, I don't actually live at the stone circle. My parents' house is on the Penzance road in St. Just. It's not far from Tregeseal East."

She nodded, satisfied, then pulled a small object out of a pocket and held it up. It was a polished carnelian egg dangling from a fine gold chain. "Put out your hand," she said, swinging the blood-red egg like a pendulum. Harry reached out for it, but she pushed his hand away. "No," she said, "don't touch it. Just leave your hand where it is."

The major had a quizzical look on his face, though he didn't interrupt. The motion of the carnelian was altering. After a few seconds the pendulum's path rotated through a full ninety degrees, and now it was swinging directly in line with his hand. Miss Sheehy hadn't moved her own hand at all.

"Right," she said, putting the pendant back in a pocket. "There you are. Put your kit together. I'll have the car ready in fifteen minutes."

"What about my family? Will I be able to write letters from wherever it is I'm going?"

"Ah," said Miss Sheehy, "That you will, but the post may be a wee bit... delayed at times, shall we say. Censored, too, more than usual. I'll make sure we notify your people that your correspondence may become irregular for a while."

Harry found himself being led out of the office.

"Wait—"

The major shook his head. "Orders," he said. "Do what she says and don't ask questions. I'll tell Will you've been detached, never fear. Good luck to you, and a safe return!" He held out his hand, and Harry shook it numbly.

The next few minutes were a blur. Running back to his dormitory hut, Harry started packing. The job was over almost too quickly. At last he picked up his bag and strode out once again into the cold night air.

Harry could hear artillery pounding away at some threatened German advance off in the distance. Across the field he saw the running lights of a Vauxhall staff car pulled up in front of the administration building, so he shouldered his bag and walked toward it. As he passed by the pilots' club the sound of gramophone music could be heard: "I wonder who's kissing her now". He had to resist the urge to whistle along with the song. *Now why am I feeling so happy?* he asked himself. Was he relieved to be taken out of danger at least temporarily? Was it a kind of cowardice? No, Harry decided, it was that he didn't want to kill again. That was it, a reaction to the day's fighting. But of course whatever this strange assignment was to be, no doubt it had something to do with the war and with combat. The logic of this reflection did nothing to dampen his spirits, however, and he was feeling quite chipper as he got into the long black automobile.

Miss Sheehy was sitting in the back seat. She nodded to Harry as he got into the car and closed the door. The chauffeur

revved the engine. No, come to think of it, that was a chauff-
euse, wasn't it? Curiouser and curiouser.

The driver threw the car into gear, and the Vauxhall lurched
into motion. As they rolled away, Harry's last token of
Droglandt was the cawing of a crow. To his ears it sounded like
laughter.

CHAPTER 2
NIGHT FLIGHT

Harry and Miss Sheehy sat in silence for a while as they rode through the darkness. All Harry could see of the driver from his seat directly behind was that she was a brunette, but she seemed to be handling the car quite well, changing gears with no apparent effort and driving with all the speed possible on the dark broken-up dirt road.

Harry had a hundred questions to ask, but he felt that Miss Sheehy must know full well that he was burning to find out what was going on, and he'd be damned if he asked now only to be rebuffed. And anyway, the driver was interesting in herself. So far, she hadn't said a word, hadn't even turned her head so her face could be seen, but Harry was curious about her anyway, merely on the basis of her skill at the helm of the car.

After half an hour driving through the darkness, they passed through a series of checkpoints before entering the big base town of Saint-Omer, one of the largest aerodromes in France. Harry had come through here the week before on his way to Droglandt field. At this point he expected to be escorted to some headquarters building for a briefing from an officer, or perhaps to be delivered to a dormitory for the night. Instead they turned directly onto the airfield where a ground crew was working on a large and unfamiliar aeroplane with French markings.

At last Miss Sheehy spoke up.

"Here we are, Lieutenant. Marie will take you the rest of the way."

"If you please," said Harry, feeling like a child asking a question of a schoolmistress, "where am I going?"

"Carnac," she said. "Heard of it?"

Harry shook his head. He had the vague idea it might be the name of an ancient temple in Egypt, but he hesitated to volunteer the suggestion, sure it would be incorrect. Most likely it was another small airstrip on the front somewhere close by.

"Not at all," he said. "Will there be a briefing there?"

Miss Sheehy smiled. "I doubt it. As far as you're concerned it's just a transit point. You'll get your briefing when your journey is over."

The driver, Marie presumably, opened the passenger door and Miss Sheehy stepped out. Harry stayed where he was, thinking he would now be driven on to Carnac, but with a gesture she indicated that he must leave the car as well.

Harry looked on as Miss Sheehy re-entered the car on the driver's side. He had assumed from her remarks about Cambrai that the French two-seater they'd parked in front of would be Miss Sheehy's transport to that destination.

Miss Sheehy called out from her position in the front of the car: "Don't forget your kit, Lieutenant! And it might be a good idea to take a few minutes for yourself now. It will be rather a long flight, I'm afraid."

"Oh, yes."

He pulled his kit from the car and shut the door. Without any further farewells Miss Sheehy threw the car into gear and performed a tight U-turn to head back the way they'd come.

Marie approached him, holding a large bag of her own. For the first time Harry had a good look at her. She was shorter than Miss Sheehy, with dark hair and a cheerful manner. Harry thought she might be about his own age, where Miss Sheehy was probably a few years older. Under her black tailored trench-coat she wore some kind of French women's auxiliary uniform.

"Allo," she said, holding out her hand.

Harry took it gingerly, and gave a sort of half-bow, not sure whether he should attempt a French greeting or not. He had the usual level of public school proficiency with the language, but he wasn't fluent, and he didn't want to provoke a conversation he couldn't understand. In the end he decided to split the difference, so as not to appear entirely uncosmopolitan.

"Hello," he said. "Enchanté."

She smiled, which Harry found very appealing, and immediately confirmed his fears by reeling off a paragraph of incomeprehensibly rapid dialogue. While he was formulating his response she rescued him, having already recognized his problem.

Using the universal method of communication with a barbarian (closer, slower, and louder, with exaggerated movements of the mouth), she said "Dix minutes, yes? Nous volerons. Long flight, hein?"

"Ah yes," he said, "je comprends."

She pointed at a Nissen hut across the way. "Le pissoir."

"Oh, ah, merci."

"Dix minutes." She flashed both hands at him, fingers splayed in case he'd missed the point, and then turned back to the biplane, addressing herself in a rapid stream to a man in a French pilot's uniform who was overseeing the work of the ground crew.

Harry shouldered his bag and trudged over to the hut Marie had indicated. The pissoir was vacant, so he was left alone with his thoughts for a few minutes. Now the meaning of Marie's remarks percolated through his numbed mind in a sort of delayed-action translation. "Nous volerons." That meant both of them would be flying, presumably to Carnac, wherever that was. The unfamiliar aeroplane was a two-seater. Did she expect him to pilot it to an unknown destination? At night, for pity's sake? Ridiculous: impossible. He'd be lucky to get off the ground, much less find his way to some obscure map coordinate for a night landing with just a compass and a chart. Perhaps that Frenchman she'd been talking to would be pilot. But then there would hardly be seating for all three of them. Could he have misunderstood the conjugation she'd used? But how could you get "nous" wrong? Then too he wasn't really equipped for a long night-time flight in December. He had his sidcot flying suit, his scarf, goggles, and gloves, but it was bad enough in that gear during the day. At night it would be freezing cold in the sky, with the bitter wind of their flight possibly making things very dangerous indeed.

On edge with these thoughts, Harry walked back to the aeroplane being readied on the airfield. There were spare fuel tanks bolted on either side of the fuselage, and the guns had been removed, but the thing was recognizable as a biplane bomber.

Marie addressed one of Harry's concerns immediately as he walked up to her side where she was inspecting the bomber. She handed him a thick knitted balaclava mask with extra-large eyes cut out to make room for goggles, and a heavy quilted white cloak made of silk and stuffed with down. "Pour le froid," she said.

"Merci." Harry gestured uncertainly at the biplane, trying to frame a question about who would pilot and where he should sit.

"C'est un Breguet-14," she said. "No guns or bombs. Pour gagner du poids, yes?"

At least he'd heard of the bomber. It was indeed supposed to be a good one. At last Harry managed to get his meaning across, and Marie pointed at the rear seat, relieving Harry's mind about the need for him to pilot the aeroplane. The Frenchman—the pilot, he assumed—said something incomprehensible to him, and handed him a thermos: Harry hoped it was full of coffee, not tea. Then he slapped Harry on the back and said, "Tous à bord!"

Harry put on his flying gear including the fancy mantle he'd been offered. He clambered up into what would normally be the rear-gunner's seat if the bomber was mounting guns. He had to wedge his bag into place in the cramped space around his knees. At this point he was surprised to see Marie put on her own helmet and goggles and climb into the pilot's seat.

Harry had read about a few daredevil female pilots in the last few years, most seeming to be dilettantes at best. But he'd never heard of a woman flying a bomber out of Saint-Omer. It hadn't occurred to him that Marie might actually be the pilot, but at least that explained the seating arrangements.

Harry had some misgivings based on his assessment of the absolute difficulty of a long night flight, but he wasn't one to reject female mechanical competence out of hand. Marie had impressed him with her driving skill, and if she was a pilot of any standing whatever she undoubtedly had more hours in the air than he did. Still, it was a surprise. He hoped for both their sakes that she was quite familiar with the trip to Carnac from here in Pas-de-Calais. Without a lot of experience both of route and destination, night flying could be a chancy thing. It was easy enough to get lost in the daytime, and at least during the day you could see where to make a forced landing if you had to.

After settling herself in, Marie turned to face him. They wouldn't have much chance to talk during the flight. The roar of the bomber's big engine and the rush of the wind would make it necessary to scream to be heard, even through the speaking-tube that connected the two cockpits.

"Nous partons pour la Bretagne. Il est quatre ou cinq heures pour Carnac. Ne vous inquiétez pas, je suis une aviatrice qualifiée."

He was regretting that "enchanté" now as she still seemed to have an overblown notion of his competence with the language. But this wasn't too hard to make out with a bit of thought. Bretagne: that was Brittany. They'd be flying across the whole breadth of the country. And what was there in Brittany that was so important, so far from the front? That explained the extra tanks, anyway. Four or five hours in the air. A dangerous flight. But what the hell. He could at least be a little gallant about it all. Frowning, he worked out a sentence, hoping he hadn't screwed up the grammar:

"Bien sûr! Je suis sûr que je suis entre de bonnes mains!"

Marie smiled widely, making Harry think he had in fact said something silly, and said "Merci, Monsieur le Lieutenant," and flashed him a thumbs-up sign. "Allez-y!" she called out to a mechanic who had been waiting at the propeller.

"What's that, then?" was the reply. The mechanic was a RFC man.

Harry translated, "She says: ready to go." He settled his leather helmet and worked the greased goggles down over his eyes. Then he pulled on the balaclava and wrapped the scarf around his collar and over his mouth and nose.

"Oh well," said the airman. "Why didn't she say so. Good luck to you. Contact!"

This needed no translation. Marie flipped a switch on her board, called out "Contac'!"

The mechanic hauled on the prop and the engine roared into full-throated life. The bomber rapidly accelerated to takeoff speed. The transition from ground to air was almost imperceptible, the first indication being the vibration from the under-carage suddenly vanishing. That dealt with one source of unease; just the takeoff alone made it clear that Marie was a skilled pilot.

After spending a few minutes gaining altitude, Marie brought the Breguet around to a heading close to WSW according to Harry's instrument panel. They were cruising now, making a little over 100 miles an hour.

The night was clear but very cold, and Harry was thankful for the extra gear. At present he was warm enough under his mantle, but he had a sense of extreme bitter chill just at hand, as on the other side of a glass window in winter when one is snug in a room with a roaring fire. A half-moon gleamed high above, empaneled in a glittering array of stars, piercingly bright even through his goggles.

Harry soon remembered the thermos. He was delighted to discover that it was filled not just with plain coffee, but with layers of coffee, whiskey and cream. The renewed buzz from the whiskey combined with the warmth of the coffee made the trip much more pleasant, despite the roar of the engine and the blast of the wind. He spent most of the rest of the flight wondering what might be awaiting him in Carnac, but was unable to come up with a plausible scenario.

Harry was at last jarred out of this futile line of thought by a change in the pitch of the engines. Was something wrong? But then he realized Marie was throttling down in preparation for a landing. Poking his head up, he looked around. Still full dark, a little before 5:00 AM. It was the solstice and sunrise wouldn't be for hours yet.

Something about the air was different now. Harry thought

he caught a whiff of the sea on the cold wind. There was almost no illumination on the ground that he could see, but just from the starlight (the moon had set behind some clouds, glowing pearlescently off to the west) he could tell they were over farming country. Looking down, he could see bare fields and the occasional dark silhouette of a stone farmhouse mixed in with patches of meadowland and light forest.

He heard Marie's distant and incomprehensible hail through the speaking tube, and she banked the bomber steeply, first to the right and then back again to the left. Harry wondered what she was doing, but then realized she was giving him a chance to look directly forward and down, a blind spot for a rear-gunner in level flight. In the distance he now saw a gleaming trail of light had appeared directly in their path. At first the nature of the light was a mystery to Harry but then he realized that searchlights were picking out a long strip on what must be their destination landing field. There seemed to be a great deal of irregularity to the ground around the strip. Was it possible they were going to land in a cemetery? Ridiculous: but even so, Harry thought he saw rows of white stones to either side of the illuminated path. Knowing how easy it was to overshoot a landing or slip to the side in a crosswind, Harry couldn't help but grow a little anxious, despite all recent evidence of Marie's expertise as a pilot.

As they began their descent Harry could see off to the sides the gravestones he thought he'd seen from miles away. They were there all right, but the scale and distance had deceived his eyes. Menhirs they were, rows and rows of them like the broken fangs of some monstrous maw. Nothing like Tregeseal East, though. That was a circular formation with just nineteen standing stones. Here at Carnac it looked like there must be hundreds or even thousands of the things laid out just like headstones in a grid—and there, was that a cromlech? This place made Stonehenge look like a mere bowling green, and even Avebury had fewer stones.

At last they approached the long swath of open ground illuminated by the searchlights. The aeroplane shuddered as Marie pulled back on the stick, killing much of the plane's remaining velocity. The nose dropped and they dropped a yard to the earth, jouncing heavily forward for a minute or so before coming to a halt just beside a makeshift refueling station. Harry could see a few Nissen huts clumped together on the sward beyond the landing strip. It was a perfect landing.

CHAPTER 3
A BRIEF ENCOUNTER

Marie turned off the engine and after so many hours enduring the roar the silence was almost shocking. Climbing out of the gunner's seat wasn't too bad, but when he dropped to the ground with his kit Harry felt some weakness in his legs after sitting in the gunner's cramped position for so long. He turned to see Marie wobbling a little herself after descending from the cockpit, and put an arm out for her to grab.

After a moment Marie released his arm. "Merci", she said curtly. Perhaps, he thought, she would have preferred to do without the assistance.

Harry tried to strike the right balance between praising her performance and not seeming too surprised by it. It was after all something he wouldn't have been able to do himself.

"Well done," he said, "C'était un vol splendide."

"Merci", she said again, but a little more warmly this time.

Harry was going to say something more, but he was interrupted.

"You've made excellent time, I see!"

The hearty voice was connected to a matronly woman in a fur wrap—possibly Welsh, Harry thought, from her manner of speaking. She looked to be around fifty or so, and though she was quite short and somewhat rotund, she carried herself with an air of authority. She had come up to them with a pair of French mechanics who had the look of resenting being hustled out of bed.

"Bonjour, Madame Llewellyn," said Marie, mangling the name. Definitely Welsh.

"Sunrise is in three hours." The woman paused for a moment. "Ah, Marie-bach, ah, la montée de soleil, er, du soleil..." She faltered. "Look here, young man, if you speak French at all, be a good fellow and tell her sunrise won't be for another three hours and change. There's something of a canteen over in that hut, and spare bunks in that hut over there, if she'd like to refresh herself until then."

Harry haltingly translated, and Marie nodded. She performed a sketch of a curtsey, charmingly executed in the white quilted mantle she still wore, and said "Merci, Madame." Picking up her bag and giving Harry a little wave, she headed for the canteen hut.

Harry said, "Mrs. Llewellyn, I presume? Second Lieutenant

Harry Tregeseal, RFC, at your service."

"Yes," she said, "the Cornish pilot, isn't it? Welcome to Carnac."

"Thank you." He paused. "It's only been five hours since I was singled out for this duty, and no one has told me yet what it's to be."

"Indeed," said Mrs. Llewellyn. "and this isn't the time for it, either. You should get some sleep now, I think. You'll need all your wits about you tomorrow. There may be a little time later in the morning for explanations."

"But—" Harry was frustrated not to learn anything more, but he was able to cut off his incipient complaint.

"Well," he said, "I have my orders, at any rate. Such as they are."

"Ha ha," said Mrs. Llewellyn sarcastically. "Such as they are: indeed. I daresay you're all in after a night flight, isn't it? I want a few more hours in bed myself. Be back here on the greensward by 8:15 or we'll come looking for you, though."

"Thank you, Mrs. Llewellyn," said Harry, "and good morning to you then. I'll take your advice."

"Good morning," she said. "You might well do. Just keep a steady head on your shoulders, is the thing. Good luck to you." And she turned away to harangue the two mechanics in a mix of broken French and Welsh-English.

After first finding a pissoir, Harry made his way to the canteen hut. He was in that sharp-edged mental state that sometimes emerges after staying up very late, in which it seems like it may be impossible ever to go to sleep again. There were a couple of benches set up at a trestle table, a coffee pot resting on a gas burner, and what looked to be a gas-fired griddle of some kind, currently not in use.

Marie was seated at the table, a coffee cup steaming in front of her. She didn't look up as he entered. As he sat down, Harry saw she had her eyes closed, that curious pendant of Miss Sheehy's clutched between her hands resting on the table. Harry could see her hands were trembling. She was muttering something. Harry thought he made out "trop... ne suffit..." Too much? Not enough what?

Moved by her distress to go beyond what he would normally consider proper, Harry reached out to cover her clenched hands with his own. She reacted with a suppressed start but didn't shy away. Her hands were very cold. After a moment Marie opened her eyes. She gave a small shudder that rippled through Harry's own body as well as her own, but she didn't otherwise move or speak for a moment. At last she said quietly, "Vos mains sont chaudes."

Harry took that to be a favorable comment. He left his hands there, and said "Le vol a dû être très fatigant. I couldn't have done it myself."

After another moment or two, she said, "You are very gallant, mon lieutenant." And she looked at him with a strange combination of shyness and bravado before bending forward to kiss his hand as it rested on hers. Harry thought it almost a formal gesture, but he felt a thrill nonetheless. Then she spoke, stammering slightly and blushing, "Ah, would—would you—Voulez-vous venir avec moi?"

Harry wasn't sure what she intended by this, but he no longer felt the least bit tired. They both stood up at once, a little awkwardly due to the placement of the bench and the fact that Harry had yet to let go of her hands. He flushed for a moment and released her. She gave a soft chuckle and stepped forward to kiss him once on the lips, very briefly. Just a touch, but it made Harry come alive in a way he'd never felt before, not with any woman, not even that one time on his second solo flight when he'd felt sure he wasn't going to pull out of a dive before hitting the ground.

Marie slipped the pendant chain back over her head, and taking Harry by the hand led him out of the canteen. They made their way to the hut Mrs. Llewellyn had indicated had spare bunks. The mechanics had finished working on the bomber and the searchlights had been turned off. The field was deserted, and only the muted rumble of a generator somewhere nearby broke the stillness of the night.

Harry had no idea what he would have done if the hut had been occupied, but fortunately it was vacant. It was the usual bare steel half-cylinder containing nothing more than half a dozen cots with pillows and blankets on each one, and no sign of recent use.

Harry approached Marie then, thinking he should kiss her. But she put her hand on his chest and stepped back. Harry was dismayed for a moment: had he misunderstood? But then she smiled and said "Permittez moi..." She stepped up to him and began undoing the buttons on his coat, and then she unfastened his shirt and trousers. At last Marie stood back and pointed at the cot. "Là-bas," she said, so he lay down there, reclining and looking up at her as she began to undress herself. Soon she was nude except for the carnelian dangling between her breasts. Harry was conscious of a certain reticence now, bordering almost on fear. Was this what he wanted? But it was too late to back out of it, and he felt eagerness too, strangely mixed with hesitation.

She raised the pendant to her lips and kissed the stone as if it was some sort of religious icon. Harry's eagerness didn't abate, but it was for a moment suspended as he involuntarily began to connect the dots he had deliberately left unlinked for the last few hours. While a part of his attention was still focused on Marie's breasts, the curves of her hips, her dark eyes, and her mouth as she licked her lips, Harry couldn't help but wonder what he was being drawn into. The odd reference to the stone circle at Tregeseal East, the strangeness of the pendant, their destination of Carnac, the fact that all these people were women...

Reaching the conclusion to her whispered chant, Marie put the pendant back around her neck. Then she climbed onto the cot. Harry looked up at her, waiting passively for her next move. She was blushing now, looking at the last hesitant rather than eager. He wondered if after all he should demur. Did she really want this? Did he if she did not?

"Marie," he said, "are you sure—"

"Ne parlent pas," she said, touching his lips with her finger. "J'ai honte." Then, seeing he didn't understand, she said, stammering, "I am—ashamed to be—éhonté, ah, ah—ashamed to be so shameless, I mean. But—but I do want this. Please, 'Arry."

Harry couldn't think what to say; his mind had gone blank and all ability to speak French had left him. He realized he was blushing now himself, but at last he nodded sharply once, fearing even to touch her on his own despite what she had just said.

She smiled then, and Harry saw that she was both relieved and happy, and he felt a surge of happiness rising in his own chest in response. There was no obligation holding him back or pushing him forward now, no sense of duty or false gallantry getting in the way. And now she was lowering her body against his own and her lips met his and it was very sweet indeed. He felt the cool weight of her pendant against his chest, and a strange tingling as well. He opened his eyes from the kiss to see the carnelian had kindled a faint glow, pulsing in time with Marie's heartbeat. Or was it in time with his own? A minute before this would have been so eerie it would have worked with Harry's reticence to shatter the mood, but now he had other things on his mind. And anyway, the entirely natural play of passion and pleasure on Marie's face as she began to move above him was of far greater interest.

♍   ♍   ♍

21 December 1917.

"As I suspected!" Mrs. Llewellyn's voice, waking him up, was not at all unkind, but nevertheless Harry experienced a surge of the most pure and exquisite embarrassment he'd ever felt, almost lethal in its intensity. She was standing there in her fur wrap, the door thrown open. The chill air and the dawn light were both streaming into the hut. Harry was supine on the cot, just as naked as when he'd fallen asleep, with Marie still on top of him, equally undressed.

"Madame! Avez-vous aucune décence? C'est scandaleux!" Marie sat up atop him but Harry suspected she was not as nearly outraged as her words suggested. For his own part he was still too paralyzed with shock even to move, much less to speak.

"Scandalous, eh? Scandalous it is when I tell you to be ready by 8:15 and already it's 8:00! Huit heures, Marie! Rappelle… Rappelle le lever du soleil!"

"Merde!" Marie was on her feet in a flash, gathering up her clothes where they lay scattered on the floor, leaving Harry to hastily pull the blanket over himself.

"Ah well," said Mrs. Llewellyn, disinterested in Marie's nudity as well as the brief flash of Harry's she'd seen. "No harm done, I suppose. We'll just have to skip your briefing. They'll tell you everything at your next stop anyway. But you'll have to hurry if you want to cram in a bite to eat before the big event! You had better be ready in twenty—no, in fifteen minutes now, or there will be the devil to pay and no pitch hot." And she swept out of the room.

CHAPTER 4
MISSION IMPLAUSIBLE

Harry dressed quickly. Marie was already leaving, though she blew a kiss to him on her way out. He couldn't imagine what could be next on the agenda. The whole experience appeared more and more unlikely at every turn, from its improbable beginning back at Droglandt field to this episode with Marie just now, and then Mrs. Llewellyn's blasé dismissal of it, as if such an encounter was only to be expected.

With the hut illuminated by the dubious glow of a late December morning just before sunrise, it was hard for Harry to believe his memories were not confused. He was certain he'd just made love to Marie, but honestly: had it really been part of —what? A pagan ritual? Harry recalled the carnelian pendant glowing with the light of their mutual passion, but for a beat he questioned the reality of the memory. Could that have been a dream? But he knew he hadn't deceived himself. These memories weren't dwindling and unravelling like those of a dream. No, they remained so sharp and certain that he was aroused once more at the recollection of Marie's kiss, with the uncanny light of the carnelian as clear and certain as the recalled sensations of lovemaking. With a bit of a shudder he tried to thrust the whole thing from his consciousness just to be able to leave the hut in some kind of good order.

At last he stumbled out into the cold chill air of a Carnac dawn. He could smell salt air, and that faint piercing cry, distant, harsh, and baleful, could only be that of a gull. Apart from the scatter of Nissen huts on a rough expanse of what looked like sheep- or goat-trimmed lawn, the site was surrounded by menhirs, crudely cut white and gray stones in serried rows on both sides of the landing strip. A ground fog swirled around the stones, looking to Harry like an overcast layer seen from above.

Beyond the ranks of smaller stones he saw to one side what looked like farm fields, and to the other some larger and more prominent stones. There, the big cromlech he'd seen on landing, a circle of menhirs, and further away a dolmen, a stone portal set into a tumulus hill.

Mrs. Llewellyn's words about a bite to eat came to mind, and Harry realized he was ravenously hungry. He hurried over to the canteen hut to find the lady herself, Marie, and a group of French mechanics eating some kind of bastard child of crêpes and griddle cakes a cook was making on the gas-powered grill.

Marie was picking dubiously at the food when Harry joined her at the table. She turned and smiled at him.

"They say, la première crêpe est pour le chien, you know? But this? Tout pour le chien."

Harry took a bite. At that moment he thought it the best breakfast he'd ever had: greasy fried batter with butter and jam. Better than the usual RFC hard-boiled egg, anyway.

Mrs. Llewellyn joined them a moment later, setting down a mug of tea at the table.

"All right, then," she said. "Here's what you'll need to do for the next transit stage. Go through your kit and your pockets and find anything iron and put it aside." She handed him a rough, blackened metal bar with silvery ends polished smooth.

"A magnet," she said. "Anything it sticks to, put aside, no matter how small."

"What," asked Harry, "will there be some kind of electrical equipment it might affect? Some kind of compass? And what about other kinds of metal? Brass or copper, say?" His goggles were bound with brass bands and he didn't want to give them up. It had taken quite a while before he got them adjusted properly.

"Electricity is beside the point," said Mrs. Llewellyn. "or rather, I think it is. But since you mention it, perhaps that's the reason for it after all. But only iron matters: if the magnet doesn't work on it, it's all right."

"I see," said Harry, though he didn't at all.

"Look you," she said, "if you overlook anything iron, you're putting Marie in danger, you understand? Even a tiny thing like a cufflink or a nail could be a hazard."

"I don't understand, I must say. But that's not important, I suppose." He started checking his possessions, running the magnet over anything that had a metal component.

"There's a good boy," said Mrs. Llewellyn, and Marie laughed. "You'd better get ready," said the Welsh matron to the Frenchwoman, "and we'll meet you at sunrise."

Marie said "Oui, Madame." She departed, leaving her picked-at breakfast on the table. Harry stole a few bites from her plate while he sifted through his gear with the magnet.

"I'm sorry," said Mrs. Llewellyn, "but we don't have enough time to tell you much at all about where you're going."

Harry found his razor, nail-clipper, pipe cleaners, pocket knife, lighter, and a service revolver to be ferrous. None of it couldn't be easily replaced. A few other metallic items had proven to be brass, zinc, or tin.

He looked up and said, "There's a chance for a few words now, isn't there?"

"I doubt you'd believe it," said Mrs. Llewellyn.

"I'd rather hear something that I might not believe than go on knowing nothing at all. You have no idea how frustrating this is, to be told I won't believe the explanation."

Mrs. Llewellyn laughed, a little bitterly, Harry thought. "You have no idea how frustrated I am myself, Harry-bach. Sure, and I know some things you don't, but you're the one who gets to go through, and I've got to stay here minding the store."

She rose from the bench. "Come on," she said, "I'll give you a few words as we walk."

Harry rose and followed Mrs. Llewellyn out of the hut. She led him across a broad field of menhirs, heading towards a small isolated hill.

"Listen then," she said over her shoulder, "and don't blame me if you don't believe any of it."

"I promise," said Harry.

"Right," she said. "You're going to a place most people don't think even exists. When you get there, you'll meet people you can't even imagine. They need your help, they say, a pilot's help. But iron is poison to them, to most of them anyway, and the way you'll be going, carrying iron on you makes it a thousand times harder to go."

"But the aeroplanes," said Harry, "the guns, the engines. All of that's got a lot of iron."

"Yes, and some of our people killed themselves sending that stuff through before we understood that it was a deadly risk. Thirty-six aeroplanes, ammunition, spare parts and tools in a single shipment along with who knows how much more stuff. Enough and more than enough to outfit a squadron. We knew it would be hard, so we got a group together for it, but we didn't know it would be a mortal hazard. Five of our best dead, half a dozen more in hospital, and not even a note saying 'sorry' back from the other side." Here she added something in Welsh. Harry couldn't make it out at all, but it was vehement and bitter.

"I'm sorry," he said lamely.

"Well, it's not your fault, is it?" Mrs. Llewellyn sighed. "And every one of us would give her left hand to be able to go through. But it's your blood and skills they're after, my boy. Someone's got to stay behind and open the gates, and we're the only ones who can do that."

"Wait," said Harry. "Who are all you people, anyway? Where do you come from? And why is Brigade doing what you ask?"

"Ha," said Mrs. Llewellyn, "that's a good question. The second one, I mean. It'd take too long to explain where we come from and why, but your brigade is just following orders, same as you."

"Orders from where?"

"From the Crown, of course. Who else do you think could command such a hare-brained diversion of resources from the front?"

"Oh." Harry was stunned briefly, but it made a sort of sense.

"Such a surprise it must have been to our blessed royals, too. Bunch of Germans as they are. Little did Victoria know when she crossed over from Saxony to sit on the Stone that the geas would bind her and all her line."

Harry supposed she meant the Stone of Scone. Of the hundred questions she had already given him to ask, it was hard to choose just one at a time. "Geas? You mean some kind of magic spell?"

"Yes, my boy. And magic's going to open the way to your destination. Still believe me?"

"Whether or not I believe you, I don't want to stop listening. Tell me all you can."

"Ah," she said, "now we come to it. This is the part where the dashing young lieutenant looks at me like the old lady should be put away someplace with close monitoring and caring nurses."

"I don't think you're all that old," he said.

Mrs. Llewellyn snorted. "Thank you kindly. But you'll reserve judgment on the funny farm, eh? Well, let's see how you take it, then. You're going to fairyland, aren't you? Where else did you think it would be?"

Harry blinked. "Fairyland? You mean little people with wings? Like those things Conan Doyle is on about?"

Mrs. Llewellyn barked laughter. "Not half," she said. "There are some different kinds of people in—in the other world, you might call it, and I believe some are very queer indeed."

A faint chiming could now be heard. Mrs. Llewellyn took a big old-fashioned pocket watch out of her handbag, pressed the stem to make it stop. They were making their way around the low hill now.

"And here we were getting on so well, too. Pity, we're out of time. Come on, it's almost sunrise."

"What? Wait—"

But Mrs. Llewellyn was almost scurrying now, and Harry had to hurry behind her to keep up.

"Sorry, my boy," she said over her shoulder, "No time. Oh wait. One thing I should say. I'll say it as we walk, right? About what you got up to with Marie earlier. Don't be shy now! I only wish I was young enough—well anyway, that was well done, I'm trying to tell you. The stupid girl didn't let me know until just a few minutes past how low she'd been on, er, well, call it the fuel she'll need to send you through. But let's say you topped off her tank, eh?"

Harry was blushing too intensely to reply.

Mrs. Llewellyn paused a moment, patted his cheek in a kindly way. "There, there. All's well that ends well, isn't it? But just so you know, she told me all about it—"

Harry made a muted strangled sound, but Mrs. Llewellyn chuckled.

"She told me, I say, that she's sorry that it must have seemed so strange to you, and more, she said she hopes it didn't feel, like, what did she say? Oh, yes, *un engagement mécanique*, she said. Listen, Harry-bach, I'm trying to say she speaks well of you and she doesn't want you to think she was just using you, understand?"

"Oh," said Harry weakly. "I see. But—"

"Look you," said Mrs. Llewellyn, "she's going to be already starting the ritual. You're not going to have time to chat. But when you get back from, well, over there, you'll look her up, won't you?"

"Of course—"

"I just want to make sure you understood, that's all. And here we are."

They rounded the tumulus and now Harry could see the dolmen, which was built into the east side of the hill. The three stones of the dolmen formed a lintel over the mouth of a passage heading west into the base of the hillside. Most of the ground fog had already evaporated, but the narrow entrance was still surrounded by an eerie puddle of the stuff a good ten yards across lapping at the stone. The passage was dark in the murky December dawn and looked very forbidding. A leather satchel had been placed near the opening.

Marie was standing in the midst of the pool of fog, clad now in a heavy blue-gray robe. She was holding the carnelian pendant out like a censer. Her eyes were closed.

Harry started to walk over to her, but Mrs. Llewellyn put a hand on his shoulder and whispered: "Shh! She's already begun. Don't disturb her. This is the Kercado dolmen, the gateway you have to go through. She'll tell you when to enter, don't worry. Take that pack with you too, when you go. It's post for the other boys."

"What about me?" Harry couldn't help but whisper back.

"Not to worry. In our world the passage goes to a chamber in the center of the tumulus where it ends, but if all goes well you will go straight on through to the far side. There's a second passage, you see. Or rather, you wouldn't see it if you just went in there on your own. It's in the other world, isn't it?"

"Oh." Even with the evidence he'd seen thus far, the otherwise inexplicable orders he'd received and the apparently supernatural phenomena he'd already witnessed, Harry couldn't quite make himself believe in fairies or in wherever it was he was supposed to be going. *But what the hell*, he thought. Might as well go through with it.

Mrs. Llewellyn patted him on the shoulder. "I'll say au revoir now, and good luck to you too, young man. There's some nasty business going on over there, and there are people, of a sort, who need your help. Also some who probably don't for the matter of that, but put that to the side. They'll tell you more and better than ever I could in the other world, I'm sure, and you can make up your own mind when you see what's what."

"By the way," said Harry, "how am I supposed to get back?"

Mrs. Llewellyn chuckled. "Starting to think it's all real, are you, Harry-bach? Never fear. Our people can send you over there, and you can come back the same way for as long as the passage is open. We've been getting post and such coming regular for a while now, so you can be sure the paths run in both directions."

Mrs. Llewellyn pulled a pendant out of her blouse. Harry was expecting another carnelian, but this was a finely figured miniature of a horse, carved of alabaster or some other pellucid white stone.

"Now then," she said, "the folk on the other side tell us most of the old gods are dead, but the power's still there in earth and sea and sky, and I won't accept that they've vanished completely."

She kissed the figurine, put it back in her blouse. Harry was about to speak up, but she took both of his hands in hers, and brought them together between them. "My family have been her faithful servants since time out of mind," she said, "and I believe she's done right by us down through the years. So may Rhiannon's blessings be on your head young man, and keep you safe in the skies of the other world. And may the Bendith y Mamau treat you well, or as well as they can, anyway."

Harry was a member of the Church of England, but at a very young age he had decided for himself that the question of the existence of God was not merely unprovable but irrelevant. For some years now he had only attended church services to oblige others. Harry usually felt aloof and superior in the presence of any sort of ritual but in the face of Mrs. Llewellyn's warm and well-meaning invocation he felt himself blushing, as if he didn't deserve the blessing.

She released his hands, and Harry stammered a lame thank-you. Mrs. Llewellyn was about to reply when she cocked her head and looked off into the hazy sky glowing softly in the east.

"It's time," she said. "I'm off then. Good faring to you." She raised her hand in what looked like another ritual gesture, then tapped him on the nose. Chuckling to herself, Mrs. Llewellyn turned and started walking back the way she'd come.

CHAPTER 5
DOWN THE RABBIT HOLE

Harry saw that Marie had raised her pendant up to eye level and was holding it out before her. At that moment the first rays from the rising sun illuminated Marie's position, and the stone caught the light causing it to shine a brilliant red.

"Now! Le passage est ouvert! Go, 'Arry!"

There was a note of urgency in Marie's voice, so Harry ran to the dolmen. He paused to hoist the leather pack over his shoulder with his kit. It was bound with a lead seal and stenciled: *Army Special Post*. He paused for a moment at the entrance, turned and waved. Then he entered the dark passage, ducking under the heavy stone lintel. He heard the raucous call of a crow that must have been perched atop the tumulus.

The passage was awkwardly narrow. The transition from light to shadow was almost blinding, so Harry had to slow down to avoid tripping over the irregular floor. There was a strong smell of earth here, and something else too, a sort of moldering decay. Where he was standing was partially illuminated by light coming in from the entrance, but further in everything was dark. There was no sign of an exit on the far side.

Harry moved as quickly as he could. After a few dozen steps, he sensed more than saw a widening of the passage ahead and to his right. This must be the central chamber Mrs. Llewellyn had mentioned. He took a step inside.

Harry felt a sudden nauseous disorientation, exactly like the first time he'd gone into a spin. He tried to fight the sensation off but had to drop to one knee. As he crouched there, one hand on the ground to stop from falling flat on his face, he saw a spot of light moving clockwise. Or was it his head that was moving? That must be the passage entrance. Had he gotten turned around? He looked over his shoulder—a mistake, he almost threw up from the sickening sense of everything whirling around him—and there was another spot of light, much brighter.

At last he staggered to his feet and confirmed that there were two entrances visible now, just as Mrs. Llewellyn had said there would be. The darker of the two was in front of him, which made sense if it was on the west side of the tumulus. Harry started moving again, first at a walk, then at a shambling trot. Just before reaching the entrance he looked over his shoulder but saw nothing but darkness behind him. He turned back and—

♍   ♍   ♍

"Moghrey mie. Welcome to fairyland."

Harry started, and opened his eyes. For a moment he was confused. The world seemed topsy-turvy. Then he realized he was lying on his back on the ground, and a sandy-haired man in RFC uniform holding out his hand; presumably he was the one who'd just wished him a Manx good-morning.

The officer was wearing a captain's three stars on his shoulders. Harry reached out his hand, and the captain hauled him to his feet. For a moment he felt faint, and he might have fallen except for the other's grip on his hand and shoulder, but then the world stabilized.

"I'm sorry sir," said Harry, "but what just happened to me?"

"You passed out," said the man. "Something about coming across tends to knock one for a loop. Nothing to worry about, though. I take it you're Tregeseal?"

"Yes sir."

"Quirk comma Arthur: brevet-major and your squadron commander now, such as I am. Still waiting for the insignia to show up, in case you're wondering."

"Honored," said Harry, and saluted as crisply as he could, feeling as usual as if he was a stand-in unexpectedly called to play a military role in some stage play. "Second Lieutenant Harold Tregeseal reporting for duty, sir."

Major Quirk tossed him a casual salute in return. "You can lay off the spit and polish if you like. We're two of the only ten army officers in this whole blessed world. No stuffed-shirt colonel is going to be breathing down your neck and telling you your slovenly tie knot is a clear sign of moral decay."

From his tone of voice, Harry had the idea Quirk might actually have heard words to that effect not too long ago.

Harry looked around. It was warm here, more like late June than the chilly December he remembered, and the grass was much more lush and green than he'd seen around Carnac. The trees still had their leaves. Harry had never seen such verdance before in England or France, not even in a greenhouse or at a botanical garden.

The tumulus and dolmen looked similar but not identical to the one he'd entered a minute before. He was on the west side, so the area was shadowed by the bulk of the hillside. The rest of the landscape was different, though: no rows of menhirs, no cromlech, and no farmland either, but heavy undergrowth

30

everywhere except where an area had been cleared around the tumulus. The far side of the tumulus at Carnac—a low isolated hillock—should have allowed for a view of any number of landmarks he'd just walked past minutes before. This here was a lightly wooded meadowland, but the edge of what looked to be a densely forested area stood a few hundred yards to the west, and he remembered no such woods. Harry was sure beyond doubt he was no longer in Carnac. And yet it was still just after sunrise.

"Where do you think you are, by the way?" Asked casually, but it occurred to Harry this might be a sort of test. He answered slowly and carefully.

"I was told I was being sent to some kind of fairyland."

"Indeed?" In a neutral tone of voice.

"Yes, sir. It does appear to me that I have been transported to an unfamiliar place, and the similarity of that dolmen to the one I remember entering a minute or so ago is consistent with what I was told."

"But where do you think you really are? I mean, what do you really believe?"

Harry paused for a moment to compose an answer he hoped would be acceptable.

"Frankly, sir, it's hard for me to believe in fairyland. But I don't think it's some kind of deception. Obviously I'm not where I was a few minutes ago, and it might be another world. I have to withhold judgment for now."

"Not bad," said Major Quirk. "You pass, I suppose."

"Sir?"

Major Quirk laughed.

"Oh, just wondering how credulous you might be. Or how incredulous for that matter. A couple of us have grown up with some slight understanding of these matters, but for most it's just old-time stories. And those stories don't give a true account of this world, either."

"But what's the real situation, then?"

"We're still working that out, to be honest. The first few of us have only been here a week or so, and the briefing we had in advance was, well... not very detailed, let's say."

Major Quirk picked up the heavy post bag Harry had lugged through the passage. Even considering he'd just been promoted, Quirk was the most un-majorly squadron officer Harry had seen in his admittedly limited experience. Not that Major Russell of 32 Squadron was a stickler or a stuffed-shirt, but in the event he wanted a bag moved he would have told his adjutant to do it and the adjutant would have found an enlisted man to perform the chore.

"Come along," said Quirk, "and I'll give you some of the background on the way to the aerodrome. Hartshorn is around the other side with a wagon. Thought it best to meet you myself till you got yourself up on your feet again."

Major Quirk led Harry around the far side of the tumulus. The eastern hillside, now illuminated by the early morning sun, was a blank slope of grass and brambles but there was a beaten track here and a wagon was waiting past a small grove of trees. Beyond that to the north and east were lightly forested rolling hills, to the south a stretch of meadowland and then an arm of the dense woods Harry had seen to the west. The eastern sky was bright now with the newly risen sun, overhead the most striking azure Harry had ever seen. In the west the sky was somewhat darker, with an almost purple cast near the horizon, above the line of trees.

Everything seemed familiar and strange at the same time. The colors of the sky, of the forest, and of the meadowland were richer and more intense than in England, and yet Harry had a sense of being back home again, home in a place he'd never been before.

"Don't stare at Hartshorn or ask him anything," said Quirk in a low voice as they walked down the path. "These folk are scared half to death of us as it is. Think we're some kind of monsters, I suppose. Anyway, they don't speak English. I just call him Hartshorn because he won't tell his name. Some kind of superstition. His village and some others nearby are providing us with food and such, though they'd much prefer not to. But they obey their lords. Might as well be the dark ages as far as that goes around here."

As they approached the wagon, the first thing Harry noticed was that it was drawn by a pair of stags—not reindeer but ordinary red deer, wearing girths, collars, and harnesses as if they were horses. A slight figure in a ragged tunic and trousers and a broad drooping black hat sat on a box at the front, idly swish-ing a crop in the air. As he heard them approaching, he tensed up, hunching over and hiding his face under the brim of his hat.

Major Quirk addressed the local. It sounded something like Irish to Harry's ears. The hunched figure nodded jerkily, and he raised a hand to his forehead, but he didn't face around.

Harry and Major Quirk put their bags in the wagon, and then climbed in. The driver twitched his crop in a quick double-tap at the two stags' flanks, and they struggled for a moment to get the wagon into motion.

"Well-trained they are, those animals," said Quirk, "and willing, but you can see they're not good with heavy loads. Horses are reserved for the lords, however, and they've got no oxen around here so the villagers have to make do with deer."

"I see," said Harry.

It was good to sit down here, sprawled out in this wagon smelling of hay, rolling gently along. Harry really didn't feel all that tired—his eyes weren't heavy—but he had the sense that fatigue was waiting very close at hand for an invitation.

"It's just a couple of miles or so to the aerodrome," said the major, "but it'll be the better part of half an hour at this pace. Just as well. Gives you some time to learn what's what.

"Thank you, sir," said Harry. "It seems like I've been waiting forever to be briefed, but I guess it's only been nine hours or so."

Quirk chuckled. "They briefed me before I went through," he said, "but only because I was supposed to take command. And even then, it turned out half what they told me wasn't quite right. Just to save time, I've written up a few key points."

Major Quirk took a folded sheet out of his breast pocket. Harry looked at the proffered page. It was typewritten and looked to have been mimeographed.

♍　　♍　　♍

Notes for new pilots attached to Elfshot Squadron
* You are here because you're a pilot, and because some close female relative of yours is of a particular Celtic bloodline that allows passage to this place. That relative may or may not know herself to be part of a sort of sisterhood entrusted with managing the gates between our world and this one.

* This is indeed another world, but a world with what seems to be the same Sun, Moon, and stars, the same air and gravity, and the same plants and animals. Geography is very roughly similar to that of Europe (see map).

* You are here because our royal family has inherited an obligation from long ago to assist the rulers here should an urgent need arise. HM George V has chosen to honor the request for assistance which the sisterhood passed on from the rulers of this place. Neither the King nor anyone in government had any idea of the existence of this obligation or of this world

and its people until a couple of months ago.

* This part of the world is inhabited by people who seem to be related to some of the folk out of the Irish Lebor na hUidre and the Welsh Mabinogi. They speak a form of Gaelic, but the prince who deals with us has fluent English, as have all of our native mechanics. There are supposed to be other races too. As yet we haven't met any of them save one other type, the kobolds who serve as our enlisted men.

* You came to this world by means of a magical ritual. There may be some kind of science behind it, but not that we've figured out. Some of the fair folk are said to be able to wield a kind of magic, a sort that can charm, deceive, or confuse, but most can't do much more than that. However, the magic that brought us here is more substantial. It was originally taught to the sisterhood by the fair folk here and works with their cooperation and consent. Almost all magic fails or becomes much more difficult in the presence of iron. Most of the people here consider iron to be a deadly poison, and won't go near it.

* Our mechanics, guards, and servants at the aerodrome are kobolds, one of the few races here that can bear the touch of iron. They are refugees from the Unseelie court (see below), and are serving as enlisted men would in a regular squadron. So far they've done a good job; indeed they are responsible for setting up the aerodrome buildings from requirements sent on ahead before the first of us arrived. Unlike some of the other locals, they are quite forthcoming and eager to please. However, please remember they are natives and they have their own peculiar ways. *IMPORTANT: Speak to the O.C. about certain peculiar aspects of kobold culture as soon as possible after reading these notes.*

* The region here that corresponds to Western Europe is (or was) divided into two loosely organized kingdoms, each with a high king or queen and subsidiary local rulers. These are the Seelie and Unseelie courts of Scottish legend. The Seelie Court is to the west, like our side in our own war, and the Unseelie Court is to the east, like the Triple Alliance. However the Unseelie court is not the enemy here, but a sort of a victim. The ruler of the Seelie Court is High Queen Medb.

* For a very long time ("time out of mind", at least a thousand years, probably a lot more), the Seelie and Unseelie courts were hostile and squabbled bitterly from time to time, but were never actually at war. Recently something unprecedented and horrible has befallen the Unseelie Court and is threatening the Seelie court as well.

* The threat manifests itself as enormous floating pods, bigger than dirigibles, which rain a sort of heavy particulate smoke with long-term poisonous effects. The entire realm of the Unseelie court has become covered with this stuff. The people around here call this "the Shroud". The stuff poisons the land and people in such a way as to kill most and turn others into mindless thralls, who have been raiding villages and holdings on the Seelie side of the border. No one in the Seelie court has any idea where the Shroud came from, and it has completely ruined the Unseelie kingdom. And now the pods are close to the border of the Seelie kingdom, hence our presence. The Seelie knights—light cavalry lancers, really—can fight the raiders, but they can't reach the pods, and it's hoped that we can shoot them down. If we fail, the Seelie Court may be destroyed just as was the Unseelie Court, and who knows but the Shroud may expand to cover the rest of this world as well.

♍   ♍   ♍

Somewhere around the end of this document, Harry realized that in fact he was tired after all; on the point of dropping off, in fact. As his eyes closed, he heard as if in the distance Major Quirk's voice.

"Any questions? Oh... never mind."

♍   ♍   ♍

Harry woke with a start. The cart had just stopped at a small hillock which Harry realized after a moment was actually a sod house, the earthen walls as well as the roof completely covered in foliage.

The driver said something low and unintelligible over his shoulder. The major replied with what sounded like it might be a thank-you, and then turned back to Harry.

"You slept for ten minutes or so. We're at the outskirts of the local fairy village. North and west there's more of these houses on the edge of the forest. We'll walk the rest of the way to the aerodrome. These folk won't come any closer unless the lords make them. I think all the iron puts them off."

They clambered down from the wagon, shouldering their bags. The driver muttered what might have been a goodbye and twitched his whip, sending the wagon down the path, which wound around the sod house to the left. Major Quirk pointed off to the right as the cart rolled off.

"We'll go over a couple of hills and you'll have a nice view of the airfield."

They started off, struggling somewhat to climb the soft grassy slope of the hillside. Thinking about the aerodrome, a question occurred to Harry, one of a great many that were fighting for precedence in his mind.

"Sir, I understand that to get here I passed through a dolmen which somehow has passages going through two worlds. But that's a pretty cramped entrance. How did they get all the aeroplanes, the machines, the tools, the fuel and so on through?"

Major Quirk laughed. "Good question. Of course, they didn't take everything apart and pass it by hand through that little tunnel. Fortunately, the Wayland's Forge gate back in Oxfordshire has a sort of above-ground extension. The sisterhood was able to send a great deal of matériel between the worlds from the figure of the Uffington White Horse, which is on a hilltop, so they could just load the goods and fuel and so on onto horse wagons."

"Oh. But you said Oxfordshire. That's got to be around 300 miles from Carnac, isn't it? And what about the Channel?"

"Well, there's no English Channel here, to begin with. What would be Britain and Ireland in our world is a sort of big peninsula with no water cutting it off. And anyway, the distances and locations of the gates in the two worlds don't match up. But even though it was closer to 100 miles than 300, with no Channel to cross, it was a still a good long way to wrangle all those hundreds of tons of stuff over the dreadful roads they've got in this country. We've got one Avro two-seater along with our scouts, so at least we were able to fly the aeroplanes over here. One at a time. That's what we spent most of last week doing. Seventy-two bloody flights back and forth. But the ground transport for all the cargo took most of this last month. We've only managed to set everything up just recently. Couldn't have done it without the kobolds, of course. No one else around here would be willing to get within a hundred yards of that much iron."

Harry and the major had reached the top of the hill they'd been climbing. They paused there for a moment, Harry taking the opportunity to look around. Off to the left—to the north— Harry could now see an array of the little hillock-houses of the villagers, each with its own vegetable garden out in front. A few figures here and there were moving around the area. On the far side of the houses he saw a broad commons in which a flock of sheep was grazing. Beyond that, an extensive area of tilled fields. Ahead and to the right the prospect was blocked by more hills.

The difficulty of transporting goods from world to world suggested another problem.

"How are we set up for fuel, sir, if I may ask?"

"It's our biggest headache, since you mention it. We've got around 50,000 gallons of petrol at present, which would be fine for a field at the front that has tankers coming through every week. But of course, that's all there is in the entire world over here. It's enough for something more than two weeks of work if we fly 20 times a day. Thank heaven it doesn't need to come across in steel tanks. And there's another shipment en route, so I'm told. But it's going to be a continuing problem getting the fuel tanks to the aerodrome here without any proper transports but horse drays, and relying on the locals to do all the work. Even if we were able to get some lorries over here, they'd probably have a terrible time in the mud, but the lords absolutely forbade the idea."

"Sounds like a big problem."

"Rather. But needs must. We'll just have to make do."

They started trudging down the slope of the hill. The valley was covered in a profusion of wildflowers: daisies, buttercups, bluebells, and willowherb, among the few types Harry could identify. Stippled patterns of white, gold, blue and purple were splashed around the landscape like daubs of paint among the rich green grass and clover. Here and there bees buzzed about. It was slow going, but very pleasant.

Harry spoke up again. "From what I've read, these kobolds sound like remarkable people. How long have they had to learn our engineering methods? You gave me the impression this whole country is back in the stone age."

"Well, bronze age might be more to the point for most of the fair folk," said Major Quirk, "or iron age for the kobolds, until recently. But they are very clever and hard workers, and I do believe we've kicked off a miniature renaissance. Some engineering textbooks were sent across a few months ago, and by the time we came here ourselves we found the kobolds had managed to come up with a functional machine shop of what you might call the Victorian era almost from scratch. And since we sent a heavy generator across with the aeroplanes, they've learned to use electricity, too."

"A thousand years of progress in a couple of months? That's hard to believe."

Major Quirk paused. They were climbing the slope of a second hill now, completely surrounded by nature. These hills were mostly grassy at their tops, with the occasional little copse of trees, but the slopes were more thickly grown in and they had to pick their way around bushes and brambles at times.

"Yes. Very clever people. I should tell you something up front about them, though."

"Yes, sir?" Harry could see that the major was hesitant to speak for some reason.

"It's, well, a bit of an awkward subject..."

Harry remained silent. He couldn't think of anything to say, though he was conscious this was making it hard for Major Quirk to continue. At length, the major shook his head.

"No sense beating around the bush," he said. "So this is the kobolds. As far as I can tell, they are one and all cheerful honest workers, technically brilliant mechanics, and happy to get out from under the thumbs of the lords of the Unseelie court. In just about every way they make perfect airmen: mechanics, batmen, guards, and so on. I mean, everything we'd usually get from enlisted men in the RFC, the kobolds have been able to provide, and with remarkably little training. And what's more, we're the only other race of iron-workers they've ever heard of, we don't live under the rule of the fairy lords and ladies, and we're the ones who came up with all this science and engineering. So they practically idolize us."

Here the major paused again, and after the silence grew uncomfortably long, Harry felt he had to say something.

"But I suppose there is some problem, nevertheless, sir?"

"Yes." The major shook his head. "Or rather, I hope it won't be a problem. It's, well, not their fault, I think. For every one girl-kobold, a good dozen or more boys are born."

"Really, sir? How very strange. Is this the case for any of the other fairy races?"

"No. Or at least, not that I know of. But you see, that means that their society isn't at all like ours. They don't have husbands and wives, nor regular families and relations. I gather the boys grow up in what you might call herds and the rare precious girl-child is kept apart. I'm afraid the kobold women spend most of their lives with child, the poor things. As you can imagine, they must each have a great many children or the race would die off. So as regards, er, male-female relations, even without marriages or anything like that, the average kobold male will hardly ever have the opportunity to make love to a female. But even so they are not, well, chaste..."

Harry thought he understood what Major Quirk was trying to get at.

"You're saying they're homosexuals, sir?"

He felt strange even saying the word out loud. At his public school, the whole subject was beyond the pale, absolutely forbidden to be discussed, worth a caning or even an expulsion if one was overheard.

"Queer as the day is long, the lot of them," said Major Quirk. "Actually, I suppose that's not quite right. Of course they have the usual relations with their women when the opportunity arises, but for most of their lives..." The major trailed off.

Harry shook his head. "It's hard to believe. And these are our mechanics? Our servants?"

"Yes," said the Major. "And I think they don't quite understand the idea of a sexual taboo. They seem to think it's some kind of joke, or that we don't really mean it. Evidently the other fairy races have no very strong notion of the taboo either, but being divided more evenly male and female, it's not so ubiquitous a practice since they form the usual families with marriages and in-laws and so on."

"You're saying they will approach us, sir?" The idea was appalling.

"Well, yes. They probably will. And while I must say that for my own part, I have absolutely no objection to what any two civilians wish to do in private, and heaven knows there is not enough love in the world as it is, or we shouldn't be fighting this terrible war in the first place..."

Here Major Quirk seemed to realize he was wandering off the subject.

"I say, as tolerant as I like to think I am, one of the forms of politesse the Army seems to have omitted at Sandhurst is how to tell your not-quite-human orderly that you don't want to sleep with him, not just today, but tomorrow too."

Harry thought for a moment, unsure at first how to respond. After a pause, he said, carefully, "I understand this could be difficult. Not perhaps so much in saying 'no' to a kobold so much as with respect to the discipline of a squadron and its officers."

"Very good," said Major Quirk. "I'm relieved to hear you take my meaning. I have nothing to say as regards the brothels and camp followers convenient to a flying officer with a day or two of leave who is stationed in France, or for the matter of that at Northolt or Biggin Hill. But while we are here we will have little opportunity for leave, and the local villagers are unlikely to be very welcoming in that regard."

"I understand," said Harry, and considering what might be an enforced period of chastity his thoughts flashed involuntarily back to his time with Marie, just a few hours before. He hoped he wasn't blushing, for who knew how it might be taken in the current conversation.

"So you see," said the major, "while in civilian life I would have nothing to say on the subject at all, as a squadron commander I must be concerned with discipline and morale, and I rather think that sleeping with the enlisted men is not good for either."

"Of course, sir."

"But on the other hand," said Major Quirk, "I will not tolerate any abuse of these people, either. I mean of course there are many who would regard, well, a homosexual advance as an affront, an intolerable affront at that. But some of these kobolds just don't seem to understand they are giving offense. And our operations here are completely dependent on their good will. They seem perfectly happy to submit themselves to our orders, and I daresay they might possibly tolerate abuse from our people, apparently being used to this kind of treatment from their former lords. But I won't have it, not either way."

Quirk's voice turned stern. "If any of my officers does fancy one of these people, I hope he'll keep his lips sealed and his breeches buttoned and pine away in proper British silence. But if any officer takes offense at a proposition, he will keep his temper and respond with what civility he can muster. Is that clear?"

"Yes, sir."

"Good. I may have exaggerated the kobolds' forwardness somewhat, but it's just as well to be prepared. No doubt they will eventually come to learn our ways and the whole thing will be less of a problem."

"Yes, sir."

"We're coming up on the aerodrome now," said the major. "You'll see the grand vista from the top of this hill. Are there any other questions you'd like to ask before we arrive?"

"Only a thousand, sir," said Harry, "but I have so much to digest at present that it would be pointless to ask anything further now. I am very grateful for your kindness in giving me so much of your time."

"Think nothing of it," said Major Quirk. "There will be plenty of time for more questions and discussion later on. In fact— *what the bloody hell is that?*"

It was a klaxon. Harry had never heard one before at the front. For the brief week he'd been at Droglandt field, the Germans hadn't attacked even once, but the meaning of the sound was unmistakable.

CHAPTER 6
BURNING THREADS

"Come on!"

Major Quirk dropped the heavy post bag and started scrambling up the face of the hill, so Harry emulated him, dropping his kit. They reached the crest at about the same time. Harry saw down below a broad stretch of meadowland to the northeast in which an aerodrome had been built, the near edge of the closely mown field perhaps two hundred yards away at the bottom of the hill.

At first Harry couldn't quite understand all that he was seeing. It was an ordinary-looking RFC aerodrome, quite similar to Droglandt field, even down to the flagpole with the Union Jack at the peak. However, there were no steel Nissen huts here. In their place was a dozen neat half-timbered cottages and one larger building of the same type. In front of the wood-framed open hangars—almost identical to those at Droglandt— a row of biplanes was pegged down and a number of figures were running toward them from the cottages. Apart from these homely elements, Harry also noted a deep ramp on one side of the field leading underground, with a tall smokestack next to it along with what looked like air ducts piercing the earth. But all this was easily grasped in a moment's glance at the scene.

What Harry couldn't make out so quickly were the crystalline objects drifting through the sky towards the aerodrome from the east. Several hundred of the things, looking like gigantic chunks of rock candy a yard in length, were moving in a loose grouping across the landscape. These things were so alien to Harry's understanding that he was unable at first to judge their nature and scale. Watching them moving above the meadowland for a moment, he realized that the crystals were connected to cables dangling from points high above the field. The cables were many hundreds of feet long, no more than thin black threads at this distance, and each was strung with around twenty crystals. These threads of crystals were moving west into the eye of the wind, trailing diagonally down and to the east as if being towed from above. Looking up Harry thought he saw some cloudlike blots, hard to make out, at the tops of the strands. At present the lowest bead of the leading thread of crystals looked to be a good hundred feet above the ground, but in addition to moving west the thread was also dropping slowly downward. It wouldn't be long before they began to trail through the meadowland, and then through the aerodrome itself.

"What *are* those things?"

"I don't know," said the major, "but someone's got the right idea. Getting the exposed machines off the ground before they get here. Let's run. Maybe we can help out."

Harry and Major Quirk hurried down the long shallow face of the hill towards the airfield and the row of parked biplanes. The combination of the grade and the irregular ground made it hard to go all that fast, and by the time they had almost made it to the near side of the airfield the lowest crystal bead of the first of the aerial threads was already touching ground, perhaps a quarter mile beyond the far side of the aerodrome. There was a flash in the distance and what looked like a puff of smoke or mist, and the spot where the bead touched turned from green to brown. Harry realized the grass had been burnt away. The thread dragged onward, tangling for a moment in a small isolated copse of trees. There was a cascade of small flashes as several beads all erupted at once and the copse burst into flames. The remaining length of crystal-bearing thread must have detached from whatever was towing it at that point, because it fell downward and forward like a cable breaking loose from an observation balloon. A linear path almost a thousand feet long was burnt through the meadowland in just a few seconds, the last crystal impacting harmlessly a hundred feet or so beyond the far side of the airfield.

"That one dropped too soon," said Major Quirk, panting.

Crews were already bustling around six of the twelve scout biplanes exposed in front of the hangars. Harry saw that half of them were S.E.5as, easily identifiable due to their narrow fuselages and snub-nosed radiators, not to mention the Lewis guns mounted on the upper wing planes. The SEs were painted blue and white with the usual RFC red, white, and blue roundels. The other machines were Sopwith Camels, shorter and wider in body, in green and brown camouflage pattern.

Breathing hard, Major Quirk and Harry arrived at the row of aeroplanes as the first of the Camels was being readied for take-off. A work crew was hauling the tail around to face into the wind, and the engine was revving up. A uniformed figure came running up to them as they arrived. It was another RFC captain, a heavy-set man with improbably bright red hair.

"Sir! We're evacuating as many machines as we can before those things hit ground."

They paused for a moment as the Camel rolled by and started its take-off run.

"Good! Ready two more. My Camel and... what do you fly, Tregeseal?"

"Ah, I'll take one of the SEs up, sir, if you please." Harry thought this probably wasn't the ideal moment to explain he'd never actually touched one before.

"Right," said Major Quirk. "No need for anything fancy or heroic. Just get out of the way of those things, and land when the—when the attack is over. Understood?"

"Yes, sir."

The major turned to the other officer. "Make sure the kobolds get underground as soon as we're in the air. We don't need them being heroes trying to save any of the aeroplanes we can't get off the ground."

"Yes, sir. Will do." The officer turned to run back towards the hangars. He paused when he was well in view, waved his arms and shouted, and another group of uniformed figures ran out. The officer pointed towards two of the biplanes, a Camel and a S.E.5a.

"All right," said Major Quirk. "Let's see if we can get off before those things drop on our heads. If you can't make it in good time, don't be a hero yourself either. Just run for that ramp to the underground level. Looks like these crystal bombs can't penetrate earth."

"Yes sir."

Major Quirk was already jogging over to one of the unoccupied Camels. Harry turned to the S.E.5a he'd picked out and saw a figure in an enlisted man's uniform was standing there, back turned, gesturing towards a group who were running over from the hangar. He looked up and saw that several more of the threads had dropped, some blasting furrows into the far side of the airfield. More were still in the air, and these looked like they might come down amongst the buildings and aeroplanes.

"Is this scout ready to go?" Harry called out to the figure—a kobold mechanic, presumably—who was still waving the group over. From the rear the mechanic looked like an ordinary enlisted man dressed in a regulation RFC uniform down to the corporal's chevrons on his sleeves.

The mechanic turned around. Harry saw that beneath his cap his face was reddish-gray, with red irises to his eyes and lips a sort of red-black in color. But apart from the coloration his features seemed ordinary enough.

"All fueled up, and we'll have you away in a moment, sir."

Spoken in a perfectly clear received pronunciation with no trace of accent.

Harry clambered up into the cockpit. With the propeller a few yards from his face, and the tiny rectangular windshield not inspiring much confidence, he realized he was about to have a problem.

"I say," he called out again, "I don't suppose there are any spare goggles about?"

"One moment, sir!"

The corporal called out and one of the other men (kobolds, presumably) approaching in the ground crew turned and sprinted back toward the hangar. Meanwhile, Harry took a look at the cockpit.

The instrument layout was unfamiliar, but at least the rudder bar and control stick were obvious. Where was the fuel pump selector? The oil gauge? The whole board was a blur. There, that must be the throttle and mixture levers, anyway. And what was that handle? For the radiator shutters? No way to tell without pulling it. There, the crank for the booster magneto.

By now the rest of the group of airmen had arrived (should that be air-kobolds?), and they were releasing the cables that held the biplane pegged to the ground and removing the chocks from the wheels.

"The major says to head underground as soon as I'm off," shouted Harry.

The mechanic corporal turned back to Harry. He had been directing the efforts of the other members of the ground crew. "But—but what about the other aeroplanes? We can wheel them underground—" The corporal's voice was plaintive.

"Orders," said Harry. "He said to protect yourselves."

At this point one of the crew emerged sprinting from the hangar, goggles in his hands. Reaching the aeroplane he tossed them up to Harry and then bent over panting, hands on his thighs. Harry worked the strap over his head and lowered the goggles. They weren't greased or fitted properly, but they would have to do.

"Are you ready, sir?" The crew chief turned the propeller twice, slowly. He'd already primed the engine, and this would would start some oil through the system.

"Ready." A profound lie.

"Switch off."

Harry looked for the switch. It wasn't in the same place on the board as in the DH.5. After an embarrassing pause, he located it by the magneto, or he found some switch anyway, and what else could it be? Actually, there were two of them, ident-ical, side by side. Two magnetos? Must be. What a luxury!

"Power off," he replied, hoping he was right about the switches and that they were flipped in the right direction. He cranked the booster handle to charge electricity for an engine start-up, and worked the hand-pump to provide some initial pressure in the fuel line.

Then the mechanic looked up. "Contact!"

Harry flipped the switches. A needle pulsed.

He shouted back: "Contact!"

Harry was surprised when the engine roared into life with no need for the usual haul at the propeller. Must be some special feature of the dual-magneto system. The propeller immediately started to spin up. The engine was giving off a beautiful deep-throated roaring purr, like a lion pretending it was a tabby.

Even at idle the prop wash was a powerful blast of wind to the face, and Harry was grateful for the goggles. Possibly he would have been able to hunch over just behind the glass to shield his eyes, but that would have made things extremely unpleasant for his untutored first-ever flight in this aeroplane.

The crew lifted the tail of the biplane and hoisted it around to face the wind, and Harry tried to keep in mind what he needed to do to take off in this unfamiliar machine. It would have more power than he was used to, but on the other hand with the big stationary engine it must be heavier too. He'd keep the nose down an extra-long time while making his run, because there appeared to be plenty of room to take off and it would be best to exceed the unknown minimum take-off speed just to be safe. No more time for preparation: those floating threads must be getting awfully damned close... He waved his hand above his head, opened up the throttle, and tweaked the mixture a little towards lean. The SE surged forward and he was off.

In just a few seconds the SE's tail lifted and he was having to hold the stick down to keep from taking off before he was ready. The SE was moving a lot faster than he was used to. He'd been expecting the better part of fifteen or twenty seconds of picking up ground speed, but he'd already reached DH.5 take-off speed in less than half that time. Engine revs sounded way too high, but maybe that was normal for this machine. Harry had no time to look for the tachometer or at the airspeed gauge just then as he was taking off on feel alone. The lengthy strip of cut lawn was coming to an end far faster than he'd expected and it would be a sad cock-up to nose over hitting some hidden boulder in the rough area beyond the airstrip, so he pulled back on the stick.

Harry thought he'd been gentle enough, but the biplane leapt into the air at a shockingly steep angle, pressing him back into his seat. It took all of Harry's remaining composure not to push the stick down and crash immediately on takeoff. By the time Harry had managed to force his scout into something resembling a conventional angle of ascent, he was over a thousand feet up, well away from the airfield, already somewhere west of the fairy village.

Before trying his first actual maneuver after taking off in the aeroplane, Harry spent a few moments looking at his instruments. *Jesus*, he thought, *the tachometer's pegged*! It was reading above redline: that couldn't be good. And yet the engine sound was fine and neither the oil pressure nor the temperature gauges seemed to be complaining. Still he thought he'd better throttle down to something resembling a normal rev level and maybe adjust the mixture back towards rich, too. His airspeed gauge was reading something strange as well, the needle hovering around 135 MPH. Ridiculous—no aeroplane could go that fast on ascent or even in level flight—there must be something wrong with the indicator. But he was definitely going much faster than his old DH.5 could have managed. After cautiously sliding back the throttle lever, he was able to get the tachometer needle back into its proper range of motion, eventually settling his airspeed at 120 MPH with just 50% throttle, what he thought he remembered as the S.E.5a's rated top speed.

At this point Harry had been flying west for the better part of a minute. He looked over his shoulder and saw the crystal-bearing threads were still in motion over the aerodrome. He'd have to turn back to get a better view. It was with a little trepidation that he banked gently into a turn, wondering how sensitive the aeroplane would be to the rudder and ailerons. But he had no cause for concern. The greater power of the inline engine combined with some inherent qualities of the airframe to make for an unusually stable platform in the air.

And then he had the vantage to look down at the airfield, which was sweeping majestically into view as Harry completed his gentle turn. The last of the crystal-laden threads was in the process of draping itself across the length of the aerodrome. From this angle, he could just make out the vanishingly thin material of the thread itself, with one of those crystalline bomb-beads attached every ten yards or so along the length. A length of it fell diagonally across one of the hangars, and he saw the canvas roof disintegrate in a jagged tear several yards across. There was no way to tell for sure what was happening below the roof, but he saw some ominous-looking dark smoke curling up from several other rents that had already been torn through the material.

Seeing the damage lit a fire in Harry's gut. He wanted to retaliate, but there was nothing obvious to shoot at. He saw that a few of the cottages had also been damaged by the crystal bombs, one completely destroyed and two others with roofs burnt or staved in. There was no sign of any follow up attack, nothing moving on the ground so far as he could tell. There were no more crystal bombs in the air, either. It looked like all of them had now dropped. But something had been carrying those cables, bombers of some kind, maybe dirigibles judging from their slow speed. They must still be nearby.

For a moment Harry juggled priorities in his head. He was feeling the weight of an exhausting day now, the most exciting and distressing of his life by far, but his fatigue was balanced by anger. This was obviously a preemptive attack by whatever force was behind the Shroud. Somehow the enemy had learned of the squadron's existence and realized they were a threat. No doubt there were all kinds of intelligence ramifications if he had some better idea what was going on, but for now Harry just wanted to strike back somehow, if only as a gesture. It was funny, he thought, how he already identified with the squadron, not yet even having been introduced to the other pilots, but there it was.

So Harry continued to fly, looking for any sign of the things he had seen before towing the threads. He had just passed over the field heading east. In another minute he'd have left the aerodrome well behind. And then he was in amongst the things. It was a loose formation of a dozen floating tugs that had by now climbed to 2,500 feet. They reminded him somewhat of observation balloons—the Germans called theirs *Drachen*— vaguely sausage-shaped objects perhaps 100 feet in length, trailing broken bits of thread behind them like tentacles. There was something oddly indistinct about the things. It seemed they were made of some kind of half-transparent material. Clearly the tugs were self-propelled, but Harry saw no engines, no propellers, no gondolas. The surfaces of the things were rippling, so perhaps they moved in some fashion like a jellyfish, though that didn't seem right, not through the air. The tugs appeared to take no notice of his passage. It shouldn't be too hard to line up a shot...

It took Harry what seemed like a long time to turn back towards the floating tugs, having overshot them by the better part of a mile before managing to line up again. But as they were only moving at a trot, perhaps ten miles an hour, there was no great rush. At length he found himself in position, about 1,000 yards above and behind the trailing floater, and at the last minute it occurred to him to check the guns and the synchronizing gear. It would be a shame to shoot his propeller off. He cocked the Vickers gun. The breech was set into the dashboard so it was right there at arm's length. He looked up and decided not to worry about the awkwardly mounted Lewis gun above his head. He'd have to stand up in the cockpit to ready it for firing and that was more than he was prepared to risk just then.

Closing at well over 100 MPH, Harry came up on the first aerial tug shockingly fast. He pressed the trigger button on the control stick and heard the gun rattling. He only had a time for a short burst before he had to pull up to avoid running right through the target. Harry passed over the tug so quickly he had only the impression of a burst of flame below him, and when he banked to take a look, he saw a cloud of smoke, nothing more; the floating vessel had caught fire from his shots and had been completely consumed in just a few seconds.

Well, then: that seemed easy enough. It took another five minutes for Harry to destroy the entire little flotilla, spending almost all his ammo on them. They must be inflated with hydrogen, he thought, just like the German Drachen balloons, but it seemed there was hardly any material to the bodies of the things, and that highly combustible as well. You could punch a lot of bullet holes in a military balloon or zeppelin without causing a fire, but Harry's bullets shredded the thin skin of these tugs and gouts of gas caught fire immediately, ignited by the burning phosphorus in his tracer rounds. After the fact, Harry was relieved to observe there was no sign of any kind of pilots in the floating tugs. The things seemed autonomous and at the same time completely unconcerned with their own destruction.

It occurred to Harry now that it was over that he had probably disobeyed orders in pursuing and shooting these tugs down but there had been no danger at all, nothing to be worried about. In fact, Harry felt he was probably more at risk in making a safe landing than in the engagement with the tugs. This could well be a problem in an unfamiliar, over-powered, extra-heavy machine.

It took Harry a good ten minutes to line up a descent that made him feel reasonably happy about his prospects. There were no other aeroplanes in the sky, so he must be the last pilot to return from the emergency evacuation.

Fortunately there were no cross winds at all, and the S.E.5a exhibited a beautiful stability even at low speed, so he didn't have to perform any last-second maneuvers to align the scout for landing. Harry felt a moment of panic when he pulled the stick back at 60 MPH a few feet off the ground and the scout not only showed no signs of stalling but actually gained a few yards of altitude, but he had plenty of space ahead of him still, and he wound up dropping the S.E.5a heavily to the ground, going a good ten miles an hour faster than he would have preferred. The ground was flat, the lawn was clear, and he trundled to a safe stop without hitting anything, stopping at last just in front of one of the hangars.

♍   ♍   ♍

It was only when he climbed down out of the cockpit that the weight of the day's events finally hit home. On touching ground Harry staggered more drunkenly than Marie had done, hours before, and he wound up leaning on the fuselage just to remain upright. Now his eyelids were heavy enough that just letting them close and falling asleep on the spot seemed like a reasonable option. Still he had enough composure to stand up in some semblance of an alert and attentive posture when he heard footsteps approaching. It was Major Quirk and the red-headed officer, followed by a group of kobold mechanics.

"I say, Tregeseal, are you all right?" Major Quirk put a hand on Harry's shoulder.

"Yes, sir. I'm sorry, sir. Just tired. Didn't sleep on the flight from the front to Carnac." Harry didn't mention the couple of hours he'd dozed off with Marie in his arms. To his mind that didn't really count as rest. For all practical purposes he'd been up for well over 24 hours now, and with the stress of the day Harry thought it should probably count more like 48. He'd spent more time in the air in one day than he had the entire week he'd been assigned to 32 Squadron.

Major Quirk peered at him quizzically. Harry would have been embarrassed if he wasn't so exhausted.

"I suppose you'd better get some sleep, then. I'll send some-one to fetch your kit bag. And hey, that reminds me, post's here! Well, come on. We'll find you a cot. Can't have you wobbling back and forth like that. Unmilitary, don't you know."

Harry was about to allow himself to be led off by the other officer, whose name he still didn't know, when he paused and turned back to the major, a little ashamed it had taken him so long to ask the question: "Was—was there much damage done, sir?"

"Not too bad," said Major Quirk. "Three scouts damaged, one totalled as it caught fire. Some minor damage to the buildings that's neither here nor there." He paused, frowned. "And one bloody fool of a mechanic got himself killed, too, standing up on the nose of a Camel trying to bat one of those damn crystal bombs out of the way with a broom. Count their lives too cheaply, they do..."

For some reason everything was dark now. After a moment of dull confusion, Harry realized it was because his eyes were closed.

"Oh, for heaven's sake. Devlin, lend a hand now..." The major's voice, sounding very far away, was the last thing Harry remembered before he fell asleep on his feet.

CHAPTER 7
ELFSHOT SQUADRON

A Flight	B Flight
Capt Ryan Devlin*	Capt Rhys Jernigan*
Lt Ewan Carstairs	Lt David Powell
Lt Donald Graham	Lt Aidan Murphy
2nd Lt Brian O'Meara	2nd Lt Harold Tregeseal
2nd Lt Alasdair MacLeod	(unassigned)
(unassigned)	(unassigned)

*=Flight Commander

"Wake up, sir."

Harry awoke to a moment of confusion. This wasn't his bunk, and he wasn't in his dormitory hut at Droglandt field. Then in a sort of a flash he recalled the past day's events all at once. It was like waking up falling out of the sky, only to land a moment later in a pile of soft mattresses. He was lying on a cot in a small half-timbered room. He supposed he must be in one of the airfield cottages. Someone had taken off his boots and tunic before putting him to bed. The clothes were draped neatly over a chair and it appeared that his boots had been polished. There was another cot set up across the room. Presumably he'd be sharing when more pilots arrived.

Looking up, Harry saw a kobold in a RFC private's uniform bending over him. He recoiled in surprise, and was a little ashamed of himself before he remembered what the kobolds were supposed to be like. *Jesus,* he thought, *he's been here with me while I slept.*

"It's four o'clock, sir. Squadron officers' meeting in thirty minutes."

"What? Oh. Yes."

Harry struggled for a moment to clear his head, then sat up, swinging his legs over the edge of the cot. He must have been asleep most of the day. He saw that the kobold was holding a tray. What was that on it? An egg cup? With a cozy, no less.

"Is that a hard-boiled egg?"

"Yes, sir. I understand it's the custom in the RFC to eat an egg after waking up. Isn't that right?"

"Er, I think that's intended as a dawn patrol breakfast. Not really meant for tea-time."

An almost comical expression of dismay appeared on the kobold's face. For a moment, Harry had the idea that he was being made game of, but then he decided the kobold was in fact seriously upset at making a mistake.

"However," said Harry, "I won't turn it down." He reached out, removed the cozy, took the egg, rapped it against a convenient shelf next to the cot, and began to peel it. For a moment Harry felt rather foolish. Was he really going through with a sort of dumb-show to spare the fellow embarrassment? Then the aroma of the egg reached his nostrils, and he realized he was hungry.

"Oh," said the kobold, apparently remembering something. He started to bow, but cut it off in the middle and converted the gesture into a salute. "Private Lambeth. I'm assigned as your batman."

Lambeth, he thought, *Really?*

"I see. Well, a pleasure to make your acquaintance, I'm sure."

Harry realized at this point he'd decided to be polite to the kobold. *What the hell,* he thought. *It's not like I'm in any danger from him.*

The kobold smiled. "Looks like this cottage isn't quite up to snuff yet, sir," he said, glancing around the room. "No wash-bowl, no water jug, no tea-kettle. A bit dusty, too. Permit me to tidy it up for you."

For the next two minutes, Harry felt rather self-conscious as he finished his egg, trying to avoid staring as Lambeth bustled around the room. He wasn't sure whether it was due to the kobold's presumed sexual preferences or simply due to the obvious fact that Lambeth was a member of a race he would have said confidently the day before was entirely mythological. Possibly both. At first he tried to avoid staring, but eventually he decided it would be inhuman not to study the kobold for a moment or two at least.

Apart from his reddish-gray skin, at first glance Lambeth could pass for an Englishman, but the more Harry looked, the more alien the fellow appeared. He was a bit on the short side at around five and a half feet tall, but there were plenty of shorter officers and men in the army. The breadth of the kobold's shoulders might have been a bit out of normal proportion for his height, but a human smith or a weightlifter could easily have the same build. The kobold's face was ordinary enough in its shape: somewhat sharp-featured perhaps, but still perfectly normal for a human.

On closer study, though, the kobold showed some other unusual features which taken together made him look more inhuman. There was a curious quality to his skin that looked quite unnatural when Harry finally noticed it. It was if the kobold had no pores, no body hair, just smooth and featureless skin—though now that he was paying attention, Harry saw a scattering of small scars here and there on Lambeth's hands and wrists, and a few similar marks on his face. The deep red irises of the kobold's eyes were flat and completely devoid of the usual striations found in human eyes, and this gave a rather disconcerting feeling to looking him in the face. When he smiled, he showed teeth that looked more pointed than normal. The most extreme difference was his fingernails, which were almost claw-like. They were either clipped or grew naturally into a sort of curved triangular form that looked quite sharp, and were thicker and more prominent than a human's.

Someone had fetched Harry's kit bag from where he'd dropped it on the hill behind the airfield. Opening it up to look for his shaving gear, he remembered that he'd left his razor behind. Oh well. He thought no one would mind a bit of stubble around here, and anyway he really only needed to shave every other day. But perhaps there were some spares he could borrow.

"I say, Lambeth," he said, "would you mind fetching that missing washbasin and some water? I'd like to clean up a little before this meeting."

"Of course, sir."

Harry realized he had breathed a sigh of relief on the kobold's departure from the cottage. It was a little embarrassing, really. Harry was accustomed to thinking of himself as tolerant, liberal, and not encumbered by prejudice, but he'd never considered sexuality to be a subject for which tolerance was required. Anyway, he was happy to be able to change his clothes without Lambeth being present.

He had only just buttoned up when the kobold returned with the washbasin and water. The ritual of splashing a little water on his face settled some of his unease, and as he dragged a comb across his head he felt a little calmer. Conscious of his discomfort in the kobold's presence before, Harry made an effort to thank him, but the words sounded stilted in his ears.

"Lambeth, do you know much about our world? I mean, where we pilots come from?"

The kobold looked up from where he was setting up a towel rack.

"Only what I've gathered from your newspapers and a few novels, sir. I don't have much confidence in my understanding. There's no way for me to distinguish factual details from fanciful ones."

"Novels? Really? You've read our novels?"

Harry grew interested despite himself.

"Yes, sir," said Lambeth. "I believe there has been a certain traffic in such things for a long time. Stories, poems, engravings, sketches, things like that. Nothing practical or useful until very recently, though."

"A long time? I thought the connection between our worlds was a recent thing."

The kobold shrugged. "Perhaps it was, sir, for actual passage. But I understand your people have been transporting packages for quite a long time. In return for items from our world: crafts, minor enchantments and such."

Harry asked, "But weren't you subjects of the Unseelie Court? How did you get your hands on this stuff?"

"We only did so very recently, sir. All this traffic was for the pleasure of the high lords and ladies of the Seelie Court, but a few months ago when it became clear that we might be of some use to them in this crisis, they sent a few crates of books to our camps, and even a few language teachers. The competition over them was fierce, but I did manage to get my hands on a few novels and plays. Dickens, Dumas, and Marlowe, and a book of poems by Baudelaire that I think our former masters of the Unseelie Court would have treasured. I'm not sure how accurate a picture they paint, of course."

"Well," said Harry, "I had no idea." He decided to take the bull by the horns. "But the reason I asked how much you know about us... listen, do you understand that none of us pilots have any experience of people so different from our own kind?"

Lambeth nodded. "So I'm given to understand, sir. I know you do have different races, but more similar to one another than the various folk here."

"Yes. But what I'm trying to say is, I may seem, well, uncomfortable around you at times. I was completely unaware of this world's existence a day ago, and it may take me a while to adjust."

So much for the bull and the horns; he'd completely avoided saying what he meant.

Lambeth stared at Harry for a moment, obviously astonished. Then he blushed, his face turning a bright red. "Sir," he said, bowing. "You honor me, but I don't know that you need to have such consideration. It's not a servant's place to complain of his master's behavior. If I do make you uncomfortable in any way, it's my fault, not yours." He paused, then looked up from his bow. "It's not—It's not about that egg, is it, sir? I hope that didn't seem strange?"

Harry laughed. "No, not that. It's—Well, I'll talk to you more later. I suppose I had better get ready to go this meeting."

"Yes, sir."

Harry buttoned up his uniform tunic and secured the Sam Browne belt that went over it while Lambeth resumed cleaning the cottage. All things considered he thought that exchange hadn't gone that badly, anyway.

There was a knock on the door, and an RFC officer opened the door and stuck his head in before Lambeth could answer it.

"Tregeseal?"

"Yes, that's me."

"Good. I'm Jernigan. Call me Rhys. You've been put into B Flight with me, so I thought I'd drop by and say hello."

He held out his hand, and Harry shook it. Jernigan had three stars on his cuffs, making him a captain. He looked to be two or three years older than Harry. Jernigan had a narrow blade of a nose and bright blue eyes, deep-set in a long triangular face, to go with his black hair.

"Right. Come on, then. We've got about five minutes till this meeting, might as well chat a bit while we walk."

They stepped out into the fairyland afternoon, and once again, Harry was struck by a strong sense of unreality. This time he thought it was caused by the warm breeze, the golden sunlight slanting downwards from the west, and the unaccustomed sight and smell of greenery all around, all so different from the bleak start to winter on the front he'd just been getting used to.

"You're an SE pilot, then, are you?"

Harry thought he'd better answer this question with complete candor. "Actually, not. Or rather, not until today. I thought I'd prefer it to the Camel. I understand we've been waiting to get S.E.5as in 32 Squadron for months, but for now we're still flying De Havilland Fives."

"Oh. But aren't those rotaries like the Camels?"

"Yes," said Harry, "but I'd just as soon not pilot a machine that will go into a spin if I take my foot off the rudder. Besides, when this is over and I go back to 32 Squadron, I might as well put some time in on the machine that they'll be getting."

"Ah," said Jernigan, "just so. Well, for the moment anyway

we're outnumbered by the Camel jockeys. Crazy bastards. Even the major flies one when he goes up himself."

"I suppose they must have their good points."

"Well, they do have two Vickers guns to our one, but then they don't have the Lewis gun, for what it's worth. They've got maneuverability, but we've got much more power for climbing, and the fixed engine makes for a much more stable firing platform. And I suppose you must have noticed the speed boost?"

"Oh yes, I was wondering about that. I thought my instruments must be on the fritz."

"The kobolds," said Jernigan. "Got their hands on the plans for a superturbocharger from somewhere. Look under the bonnet and you'll see some contraption hooked up to the carburetor that would shock the chaps at Hispano-Suiza and Wolseley."

Jernigan was leading Harry towards the large building he'd seen before. A corner of the roof on one side of the structure had partially collapsed as a result of the recent attack, but for the most part the building still appeared to be sound.

"Seriously? What does that do to the fuel consumption? To the mixture?" Harry was shocked. Superchargers were still experimental, not yet in use with aeroplane engines.

"Well, it does burn a bit more fuel, but the mixture controls seem to work pretty much as before. Ludicrous increase in power, though."

"Remarkable. And they just went ahead and did that on their own?" Harry wasn't sure what would happen to a mechanic who attempted an impromptu engine modification in an ordinary RFC squadron, but he guessed it would be nothing good.

"I believe they asked permission to take one of the Viper engines apart to tinker with it, and some genius must have taken the idea out of some technical journal or other."

"I see. Well, if the supercharger is such a success, hadn't we better write it up and let someone on the technical staff back home know about how well the thing works?"

Captain Jernigan stopped walking. He looked a little unhappy. "Well, perhaps it's better if we don't. You see..." He trailed off for a moment, then continued. "These machines are rather finely tuned, isn't it? Hydraulics, pumps, revs, mixtures, and so on?"

Harry nodded, but he wasn't sure what Jernigan was driving at.

"Right, so the machines we are used to—I mean, the

machines we were flying back in France—they're designed to run at full throttle. Oil pressure is always on the edge of blowing a gasket. Revs are just below redline most of the time. Look cross-eyed at some of these aeroplanes and they'll fall apart. And almost every time you land, you need maintenance, am I right?"

"Yes..."

"And even then, half the time you take her up and the fuel line clogs, the engine overheats or freezes, a cylinder goes out of timing, a spark plug burns out, the engine throws a rod, or maybe the oil gauge explodes in your face when you try to pull up from a dive."

"Yes, but—"

"So you increase the engine power by twenty, thirty, maybe even fifty percent, increase the revs, the pressure, the stress, everything, but keep the same design, all the same engine components. All you're doing is strapping a supercharger onto the carburetor. You'd be lucky to take off and land in one piece, wouldn't you?"

A light dawned.

"I take your point," said Harry. "You'd have to redesign the whole thing almost from scratch for more power. But if even the latest Wolseley engines are so delicate, how is it we're allowing the supercharger on *our* aeroplanes?"

They'd paused at the door to the building. Someone had installed a big sign over the lintel reading "Elfshot Squadron" with the squadron device set below the words, a cupid's bow and arrow superimposed over a bright red heart. Another group of officers was walking towards them now from across the field.

"It's the kobolds again, naturally," said Jernigan, shaking his head.

"What do you mean?"

"Of course. You're new. You don't know. They *say* they don't know magic at all. They *say* they're just good with tools. They *say* they know nothing compared to what a real engineer at Hispano-Suiza or Gnome-et-Rhône knows. But I swear if they tune your engine you can run it at the redline for a week with nothing blowing. Hit the oil gauge with a wrench, it'll probably just laugh at you."

"Oh."

"So that's the problem, isn't it? Say we send this design off to some staff engineering officer back in Home Establishment. Sure it will probably work at first, but for how long on any given machine?"

At this point the other officers arrived, and there was a pause while Harry was introduced. Despite his best intentions, Harry had some problems working through the memory game of names, faces, and handshakes, but a few flashes of association remained.

Alasdair MacLeod: A huge blond man with a big round face, a thick brush of a moustache, and a broad Scots accent he struggled at times to suppress. He seemed rather restrained and taciturn at first meeting, but Harry later found him to be more loquacious in private conversation. For some reason Harry liked him instinctively on sight, though he barely said a word at their introduction. A Camel pilot in A Flight.

Brian O'Meara: A wiry, athletic officer from Limerick. A chess player: his first question to Harry was if he played and Harry was forced to demur. Another Camel pilot. Harry later learned he was a fierce republican who had only just managed to avoid entanglement in last year's Easter Rising. He had volunteered for the RFC on the grounds that Ireland would sooner or later—hopefully sooner—need an air service of its own.

Aidan Murphy: A pink-faced Irishman out of Wexford. He must have been at least 18, but looked younger. However, he was a full lieutenant, and had three months of flying experience at the front. Murphy seemed rather shy and self-effacing at first, but when he spoke, he displayed an incisive intelligence. Not political at all, he had been convinced to volunteer by his mother, an active member of the sisterhood. Murphy was in Harry's flight, an S.E.5a pilot.

Donald Graham: A dark-haired clean-shaven man, Scottish by name and accent, always a solemn look on his face. He gave the impression of scholarship in some capacity or other, possibly holding some university appointment or maybe some kind of attorney or barrister. Harry guessed he was 25 or so, a few years older than most of the other pilots, and he was the only pilot wearing a wedding band. He spoke slowly and carefully, in complete sentences, and while his voice was redolent of the north his vocabulary was pure English. Graham was a Camel pilot in A Flight.

David Powell: A Welsh S.E.5a pilot in Harry's flight, Powell was burly and compact, with a broken nose that had healed badly, looking a little off-center in his craggy face. Harry later learned he'd been a middleweight champion at the University of Wales. Powell looked laconic and sleepy at first glance, and none too bright, but he proved both voluble and eloquent and in fact had been studying poetry and literature before the war interrupted his education.

Ewan Carstairs: A slender boyish man, presumably Scottish by his name, he seemed to Harry to be the polar opposite of MacLeod in all respects, from his slight build and sharp-featured face down to the inexplicable antipathy he felt at their first meeting. There was no trace of the Scots in his voice at all. He could have been born and raised in Surrey for all Harry would have guessed. Another Camel pilot from A Flight. His handshake and greeting was cordial enough, but there was something in his face that seemed to Harry to express disdain. But perhaps he'd misinterpreted the man. After all, there was no reason for such a reaction.

♍   ♍   ♍

The eight pilots entered the building, a mess hall with attached kitchens. The interior was substantially intact, but the sky was visible through the section of damaged roof Harry had seen from the outside, and an area of wall and floor beneath the gap looked like it had been partially burned.

Most of the space in the dining room was taken up with trestle tables and benches, but one area had been cleared and looked to be reserved for recreation, with a dartboard on the wall, a few table games stacked on shelves, and somewhat to Harry's surprise, a harpsichord made of polished ebony and faced with ornate silver trim. A holstered pistol in its belt was resting on the case. Major Quirk was sitting on the instrument's bench, chatting with the red-haired Captain Devlin over a clipboard. He looked up as the pilots entered.

"Welcome, gentlemen," he said. "Please sit down. We have a lot to cover. Tomorrow will be our first day of real operations."

The pilots found seats on benches facing the major. Quirk glanced at Harry. He played a few bars of "Beautiful Dreamer" and smiled. "So glad you could make it, Tregeseal. I see you've already been introduced."

"Yes, sir."

"Right. Let's begin." He stood, picked up the clipboard, flipped through it.

"First of all," said the major, "I imagine some of you may be interested in our security arrangements. We'd assumed that our presence here was unknown to the enemy, but obviously that's not the case. There are supposed to be lancers—knights of the Seelie Court—patrolling in the area, but if they saw those flying threads coming they didn't see fit to warn us. I have the idea there aren't all that many of them, however, and so it's quite possible they simply weren't in the area at the time."

Quirk coughed.

"Well," he continued, "be that as it may, clearly we can't have those blasted things drifting in without warning. I'm having some of our spare guns set up on the perimeter—they ought just to be able to reach those flying tugs as they come in for an attack. I've also detailed three squads of kobolds to establish camps about five miles away, to the east, northeast and southeast. Each group has a pair of guns along with some signal rockets and flares. That should give us plenty of notice next time. If there is a next time."

"Next," he said, flipping a page, "Operations. I had hoped to be able to assemble a full squadron roster and give everyone enough time to gain familiarity with their flight-mates and the place in general, but this attack can't be ignored. It may mean a new offensive on the part of the enemy. We'll just have to train up new pilots as they arrive and fit them in. I'm told we will be getting a few more in the coming week, but I don't know after that. Apparently there aren't that many pilots with the right bloodlines.

"Anyway, we're going to do a reconnaissance in force to-morrow morning. Both flights together. So far as we knew before today the enemy has no air defenses at all, but since no one told us about these bombers we'll just have to be wary. If nothing else, those things might make for the equivalent of dirigible barrage balloons."

Here the major paused for a moment and flipped a page on his clipboard.

"Speaking of the bombs, I'm sure you're wondering just what they are. They're chemical weapons. Incendiaries. A couple of them survived impact with the ground, and we'll have a brief demonstration of what they can do after this meeting.

"A certain pilot," here Major Quirk looked at Harry, "saw fit to disregard my instructions regarding safety-first earlier today, and perhaps we should pause for a moment to hear his report. Lieutenant Tregeseal, if you would be so kind."

Harry stood up. He had been preparing himself for this moment, though he hadn't been sure whether it would be brought up at the meeting or if he would have to report his little action in private.

"Yes, sir. I'm sorry sir. I have no excuse except to say that I was angry at the attack, and as it took me a while to familiarize myself with the controls of my aeroplane, I was in the air longer than the rest of the squadron. I happened to see a group of the, er, enemy vehicles returning eastwards, and I thought it would be a shame to let them go on their way."

"As you may or may not be aware, Lieutenant," said the major dryly, "discipline and obedience to orders is considered to be a mandatory part of army life. Shocking, yes, I know." He paused, and Harry heard someone trying unsuccessfully to suppress a snort at his table.

"But as it happens," Major Quirk continued, "if rumor is true the flying corps is about to be separated from the army and reformed as an independent service, and among pilots individual initiative and an aggressive temperament are said to be virtues, or so I've heard. So let's consider this little episode a wash as regards praise or blame, and just tell us what you did and what you saw."

Harry recounted his little engagement with the floating tugs.

"Well I suppose that's a good sign, at least," said Captain Devlin. "If the pods in the Shroud are equally flimsy and are likewise inflated with hydrogen, they should be easy targets."

"Yes," said Major Quirk, "we can hope so. We'll be loaded with Buckingham incendiary ammo, same as they developed to defend against the zeppelins. No worry about the Germans saying it's a war crime to use it, after all. But I should like to remind the squadron that there's a reason most of us aren't fond of balloon-busting back on the front. Archie doesn't like it when you try to shoot down his observers, and for all we know the enemy has something like Archie over here as well, so I'll thank everyone to stay alert and take nothing for granted on our first patrol."

There followed some technical discussion of the plan for the next day's operation, and then Major Quirk called for questions. There was the usual initial silence, but after a moment Harry was surprised to see Lieutenant Murphy raise his hand. He'd thought the young Irishman too shy to speak up.

"Pardon me, sir," said Murphy, "but do we have any better idea of who the enemy is, yet? What they want, what their resources may be? Anything like proper intelligence at all, sir?"

Harry thought it was a rather confrontational question, under the circumstances, but Major Quirk didn't seem annoyed to hear it.

"Those are good questions, Lieutenant," he said, "but I'm afraid there are no answers as yet. This is one reason why I keep repeating these cautions. We simply don't know enough about what's going on. The one thing I am confident about is that our hosts on this side of the line are as worried as we are about the Shroud."

That provoked a question from Harry. He raised his hand.

"Yes, Tregeseal?"

"About the Shroud, sir. Is there some pattern to its movement? How long do we think it will be until it begins to approach our position, or other possessions of the Seelie Court?"

"Another good question," said the major. "None of us have seen it moving at all. But at least we've reports from the kobolds and some other refugees about how it moved when it was expanding to cover the lands of the Unseelie court. When the pods are in motion, they are said to make no more than a mile an hour or so, and after a day's movement they pause for a while, as if to rest. That's just past behavior of course. We don't know if that's their limit or not. But the line has been static for a couple of months now, since the entire expanse of the former lands of the Unseelie court were covered. Possibly the enemy has to consolidate its holdings in some fashion before resuming its expansion."

"Is it possible that the Shroud won't move to cover the Seelie Court lands at all?"

"Yes. But of course, from *their* point of view, I mean, the point of view of our hosts in the Seelie Court, it would be foolhardy to assume as much. And this recent attack suggests not only that the enemy regards us as a threat, but that it has no particular compunction about an attack outside its own lines."

"I see," said Harry. "Thank you, sir, but if you don't mind, one more question. These refugee reports. Do they suggest where the Shroud came from? Did it move into the Unseelie Court lands from somewhere outside their borders, or it did it somehow arise there?"

"Sadly, we've got no answers. The only refugees were from isolated communities on the western borders of the region—mostly kobolds, actually—who both recognized the Shroud as a threat and were able to move fast enough to escape its influence."

"Thank you, sir." Harry sat down, disappointed.

"All right," said Major Quirk. "Let's proceed outside for an object demonstration of the enemy's capabilities." He nodded at Captain Devlin who picked up the revolver from where it had been resting on the harpsichord case.

The officers filed outside, and the major led them to the far side of the building, where a path of blasted and burned spots could be seen starting from the damaged corner of the building and extending east on the lawn towards the edge of the airfield. Two dozen similar tracks had marred the surface of the field. Here, though, one of the crystal beads nestled on a patch of brambly bushes.

"Careful not to touch it," said the major, "nasty stuff in there. But do walk up and take a look."

The crystalline object was about a yard long. Harry saw that while the overall shape was that of a hexagonal prism, on one end the sharp geometrical facets smoothed out and elongated, thinning to form a long slender curve, like the tail of glassy teardrop. A length of inch-thick black line, featureless but soft and flexible, was attached to the crystal tail.

"That crystal shell is something like Rupert's drops," said Captain Devlin. "Anyone heard of the stuff? You drop molten glass into water, and the stress from the rapid cooling is frozen into the glass. It's very strong, but if it cracks or breaks at all, even if it's just scratched, the whole thing explodes. That long tail is so thin that it will probably break when it hits ground or if the thread gets snagged on something, but this one happened to land just right and survived."

He took the pistol out of the holster, checked the cylinder to make sure it was loaded, and held it up in the air.

"Anyone fancy themselves a good shot?"

No one replied immediately, so the captain said, "Never mind. I'll do it. Stand well back, now. Everyone upwind, please."

Devlin cocked the revolver, took careful aim, and pulled the trigger. The crystal shell exploded into a burst of particles, shining like a million tiny diamonds in the sunlight. There was a puff and a visible cloud of vapor erupted. After a heartbeat the cloud ignited in a fireball that reached a maximum diameter of about five yards and quickly dissipated. The bramble bush on which the crystal had rested disintegrated into ash, and the lawn surrounding it turned black and burned away. A sharp pungent smell could be detected. There was something rather familiar about the scent.

"Is that—"

"Hydrogen peroxide," said Captain Devlin. "Seems to be. Very high concentration. When the crystal blows, the peroxide mixes with something extremely inflammable in an internal compartment, but we don't have a chemical laboratory to find out what. I'm no chemist, but my father used to run a hospital pharmacy so I'm somewhat familiar with peroxide.

"This isn't the stuff you put on cuts, by the way. That's just three or five percent, mixed with water. The thirty percent stuff they use in hospitals for disinfecting will burn your skin if you touch it, but above seventy percent, that's where it really gets exciting. When peroxide is almost pure anything it touches that can possibly burn or corrode at all will do so almost instantly. Nasty stuff indeed. You can imagine what would happen if one of these things hit an aeroplane in flight. The fabric and frame would just disintegrate on contact. Not to mention the pilot."

"Thank you, Captain Devlin," said Major Quirk. "I think that will be all for today. In the morning we'll take a closer look at the enemy. Dismissed."

Captain Jernigan caught up with Harry as the meeting dispersed. "There's still some daylight left," he said. "Spend them aloft, shall we? I can show off a few tricks these souped-up fives can do, and you can get a bit more used to the aeroplane before the job tomorrow. Always good to get the lay of the land, for that matter."

"Thanks," said Harry, "I appreciate the help."

They located the kobold sergeant currently in charge of the hangar. He introduced himself as Blackheath, and directed a corporal named Bromley to organize a gang to ready their aeroplanes. So far all of the kobolds Harry had seen up close looked much alike. None showed any signs of age, but then almost the entire RFC officer corps was in their early twenties so that wasn't surprising. But all the kobolds had the same sharp features, the same skin coloration, a similar scattering of fine scars on hands and face. Looking at Bromley and Blackheath side by side—two more London place-names, it occurred to Harry—hey weren't really identical, but had they been human Harry wouldn't have been surprised to learn they were brothers.

The S.E.5a that Harry had piloted that morning was designated provisionally as his personal machine. Looking it over he had to wonder why the SE mounted a Lewis gun atop the wing planes. This seemed to be holdover from the old days of unsynchronized guns. And yet the SE mounted a single synchronized conventional Vickers gun firing through the propeller. So far as Harry knew, all fighters in the current generation apart from the SE were mounting twin coaxial guns. Such guns took belt feeds of hundreds of rounds of ammo with no need for the awkwardness of standing up in the cockpit to switch small ammo drums in combat like the Lewis gun.

Twin guns were also easier to aim and zero in for dogfighting.

"Sorry," said Jernigan when Harry asked, "I've no idea. I'm just used to the Lewis gun from the older aeroplanes, I suppose."

They spent a few minutes going over the modified engine internals before running through the usual checklist.

"Tell me," said Harry to the kobold corporal—he was perched on a step-ladder beside the engine—"this supercharger: I suppose it must make the engine run very hot? But yesterday when I didn't know it was there I hardly had to adjust the radiator at all after taking off. The temperature was still in the normal range the whole time even with the tachometer pegged."

"Sir," said Bromley carefully, "you probably didn't engage the system. The lever is a bit out of the way, you see. Not part of the original design." The kobold frowned disapprovingly. "If you don't pull the handle out, it will just pass the air through."

"What? You're saying I was doing over 120 at half throttle with the turbine not even spinning?"

"Yes, sir. There is a small increase in compression even when it's just set to pass-through."

Now Harry had some idea of what Jernigan had been talking about before. Improving performance so dramatically really did smack of magic.

"Amazing. Anyway, I suppose I need to know what to do with the mixture and the radiator when the supercharger is actually working. And how do I know if I'm pushing it too hard? The tachometer was pegged even without the supercharger running."

The kobold looked embarrassed. "We haven't had time yet to machine new gauges yet with proper redlines. Revs should be safe up close to 3,000. At least the airspeed indicator will read accurately. As a rough guide, try not to go faster than 170 in level flight at 10,000 feet for more than ten minutes, or 150 at 20,000 feet."

"You're not serious," said Harry. He'd never heard of any aeroplane going that fast, except in a dive.

"That's with the supercharger engaged, of course sir."

"Is that even possible? The cams, the rods, the stress on the crankshaft, the pumps, the gaskets—surely something would give... Wouldn't the fabric just peel off the wings at that speed?"

"No, sir. Of course, there is a limit to the stress the frame can support. If you're going much faster than 280 in a dive, you're in trouble, sir, because the wings will come off when you zoom."

"280? You *do* mean miles per hour, right, not kilometers?"

"Yes, sir. Miles."

Harry was stunned. If they had aeroplanes like this back in France, the Germans wouldn't have a chance. Even von Richtofen's *Jagdgeschwader 1* would be unable to fight against such overwhelming technical superiority.

"Oh, sir," said the kobold. "One more thing, if you please."

"Yes?"

"With the supercharger engaged, your ceiling is upwards of 30,000 feet. Please don't fly much over 20,000, though, or you'll pass out for sure."

Harry didn't know what the service ceiling of a stock S.E.5a was supposed to be, but he was sure it wasn't anything like 30,000 feet. He thought no one had ever even tried to fly that high before. His old DH.5 couldn't break 15,000 feet, and in 32 Squadron they never flew anywhere close to that altitude because performance degraded rapidly as the air got thinner.

♍   ♍   ♍

Once again the propeller spun up immediately as Harry flipped the switches on the call of "Contact!", without the mechanic having to heave at it. Jernigan's aeroplane had already been run out onto the field by the time that Harry was ready, and he watched him take off. Just as he recalled from his first flight that morning, Jernigan's take-off was startlingly fast and abrupt, at a much steeper angle than Harry would have thought possible back in France.

The actual experience of his own take-off was a little less alarming this time, though Harry still wasn't used to the sudden surge of acceleration. He rose to 3,000 feet readily enough, finding Jernigan circling above him. It wasn't too hard to sideslip into formation off to Jernigan's right and behind him. At first they just flew northwest for a few minutes, leaving the hills around the fairy village behind and soon passing beyond the village fields and pastures. They began cruising along the edge of the forest Harry had noticed on emerging from the dolmen. This was the largest wood Harry had ever seen, extending indefinitely into the distance to the northwest and west.

Now that he was fully awake and had time to look around with no particular urgency to the situation, Harry found himself almost mesmerized by the improbably deep blue shell of the heavens around him. He felt as if he was getting drunk on the color. A few white clouds floated through the sky high above, looking absurdly distinct and solid as if they were made out of meringue. One of the secret delights that Harry had learned during his brief tenure as a pilot was the grandeur of the view from the cockpit, but here, flying over the fairy lands at 5,000 feet, everything he'd seen in England and France paled into insignificance in comparison. Even the engine noise seemed less jarring than usual.

Jernigan carried on northwest along the edge of the woods for a few minutes without any maneuvers, and then Harry saw him pointing down before banking into a tight arc. Harry had no trouble staying in formation, and as they turned he looked down and saw a stone structure, a fort at a high place a thousand yards deep into the forest.

They flew low over the fort, no more than 200 feet up, and Harry saw the place was surrounded by a number of out-buildings, including an extensive stables. A squadron of horsemen had formed up on a road leading east through the forest, and Harry could just make out some of the riders standing up in their stirrups looking up at him as they flew over the fort. He waggled his wings as he passed over their heads, and Jernigan executed a perfect aileron roll.

Jernigan led him back up and to the east for a few miles, and they were once again over the meadowlands, having risen to 10,000 feet in a surprisingly short time, the SE not exhibiting any of Harry's old DH.5's reluctance to climb.

Now Jernigan banked into a gentle and rather lazy right turn. This was easy enough to follow, but as they bent their course around, he gradually tightened the curve to the point that Harry would have been concerned about the prospect of falling into a spin if he'd been on his own. But Jernigan's machine was still stable, so he tried to keep bending around, tighter and tighter... Then he lost track of Jernigan completely as the Welshman had turned so sharply to the right he wasn't in front anymore. Harry straightened out, puzzled, and Jernigan dropped in immediately behind him. Evidently, he'd pulled up just as he left Harry's field of vision, and Harry had lost him completely as a result.

But now Harry understood what they were doing. It was mock dogfighting. If he'd realized this in time, he might not have let Jernigan get behind him so easily. Oh well. It was his turn to try to escape Jernigan's tailing position. He started to break left, aborted the turn and side slipped, then broke hard right, all with no luck. It was as if Jernigan was trailing behind on a tow rope. A split-S didn't work either—Harry was particularly proud of this maneuver, which was just about at the limits of his skill. But by the time he emerged from the downward half-loop pulled after an initial inversion, Jernigan was close enough to call out to had the engine noise not been so loud. But he really was very close now, no more than 50 feet away, an amazing display of skill on Jernigan's part, and the closeness gave Harry an idea. He dove briefly to pick up some speed, and pulled sharply back on the stick. Jernigan would see him soaring upwards, of course, but he was so close that it would be impossible for him to react quickly enough to follow in the same path, and now Harry could decide whether to turn left or right, reverse into something like a wingover, complete an inside loop, or roll into an Immelman headed back the way he'd come. In theory he could also just push the stick back into level flight, which might have been clever if Jernigan overshot him, but would also have risked a collision. Harry wound up trying a very radical wingover to the left, the souped-up SE angling up almost vertically before showing signs of a stall and falling back down into a tight left turn with so much airspeed lost that Harry was able to reverse direction in a very tight radius. In the DH.5 he would have fallen into a spin for sure, but the power of the SE's engine was such that it pulled him back into level flight with almost no instability at all—it was as if he'd banked a motorcycle up a steeply cambered stadium turn.

For a moment Harry thought he'd lost Jernigan when he finally completed the maneuver, but there he was again, somehow slipping back into position a stone's throw behind him. Harry couldn't imagine how Jernigan had managed to stay so close. He must have both anticipated the maneuver and guessed right about where Harry was going to end up. Looking over his shoulder, Harry saw Jernigan giving a thumbs-up gesture, and then he pointed west before breaking away from his tailing position. Harry looked west too, not understanding for a moment, and then he saw the sky over the western horizon blazing with a glorious mix of crimson and purple, a bright ruby flash vanishing over the horizon far to the west. The sun had just set, and it was time to return to the airfield.

♍   ♍   ♍

The twilight landing was easier this time, now that Harry knew the S.E.5a had a fairly low stall speed. He was able to drop easily into position, touching ground as gently as he'd ever managed before, and taxiing up to the entrance to the hangar. A gang of kobolds was ready and waiting to wheel the machine under the newly patched canvas roof.

Captain Jernigan landed a minute later, and he was out of his cockpit before the propeller had spun down. Harry walked over to meet him.

"Not bad," said Jernigan, "for no experience in a SE."

"Thanks," said Harry. "But I can see I have a lot to learn. I'm amazed you were able to stay on my tail like that. I can't imagine staying so close behind anyone trying to shake me off. Can you tell me how you did it?"

"Well..." Jernigan seemed oddly hesitant for a moment, and then he spoke up. "First of all, I have a lot more experience than you. I've been flying since '14, you know."

"Really?" Harry was surprised to learn this. Most pilots with such longevity would be promoted to field rank or even higher by now.

"Yes. Close to 3,000 hours logged, perhaps half that at the front, after a break back home as an instructor. In 1914 or '15 your old DH.5 would have been a sort of angel of war, not the clunker it is now."

"I see."

"And since you're probably wondering," said Jernigan, "there's a reason I'm still a captain. You must have done some stunting in school?"

"A little," said Harry, cautiously. It was forbidden, of course, but everyone did it. Racing down near the ground, ducking under bridges, that sort of thing. Near the end of flight school, he'd nearly smashed himself up several times.

"We do it up at the front too, you know," said Jernigan. "A year or so ago, I buzzed an annoying army staff car buggering about near my airfield as if it owned the place... Turned out it did."

"What do you mean?"

"Oh, it seems Trenchard doesn't like being mock-strafed by his own side."

"Trenchard? You mean *General* Trenchard? *Chief of Air Staff* Trenchard?"

"The very same. Head of the whole flying corps. But that put the kibosh on further promotions for the duration, I'm afraid. Honestly, I was lucky not to be court-martialed, but I had a DSO and all that, back when there weren't that many of them, so they just shoved it under the rug."

"I'm impressed," said Harry, and Jernigan grinned.

"But you were asking about that mock dogfight," said Jernigan. "Let's see. I got behind you by cheating, of course. You didn't know what I was doing when I started that silly inward spiral turn. Then you tried to shake me off the usual ways, and I stayed on you through sheer skill, if I say so myself. Up until just before the end."

Harry nodded. "But what about when you were right behind me? How could you possibly figure out what I was doing when I pulled up?"

"I was showing off, of course, staying so close. No need to do that in a real fight." Jernigan stuck his fingers out as if they were guns. "You'd already be shot down. But you mean when you did that sort of wingover-stall thing? You might say that was sheer luck..."

Jernigan trailed off. He seemed to be making his mind up about something.

"Well," he said, "in for a penny, I suppose. No harm in talking about it here anyway, of all places. Just that I've got used to keeping mum about it."

Jernigan took something out of his pocket. He held it out for Harry to take a look at. It was an amber sphere, perhaps an inch and a half in diameter, held in a gold fitting like a claw, a fine gold chain depending from the fitting.

"My aunt gave this to me when I entered as a pilot back in '14. Didn't hold with superstition at the time, but you know, would have been rude to turn it down. Nice looking thing, isn't it? Got a feather inside the amber. Good token for a flier to carry, right? Anyway, I went through the Fokker Scourge of '15 in an early-model B.E.2. You remember what the press called that aeroplane at the time?"

"Fokker fodder, wasn't it?"

"Yes," said Jernigan. "And the German nickname for the machine was *cold meat*. I'm serious. The aeroplane was totally outclassed in every way as it was, and then that damn Dutchman Fokker came up with his synchronizing gear and it got even worse. No point in having a rear-gunner when the hun is shooting at you from the front. Three times, I'm telling you, I was the only one to make it back in my flight."

"Jesus," said Harry. "I knew it was bad back then, but I had no idea how bad."

"Not every squadron was hit that hard, but mine was disbanded. We ran out of pilots too fast for replacements. Never took any damage myself, though, not even a dud engine the whole time. So you understand I started to put a little stock in this charm, don't you? Eventually I was reassigned to a new squadron supplied with Nieuport-11 scouts—my God, what a change from those blasted B.E.2s—and finally we began to get our own back a little. I had one day where I shot down five Fokkers. Got a line in the Gazette, DSO, promotion, leave—you name it. This was before that little strafing incident, you understand. Back then I thought that I was winning based entirely on skill."

"You're not saying this talisman was what saved you?" Harry realized he sounded incredulous, maybe offensively so. "Listen," he said quickly, "it's not that I'm doubting you. I mean, here we are, after all. It's just—well, if this thing can protect you in the air, makes you lucky, whatever... what *can't* happen? It's as if I don't know how the world works anymore. Are you sure it was the amulet that did all this?"

"I'm afraid I am. And I know what you mean, too. A lump of amber that somehow knows when I'm flying, that does all these things... it doesn't even begin to make sense."

They were both silent for a moment, and Jernigan spoke up again.

"But that's the way it seems to work. I got back home on leave after my promotion, and my family had a bit of a to-do for me. My aunt had perhaps a bit too much punch to drink, and she asked if the Badb was keeping me safe."

"The what?"

"I had no idea what she was talking about at the time either. But it turns out Badb Catha is one face of the Irish Morrígan war goddess. The battle crow, they call her. Anyway, I thought it was rather odd. After all, we're Welsh, you know. So I said, my dear Anti Ellen, what is it you're on about now? We've no Irish blood, or do we? And she gets a bit talkative, being somewhat drunk, and she tells me the amber has got an enchantment on it from the Irish goddess herself that will protect the bearer from danger in the sky."

"I'm not sure I know what to say," said Harry. "Are you telling me that your Badb Catha is a real living goddess? With real power, I mean?"

"Listen, Tregeseal, I'm not saying it myself. And she's not *my* goddess. But I can tell you the thing does work. And if it's not really the amber that's doing it, but a goddess... well, it may not make much sense, but it's just a little bit less crazy, isn't it? I mean to say a lump of amber can't do anything by itself, but maybe a goddess *can*."

"But the goddess couldn't protect you without you carrying this thing? She can reach between the worlds, change the course of a dogfight, do all that, but she won't do it if you don't have the talisman? And if someone else picked it up, a German, say, she'd do it for them too?"

"Believe me," said Jernigan, "I'd like a better explanation myself but I'm just a pilot. I wasn't raised on this stuff anymore than you were."

"All right," said Harry, "I'm sorry to press you so hard. I just want to try to understand, because it sounds so crazy on the face of it. I suppose your, er, Aunt Ellen, she's in this sisterhood, then, is she?"

"Righto. Didn't know it at the time, of course. She never got *that* drunk. So I get back to the front, and now I realize just how lucky I've been in the air: or maybe the effect gets stronger somehow now that I know I have it. If some hun is on my tail, his guns jam. If I spot one and dive on him, he won't see me until it's too late. I'm leading a charmed life up there, and it's not long before I get a little sick of it. Not so sick I fly without the charm, mind you—I'm not suicidal. But it's not right to be slaughtering Germans up there like pigeons with nothing coming my way."

"I understand," said Harry. "To be honest, I felt pretty bad on my first engagement. We attacked three Germans unawares, with a two-to-one advantage. Uh, yesterday, it was, though it feels like a year ago now. I know it makes no sense in wartime, but how I felt was this: what business is it of mine to be shooting down some poor bastard that doesn't even know I'm there? Made me feel dirty."

"Yes. I know the feeling well. You do feel different about it when it's one of your mates who's been shot down the day before. Then you want revenge. But after we got our Nieuports, we had the advantage for a while. Same Lewis gun as on the SE, by the way, though I grant you the Vickers is far superior now. The war almost seemed winnable there for a shining moment or two. But then of course the Huns came up with the Albatross D.I, and it was the whole thing over again in '16, and again in bloody April this year with the D.III."

Jernigan stopped speaking for a moment, maybe realizing all that he'd been saying, and for how long he'd been going on. He passed a hand over his face, rubbed his eyes.

"Sorry," he said, "going a bit far field from the topic. But that's how I stayed on your tail. Magic. You pulled up for that vertical maneuver, whatever it was going to be, and you were quite right: I was too close on your tail to follow directly, so I put my hand in my pocket and just sort of *felt* what the best thing to do would be, nosed underneath you and pulled my own Immelman with a bit of left slip, and you came out of your wingover right in front of me like we had planned it in advance. No credit to me at all. Anyway, I really am sorry for bending your ear with all that stuff."

"It's no trouble," said Harry. "In one week at the front, I haven't had time to learn anything really of what this war is like, but to be honest, that one fight yesterday was enough for me."

"Sure enough," said Jernigan, "and that's the sane response, isn't it? If they felt that way in the high command, there'd be no war in the first place. Pity, that. For now, though, enough talk: it's dinner time."

♍ ♍ ♍

Dinner was a mix of the elaborate and simple. Like every other service that would usually be performed by enlisted men or NCOs, cooking was done by the kobolds. They served and cleared the table as well. The squadron sat down to eat in the refectory, white tablecloths covering the trestle tables, and a shining display of silver plate on the tables, all exquisitely wrought, the work of fairy artisans. The meal itself, however, was peasant food—wealthy peasant food perhaps, since it was dominated by roast mutton—but very plain, accompanied by an endless supply of brown ale that went down very well with the food.

"I hope you gentlemen liked that mutton," said Major Quirk, as the table was cleared. "We'll be eating a lot of it, along with goat, venison, and the occasional chicken. The barley bread's not bad, I must say, and the soups are generally passable, if uninspired. I'm afraid the cook doesn't have much notion of a sauce, though. No fish and no potatoes. Turnips and cabbage for those who like them. Good English peas, at least."

There was a pause while the table was cleared, and the pewter tankards were replaced by crystal goblets carried in by the white-gloved kobolds acting as waiters for the meal.

"Oh sure," said Lieutenant O'Meara, "the food is a wee bit dull as may be, but the wine! Now that is nectar for you. And with such a drink at hand, ambrosia is unnecessary."

"Indeed," said Quirk, "we've half a dozen cases stowed away, and more promised when we run out: another token of Prince Nuada's generosity. Not a single distillery in the whole realm, but they certainly know how to treat a grape well. And in token of that..."

Major Quirk picked up his glass, and stood. "Gentleman, the

King."

The squadron followed suit for the loyal toast, and Harry tasted the drink. He was not a connoisseur of wine, usually preferring ale or liquor when he drank, but O'Meara had the right of it. This was nectar such as the gods themselves wouldn't scorn. Later he heard Powell put it like this: suppose it was possible for a man to go without water for so long that he forgot what drinking was like. Perhaps he somehow went an entire lifetime without a drink. The withered fellow comes tottering home after a long day's work under the hot sun, and sees a tumbler of ice-water someone has put out. He doesn't recognize it at all, but nevertheless he takes a sip, and at last he realizes what he's been missing. That was the feeling of drinking the fairy wine, a feeling that was strangely divorced from the actual flavor.

Considering just the sensations on tongue and nostrils by themselves, it was a good, heavy red wine, bitter with tannin, something like certain Burgundies: well enough in its way, but nothing all that special. But the buzz, or whatever it might be called that accompanied a sip, that was something extraordinary. Delightful it was, even thrilling, but also enormously satisfying. When Harry finished the glass he came back to himself with an ordinary enough taste in his mouth, and the fading memory of something indescribable, like a half-forgotten dream of heaven.

"A moment of silence for Tregeseal's first sip," said O'Meara. And then after a pause, "Well? What d'ye think?"

"I don't know what to say," said Harry. "If I didn't believe in magic before now, this would prove me wrong. If ever there is anything like normal commerce between our worlds, the Seelie Court will certainly not have to worry about balance of trade."

The dinner dissolved after that, with some of the pilots chatting over tankards of the brown ale. The wine was too precious to waste on casual drinking. O'Meara brought out a chess set and hectored Graham into giving him a game with a pawn in hand, and Harry spent the remainder of the evening getting to know the other pilots in his flight.

♍   ♍   ♍

22 December 1917.

Harry lurched in his cot. Something had woken him up from a confused erotic dream—he could still see Marie, the pendant glowing between her breasts. He'd been trying to reach her, but had been unable to move for some reason, and somehow they were drifting apart. *Christ*, he'd wanted her so badly... he realized his face was moist with tears. For a brief span he suffered the throes of that curious mix of confusion and clarity that sometimes comes when waking abruptly in a strange place. The room was murky and dark, but a few cracks of sunlight piercing chinks in the timbers and filtering through the shutters made it obvious that it was full morning already.

The knock on the door was repeated.

"Come in," he called, wiping his face and sitting up in bed.

"Good morning, sir," said Lambeth, carrying in a tray with, yes, another egg in its knitted egg-cozy. This time it was accompanied by a teapot, mug, cup of milk, and salt and pepper shakers. After setting down the tray, he opened the wood shutters, letting in a dazzling shaft of sunlight. It was well after sunrise. Late for a dawn patrol—oh yes, they weren't scheduled to fly until mid-morning.

"Squadron to assemble in an hour for operations, sir."

"Ah, thank you." Harry was fully awake now, and back in control of himself after the broken ending to his dream.

The kobold made to leave, but Harry recalled a couple of questions he'd been storing up.

"I say, Lambeth."

"Yes, sir?"

"There's a chief mechanic, I suppose? I'd like to talk to him later on."

Lambeth looked worried. "Yes, sir. That would be Sergeant Major, uh, Charing-Cross. Do you wish to see him immediately, or after you return from your flight?"

"*Charing-Cross*? Really?"

"Yes, sir. And may I ask what you wish to see him about?"

"Nothing all that important. I'm just interested in these engineering innovations your people seem to have come up with. Is, er, Charing-Cross the one responsible for supercharging the S.E.5a engine?"

Lambeth paled, then flushed. It was an interesting effect in a kobold, as it turned him such a bright red that he seemed almost to be glowing for a few moments.

"No, sir," he said, and trailed off, mumbling something indistinctly.

"Sorry, what was that?"

"That was me, sir!" Lambeth seemed distressed. He was standing at attention now, looking straight in front of him, not at Harry.

"What?"

"I'm responsible for the superturbocharger, sir. It's my fault. I'm sorry."

"Hold on, Lambeth," said Harry. "I may not be understanding you properly, and I'm not sure you understand me, either. First of all, I'm not upset about it, and second, aren't you my batman? Are you holding down two jobs, servant and chief designer?"

Lambeth's eyes widened. Harry saw his lips moving, silently framing the phrase "chief designer", and then he answered. "Sir, I was, um, reassigned."

"Who would reassign a talented engineer to be a personal servant? That makes no sense."

Lambeth paused before answering.

"Sir, you're right and wrong. Serving as batman in this squadron is the most desirable job any of us could hope for. But, well, in my case I believe it was not given to me so much as a reward, but to stop me working on the machines."

Harry shook his head. "I'm sorry, Lambeth. I don't understand at all. Why would being a servant be such a great job? And why stop you from doing your other work?"

Lambeth looked down at his feet. "It's generally believed, sir, that being a batman provides the most... opportunity."

"The most what? Opportunity? For what?"

"I don't want to give offense, sir."

"But—Oh!" A light dawned. Harry wasn't sure how to respond to this, so he changed topics. "Well, er, why would they want you out as an engineer?"

"Mechanic, sir. We're squadron mechanics—"

"Don't be ridiculous," said Harry. Now he felt himself to be on firmer ground. "No ordinary mechanic could craft a supercharger from scratch, much less figure out how to get it to work reliably with an engine that wasn't even designed for one. If it was a merely mechanical job, no doubt the machines would already have them when shipped from the factory."

Lambeth opened his mouth to speak, but didn't say anything for a time. He was clearly trying to come up with something. At last he said "Philosophical differences, sir."

"What do you mean by that?"

"I believe I was offered this position because some of the other mechanics were not—how shall I say this... they found the work I was doing not to be in harmony with the rest of the work of the shop."

"Listen," said Harry, "I realize I'm prying, and that you

would rather not answer. But you've accomplished something really remarkable with that engine. If you can bring yourself to ex-plain without violating any confidence, I'd like to hear it, is all."

Lambeth looked at him with those flat red eyes, again without saying anything for a time, and for the duration of that brief silence, he seemed completely alien and uncanny. When he started speaking again it took Harry a second to realize he was hearing intelligible English: that was how far he'd seemed to depart from humanity.

"Sir," said Lambeth, "if you would truly like to hear about this... situation, I will tell you. But I think it will take a while to explain. Perhaps we had best leave this discussion for another time? This afternoon, if all goes well?"

"All right. Thank you, Lambeth. One more question, though, if it's not a private matter. Why do you all have names of places in and around London?"

Lambeth smiled, looking relieved. "Oh, that. No sir, there's no difficulty explaining. We prefer not to speak our true names where others can hear. The lords and ladies of the courts can use them to conjure with, you see, and well, not that *you* would do such a thing, but at the time... Well, when Major Quirk read us into service with the squadron it was necessary to provide names rather expeditiously, and the only source of a large number of proper English names that was convenient was a map of London and nearby towns. We'd learned of course from our reading that many English family names are based on places."

"Oh," said Harry. "That makes sense, I suppose. And of course, you're right about the naming convention. My family name is a place-name, too. I'm sure there are quite a few families named Lambeth in my world. Not so many named Charing-Cross, however..."

CHAPTER 8
THE SHROUD

The pilots of Elfshot Squadron stood in a somewhat disorderly line in front of the north hangar, listening to Major Quirk's address before their first formal operation.

"...assuming no resistance, A Flight will approach to approximately one mile of the Shroud. At that time, the launch of a red flare will mean to begin a cautious attack on a single pod, the target to be determined by Captain Devlin. Meanwhile, B Flight will be watching over us from the upper layer, and will only engage if A Flight runs into difficulty. If at any time a green flare is fired, all aircraft will disengage and return to the aerodrome.

"Now then, seeing as those thread-tugs were used offensively we should not be surprised to see them used defensively as well. Think of them as mobile barrage balloons whose cables are studded with mines. Should these, ah, vehicles indeed be deployed around the pods, we will want counts of their numbers as well as detailed observations regarding their behavior. All pilots will be responsible for paying careful attention to these details, but I especially want the pilots of B Flight to take note. If all goes well you gentlemen will be well above the pods with nothing to do except watch, and will be able to observe the enemy's configuration and any defenses they may have.

"I will fly with A Flight for this job. Both flight commanders will observe my scout for signals. Other pilots will no doubt see the flares as well, but will follow their own flight commanders' leads. I want no individual heroics today. Is that clear?"

There was a general vocalization of yes-sirs.

"All right, then," he said. "Let's go. A Flight to depart first and cruise at 10,000. B Flight will follow at an altitude of 13,000 feet."

♍   ♍   ♍

Harry waited in the cockpit with the rest of B Flight's aeroplanes lined up ready to go alongside his own aeroplane, watching A Flight's departure. Major Quirk had taken off in his Camel first, and now the rest of the Camels followed, ascending in a beautiful line abreast. Their initial acceleration was markedly less than that of the supercharged S.E.5as, and their climb angle was more natural-looking.

Now it was B Flight's turn. Jernigan lost no time, the

streamer on his machine's tail that signified his status as flight commander trailing straight behind as he rocketed upwards. Powell and Murphy were just behind him to either side, and Harry took up the fourth position in the abbreviated chevron formation. They engaged superchargers almost immediately to gain the superior altitude required by their mission briefing, and then throttled down to avoid actually overtaking A Flight. The edge of the Shroud was a little more than half an hour to reach their destination.

It was warm enough again this morning. A lovely day really, but not quite ideal for flying. There was a high thin haze that reduced visibility somewhat at a distance, though it gave a pretty golden cast to the sky. Still, the air was clear enough to see good long way before ground features smeared out into a yellow-brown blur, and the lack of clouds meant there would be no surprises in the air, not that they expected to be intercepted in any event. At first the Shroud was merely a line of darkness in the east, but as they flew on it rose steadily over the horizon until at a distance of around ten miles it appeared as a vast imposing curtain of darkness 10,000 feet in height. With the sun well above the Shroud, the light was such that it was impossible to look through it to see any landscape. From B Flight's position, rising to 13,000 feet, the Shroud changed in aspect from a wall into a sort of smoky black tabletop surmounted by shallow conical forms that represented the locations of the pods spewing the black stuff outward and downward.

As they approached the Shroud more closely, more details became apparent, and at last Harry had his first view of one of the pods, spotting it at a range of around five miles. It looked something like one of the floater-tugs he'd seen the day before, but vastly larger, dwarfing even the biggest zeppelins of the Luftstreitkräfte, which themselves were now exceeding 750 feet in length. On its own the pod would have been visible from much further away, but it was effectively camouflaged by the smoky haze of the Shroud itself, being the same color. It was hard to determine the pod's size very precisely with nothing to act as a nearby scale reference, but Harry thought it was a bloated disc well over 1,000 feet in diameter, which would give it enormously more volume and lift than the elongated narrow forms of the German airships. The previous day Harry had noted a certain biological quality to the floating tugs, and this pod looked even more like a living thing. Its body was constantly rippling, with great undulating waves moving slowly through the material of its skin. A sort of ragged skirt or frill of material seemed to be hanging down beneath the thing, though it was hard to make this out due to the combination of the over-head view-ing angle and the effusion of smoke or dark-colored gas that the thing was emitting in great billowing blasts from its underside. Like the tugs, the pod had no visible propulsion system, but it was holding steady in the face of a moderate westerly wind, and Harry doubted it was tethered to a 10,000 foot cable.

Harry was also able to see a number of the other pods in the region. It looked like there was one every mile or two up and down the western front of the Shroud, set back a thousand yards or so from the edge of the smoky clouds. It looked to Harry as if the pods further east were much more sparsely laid out, perhaps 10 miles apart from one another in a grid pattern. If that was an accurate estimate, and the same pattern continued further inwards, that meant there might only be hundreds of the things in total. It was an awesome amount of matériel, considering the pods as military vehicles. It would take all of Europe working in concert to produce that many zeppelins.

There were no signs of activity or alarm from the pod or from the Shroud as a whole as the squadron approached, and at last they took up a station around a mile from the nearest pod, A Flight circling at 10,000 feet, and above them B Flight exe-cuting the lazy figure-8s more usual for observation aeroplanes. 3,000 feet beneath Harry the Camels looked no larger than flies, and it was easy to lose track of them against the dirty gray backdrop of the Shroud.

But there it was. The red flare, a brilliant point of light far below. Major Quirk was hanging back and circling in case another signal was required, but A Flight was moving in for the attack. In the absence of any visible resistance or defenses, Captain Devlin had determined that a long line astern was in order, allowing pilots behind to see the effects of the lead pilot's attack. The line was a half-mile long, the pilots about 200 yards apart from one another.

Devlin was approaching the pod now, coming in from above with a gentle rate of descent, as if strafing a trench. He was two hundred yards from his target. One hundred, and the captain opened fire. Harry could just barely make out the distant flicker of tracers. This was about the maximum distance at which you could count on hitting anything in a dogfight, but the effective range of the Vickers gun was much longer, and though accuracy fell off rapidly with distance, the size of the pods was such that it would be virtually impossible to miss.

A flash of fire from the pod! Not a huge explosion, but a disappointingly small puff. Harry thought it was no more than 20 feet in diameter, a mere scar on the vast face of the pod. Unlike the floater-tugs which went up with a single burst, the pod structure must be built up of gas cells like a zeppelin. Harry supposed it was too much to hope that a single spark would instantly destroy the entire pod. German zeppelins were notoriously tough, able to stand repeated scout attacks without catching fire.

But Devlin was continuing his strafing run. He stitched a line of explosions for over two hundred yards along the upper body of the pod before zooming upward to break off his attack as he got too close to the upper deck of the pod for comfort.

Now it was the turn of the second pilot in line. Another long line of explosions, parallel to the first. The skin and interior structure of the pod must be rather resistant to flame, much tougher than that of the tugs, as the explosions died out without seeming to propagate. But the thing had sustained a fair amount of damage. Yes: it was beginning to heel over, slowly and majestically, and was drifting eastward now, as if the pod had lost whatever propulsive effect had been keeping it from moving with the wind.

Devlin had performed an Immelman turn at the top of his zoom, and was heading back west, the second pilot now following at the beginning of his zoom, and the third in line beginning his attack run. Another line of explosions started across the bloated disk of the pod, and this time several of the explosions merged and formed a larger and more intense conflagration. And now the flames weren't dying away.

A large hole opened up in the center of the pod's upper surface. At first Harry thought it was some kind of catastrophic failure, the pod coming apart, but then he realized it was a giant orifice or portal of sorts, dilating like an iris. A scattering of objects were being launched upwards from the interior of the pod. The objects were too indistinct for Harry to make out clearly at this range. But the third Camel pilot saw them and broke off his strafing run early to avoid colliding. The fourth pilot, on his approach a hundred yards away, broke hard right with the heart-stopping abruptness of a rotary-engine aeroplane, aborting his attack entirely.

As the launched objects flew upwards from the pod Harry could make out sparkles of reflected sunlight in the area. It

wasn't the objects themselves that were sparkling, it was—
Crystal bombs. Of course. These must be thread-tugs, or something very much like them, deploying their cables from some interior compartment as they emerged from the pod. The tugs had
been launched at a higher velocity than they had been traveling
the day before during their attack on the airfield, but even so
they had nothing like the speed of one of A Flight's Camels. It
looked like they could present no real danger now that the
attack had been broken off. Possibly if launched ahead of time
and not noticed at all by the attackers they might be dangerous, but it was too late for them do anything at this point.

The whole pod was listing badly now, bulging clouds of
black smoke shot through with reddish flames gouting forth
from the dilated central orifice as well as from wounds blasted
through the dorsal surface by A Flight's strafing runs. It slid
slowly down into the turbulent darkness of the Shroud, like
(Harry thought) one of the stricken battlecruisers foundering at
the Battle of Jutland the year before. The pod took a good thirty
seconds to sink so far beneath the surface of the Shroud as to
become invisible in the murk, and shortly thereafter a huge indistinct crimson glow could be seen through the smoky stuff of
the Shroud, descending rapidly and fading away. Then without
warning the whole upper layer of the Shroud was distorted into
a bulging bubble of smoky stuff a thousand yards across, and
ten or fifteen seconds later Harry heard the extended boom of a
large explosion. The remaining gas in the pod must have finally
ignited all at once somewhere down in the depths of the
Shroud.

A Flight reassembled its formation west of the Shroud, near
its original point of departure for the attack. Harry had lost
sight of the tugs or whatever had been launched by the stricken
pod—the Shroud in the area, reacting to the pod's explosion,
had expanded, lofting hundreds of yards above its former
ceiling and obscuring any details beneath the surface—but
Harry thought they could present no immediate threat in any
event. He watched in fascination as the smoky body of Shroud,
now no longer being generated from above, started simul-
taneously to sink and dissipate. Over the next two minutes, the
air around the former position of the pod didn't clear entirely,
but the Shroud became much thinner. Smoky billows from
adjacent pods in the pattern continued to feed the area, but
Harry thought he could now just make out the landscape far
below.

And there it was, the green flare. Time to go home. Harry

thought it would be just as well to take one last look at the overall pattern of the Shroud and the nearby pods. He'd lost his wider focus during the spectacle of A Flight's attack. That was when he saw the sparkles above and around the two pods north and south along the line.

♍   ♍   ♍

Back at the aerodrome B Flight fulfilled its escort role by remaining in the air circling while A Flight landed first. At last Harry was able to land, and he vaulted down from his cockpit and rushed over to Jernigan's scout while the flight commander was still seated, fiddling with his goggles.

He climbed up on the lower wing plane. "Rhys, did you see the launch?"

"What? You mean those thread-tug things? The pod launched a flight of them just before it went down. Think they might have been caught in the explosion? I didn't see them again after the Shroud settled."

"Yes," said Harry, "but the two nearest pods also launched. Could be more, even, but the others were too far away to see clearly."

"Oh. Good job of spotting. Did you get any idea of their numbers or movements?"

"No. I just noticed those crystal bombs sparkling in the sun around the pods, and then the major signaled to return home. Hard to say how many there were. I would have had to fly over there to see for sure what they were doing."

"Bother." Jernigan climbed out of the cockpit and he and Harry descended to the ground. "I suppose we'd better tell the major. Could be they're going to attack with them again."

They were joined by Powell and Murphy. Murphy had also spotted the launches from the nearby pods.

The pilots of A Flight were standing in a group around Major Quirk, animatedly discussing the way the pod had gone down under their attack. Jernigan almost had to shoulder his way into the group to make his report.

"Damn," said Major Quirk. "Of course, we knew we were sending them a signal with today's job. I was going to order defensive patrols in any event starting today, but it's going to be painful with so few pilots. We'll have to fill out a rota."

"Hmph." Jernigan rubbed his chin. "Well, I'll take the first patrol. Those things are so slow, it'll be almost sunset by the time they get here, if they're coming at all. I'll see if I can't intercept them. If I don't find them in an hour, I'll come back and circle for the rest of my time. Could be they were just launched defensively, anyway."

"Let's hope so," said Major Quirk. "All right. Ryan, if you don't mind, I'll need you for a few minutes to work on the patrol schedule. Everyone else: good job today, and we'll come up with something resembling a plan for future operations by dinnertime. The rest of the day is yours. Or rather, it will be after you write up detailed reports of what you did and saw. We won't want to miss anything that happened today, so I'll trouble you to be a bit more verbose than 'sighted pod; shot down same.'"

♍   ♍   ♍

Lunch was a cheerful affair, over cold mutton sandwiches. The awesome spectacle of the stricken pod was apparently even more dramatic from up close, as the pilots of A Flight couldn't stop telling and retelling their accounts, embellishing details, and cheering each other on. Harry and Powell added their perspectives too, but Murphy was quiet.

"Come on, Aidan," said O'Meara. "Don't be so glum. The bastards have no air defenses. This whole thing will be a lark, don't you think?"

The young Irishman forced a smile. "Sure, and you're probably right. Just thinking, though. That's an awful lot of gasbags they've got out there. Can you imagine the factories they must have cranking those things out someplace? The machines, the workers, everything? I can't. I don't think they exist, myself."

"You've lost me," said O'Meara. "What are you saying now?"

"Don't you think those pods looked more like living things than machines? I'm guessing they're grown or reared somehow, not made."

"Well," said O'Meara, "maybe so. That pod certainly didn't behave like it had any crew on board, anyway. But that will just make things easier, won't it? It'll be like birding. Not much they can do except go down when you shoot them, eh?"

"I hope so. It's just, well..." Murphy trailed off.

"Come on, out with it, man."

"There's nothing like those pods in our world, right? Nothing like that in any old story from the fairy tales or the old books, either. We can't make anything that big that flies, and for the matter of that, there's nothing alive in our world that big that swims or walks either. We've got no idea where it came from, if anyone's behind it, or even what they're trying to do. It's just completely uncanny. It's not reasonable that's all the enemy's got, but we have no idea what else they have because whatever the enemy is, it's like no one and nothing we know about. So I'm just thinking we might be celebrating a bit early, is all."

"Maybe so," said O'Meara, "but there's no point to worrying about all this stuff we don't know. If they start mounting machineguns on the pods, we can worry about that after we see the muzzle-flashes. Or rather, begging your pardon Aidan, if they shoot giant mushrooms at us from the ground instead of proper Archie, we'll know it when the damn things go flying by the cockpit. But until then there's no sense staying up at night imagining what might happen. Am I right?"

"Aye, that's what I'm thinking, as well." said MacLeod.

Murphy smiled again. "Frankly, I think you've probably got the right of it too, Brian, even if I was the one to come out with that gloom and doom stuff. I wasn't going to say anything, but you did ask what I was thinking about. Could be we'll be done with all this in a month. Maybe we can shoot down ten or twenty pods a day and clear the entire front in a few weeks."

There was a pause as this was digested.

"Right then," said Harry, "I suppose I should write up my report. Where do we keep the stationery?"

"Underground, it is," said MacLeod. "Bluidy great quarter-master's paradise they've got squirreled away doon below. I'll see you over there."

They walked out onto the airfield, toward the broad earthen ramp with its accompanying smokestack.

"How long have you been here, Alasdair?"

"A week, noo," said MacLeod. "Number three over here, I am. The major and Devlin have been here a wee bit longer. Still got to pinch myself from time to time to be sure I'm nae dreaming, ye ken?"

"Oh yes," said Harry. "I get dizzy just trying to work out the implications, what this all means. It's hard to believe it's real, for sure."

"A right scunner it is, aye. And here we are." They'd arrived at the ramp, a good fifty feet wide and perhaps three times that in length, obviously leading down into an underground level. It was a difficult twenty percent grade down the main path, but steps had been cut along one side. The ground here was a hard dry clay, and Harry imagined it would be rather treacherous in the rain.

"Mind the grill, noo," said MacLeod. At the base of the ramp, there was a span of iron bars in a grid over a gap, presumably intended as some kind of drainage. There must be some kind of sewers below, though where they led Harry had no idea. Even assuming natural caverns down here, he wondered at the work that must have gone into the excavation. Wouldn't it have been easier to build above ground?

Crossing the grilled drainage space, Harry and MacLeod emerged onto a hard stone floor in a chamber about thirty feet across. Well, that confirmed his guess about caverns. The ceiling was supported by timbers, but the floor and some of the walls were rock, showing signs of excavation. It looked like limestone here, or dolomite. Electric bulbs were hanging from the ceiling here and there, providing a modest illumination to the chamber, which was bare except for a few passages leading out.

"Storerooms off that way," said MacLeod, pointing to the left. "Straight on for the kobold workshops. They live down here, ye ken? Troglodytes. Proper moles, the lot of them."

A kobold was even now emerging from the far passageway.

"Ah, sirs," he said, saluting, "can I be of some service?"

"Sure," said MacLeod, "the laddie here is after some writing supplies, and I'm seeing him around. In there, eh?"

"Of course. There should be someone on duty in the store-room."

Harry had been wondering how the kobolds had managed to make such huge technical advances in so short a time, and how they had managed to improve the performance of the squadron aeroplanes so markedly. Now, motivated by a random impulse, he spoke up.

"And I'd also like to take a look at the workshop, if that's all right."

"Um. Well, of course." The kobold hesitated. "I'll just fetch the sergeant, then, shall I? Was there something in particular you wanted to see?"

"Oh," said Harry, "nothing in particular. It's just I'm an engineering student, or I was until recently, and I wanted to take a look at your work."

"I see. An engineering student. I'll fetch the sergeant. You might as well look into the storeroom first, sir."

The kobold departed hurriedly.

"Och, noo you've done it," said MacLeod.

"What?"

"Listen noo, you're an officer and a pilot, sure, that's bad enough, but you're also a bluidy engineer, so you said. Can ye imagine what it would be like if the sainted James Watt, his ain self-wearing wings and a halo descended from heaven into your engineering school quadrangle and asked to sit in on a class. I'll be nae trouble at all,' he says, 'ye won't even ken I'm there.'"

"Oh. I suppose I shouldn't have asked."

"Too late noo," said MacLeod. "Just dinna cause a stooshie. I mean, dinna make a fuss when they show you around. Say something cross and the daft bairns will think they failed you somehow. Poor buggers got nae sense of themselves."

"I see," said Harry. "I caught something of that from my batman, but I didn't realize they were all so shy."

MacLeod looked embarrassed. He pulled on the end of his moustache before replying.

"Well, shy's one way to put it, I suppose. They're right shy about some things like that. It's like they hae no pride at all, and you can crush them with a harsh word if you like. But don't you set foot in their living quarters, or you'll learn what shy ain't."

MacLeod was blushing now, his big pale face gone quite pink.

"You mean—"

"My first day here, I'm looking around masellie, and the buggers haven't learned yet we're different from them. I just sort of find my way into their quarters, naebody stops me..." He broke off for a moment, then continued.

"Listen here, I'm from a Navy family, and I was reared on stories of wooden ships and iron men, ye ken? Back in the old Royal Navy, a century past and more I mean, some old man o' war would be at sea for months on end, and they would come into port and give nae leave to the men, be right off cruising for another six months as soon as they completed their stores. Well, the captain wouldn't want nae mutiny on his hands, so he'd let the working girls from shore onto the ship, wouldn't he? Back then they had these crowded lower decks for the sailors, nae cabins, nae bunks, just one big room. You can imagine the kind of deviltry they'd get up to doon there with whores aboard, nae privacy, nae shame at all. So it was the same thing in there with the kobolds, but without the girls if you take my drift."

"Oh," said Harry. "That must have been quite a shock. Major Quirk warned me about them when I first came across."

"Made me sick to my stomach," said MacLeod. "Said a few harsh words when I got out of there. Regret it noo, though. I was black-affronted. Ashamed of myself, I mean."

"Really?"

"Aye. None of my bluidy business what they get up to amongst themselves, eh? Nae in Selkirk noo, nae my country, nae my place to say a word. Think I brought a couple of the poor buggers to the point of tears with what I said, and it made me feel small afterwards. They dinna fight back, you see. I apologized later, when I calmed down."

"They do seem to be working very hard to please," said Harry. "I hope I'm not going to make problems with this workshop visit."

"Dinna fash yerself," said MacLeod. "I think they may finally hae figured oot we're nae going to kill them if they make a false step, and they're learning we're nae fond of—well, the kinds of things they like. But still, you may as well walk with a care down here. You wouldn't want to give them the wrong idea, now would you?"

"Rather not."

They turned and walked into the storeroom. It proved to be a chamber packed almost solid with crates, all bearing Army stencils. A bare bulb hung over a wooden counter at which a kobold in a corporal's uniform was poring over a book.

The kobold started when he noticed them, hastily placing the book face-down to save his place.

MacLeod peered down at the volume. "Och noo, that's just what's needed. Of all the authors to send over here..."

Harry had to smile. It was *The Importance of Being Earnest.*

"Sir? Ah, can I help you?"

"Just some stationery supplies," said Harry. "Paper, something to write with. Perhaps a clipboard."

"Bond paper, sir? Or a notebook? We have regular and mechanical pencils, but no fountain pens, only dip pens."

Harry wound up with a parcel including one of every kind of writing implement they had in stock, ink, blotter paper, and a pencil sharpener. He was bemused by the sheer abundance of stuff they seemed to have stockpiled here.

"I don't suppose you have any spare razors down here, do you?"

"That we don't sir," said the kobold, "but I'll have one of the crews run one up for you if you like."

"Pardon me?"

"We've got a number of forges here, of course. It will be no problem at all to make a small sharp blade for you. Will a bone handle do?"

Harry blinked. He supposed he shouldn't be surprised. Kobolds were famous as smiths in fairy tales, after all.

"Thanks," he said, "that would be terrific. But where did all this other stuff come from? It seems, well, rather luxurious, doesn't it?"

MacLeod shrugged. "Nae doubt the brass passed a list of everything a regular squadron gets on to some clerk someplace in some H.E. warehouse and just bundled it all together. On top of a hundred and fifty tons of aeroplanes, guns, and ammo, and the same weight in fuel, a ton of office supplies is naither here nor there, really."

"Sir! The workshop is ready for your inspection!" A kobold sergeant had just entered the room, a little out of breath.

"Dinna keep them waiting," said MacLeod. "I'm sure it will be educational and all of that, but I'll pass, myself. I've my own report to write, after all." He relieved Harry of his parcel. "I'll just put this doon in your cottage for you."

♍   ♍   ♍

The workshop area proved to be an extensive set of inter-connected chambers, dimly lit by the occasional bare bulb suspended from the ceiling. The sergeant showed Harry to one of the shop workstations.

Here a Gnome Monosoupape rotary engine taken from a Sopwith Camel was laid out neatly on a bench fully dis-assembled. Every connecting rod, every valve, every cam and pin was sorted away in its own place, the stripped engine block mounted on a test frame. Harry had never seen a disassembled Gnome before and he paused for a moment, fascinated by the neat array of shining metal parts. The two big French rotary-engine firms Gnome and Le Rhône had recently merged, but they still maintained separately named engine lines.

"Was there a fault with this engine?" Harry wanted to know. "Have you broken it down to get at the problem?"

"Oh no, sir," said the kobold in charge of this station, a corporal named Kensington. "We're just tuning it."

"You tune it by taking it completely apart?"

The kobold looked nervous. He said at last, "Well, sir, it's the tolerances. And... and the metal."

"I'm sorry," said Harry, "I don't understand."

The kobold was apologetic.

"Sir, you know we have enormous regard and admiration for the designers of this engine."

"And?"

"Well sir, this model has a much simpler design than the Le Rhônes. We have the manuals for other engines to compare. The number of parts has been reduced, and the single valve simplifies the operation considerably. But the design cost is lower power. The Le Rhône 9R produces 170 horsepower at the same weight as the Monosoupape, with almost the same fuel usage. This engine only supplies 150. Why would it be chosen for the Camel?"

The kobold paused, swallowed once, then he continued. "Sir, we don't know how to design engines at all. It's not something we can do ourselves. But we can understand the design when we read the plans and take it apart ourselves. This engine consumes nearly as much oil as it does fuel. And the oil is sprayed out into the prop wash when the pistons cycle. You must get it all over your suit when you fly."

Harry had never flown an aeroplane with a Mono, but even in the DH.5 there was a constant spray of castor oil from the engine, to the point that some pilots suffered notoriously from the laxative effect of accidentally ingesting the stuff. With a rotary engine you had to be sure to pack clean handkerchiefs to wipe off your goggles. It could take a good long time after a flight to clean the dirty oil off your face, and it worked its way into your flight suit after a while too.

"I imagine the idea was to reduce the number of points of failure," said Harry. He wasn't certain of the goals of the designers at Gnome-et-Rhône, but he'd taken apart a 1915 vintage Le Rhône 80 himself back in flight school. The Le Rhônes were considerably more complicated, and the older ones required almost constant maintenance.

"Points of failure..." Kensington repeated the term, but more in wonder at it than in agreement.

"Yes," said Harry, "a simpler design with fewer parts means it will likely last longer before it fails. The Mono is supposed to be very reliable."

"Sir, sir," said Kensington, almost hopelessly, "how is it that your engines fail? We don't understand. They can't have been designed to fail! That makes no sense!"

"Well, you know," said Harry. "These engines are under incredible stress in the air. They run at their limits to give the maximum horsepower, the maximum torque. There's an awful lot of stress on the connecting rods, the cams, the crankshaft. And the combustion... the hot gas corrodes the valves and fittings. After a while they'll just disintegrate if you don't replace them."

"Your war must be a terrible thing," said Kensington. "These engines... they must have been running for thousands of hours without maintenance. I'm so sorry you pilots have to fly in such conditions."

"What do you mean?"

"These parts," said the kobold. "They're all *wrong*... The pistons are out of true. They practically rattle around in the cylinders, and they're often a full tenth away from being circular! The rods have flaws in the metal. The whole thing hardly fits together without forcing. And then there's the balance. The engine wobbles on the shaft, sir! That can't be right! These engines must have seen an enormous amount of abuse before coming here."

"Listen," said Harry, "I'm afraid you're making a kind of mistake here. It may be that our designers can do work you find admirable, but our machinists don't seem to be up to your standards."

"Sir?"

"These engines," said Harry. "They have to be new from the factory. Tested for a few hours, but probably never flown even once before coming here. These loose tolerances you're talking about, the flaws in the metal, the irregularities—that's the best they—the best we can do, I'm sure. Some of the work may be rushed due to the urgency of the war, but I doubt it would be all that much better in peacetime."

"The best you can do?" The kobold corporal was shocked.

"Yes. That's why I'm down here. Not to make sure you're all wearing your uniforms properly and keeping a clean workplace, or whatever it is an officer is supposed to look for in an inspection. I want to find out how you managed to increase engine performance without redesigning everything. And it looks to me like you're doing it by replacing all the parts, one at a time, with your own work. Is that right?"

"Oh," said Kensington, taken aback, "not *all* the parts. Your beautiful Wolseley Vipers have aluminium blocks. We haven't got the plans or the minerals for an aluminium foundry, not to mention the power. And even though this Gnome has a steel engine block, we're going to keep it as is for now. It would take too long to forge a new one from scratch."

"But the pistons, the valves, the rods, the cams, and all that. You're going to swap them out, right?"

"Well, yes. It's easy enough to mill and lathe out new parts like those."

"Right then," said Harry. "That's what I want to see. I want to see you cutting a new piston out of a steel blank. I want to see how you make it so perfectly circular. What did you say? A tenth deviation in cylindricity is too much? You mean a ten thousandth of an inch, right? A tenth of a mil?"

"Yes, sir. We will turn a piston that is circular to within a hundredth of a mil in all diameters."

"I see..."

♍   ♍   ♍

"Tregeseal! There you are." Jernigan's voice snapped Harry out of a reverie of concentration so intense it was almost dreamlike. He'd been focusing on the quick and eerily coordinated actions of the kobold work crew as they turned another piston on an engine lathe.

"Oh." He shook his head, blinking. "Rhys. What time is it?"

"Half past three. Have you been down here all day?"

"Looks like. Let me just say goodbye." Harry turned to Kensington. "Corporal, thank you very much for the chance to observe your work. Frankly, you amaze me with your skill."

The kobold stepped back from the lathe. He seemed embarrassed at this praise. "Oh, sir, it's no problem at all. Really we should be thanking you for the chance to show what we can do."

Harry looked around. The hundred or so kobolds who had stood to attention around the shop for his inspection had long since gone back to work on their various tasks, and he had no idea where the sergeant who had been escorting him had gone off to. He paused to compose a little speech, and raised his voice to be heard a distance away.

"It's been an amazing experience. I'm deeply indebted to you for showing me how you work, and also to all your colleagues here for disrupting their schedules just for my pleasure. I'm enormously impressed with everything I've seen. Frankly, the precision, the speed, and the sheer mastery you display in your work would be unbelievable in any factory back home."

"You honor us, sir." Kensington was obviously pleased, and for a moment he was almost overcome with emotion. His crew suddenly bowed, a completely non-military gesture, imitated almost immediately by the rest of the kobolds elsewhere in the workshop.

Now Harry was the one to be embarrassed. "Oh. Well... Thanks again. I'll come back when I can."

They were on their way out of the underground complex when a kobold came running up to Harry. He recognized the corporal who had been tending the supply stores earlier in the day.

"Your order, sir," he said, handing over a bone-handled

straight razor with a folding blade.

"What, already?" Harry looked closely at the steel. Curious wave-like patterns could be seen in the metal. The handle fit his hand quite well. "I suppose I shouldn't be surprised, though. Thanks very much."

Harry made to test the edge with his thumb.

"Sir!" The kobold caught at his arm. "Please don't do that. It's *sharp*."

"Oh."

"You shouldn't need to strop it for a while," said the corporal, "but when it begins to dull, your batman will get it sharp again for you."

Harry wanted to say that he was perfectly capable of sharpening a razor blade for himself. He realized that the kobolds had only been using machine tools for a month or two, but they had been making steel blades for many hundreds or possibly even thousands of years.

"Righto," he said. "But I'm deeply appreciative of the work. Thanks again."

The kobold's extreme pleasure at this simple remark was obvious, and it was impossible for Harry not to smile at the rigid correctness of his salute.

"Looks like you made some friends," said Jernigan as they walked up the ramp to the surface.

This took Harry aback for a moment. But he supposed he had made friends at that. For the last three or four hours he'd been surrounded by a hundred or so of the kobolds, observed a work-crew of six very closely, and he hadn't felt even a little distanced from them. None of that distressing sense of the alien, or the other. And their presumed personal habits hadn't even come to mind.

"Yes, well... Remember we were talking about how they had souped up our scouts? I wanted to see just what they were doing."

"Did you figure it out?"

"Not exactly. I think you said it was magic. There's definitely something extraordinary about what they can do, but I'm not sure I'd call it magic, so much as an absurdly fine sense of—I'm not sure what it is, exactly. A sense of shape? Of material? I think they can visualize the whole engine and all the parts, both as they are and as they should be... And they can tell somehow when something is out of true, even by a hundredth of a mil. It's as if they have vernier scales built into their fingertips. I can't explain it, and I don't really understand it anyway."

"Frankly," said Jernigan, "all that really matters to me is an extra 30 or 40 miles per hour, and being confident the oil gauge isn't going to explode when I pull up out of a dive."

"The other thing they have going for them," said Harry, oblivious to Jernigan's remark, "is their teamwork. It's as if they each know what the rest of the crew is doing without saying a word. Have you ever heard of five or six machinists using one lathe all at the same time? Now that really is uncanny."

"Never touched a lathe in my life," said Jernigan. "I'm afraid you're out of my depth."

"Oh. Well—Hold on, I've been so involved in all this, I completely forgot about your patrol. Did you encounter anything?"

"No, actually," said Jernigan. "Not a blessed thing. That launch you saw must indeed have been a defensive one. Or a reflexive one, maybe."

"Hm?"

"I heard Murphy's theory that these things are all living, not constructed. I'm wondering if that might not be true."

"I think it's at least conceivable," said Harry. "The floating tugs looked something like jellyfish to me, up close, and we didn't see anything like a gondola or a cabin on those pods. Really, it seems more like something out of H. G. Wells than anything you'd ever imagine in connection with fairyland. But there's one thing for sure."

"What's that?"

"That attack on the airfield yesterday. That wasn't reflexive. That was preemptive. Someone knows we're here and they don't like us much at all."

♍   ♍   ♍

"I've posted a duty rota for the next few days," said Major Quirk.

The officers of Elfshot Squadron were assembled in the refectory prior to dinner. Harry had hastily written up a report and turned it over to Major Quirk, who'd appeared rather distracted, engaged in discussion with Captain Devlin.

He had looked around for Lambeth, intending to ask him more about the kobolds' work, but hadn't been able to find him. Harry knew he could pass the word for his batman to one of the kobold sergeants, but he felt uneasy about doing this just for the sake of a private discussion.

Meanwhile, Major Quirk was addressing the pilots, some notes in hand.

"This work schedule is based on the lack of resistance we've seen thus far. We must anticipate the enemy will respond to our attacks eventually, but until they do, we're going to exploit their passivity. Starting tomorrow, in good weather A Flight will attack pods along the edge of the Shroud in a morning mission. From dawn until one PM or so, individual members of B Flight will patrol the general area of the aerodrome on east to the Shroud, alert for any signs of another attack by thread tugs. In the afternoon, B Flight will go after the pods, and A Flight will take over the defense. So that will be two flights a day for everyone.

"We're not equipped for night patrols at present, so we're going to have to rely on our outlying kobold squads to spot any attack after dark. There's a good chance that the enemy needs light to navigate, so let's hope we don't get woken up by that damn klaxon.

"This morning we saw A Flight bring a pod down with two full strafing runs and part of a third. Based on that, the flight commanders and I believe that it's reasonable to expect two scouts to be able to bring down a pod in no more than two strafing passes, though the Camels will have an advantage due to their twin guns. That works out to four to six pods downed per flight per sortie, quite likely more as new pilots arrive, and as we gain experience with pod-busting. If we can shoot down ten pods a day, by our estimates we will have made a substantial dent in the Shroud over the course of a couple of weeks.

"Of course, the enemy may have some kind of resources we haven't seen yet, but until they show them that's the plan. Questions?"

O'Meara spoke up. "You mentioned new pilots?"

"Yes," said Quirk, "two more are coming tomorrow. That may be all for a while, though. There are a few more in flight school, but I don't know when they'll be ready. It doesn't look like we'll be able to fill out C Flight any time soon, and replacements will be thin on the ground. So please try not to die."

Harry approached Major Quirk as the meeting broke up. He was talking to Captain Devlin about the fuel supply, but he turned as Harry walked up.

"Yes, Tregeseal?"

"It's nothing much, Major, I just had a few more questions about the set-up here. Nothing urgent."

"Well, go ahead. No time like the present."

"All right," said Harry. "I was wondering about the kobolds. I mean, as enlisted men. Who had the idea they should serve in that role? I mean, they've got uniforms and everything, and they seem somehow to have learned how to behave more or less like soldiers without any proper training. But what I mean is, they're not soldiers in the Army." Harry paused for a moment, looked at the expression on Quirk's face. Devlin was grinning. "Are they?"

"Well..." Quirk looked uncomfortable. Devlin laughed.

"The major is a bit shy on the topic. You'll have to excuse him. But I suppose you haven't visited his office yet?"

"No, why?"

Quirk sighed. "You might as well. Everyone else has. Nothing to be ashamed of, I suppose, it's just a bit..." He trailed off again.

"Come on," said Devlin, and they walked together to one of the cottages Harry hadn't yet been into.

There was nothing very special about the office itself, just another one of these half-timbered cottage rooms, this time with a desk and filing cabinets instead of cots and dressers. There was an ornate document pinned to the wall, written in fancy copperplate, decorated with multiple seals and ribbons.

"There you go," said Major Quirk. "I think that will answer your question, partly, anyway."

The document began "His Majesty George the Fifth, by the Grace of God of the United Kingdom of Great Britain and Ireland and of the British Dominions beyond the Seas..." The ornate script was hard to make out, but in skimming it Harry was able to pick out the phrases "Our Trusted and Loyal Servant, Major Arthur Quirk"... "Ambassador and Minister Plenipotentiary to the Seelie Court"... "Imperial Viceroy and Governor-General in the Fairy Lands"... and there was no mistaking the signature—George R. I.—Rex Imperator.

"He can negotiate treaties and declare war on His Majesty's behalf." said Captain Devlin. "Merely creating a new squadron and inducting a group of natives as enlisted men is a trivial matter for such an exalted personage as the major. How many guns do you get, next time a Royal Navy battleship visits the airfield? 19? Or is it 31 like the Viceroy of India? Really, he could raise an entire army corps if there were enough volunteers about."

"Ridiculous, isn't it?" Major Quirk was embarrassed. "Never even attended a royal levee before this whole thing started. Don't have a coat of arms, much less any initials after my name. But the fairy lords like the forms of royalty."

"Just don't call him 'Your Excellency'," said Captain Devlin. "His Excellency doesn't like it."

"Bah," said Quirk. "I suppose this pretty parchment will be a lark to show off after all this is done, assuming I don't have to burn it. So the kobolds really are soldiers, for what it's worth. But I don't know who exactly had the idea originally of using them as enlisted men. It must have been one of *themselves*, since they were aware of the kobolds' ability to handle iron. But that was all worked out before I was sent over here. I suppose it's just a fortunate accident that they turned out to be such skillful mechanics."

♍   ♍   ♍

Dinner was a little muted this evening, as some of the pilots struggled to come up with topics of conversation apart from the immediate prospects for work for the squadron, a forbidden subject during the meal.

"One thing I don't understand about this pilot shortage," said Powell. "I gather that sending iron across from our world is a very big deal, and that some of the women on our side even lost their lives attempting it, in that one big shipment." MacLeod shook his head, and there was a general expression of sorrow.

"But is it so hard to send ordinary pilots across? Is it harder to send someone with the wrong bloodlines than to send a hundred tons of steel and supplies?"

"I know the answer to that one," said Jernigan. "I asked it just before I came over myself."

O'Meara guessed: "Something to do with keeping the secret?"

"No, that's not it. David has it backwards. It's not the difficulty sending some ordinary Englishman of a pilot, it's the difficulty the pilot will have in coming across. You remember feeling sick or fainting, don't you all?"

There was a murmur of assent.

"It's a lot worse for most people, even for someone who's as pure-blooded Celtic as can be, just not in the right family. Making the crossing is deadly for someone with the wrong blood, is what I was told. It's not exactly logical, but I suppose it's something to do with the old tynged or geas or whatever magic it was that set up this whole thing in the first place, back in the old days."

"Oh," said Powell, "that makes some sense, actually. But if

98

the tynged was set up a couple of thousand years ago or more, shouldn't there be thousands or even millions of people with the right blood?"

"You're following in my footsteps," said Jernigan. "I asked the same question. But no, for each family, there's one principal female bearer of the flame in every generation. You've got to be something like a first cousin or closer to be able to make it across without suffering a stroke. So perhaps there are a couple of dozen families who are in on the secret, and another several dozen who somehow lost their knowledge of it over the years but still have some woman with the right blood. But you can imagine most of them don't happen to have close relatives flying for the RFC or the RNAS."

The conversation became more general after the loyal toast. O'Meara, having failed to corral anyone for chess, was looking sadly down at a Ludo board that Murphy and Powell had set up. He sighed and pulled up a chair. Evidently the game was better than nothing. Jernigan was attempting *Für Elise* on the harpsichord, but not to widespread acclaim, and he gave up on it half-way through. Major Quirk pulled Captain Devlin away from the company to help with paperwork, and the remaining pilots stood in a cluster carefully sipping a second glass of the fairy wine, two bottles of which had been served up to commemorate the squadron's first victory.

"So, Tregeseal, did you enjoy your time underground with the kobolds?" Carstairs' tone was light, but Harry thought he detected an eager vindictiveness lurking beneath the surface.

"Rather," he said, deadpan. "Their technique as machinists is incredible."

"Oh? And is that the only kobold technique you studied?"

Harry laughed. "Really, Carstairs, if that sort of thing interests you, perhaps you should investigate it yourself? Not my cup of tea, but I wouldn't want to stand in your way."

"What? What are you saying?" Carstairs flushed with anger. Harry was convinced if they'd been alone the other pilot would have raised his fists, but he seemed to be conscious of the casual attention of the men nearby.

"Nothing more than you just did, old chap," said Harry.

Carstairs either didn't understand or chose to ignore Harry's remark.

"It just makes me sick, is all, having to rely on these... creatures. It's monstrous that we should have to put up with this kind of behavior right under our noses!"

Harry's feeling about Carstairs changed abruptly from

annoyance to something like pity. He thought, *what the hell*, and decided to talk to him directly instead of fencing with him.

MacLeod's little talk was still in his head, and it seemed very apt now.

"Frankly Carstairs, I feel a little uncomfortable around them myself. But you should keep something in mind, I think, before you let yourself get so angry."

"What's that?"

"They're not human, you know. Right now we're not only not in Europe anymore, we're in a different world. It's their world, not ours, you understand?"

"Yes, but—"

Now Jernigan spoke up. He had been sitting at the harpsichord, not part of the group, but it would have been hard for him not to overhear the exchange. He got up and joined the other pilots, interrupting Carstairs.

"Have any of the kobolds done anything to offend you?"

"They'd better not!"

"Well, suppose one did," said Jernigan. "I mean to say, think of the worst, the most offensive offer one of them could make. I gather it's their way of being friendly, amongst themselves. So what? How does it hurt you? You smile and say 'no thanks', is that so bad?"

"*Jesus!*" Carstairs was upset again. "What, am I the only one? No one else thinks there's something wrong with being forced to work with an entire race of sodomites?"

Graham answered this time in his slow measured way, his manner of speaking making him seem a good twenty years older than his actual age.

"I do sympathize with you, Ewan," he said, "but I find to my surprise I don't feel quite the same way. My batman offered himself to me the night before last, in the most direct terms imaginable. You will understand why I do not repeat his words verbatim. I think if I had been back home or at the aerodrome in Coudekerque and someone spoke to me that way, I would have probably struck him, and I might have felt it necessary to charge the man formally if he was in the service. But here I found that I felt no outrage, no animosity, merely a mild surprise. There was a certain forthright innocence to the offer to which I simply could not take umbrage. In fact I found myself taking great care to pose my demurral as gently as possible, so as not to hurt the fellow's feelings."

Harry was a little surprised that the company didn't seem to be very sympathetic to Carstairs' position. And he was surprised again when Carstairs closed his mouth and shook his head before saying anything more: he'd recognized that he was receiving little support and had managed to take himself under control.

"I wouldn't have been so kind in the face of such an outrage," he said to Graham, "but I suppose if they keep their distance, there's nothing more for me to say on the subject."

"There's still half a bottle left," said Jernigan after a pause, "be a shame to waste it, eh?" The moment passed, as the pilots held out their glasses for a measured inch of the remaining fairy wine. Harry could see that Carstairs was relieved no longer to be the focus of attention.

♍   ♍   ♍

When he returned to his hut, Harry found Lambeth laying out one of his spare uniforms in the room's dresser. His clothes had just been cleaned and pressed. It seemed to Harry that the kobold was more subdued than he'd seen him before.

"Hello, Lambeth. I looked for you earlier, to continue our conversation of this morning."

The kobold looked up. Harry couldn't make out his expression. "I'm sorry, sir. I would have come, of course, if you called for me. Congratulations on your successful mission."

Harry sat down on his cot, started taking off his boots, waving off Lambeth's help. It was one thing to allow the kobold to do all his chores, but actually being undressed by a servant seemed a bit much.

"I thought I might see you down in the workshop," Harry said. "I visited during the afternoon."

"So I heard, sir." Lambeth turned back to the dresser, finished folding a shirt.

"It was a remarkable experience. Your people's technical skills go well beyond what we are capable of. You've only had a month or two with these machines, and yet you kobolds can work with greater speed and precision than any machinist I've ever heard of."

"You honor us, sir." Lambeth had said this before, as had Kensington that afternoon. This time it was said in a flat quiet voice, without enthusiasm.

"I'm also very impressed with the teamwork I saw."

Lambeth said nothing.

"I watched Kensington and his crew working for quite a while," said Harry. "To be able to work together with such precision and such extreme levels of cooperation with hardly a word said over the course of a complete engine rebuild... It must be very gratifying to work on a team like that."

"Yes, sir." Lambeth's voice had some emotion in it now. He'd finished folding and putting away Harry's uniforms. "You are scheduled for the first patrol tomorrow morning, sir. Sunrise will be at 8:41, but there should be enough light at 8:15 to take off. I'll wake you at 7:30, if that will be all right."

"Fine, Lambeth, but—"

"If there's nothing else, sir, may I be excused for the rest of the evening?" The kobold looked down at his feet, and Harry thought he was ashamed for some reason.

Harry hesitated. Did he really want to deal with this now? It would certainly be easier to pretend he hadn't noticed anything unusual about the kobold's manner. But perhaps because of Carstairs' remarks earlier Harry felt that it would be wrong to let it go.

"Not yet, Lambeth. Look, pull up a chair, sit down."

"Sir?"

"You're obviously unhappy about something. I suppose it has to do with what we were going to talk about today. Your work as an engineer." Harry waved a hand as Lambeth was about to say something. "Or mechanic. Whatever. Do you want to tell me about it?"

Lambeth looked up. His eyes widened for a moment, then narrowed. But he slid the room's one chair out from the corner, and sat down rather stiffly.

"It's... Sir, should my state of mind matter to you? Begging your pardon, sir, but why should you care?"

"Come on, Lambeth," said Harry. "Here I am, a stranger, newly come to a strange world I never even imagined existed before yesterday. But today a member of an entirely new and unknown race is my servant, though by rights he should be working as an engineer, which as it happens is what I was studying to become before I joined the army. How should I not be interested?"

"Oh." Lambeth blinked. "It didn't occur to me you might see it that way. That makes sense."

"I know I'm prying," said Harry, "and don't think just because you're assigned as my batman you have to answer. If you want to keep it private, just say so. But I'm interested in your people, so if you can talk to me about your problem without being too uncomfortable, I'd like to hear it."

"Sir. Ah... I don't want to talk about anything you would

find... distressing.”

Oh Christ, here we go, Harry thought. *But I asked for it.*

“Don’t worry about that,” he said, “I’m asking you, after all.”

“Very well,” said Lambeth. “I’ve thought about this some, but I’ve never talked it out before, so please forgive me if I seem to be going on and on. Sir, you said that you had never imagined our world, or the people in it. I think the same thing applies to us.”

“Huh? What do you mean?”

“Oh, we knew in a vague way that your world and people existed, but the Unseelie Court didn’t have the same commerce in books and so on as the Seelie Court. So it wasn’t until a couple of months ago that we learned anything about you and your world.”

“I see,” said Harry. He wondered where the kobold was going with all this.

“You should understand what our situation was in the old order of things. The Seelie Court was always bigger, better organized, more powerful than the Unseelie Court. For a long time, we kobolds were the Unseelie Court’s last resort against an attack. We had iron blades and bows with iron arrowheads. We could defeat five or ten times our number with weapons like that, and *themselves,* well they hate the idea of facing such weapons. If there had been more of us, probably our masters would have tried to conquer the Seelie Court long ago, but they were always afraid we might be defeated with numbers, and then where would they be? So they never had us fight, which is just as well because we didn’t really want to use our weapons anyway.”

“Good for you,” said Harry. “Not your fight, after all.”

“Yes, sir,” said Lambeth. “But the lords and ladies of the Unseelie Court were afraid of us too, despite the fact they needed to use us as a threat. They all hated the idea of people with iron around them. We had to live apart from them, which was what we wanted too. They weren’t very nice people, for the most part.”

“So I’ve heard.”

“I’ll skip over them for now, sir. But we lived like that for a long time, isolated in our caves and mines, making iron weapons and not using them. But there was nothing else for us to do, really. And then the Shroud came.”

“What was that like?”

“Forgive me again, sir,” said Lambeth, “but I’ll talk about that more another time if you like. I need to get to the point or you'll be sitting here all night. We were lucky that two of our mining communities were on the western border. We were able to flee to the Seelie Court, and beg them for refuge."

"That must have been a desperate time."

"Oh yes sir. And we still don't know what happened to our people elsewhere in the kingdom. The other mines are mostly all the way on the far side, to the east. That's one reason we're so happy to serve you now: we want to rescue the rest of our people. But as for the Seelie Court, well, we were their oldest fears come calling, begging for help. They'd hated us for so very long, but now we had delivered ourselves into their power. They kept us penned up in camps on the border. Not nearly enough food, and sleeping out in the open air... But I suppose it could have been worse. They could easily have slaughtered us out of hand instead. We were in no state to resist at the time."

"I'm sorry to hear about it now," said Harry.

"You're kind to say so, sir." Lambeth smiled then. "But things did get better. Someone in the court figured out that your aeroplanes might work against the Shroud. Eventually they realized you would need mechanics. That's when they let us have food, tools, proper housing, and so on. And that's when we got those books that told us about your world. And about you, sir. About your people I mean, and about your discoveries in science and engineering."

"I see."

"I'm sorry I took so long to get to this point," said Lambeth, "but you have to understand how marvelous those books seemed to us. You'd made such wonderful strides in every way. Better steel: the blast furnace, the Bessemer converter, all these wonderful new alloys! It was like a miracle. And what had we been doing all those years? Hammering out the blooms from crude stone furnaces to make our horrible mild steel the same old way, every generation for hundreds, even thousands of years, exactly the same."

Lambeth's voice was full of passion. To Harry he sounded almost like a preacher in one of the nonconformist sects.

"We felt so *stupid*," said Lambeth, "or at least, I did. None of your innovations had ever occurred to any of us. We didn't even have the idea of machines, not proper ones: nothing more complicated than a hand-powered lathe. But you had steam engines! Internal combustion! Electrical generators! Such beautiful inventions! It all seemed so obvious once we saw the plans and read the manuals."

Harry nodded and said, "But you learned all that stuff in

only a month or two and built your own machines from scratch just on the basis of having some documentation? That's amazing. We could never have done all that. It would have taken us many years. And there's millions and millions of us in our world."

"Yes, sir," said Lambeth. "But we didn't know that. I think not even until today did we know that... that you have, um, *problems* actually making things. We just thought you were like gods."

"Far from it, I'm afraid."

"So now I've come to the point of all this. I was reading one of those books and wondering how it was that you had made all these strides and we had done nothing new in thousands of years. And I thought, maybe it's our—it's our—"

Lambeth's voice stumbled, came to a stop for a moment, then he resumed.

"What you called teamwork before, sir. It's a lot more than that for us. It's, well, I think there's no word for it in English. Accord? Mutuality? But make it much stronger."

"How about *rapport*? It means a closely-knit relationship between two people, especially one built on trust and understanding."

"Oh, that *is* a better word. Is it French? But just between two people? What we have is well, it's for *all* of us, but especially for our crews. Five or six of us at a time. And, uh, begging your pardon, sir..." Lambeth trailed off.

"Yes?"

"With us, anyway, it's connected to sex."

"Oh." Harry had managed to put the kobolds' sexual proclivities out of his mind for a while. Now though, involuntarily, the combinatorics of the five- and six-man teams he'd observed working on parts and assemblies in the workshop passed before his mind's eye, and he blushed, despite himself.

"I'm sorry, sir." Lambeth paused. "I know it makes you uncomfortable to talk about it. The major has been trying to explain this to us for some time now."

"I *am* uncomfortable, Lambeth," said Harry, "but the fact is I feel embarrassed that I am. I thought I was grown-up enough not to be."

"As you say, sir," said Lambeth. "So when we're working on something together, we know what needs to be done, and we do it. If someone needs help, we help, and we don't have to ask for it, and we don't have to say we're helping, either; we just know what we're doing."

"I begin to understand," said Harry. "Watching Kensington's crew yesterday... it was almost like watching a choreographed dance."

"I'm sure they would be delighted to hear you say that, sir. But in reading your books it became clear to me that's not something your people are able to do. Not usually, anyway. The characters in your stories never seem to know what other people think about them. Not even—not even when they're in love."

Lambeth paused for a moment, overcome with emotion. Despite his recent avowal of maturity, Harry thought it just as well not to ask why.

"So what are you saying? Do you think that your team rapport interferes with innovation? Is that it?"

"Yes, sir," said Lambeth, "I thought that. It could be that as a people we're essentially handicapped that way, but I thought that our way of working together might be the thing that was holding us back, if you see what I mean."

"And you tried to do something about it? Hence the supercharger."

"Yes." Lambeth began to speak faster, a nervous enthusiasm informing his words. "It was very hard, but I decided to try something new on my own. Even though it was a failure, I mean, even though I wound up just copying the design out of a journal, it was still not our way of doing things. The thought of going against the established design of the aeroplane, that was ... very distressing to my team. To me too, really. I had to force myself to work on it on my own. The idea of changing a design, it's nothing to you, am I right, sir? But it's shocking to us. When the supercharger was finally done, it was obviously an improvement. When I showed it to your Captain Jernigan a few days ago, he told us that if it made the aeroplane faster, we should put them on all the S.E.5a scouts. So then it was part of the design, and there was no problem anymore, and now all the crews can work with the supercharger. But actually making the change... that was horrible. It was like walking naked and blindfolded above ground. Anything could be out there. There was no telling what would happen."

Harry smiled. He had the feeling he was talking to a younger brother, now. A queer red-skinned younger brother, to be sure, but he realized he was feeling proud of Lambeth's accomplishment.

"I guess that's what invention is like sometimes," he said, "or anything creative, really. You can't know in advance how it will work out. You just have to risk it. But you did it, though, didn't you? Wasn't that a success? Why did you call it a failure?"

"Oh." Lambeth looked unhappy. "I wanted to make a supercharger from first principles. I wanted to design it myself to be ideally suited to the Viper. But I couldn't. I just copied someone else's design."

"Listen," said Harry, "didn't I tell you before there is nothing trivial about this? I learned about this in school, just before I went off to become a pilot. Some of my instructors consult for the Royal Aircraft Factory. I heard they've been experimenting with superchargers. In fact, I believe they tried supercharging a BE.2 last year and almost blew it up. Where did you get your design?"

"It was published by a Mr. Ellor, I believe."

"Right," said Harry. "That's the man in charge. The design doesn't work, you see. I think it was something to do with the gearing. Or rather, it didn't work for him. You must have done something to fix the problems they had. Maybe you didn't make whatever mistake they made, or maybe your machining was superior, but believe me if you took your supercharger to Farnborough to show the RAF engineers, they'd be shocked that you got it to work."

"Oh," said Lambeth, "but if it was just the machining—"

"For pity's sake," said Harry, "not only is this engineering of the highest order, but if it was even possible for us to do it at all it would take weeks or even months of effort with a big team of machinists and designers working together. How long did it take you on your own? A few days? Humility may be a virtue, but you've got to accept you've done something extraordinary here."

"Well, if you say so, sir." Lambeth was blushing again. It would have been annoying, Harry thought, if there was the slightest bit of false humility to his attitude, but it seemed that the kobold was honestly unable to credit the excellence of his accomplishment.

"Anyway," said Lambeth, "that's why they made me a batman. They didn't want any more, umm, *unmutuality*, but at the same time they had to accept that what I did was good work."

"But what about you?" Harry wanted to know. "It can't be right to exclude you from your job as a machinist. I assume you enjoyed it. I mean, you enjoyed the technical work."

"Well, yes. But it's very nice to be a batman too. I can have talks like this one, you see. Everyone will be thrilled to hear about this, I mean, if you don't mind my telling them." Harry waved his hand and Lambeth smiled cheerfully. "Anyway, it won't be forever. And to be honest, I didn't understand at the time that I was upsetting the others, and that was very wrong of me. It was a kind of madness, you see. If I'd known the effect I was having I never would have gone forward with it."

"Really?"

"Oh yes, sir. The feeling of working together as a team is... well, it's the highest value we have. It's what we live for. It's not worth breaking that up even for an extra forty miles per hour."

"Well," said Harry, "thanks for taking the time to explain all that to me. For my own part, I'll take the forty miles an hour, so I certainly appreciate your work myself."

"Thank you very much sir." Lambeth seemed hugely relieved. Harry wasn't sure why until some minutes after the kobold departed; and then he realized Lambeth never had really explained why he'd been moping around before.

CHAPTER 9
STORK AND UNICORN

A Flight	B Flight
Capt Ryan Devlin*	Capt Rhys Jernigan*
Flt Lt James Buchanan	Lt David Powell
Lt Ewan Carstairs	Lt Aidan Murphy
Lt Donald Graham	2nd Lt Harold Tregeseal
2nd Lt Brian O'Meara	Sous-Lt Robert Moisan
2nd Lt Alasdair MacLeod	(unassigned)

*=Flight Commander

Again, there she was in his dream, drifting away from him somehow. Harry made a convulsive effort of will, and the strange paralysis that had been gripping him broke down. He reached out and took Marie's hand in his own, and she smiled at him. In the dream he closed his eyes, content just to hold her hand.

♍   ♍   ♍

23 December 1917.

Lambeth woke Harry before dawn for his defensive patrol. He remembered the tag end of his dream still, that wonderful sense of relief and happiness he'd felt when he'd at last managed to touch Marie's hand with his own, doubled and redoubled when she smiled at him in return.

Harry ate his hard-boiled egg by candlelight with a contemplative air, curious what the day would bring. He shaved in front of a mirror with the kobold-forged razor. It was almost a frightening experience. His stubble offered no resistance whatsoever to the blade, which had been honed beyond even a scalpel's sharpness.

It was still almost completely dark when Harry stepped outside the cottage in his flight suit, helmet and goggles under one arm, a kerosene lantern in hand to light the way. The darkness was soft and velvety and there was a mild warmth to the air. The sky was overcast, the aerodrome almost completely unlit except for a few furtive gleams from the north hangar, but the first hints of a moderation in the encompassing gloom could just be seen in the sky to the east.

Harry was a little concerned about the overcast. If it was too low and dense and if the sunrise didn't burn it off, it would be impossible to fly at all. But though the night sky was featureless and black, there was something about the feel of the air that didn't suggest a heavy cloud cover.

As he made his careful way to the north hangar, Harry heard a medley of birds twittering and chirping in the brush around the airfield, aware of the coming dawn even before first light. They were silenced for a few seconds by the harsh cawing of a crow or a raven, perched on the roof of the hangar. He looked up, reminded of the gift of the Badb Catha that Jernigan had shown him the day before, but it was still too dark to make anything out at that distance. Moments later, the general twittering resumed.

Harry entered the hangar to see Bromley and his crew of mechanics readying his S.E.5a for flight, Captain Jernigan and Major Quirk chatting off to the side.

"Morning, Tregeseal," said Quirk. Harry remembered this time not to salute.

"Good morning, sir. You're both up early, though. I thought this was going to be a solo patrol."

"Indeed," said Jernigan, "but B Flight has to be ready to scramble, should any of us on our turns find something up there. And the major here apparently doesn't sleep."

Major Quirk smiled. "Actually, I wanted to get up early to assign Harry here some extra work."

"Sir?"

"Nothing too horrible," said Quirk. "I have to meet Prince Nuada over lunch along with Jernigan here and Devlin. There's a pair of new pilots coming through, though, and I'd like you to pick them up. Head over to the fairy village by 11:30 ack-emma. It's a noon-time passage, today. Hartshorn should be waiting with his wagon. Oh, I suppose you'll need to take a kobold with you to talk to him."

Harry said "Yes sir, will do. What are the names of the new pilots?"

"James Buchanan of the RNAS, and Robert Moisan, from the Aéronautique Militaire. Buchanan is a navy flight lieutenant, which is like a sort of senior first lieutenant in the RFC, and Moisan is a sous-lieutenant, which is the same as our second lieutenant grade."

"A Frenchman, really?" Jernigan was surprised.

"Certainly. A Breton, of course."

"Of course," said Jernigan. "I'm just wondering how whoever

it is in the brass who is managing all this was able to pry him loose. I wonder what kind of explanation they gave. I mean, you have to imagine the communication being a bit awkward, if they haven't told the French about this world and all. And what's to stop our man from revealing it all later?"

"Ha," said Quirk, "that would be interesting to find out. But I suppose the French are already in on the secret. The Carnac airstrip is operated by French airmen, after all. But I'm only an Imperial Viceroy, you know. It's not like they tell me anything."

"All right then," said Harry. "It looks like they're ready with my scout. I'll just do my preflight inspection now."

"Certainly. Oh, Tregeseal, do you have any French to speak of?"

"Some, sir," said Harry, remembering his initial confusion talking to Marie. But they'd eventually managed to communicate after all. And now he felt he was blushing again. "But I'm far from fluent."

"Well, none of us are that," said Quirk. "Buchanan flies rotaries, so he'll complete A Flight. This Moisan is supposed to be a SPAD pilot, which I'm sure you know uses a stationary engine, so in the double interest of not killing him off right away on a rotary and also of filling out B Flight's roster, I'm going to assign him to fly a SE with you and Jernigan. You don't mind if he bunks with you?"

"No, sir," said Harry.

"Fine, then. If all goes well, I'll see you before your own pod-busting sortie in the afternoon. We'll know if A Flight has learned anything new by then."

Harry completed his preflight inspection without finding a stitch out of place in the fabric, a smudge on gauge or windshield, or even so much as a speck of dirt on the venetian blind slats of the radiator grill. The rigging was in perfect shape, and even the paint job on the fabric looked like it had received a recent touch-up. Harry thought he'd never seen a more exquisite presentation of an aeroplane before. It occurred to him then that the kobolds might have gone to an extra effort. He looked around for the crew, who had started to work on one of the Camels scheduled for a pod-busting attack job later in the morning.

"Bromley," said Harry, "I must say my SE is in as beautiful condition as it's possible for mortal hands to achieve."

"Thank you, sir."

"But considering that in ten minutes or so I shall be taking off at sixty or seventy miles an hour through the field out there, kicking up a spray of dust and pollen and shredded leaves, with a fine mist of castor oil adhering to everything, corrosive hot gas blasting out the exhaust, and all manner of bugs and bits of dirt smashing into every forward-facing surface on the machine, do you suppose it's possible that this superb effort might be wasted, at all?"

Bromley paused for a moment, appeared to be considering the question seriously.

"No sir," he said at last. "We like a clean machine."

Harry wanted to suggest that if they were doing all this extra work just for him, it was completely unnecessary. No matter how uncannily skilled the kobolds might be as machinists, they couldn't realistically be capable of dusting and polishing with all that much more efficiency than ordinary human mechanics, and it must have taken them hours to bring his machine to its current pristine state. But he couldn't come up with a way to phrase his case without acknowledging some exceptional affection or at least respect they might be showing him, and he wasn't prepared just then to deal with this thorny issue.

"Very well," he said at last. "Carry on, then. My compliments to the crew." Bromley saluted, and Harry left before the effusive radiation of happiness from the other kobolds became so intense as to be embarrassing.

Harry stepped out of the hangar to check the progress of the dawn. It was still dark out, too dark for a pilot untrained in night-flying to take off, particularly with no illumination of the field, but there was a definite glow on the eastern horizon. He stood there watching as over the course of ten minutes or so the glow brightened into a soft yellow radiance gleaming in a broad swathe to the east. Well above the horizon the light diffused into faintly luminescent pink streamers that dimmed and broadened as they stretched across the sky until at last, they faded into darkness at the zenith.

As the sky slowly brightened, it became apparent that there was no heavy overcast, but instead a high haze, thick enough to block the stars but not so low as to interfere with flying. Harry thought it would probably burn off completely after sunrise. Now everything was much brighter, and even to the west Harry could see details of the landscape with the peculiar clarity that comes shortly before full daylight.

Time to fly.

The S.E.5a start-up and initial ascent again came off with the combination of remarkable ease and extraordinary power Harry was coming to associate with the kobolds' work. He circled the airfield once, refamiliarizing himself with the extra-ordinary flight properties of the souped-up scout before rising to 5,000 feet for the first leg of his patrol. They had decided that the best plan was to follow a triangular course, one corner at the airfield, another 30 miles to the southeast, and the last point 30 miles to the north, with the idea this should give a decent view of the Shroud while at the same time the patrol route would cross the likely paths of any westward attack on the aerodrome. With a circuit length of ninety miles Harry would be able to take two laps on the patrol circuit with no worries about his fuel levels, and by then it would be Powell's turn on the rota.

After about fifteen minutes in the air, with the luxurious feeling of having the entire sky to himself, the luminescence of the early morning haze faded away and the world slowly bright-ened. He turned north after reaching the southeastern corner of his patrol triangle, and Harry unlimbered the binoculars he had brought with the intention of scanning the edge of the Shroud, now only ten miles away. Gazing through the lenses Harry was relieved to see that the Shroud had not made any obvious west-ward gains. However, there was no sign of the thin spot that had been made by the destruction of a single pod in the previous day's experiment.

As Harry was approaching his second patrol waypoint the sun cleared the Shroud which at this distance formed a black wall rising some distance above the eastern horizon. Sunrise had technically occurred some minutes before, but now the act-ual solar disk was visible at last. The diffuse golden glow in the east gave way to the familiar piercing radiance of the risen sun, and the murky blue-grading-to-violet colors at the zenith were replaced by the deep azure that had impressed him during the previous days' flights. If Harry had been on a dawn patrol in France the next few minutes would have been a time to grow concerned about German attacks from the east, but here the risk of a surprise attack seemed negligible.

Still, the risen sun might well glint off the crystal bombs of any thread-tugs currently in the air. Harry swept the line of the Shroud with his binoculars, though he had to avoid looking too close to the sun itself. There were no sparkles visible, and all seemed quiet. Turning southwest toward home on the final leg of his first patrol circuit, Harry started to grow a little bored. It seemed unlikely that he would see anything worth reporting during the rest of the patrol.

On the second time around his patrol circuit, he thought it

would make a change to head down to the deck for a closer view of the landscape.

It was a positive pleasure to pull a half roll and dive in the S.E.5a. With the power of the souped-up engine multiplied by gravity the descent was an exhilarating rush of speed. In Harry's old DH.5 dives were always nerve-wracking because there was no telling what might fail when he tried to pull up. But the roar of the SE's engine was so perfectly smooth even at high speed that he felt no trepidation at all.

Diving at over 200 miles per hour—he did have to rein the aeroplane in somewhat, to keep well away from the structural limit of 280 he'd been warned of—it was less than thirty seconds before Harry leveled off a hundred feet above the ground. Out here ten miles from the Shroud the green meadowland around the aerodrome gave way to prairie with wild grasses rippling in yellow-green waves as he flew over land that was mostly flat. The grassy plain was broken here and there by streams, and he saw a few ponds as well, but no major rivers.

Zipping along above the rippling grassland, Harry felt quite alone. The landscape here had a desolate aspect despite its beauty. There wasn't a single sign of habitation or work of artifice anywhere to be seen, not even a fallow field. He could hardly imagine so much unused but obviously arable land anywhere in the world he was familiar with. It clearly hadn't been abandoned—it was just that no one had ever bothered to settle here.

But quite apart from the sense of solitude and isolation, Harry also felt a sort of yearning, almost a summons, as if the landscape was calling out for his attention. He wanted to fly on and on, to see everything in this marvelous new world. There was sure to be something worthwhile, some new vista or prospect, something no one had ever seen before from the air wherever he went. The idea of being able to see so many new sights, to explore a new world, and to fly so freely was almost intoxicating. Harry thought that if they could eliminate the threat of the Shroud, put paid to whatever mysterious enemy was behind this monstrous thing, he might be able to return to this place afterwards, and the idea gave him new energy, dispelling whatever melancholy he'd been feeling from the loneliness of the flight. It was pleasing to be able to form such a clear goal, the first he'd really had for a long time, come to think of it.

For some time now, Harry felt he'd been drifting through life, not sure what he really wanted out of it, not unhappy exactly, but with no real purpose in mind. He liked machines as well as the idea of progress, so he went to an engineering school. The notion of flying had appealed long before he'd ever become a pilot, and the experience of it was delightful now that he had achieved that status. But he'd joined the RFC—with all the striving it had taken to be accepted into the corps—in default of having anything better to do, because his country was at war and it was incumbent on him to join in. Having at last been assigned to the front, he found he could take no pleasure in destroying a human enemy. The whole war was just too stupid and wasteful to make the slightest bit of sense. As if all these millions of lives lost could somehow be justified by reckless treaties, by the foolish ambitions of generals who never even visited the charnel-house battlefields, or by conspiracies hatched a thousand miles away from the front.

Thinking these deep thoughts, Harry had been flying more or less unconsciously for several minutes. Because the glorious rush of his machine's speed was enhanced by the presence of the ground so close below, Harry had been drifting lower for some time, enjoying the racing pace and the waves of grass rushing past to either side.

So he was only around 50 feet up when bobbing up over a the crest of a very gentle rise in the seemingly endless grassland, Harry was surprised to find himself flying over a herd of wild horses, driven frantic by the sound of the engine and the unexpected sight of the aeroplane flying low over their heads. Even above the engine, he could hear the screams of the herd and the pounding tumult of their hooves.

There must have been a hundred horses scattered over an acre or two, mostly bays and chestnuts, all running wildly away from his machine. Harry immediately pulled up, ashamed at having caused this panic. He would have returned at once to his former patrol altitude, feeling rather guilty about it too, but in the chaos of the herd, he saw a single white horse, standing motionless on the crest of the rise. Harry was already 300 feet up by then, and later he realized it should have been impossible for him to make out any such details, but at that moment he was nevertheless sure it was a mare, and that she was calmly regarding him—looking at Harry, not just up at his machine. At this point it should also have been impossible for him to hear much from below, but he was sure he heard the mare's whinny followed by a full-throated neigh, and it seemed to him it was a sort of salute. Seized by an impulse he couldn't have explained, he waggled his wings in an aerial return of the courtesy before soaring up and away from the scattered herd. He was almost back at the aerodrome before he recalled Mrs. Llewellyn's figurine, and her blessing.

The remainder of his patrol was uneventful. Harry landed without incident, stopping not far from the line of five Sopwith Camels waiting to take off on A Flight's morning attack run.

"Seen anything out there?" Captain Devlin was at Harry's cockpit even before his propeller had spun down.

"No contacts at all," said Harry, "but it does look like the gap from yesterday has been filled in."

Devlin didn't seem very put out by this news. "Oh well, let's see how they do filling in today, then, shall we?"

"We'll let you know in the PM," said Harry.

"Righto."

Harry walked over to David Powell's S.E.5a, which was being readied for takeoff. Powell would be taking over Harry's patrol responsibilities for the next hour and a half. He was just finishing his preflight inspection, Jernigan standing beside him.

"Nothing to report," said Harry. "No encounters."

"Just as well," said Powell, looking up from his examination of the rudder assembly. "Strange how passive they seem to be, though, especially after that raid a couple of days ago."

"Yes. But for the moment at least, all is quiet out there. Nothing doing at all."

Harry continued, a little hesitantly, "David, Rhys, are either of you up on your Welsh mythology?"

"Not very much," said Jernigan. "Just a few dribs and drabs. Never had much interest in that sort of thing. Before, anyway. Might have been a wise move to learn more about it when I had the chance, though. What about you, Powell?"

"I'd better be up on it," said Powell, smiling, "what with competing in the national eisteddfod and all that."

Jernigan whistled appreciatively. "Sorry," he said, "I had no idea you were a bard."

"That might be going a bit far," said Powell. "But I did win the regional prize for poetry at Aberystwyth last year. Judges took no note of me in the finals, however. Why do you ask?"

"Well," Harry was a little embarrassed to explain, "there's no time now. Just want to ask you something about Rhiannon. When you get back from patrol?"

"Sure."

Jernigan looked inquisitively at Harry, but he shook his head. He wasn't prepared to talk about that strange encounter with the white mare just yet.

After wishing Powell good luck on his patrol, Harry walked back to his cottage to change from his flight suit. The package of stationery MacLeod had dropped off the previous day caught his eye, and he took a few pages of foolscap with him to the mess hall along with pen and ink to write his first letter home from this posting.

23 December 1917
XXX Squadron
XXX Aerodrome

My dear Father, Mother, and Jennifer,

When last I wrote, I was telling you about my reception in No. 32 Squadron, and my circumstances at our aero-drome not far from Ypres—which it seems everyone calls Wipers around here. But the fact is, I am "here" no longer, hence the mysterious address I've put at the top of the page. In what I must say has been an absolutely flabbergasting turn of events, I have been detached from duty after a mere week at my first RFC squadron, and assigned to a new posting which if I even attempted to describe it in print would no doubt result in this letter being censored into illegibility, if indeed you ever were permitted to receive it at all.

And Jennifer, before you ask, no, I did *not* crash my aeroplane. Your affectionate if rather dismal sisterly predictions notwithstanding, my reassignment is not punishment, but is... well, the fact is I have no idea how to put it without my words either being blacked out or burned entirely, but it's something so marvelously odd, so peculiar and unexpected, so utterly fantastic in short, that I can hardly even think how to suggest what it has to do with. Sorry for any frustration you may feel, but further explanations shall have to await my return to England. But I will say this: I am no longer anywhere on the front. In fact, I am with a new squadron I am quite unable to identify by name, number, or location, and to put your mind at ease, Mother, so far at least my duties appear to be rather less hazardous than before, though I am still a scout pilot, with all that entails.

You may have detected a hint of reticence in my last letter, about something less than universal enthusiasm in the other pilots regarding my advent at 32 Squadron. I subsequently learned what the problem was. One has to spend at least a month at the front before the other fellows really warm to one, though I do believe the ice was beginning to break even before I left. However, my current assignment is to a newly formed squadron, and I must say the collegial feeling here is most appealing and welcome. I may also have passed some disparaging remarks about the DH.5—in retrospect I wonder whether that was censored. Anyway, in my new squadron, I have the pleasure of flying the latest model of S.E.5a, an extremely powerful, stable and comfortable aeroplane superior to any-thing else in the air except possibly the Sopwith Camel.

Now I have come to the stage of the usual pleading appeals for things from home. I must say those peppermint cream things you sent to me at Upavon were quite welcome, but apart from sweets I wonder if you would be so very kind as to send me my old French textbook and dictionary, which I believe is on the shelf in my room at home.

With all my love,
Your affectionate son (or brother as the case may be),
Harry Tregeseal, 2/Lt RFC

PS: The post may well be delayed unreasonably at times because as I said I am no longer at the front, nor close to any major depot. Please don't worry if you fail to hear from me for some extended period because the way to and from my current location is, well, *convoluted* may be the best way to put it.

It was 11:00 before Harry finished his letter and emerged from his cabin into the brilliance of late morning. He passed the word for Lambeth to a kobold sergeant in the hangar, and a minute later his batman appeared from the underground level. Together they walked at a leisurely pace to through the hills to the fairy village, where they found Hartshorn waiting for them with his deer-drawn wagon in front of the same sod house as two days before. This time he looked up for a moment before hiding his face with his hat. The peasant had an ordinary enough visage at first glance, weather-worn and lined, with none of the unusual color or other curious features of the kobolds, but even so Harry thought there was something distinctly *other* about his appearance, even though he couldn't put his finger on just what it was.

"Tell him we'll spare his deer on the way there. We'll walk on ahead," said Harry. He was belatedly anxious about the timing for his delivery of the squadron's post and reception of the new pilots.

Lambeth translated, and Hartshorn tugged on his hat in response before starting his team off into a walk.

The streamside path to the dolmen was much easier to walk than the flower-choked valleys between the fairy village and the aerodrome, and so Lambeth and Harry rapidly pulled ahead of the wagon.

At this point Harry remembered the question that had been nagging about the S.E.5a's guns.

"Say Lambeth," he said, "I suppose you must be familiar with the SE design, since you worked on that supercharger?"

"Yes sir," said Lambeth a little hesitantly.

"Do you have any idea why it mounts that Lewis gun on the wing instead of a second Vickers gun?"

"Sir?"

"You know, like the twin guns on the Camels. I should think it would be much more effective to have twin guns."

Lambeth stopped short.

"I'm sorry sir," he said, "it never occurred to me to wonder at it. A question like that, *why* I mean, that's a little strange to our way of thinking. It's part of the design, so I just assumed there must be a reason for it."

"Probably there is," said Harry. "Never mind. I was just curious."

Lambeth frowned. He was silent for the remainder of the walk. They arrived at last in the vicinity of the dolmen connecting to Carnac. This was the east side, near the clearing where Hartshorn would be parking his wagon. They'd have to walk around to the far side to get to the entrance in the west.

"It can't have been much more than a half hour's walk," said Harry. "But now I'm not sure. What do you think, Lambeth?"

Lambeth produced a pocket watch from one of his uniform pockets. "It's 11:43," he said.

Harry stared at him a moment.

"Don't tell me you made that yourself."

"Actually not, sir." Lambeth handed over the watch. "We're not set up for this kind of fine work just now. It does look like an interesting device. Very detailed and delicate work compared to those engines. The escapement is beautiful. You do have *some* fair craftsmen, though why you don't put them to work on your war machines... This is the major's. It must have come across with the big shipment of aeroplanes. I borrowed it from his batman, thinking that you might want to know the time."

"Ah. That makes sense."

Harry shouldered the post bag. There wasn't much in it, just a few envelopes and a packet containing the major's official reports, nothing like the heavy pack he'd carried across from his own world. He took the letter he'd just written from his breast pocket. He'd never had a chance to ask about the protocol for posting it. But he supposed a censor—Mrs. Llewellyn, perhaps? Or some staff officer at Whitehall who was in on the secret?—would eventually review it on the other side and would black out anything inappropriate. He put the envelope in the bag, and sealed the bag with the silver tag he'd been given.

"All right, Lambeth, let's see how the transfer looks from this side. I think I must have fainted at the crucial moment a few days ago so I don't really know what it was like."

"Ah, sir, if you don't mind, I think I should wait here."

"Why do you say that? You're not afraid of being sent accidentally to my world, are you?"

"Oh no, sir," said Lambeth. "Though that would be... interesting. But you told me that just seeing a kobold for the first time was something of a shock for you. And since the transfer is so stressful, perhaps you should greet the new pilots yourself, before bringing them out to see me?"

"Oh," said Harry. "I do believe you might be right. Very considerate indeed. Well, I'll just go in and drop off the post bag, and then I suppose we'll see you in fifteen minutes or so."

Harry walked around to the west side of the hill. He glanced at the pocket watch before he passed through the dolmen trilith. 11:47. The transition from brilliant overhead sunlight to the stark darkness of the tunnel was dazzling, and he paused for a moment for his eyes to adjust.

It was a strange feeling for Harry to walk down the narrow dark corridor into the tumulus. He had a sense of his own world close at hand, though he had no idea if this was just an imagined closeness, or if he was somehow feeling the imminent opening of the passage. It occurred to him then that he might be able to go through, to return home, if only he wanted to. There it was, the central chamber, pitch black, but he could sense the widening space, and could feel the walls to confirm it. He put the post bag down, then reconsidered, moved it off to the side so no one would trip over it.

Harry turned to leave and hesitated, though he couldn't

have said why. There was no logic to a return to his own world at this time. He'd be disobeying orders—secret orders coming all the way from the King at that—and he had no idea what kind of punishment there might be in store if he did. Moreover, he had no reason to go back to the deadly senseless war, and every reason to stay here. To explore a new world, to be a hero, to save an entire fairy kingdom from ruin, who wouldn't want to do that? There would be a lot more meaning to the fight here in fairyland than in some pointless predatory combat over the blasted battlefields of the western front. His fellow pilots here were a rather pleasant and friendly group, too. Indeed, Harry had never known a group of boys or men that he liked better, even considering he'd only just met them all. Even Carstairs wasn't that bad, compared to other less pleasant individuals he'd known at school in every form and year. The kobolds were interesting people too, and sexual proclivities aside Harry was finding that he liked them. It would be a shame not to help these people out. Even the flying work seemed safer here, not to mention far less morally fraught. All these reasons made the thought of returning prematurely to his own world seem idiotic, an army of nay votes militating against the idea with no ayes on the other side. And yet... and yet... There was something about the idea of returning that was alluring, even though Harry couldn't articulate a single reason in favor of the choice.

Harry realized he'd been standing there in the dark for at least a couple of minutes, going over these arguments in his head. If he wasn't careful, he really might be caught up in whatever magic was involved in the passage between the worlds. He shook his head and started back down the passage. Now that he was walking back down the dark corridor, that feeling of being torn, that indecisiveness, evaporated completely. The thought of fleeing back to his own world made no sense at all to Harry now. Had he really been dithering in the dark there for minutes on end?

Harry stepped out blinking into the bright sunlight with something of the feeling of being reborn. Somewhere nearby a crow was giving voice, sounding like it was laughing at him. Well, he thought, he probably deserved it. He checked the major's watch. 11:59. *Bloody fucking hell!* He'd been waffling in there more than ten minutes. One more minute and he might possibly have been caught up in the transfer, if indeed it worked that way. He was wondering what could have prompted such a strange lapse when he heard a muted ding from the watch. It was noon, precisely.

Harry turned to look back at the dolmen. Nothing had changed. Should he just wait for the new pilots to emerge? But what if both of them had fainted while still in the passage? When would it be safe to enter? Harry wasn't sure whether the effect of the transfer magic would only work in the central chamber, or in the tunnels as well. He approached as close as he could without entering and peered into the darkness. For a moment he saw nothing at all, and then he saw a dim glow at the end of the passage. That must be it, the connection had been established and he was seeing the faint light of his own world from the eastern connection to the central chamber. Then the light from the far passage was blocked. Harry moved his head trying to see past the obstruction, but a moment later it proved to be caused by the emergence of two men, staggering drunkenly into the light.

These must be the two new pilots. Yes, one was in the navy blues of the RNAS, and the other in the cerulean of an officer in the Aéronautique Militaire. The French pilot was shorter than the other. He was dragging two kit-bags as well as an Army post bag behind him, at the same time as supporting the Navy pilot with one arm and carrying a leather satchel over the other shoulder—on second glance it proved to be a violin case. Harry supposed the Frenchman had come through the passage with less severe symptoms than the RNAS man, but perhaps the effect was merely delayed, because when he stepped out into the sunlight, he blinked twice and collapsed to the ground, dragging the other pilot down with him before Harry could intervene.

Harry laid the two out on the ground as best he could. His first-aid skills were only novice-level, but neither seemed to be in any dire extremity. Next time, he thought, smelling salts and a canteen would be in order, not to mention a flask, but for the moment there was nothing he could do except to prop each man's head up on his kit-bag.

After half a minute, both showed signs of recovery, but it was the Frenchman who awoke first.

"Quoi? Où suis-je?" The pilot struggled to get up, and Harry held out his hand to pull him to his feet.

"Ah, bonjour, lieutenant. Bienvenue au pays enchanté." Harry had worked this line out in advance.

"Pays enchanté? Oh. Fairyland, you mean? But of course, you are English. Thank you very much. So it's real after all!" The Frenchman's pronunciation was impeccable, quite free from any accent at all.

"Yes." But Harry was a little confused himself about pronunciation. He was set to address the man with the French version of his rank, but if he was speaking English, should it be "lieutenant" as in the Army? Better to use his French rank.

"Sous-Lieutenant Moisan, I presume?" He held out his hand. "I'm Second Lieutenant Harry Tregeseal, RFC."

"A pleasure. Robert Moisan, at your service." They shook. "And this is Flight Lieutenant Buchanan of your Royal Navy, who I suppose you must also be expecting."

The Navy man twitched, perhaps at the sound of his name, and his eyes opened. He looked up, dazed for a moment, and then sprang to his feet before Harry could try to help him up. Buchanan stood there swaying for a moment, and then mastered himself, his jaw set.

"Flight Lieutenant James Buchanan, Royal Navy Air Service, reporting for duty." Buchanan spoke in a clipped military style, with a more definitely Scottish accent than Carstairs or Graham, but none of MacLeod's broad Scots diction.

Harry repeated his introduction.

"It will be about half an hour's ride to the aerodrome," he said. "Before we head off, I should ask if either or both of you gentlemen have been briefed at all? Do you understand why you are here, or have any idea what this place is like?"

The two newcomers looked at each other for a moment, and then Buchanan spoke up.

"Frankly," he said, "I haven't the foggiest notion. I was detached from my squadron six—no seven hours ago, rousted out of bed with some kind of secret orders, but my O.C. couldn't or wouldn't provide any explanations. My transport was delayed. I was flown across the country by a French pilot who had no English, and then I was hustled into that hillside along with this gentleman by a Welsh lady with no time even to ask what was going on. After having half my personal possessions confiscated on the grounds of being magnetic, no less! So no, no briefing at all. This whole thing is entirely fantastic to me."

"Fantastic is the mot juste, all right," said Harry. "I'll try to give you some kind of briefing on the way, but no doubt the major will be able to explain things better than I can."

"Wonderful," said Buchanan. "'Major', you said? So this is an Army operation, is it? My O.C. thought as much."

"For the most part," said Harry. "I don't think there are any other Navy men among us, at any rate."

"Ridiculous!" Buchanan snorted. "So why assign me to an

Army unit? This makes no sense at all."

"There is an explanation, Flight Lieutenant. I'm not sure you'll like it very much, though. I've only been here for three days myself, and four days ago I wouldn't have believed it either."

"Hmph. Well, I'm all ears."

"In a moment, sir," said Harry. This wasn't proving to be very easy. "And you, Lieutenant Moisan? I don't suppose you had any briefing yourself?"

"Oh," said the Frenchman, "my sister told me all about it well in advance. But I must say I didn't truly believe her. Until just about five minutes ago, I really thought this was all some sort of elaborate prank."

"Your sister?"

"Yes, apparently she's part of some sort of, well, how should I put it? A conspiracy? That's not quite right. A secret society, I suppose. Anyway, if you're Tregeseal, I have a letter for you. She just gave it to me ten minutes ago." He pulled an envelope out of a pocket, handed it to Harry, who looked at it in astonishment.

"Your sister," said Harry, "she's not a pilot, is she?"

"Oh yes," said Moisan, "She said she flew transport for you last week. Marie was the one who convinced me to join our air service... and now I know why she was so insistent."

Buchanan had grown impatient during this exchange.

"Listen," he said, "I hate to interrupt, but if you would tell me what is going on, I should very much appreciate it. I'm not accustomed to being drugged and shanghaied as part of my usual service obligations."

"Drugged? What?"

"I don't faint," said Buchanan. "Not ever. And wherever I am now, it's obviously not where I was."

"Oh," said Harry, "they really didn't tell you a thing?"

"That's what I said."

Harry was momentarily perplexed. How should he start to explain?

"Listen," he said, "first of all I have the idea that fainting or something similar is common in making the transition. I don't think any drugs were involved. In fact, in my own case, I'm sure of it. Second, well, I suppose you've heard of the Seelie and Unseelie courts?"

"Fairy tales." Buchanan snorted again. "What does that have to do with anything?"

"I wouldn't have believed it last week either," said Harry. He had to admit that Buchanan's attitude seemed quite reasonable under the circumstances. "But I'm afraid to have to tell you you're in another world now. A sort of fairyland, you might call it."

"How absurd! Do you take me for a complete idiot?"

"I'm sorry," Harry said. "I know it's completely unbelievable. And I only understand some of it myself, even after three days here. I'll explain as we go. You'll have to take my word for some of it for the moment, but I think I can at least prove to you there is something completely uncanny going on if you follow me."

"Hmph," said Buchanan. "Very well. Lead on, then."

"Here," said Harry, "let me take that post bag." As Moisan handed it over, Harry asked him "I gather you have a somewhat better understanding where you are, Lieutenant?"

"Well, as good an idea as Marie could convey, since she's never been here," said Moisan. "I also had rather more opportunity to chat with Mrs. Llewellyn than Lieutenant Buchanan, as I arrived at Carnac the day before. But I'm still eager to hear everything you know. They kept me in the dark until Carnac, you see."

"I see. Well, gentlemen, on the far side of this hill there will be a wagon you can ride to the aerodrome. It's driven by one of the natives here. I gather he's not got much more standing than a serf in this country, and he's rather shy to boot, not to mention that he doesn't speak English, so it's probably best if you don't talk to him."

Here Buchanan darted a suspicious look at Harry, which he ignored.

"There's nothing about the wagoneer that will prove much of anything either way. However, I will also introduce you to my batman, who is very clearly not a human being. All the squadron officers—" he interrupted himself. "You do understand, at least, that you're joining a new squadron, gentlemen?"

Buchanan nodded, and Moisan smiled and said "Yes indeed."

"All the officers, I say, apart from yourselves are RFC men who have been sent over from various squadrons along the front over the last week or ten days. But it wasn't possible to send across airmen, so we're relying on one of the native races here for all the jobs that enlisted men would usually do. If meeting Private Lambeth doesn't convince you you're in a new world, I suppose you'll have to wait to talk to Major Quirk, our O.C."

Harry shouldered the post bag and led the two pilots around

the tumulus to the far side. As they walked, he looked over his new comrades. Buchanan was tall and thin, cutting a rather dashing figure in his navy uniform. His face was on the gaunt side, and he had pale blond hair. It looked like he might be a couple of years older than Harry, possibly 22 or 23. He clearly wasn't happy at all. Considering that he had been told much less about the assignment than Harry had, Harry couldn't blame him.

Moisan in comparison was shorter, verging almost on the rotund, with much the same dark brown hair as Marie. He seemed to be about Harry's age, conceivably a year or so younger. Moisan was pleased to be here, and was obviously excited, not upset at all. Looking at Moisan's uniform, Harry noticed an unfamiliar medal or distinction, a gold pin in the shape of a stylized flying bird on the lapel of his uniform tunic.

When they came around to the far side of the tumulus, the two new pilots both had obvious reactions to seeing Lambeth. Buchanan stopped short and goggled, his hand darting under his tunic. "Holy Christ", Harry heard him whispering.

Moisan, however, came alive rather like certain hounds Harry had known on taking a scent, and indeed the Frenchman almost seemed to be quivering with excitement.

Lambeth saluted as they approached.

"Gentlemen," said Harry, "this is Private Lambeth, a batman serving in our squadron. He's also a brilliant engineer and mechanic, as are all the kobolds so far as I can tell."

Buchanan seemed paralyzed. He said nothing, just stared.

"My dear sir," said Moisan, launching himself forward, "it is a *great* pleasure to meet you." He held out his hand, and Lambeth copied the gesture, a little tentatively.

"My word," said Moisan, after shaking the kobold's hand. Before releasing it, he stared for a moment at Lambeth's claw-like nails, then peered into his flat red eyes before finally letting go. "Such a distinctive morphology! Amazing! Wonderful! Clearly a separate species!"

Harry was about to say something, but Moisan carried on.

"Oh," he said, "I am sorry! I hope I haven't offended or embarrassed you, ah, Private. It's just, well, there must be a thousand, no ten thousand scientists who would happily sacrifice a limb for the opportunity to examine you... Oh, the papers I'll write! The academy... the institute... the royal society..." The Frenchman trailed off. He appeared to be contemplating a prospect only he could see.

"Think nothing of it, sir," said Lambeth. With his words, the spell that had seemed to paralyze Buchanan broke, and the navy pilot jerked his hand out from under his uniform lapel.

"Is it really true?" he asked. "Is this really fairyland? How is this possible?"

Harry turned to look at the Scotsman. "That's a good question," he said, "and one I don't think I can answer. At least I can tell the both of you a few things about this place, the people, and the situation we're in. But you've had a bit of a shock. It will be a short ride to the aerodrome, and I'll try to give you a first briefing as we go."

They walked over to Hartshorn's wagon.

"My word," said Moisan—he seemed to like the expression— "deer in harness! How very quaint!"

Harry looked a bit dubiously at the wagon. There would be enough room for all four of them, barely, but the team had struggled with just two passengers a few days before. "Let's walk beside the wagon," he said to Lambeth. Turning back to the pilots, "You gentlemen should ride. You'll want to recover from the shock of the passage. As I said, it was quite rough for me when I went through."

Lambeth exchanged a few words with Hartshorn as the two new pilots climbed into the wagon with their bags. Moisan cocked his head as he overheard the brief conversation.

"Proto-Gaelic," he said, "how very interesting! But no, that's not it. Some kind of fusion of Brythonic and Goidelic forms. I should add a few hundred philologists to the list of people who'd kill for this opportunity."

"You are a scholar then, m'sieur?" asked Harry.

Moisan flushed. "Please, call me Robert! As for scholarship, I'm going to be one, I hope," he said. "I was at the Sorbonne, just entered in September as a doctoral student, but my mentor —may he rest in peace—wanted me to join the war, and my sister more or less chose the air service for me. Now I understand why she did."

"A doctoral student? May I ask your age?"

"Oh, ah..." Moisan looked a little embarrassed. "I am 19, no, 20 last week, actually. I, er, was graduated early with a bachelor's degree."

"I'm 20 myself," said Harry. "What is your area of study?"

"Sociology with an emphasis on ethnology," said Moisan. "I believe the Americans are beginning to call the latter field anthropology, which seems to me rather a good name for it. The scientific study of humanity."

"I can only imagine how interesting this must be for you,

then," said Harry. "Now then, let me try to cover some of the most obvious questions you gentlemen must have." He paused, realizing he'd made a mistake. "Bother, I've forgotten the major's cheat sheets."

"Here sir," Lambeth produced a couple of folded pages. "I thought they might be needed, so I asked Hammersmith for two copies."

"Thank you, Lambeth," said Harry, relieved not to have to recapitulate it all ex tempore. "This will be much easier, I'm sure."

Harry was saw that Major Quirk had updated the page he'd shown Harry with further notes on the pods and the thread-tugs, along with a brief account of both the raid on the aerodrome and the first engagement with the pods the day before. He handed the sheets to Buchanan and Moisan.

"I'm sure you have a thousand questions, but this will answer the first few, anyway."

Halfway through reading, Buchanan snapped the page rather disdainfully. "Magic!" It was almost a snort of contempt. "Is this meant to be believed?"

"I'm afraid so," said Harry. "I'd like to think that there's some kind of science underneath it all, but what little I've seen so far hasn't shown any sign of it anyway."

"It's not science I'm referring to," said Buchanan coldly. "Any supernatural display that is not divine in origin can only be the working of the Enemy. Which would you say is the case here?"

"I haven't seen much evidence either way," said Harry. "I'm no theologian. But isn't it said that the Devil has no power to create?"

"Yes," said Buchanan. "That's certainly true. Only God has that power."

"Well," said Harry, "I don't know much about magic, except that it worked to get us here. But this world and the people who live here: it's real, and they're real. They may not exactly be Christians, but I'm pretty sure they're not demons, either. So if we are God's creations, and our world is his too, then I suppose this world and these people must be as well."

"Perhaps."

Buchanan left it at that. His remaining questions were technical, about the Shroud and its capabilities. Harry was able to describe the previous day's exploratory mission.

"I believe A Flight will have returned from their attack job by the time we get to the airfield. We should have some word if the enemy has changed its tactics at all, or if the pods are still more or less undefended."

"The enemy," repeated Moisan. "Do we really have no idea who or what they are?"

"Not yet," said Harry. "I'm told that no one in the Seelie Court has ever heard of such weapons before, and there was neither a declaration of war nor any indication who might be behind these attacks."

"Surely there are other countries in this world, though?", asked Moisan. "If this is the fairyland version of western Europe —say France, Spain, and Britain, maybe with the Lowlands and some of Germany, too—what about the rest of the world? Is there a fairyland Africa? Eastern Europe? Scandinavia? I can see there's a sort of Celtic culture here. And I suppose given the kobolds there may be a Germanic one as well. But what about the Romance and Latin influence? The Greeks? The Slavs? Something of the Near East, or the Levant?"

"I wish I could answer you," said Harry, "but we really don't know much at all yet, not even about the local area. Remember we've all only been here a week or so, and I've only been here three days. Still, I agree these are obvious questions." He turned to the kobold. "Do you understand what we're talking about, Lambeth? Do you know any other nations or peoples outside the Seelie and Unseelie Courts?"

Lambeth looked embarrassed. "I'm sorry to say that I know very little about geography," he said. "Until recently we were all living in isolated communities. But I can tell you what I've heard. They say that far to the north—sorry, I mean, northeast of here, north of the Unseelie Court's area—there's a land of giants where it's much colder most of the time, with snow and ice on the ground. They say dragons live there too, but I've never seen either giants or dragons, so they might just be stories."

"Ah," said Moisan, "it sounds like some kind of Norse version of fairyland. Jotunheim, perhaps? It would be wonderful if there were places corresponding to all nine worlds. Very satisfactory from a mythological point of view."

"East of the Unseelie Courts," continued Lambeth, "there's a very large expanse of forests and bogs, mostly rather colder than around here, but not so cold as the first country I mentioned. We used to go into the outskirts to collect bog iron. It's big enough we don't know what's beyond it. The area is mostly uninhabited, but I've heard there are some tribes of people who call themselves Leshy living there, but only in the forested parts."

"Leshy?" Harry hadn't heard the name before.

"Slavic elves," said Moisan. "Most satisfactory."

"I don't know what else to call them, sir. I've never seen them myself but I have an idea they are uncivilized cousins of the fairies here. They don't speak any of the same languages that we do."

"So," said Harry, "neither area seems like it could have spawned anything having to do with the Shroud, would you say?"

"That's right sir," said Lambeth. "And to the south and east there are some wild mountainous regions. No one lives there, and we've never heard of anyone going or coming that way. I don't know how far the mountains go or what's beyond them. We had our biggest communities in the foothills of those mountains, though, and we're hoping they too have escaped the Shroud. Maybe they went east into the marshlands. South and west—I mean more like due south of here, sir—there's a wide band of hills with only a few scattered fairy villages and supposedly some ogres too, and then you come to a long coastline and the sea. There are supposed to be some more tribes living on the coast, but nothing like a nation, not nearly as organized as the Seelie and Unseelie Courts."

Harry wanted to ask what ogres were like, but Moisan spoke up first.

"So much for the glory that was Rome," he said, "not to mention Greece. They had their own fairy stories, of course. Perhaps their areas are simply too far away for Private Lambeth to know much about."

"Yes, sir," said the kobold. "I'm sorry, sir. I know you have your world completely mapped. What we've done in all those hundreds of years while your people were moving forward... it's embarrassing. If we can get rid of the Shroud and make a country for ourselves, maybe we'll be able to do better."

They were coming up on the fairy village now. After his initial outburst and a few technical questions, Buchanan had remained silent most of the way, but over the course of the ride he had lost the edge of his irritability.

They got out of the wagon, and Harry had Lambeth bid Hartshorn goodbye, with his translated thanks. As the fairy villager led his wagon around the sod cottage, Moisan peered after him with undisguised interest.

"Are they as different from human as the kobolds?" he asked. "It was difficult restraining myself from going up to peer in his face."

"Actually," said Harry, "apart from this strange susceptibility to iron, they look more like a human race than another species."

Moisan seemed perfectly capable of standing there asking questions indefinitely, and while Harry thought the discussion would be an interesting one—he hadn't had much chance to talk with anyone this way so far—he thought he should take pity on Buchanan, who was already showing signs of impatience.

"Well gentlemen," said Harry, "it's just a short walk to the aerodrome from here. Around these hills. Hopefully A Flight will have returned by the time we get there."

Harry turned to Buchanan, as they started walking around the hill, conscious that he hadn't spoken much to the man during the ride.

"Are you a Sopwith pilot, then, Flight Lieutenant?"

"Yes," said Buchanan. "Pups and Triplanes. We just received a consignment of Camels flown over from England, but I haven't had a chance to fly one yet."

"We have them here," said Harry. "I understand you'll be in A Flight, so you'll have the chance at a Camel very shortly." Turning to Moisan: "We have no SPADs here, but I think you'll be pleasantly surprised at the performance of the S.E.5a."

"Frankly," said Moisan, "I have very little basis for comparison. Apparently, my whole career in the Aéronautique Militaire, if you can call a span of three days out of flight school a career, was designed with this assignment in mind. I had only just got to the front when they detached me from duty and sent me back home again."

"Oh? I had almost the same experience," said Harry, "though I don't think there was as much planning involved. I was with our Number 32 Squadron for just a week, at Droglandt field near Ypres. Where were you assigned?"

"Rather close by, I believe. We're stationed to the south, but I understand my squadron used to fly over Ypres sector quite recently ourselves. We might have visited your airfield some time for a party, perhaps. What a charming coincidence."

"That would have been amusing. Perhaps we will still do so when this is over," said Harry. "What is your squadron?"

Moisan tapped the gold pin on his lapel. "Escadrille N.3," he said "Les Cigognes. I'm not sure whether to be ashamed or proud of this pin, though. The day I arrived at the aerodrome, I was forced to pay 150 francs for it. I think our supply officer is making a killing on the things. I was there two whole days before leaving again for Carnac. I flew three times without seeing a single German. On the one hand I'm not sure I'm quite entitled to wear the emblem, but on the other hand... 150 francs. For that price, I'm keeping it on. Someday perhaps it will impress the girls."

"Oh," said Harry, "for heaven's sake. I'm an idiot. Everyone knows Les Cigognes. I particularly noticed the pin when I saw you at first, but I was too stupid to realize what it meant. I suppose you never met Guynemer, then?"

"Sorry, but no. He went missing back in September while I was still on my way to flight school. A charming fellow by all accounts, though: 53 victories before he disappeared somewhere north of Ypres, and supposedly very modest too. Quite unlike our current top man Capitaine Fonck, I must say."

They'd picked their way through the flower-strewn valley and were now emerging at last into the open meadowland in which the aerodrome was situated. Harry saw A Flight's four active Camels pegged out in front of the south hangar being prepared for their upcoming defensive patrols. He exhaled, and realized he'd been anxious about their prospects on the morning attack job. But evidently there had been nothing to worry about.

"And here we are, gentlemen," said Harry. "Welcome to Elfshot Squadron."

Walking across the field, Harry saw that Captain Devlin was talking to Jernigan and the other members of B Flight gathered near Devlin's Camel, so he led the two pilots that way and made introductions.

"Major Quirk is at Prince Nuada's castle or fort or whatever you may call it," said Devlin. "I'll be joining him a little later for dinner. Riding a horse to get there, forsooth, with an escort of knights! Like something out of Ivanhoe."

He turned to Buchanan and Moisan. "B Flight is getting ready for a job, so let me take you gentleman in hand for now. I'll have to leave soon for the fort, but I'll get you some lunch and answer any questions Tregeseal might not have had time for." He turned back to the pilots of B Flight. "I'll have the post sorted by the time you chaps get back."

The two new pilots followed Devlin to the mess hall, and Lambeth also left, heading into the hangar, leaving Harry behind with the rest of B Flight.

"So what did you think of him?" Jernigan asked, gesturing at the French pilot's departing back. "Speaks excellent English, doesn't he?"

"Yes," said Harry. "He seems like a decent chap. Knowledgeable in a scholarly way—he was at the Sorbonne. His sister is responsible for transfers through Carnac, so he had a much better briefing than I ever did. Even less flying experience than me, though, if you can believe it. They sent him to the front for form's sake as soon as he graduated flight school and pulled him back to Carnac almost immediately."

Jernigan shrugged. "Oh. I assumed from his pin he was a veteran. Only the best for Les Cigognes, so I've heard. If this was the front, we'd want to pick and choose his flights for a while, just like your O.C. was probably doing for you at—what was it? 32 Squadron?"

Harry nodded, quiet for a moment. He hadn't realized he was being babied along, but that probably explained why he'd flown jobs over Ypres for a week without any actual contact with the enemy until the last day. It was embarrassing, but now he felt a little better about his time at the front.

Jernigan continued "But Devlin says his flight reported nothing much changed up there on this morning's job. We'll let, umm, Moisan take a day to learn his machine—maybe I'll take him up for a joyride this afternoon when we get back, sans stunting this time."

Harry laughed.

"Anyway," said Jernigan, "once he learns the SE, he should be ready to go with the rest of us in a day or so. No dogfighting to do up there, after all. A Flight found some of those thread-tugs floating around the pods, but it seems they are too slow to be dangerous, at least as currently deployed. They got five pods with just four Camels. I hope we can do as well with four SEs, considering we have less firepower than they do."

"I was thinking about that," said Murphy.

"Oh? What do you mean?"

"Yesterday we saw A Flight strafing that pod as if it was a ground position. They traced a path all across the—the dorsal surface, I suppose you'd call it. The first attack pass started some fires, but I think those were superficial gas cell explosions, and they didn't seem to me to be spreading on their own. It wasn't until the third pass that I thought there was some real penetration, and either a number of cells went off together or else some larger inner cell exploded, and then the whole thing really went up.

"I remember that too," said Harry, and Powell and Jernigan both nodded agreement.

"So," said Murphy, "it occurred to me that it might be more

efficient to shoot straight through the thing, instead of across it. Start firing from much longer range than if you were strafing. The target's huge, and it's hardly moving at all, so it's not as if we can miss."

"Oh, I see," said Jernigan. "You're thinking the shots will penetrate better that way. Sure, that sounds like a plan. If we can ignite the core while wasting less ammo, we'll be able to take down more pods in a single job."

"Right," said Murphy. "And maybe that will make up for just having the one Vickers gun."

"We'll try it," said Jernigan. "If it doesn't work, we can always go back to strafing across the top. We'll go in pairs after separate pods, and if all goes well, we'll go on from the first pair to do another two. I'll fly with Powell, and you with Tregeseal. Same flare signal as yesterday, by the way. Red means go ahead with the attack, and green means disengage, got it? Form up again after each attack and wait for my flare before going on to the next target. And if you see something odd don't be afraid to shoot a green flare off yourself. Make sure you've got the Very pistol loaded and ready in your cockpit."

Putting on his flight suit in his cottage, Harry was reminded by the crinkle of paper he had Marie's letter, still unread in his pocket. He unfolded it with as much trepidation as eagerness, almost tempted to put it aside for later. But that would be cowardly, he thought, taking a deep breath before beginning to read.

23 December 1917
Carnac

My Dear Harry,
You have no idea how nervous I am about this letter. First there is my English, better in print I hope than in my speech, especially with Mrs. Llewellyn's kind assistance as a redactor. But more than that, there is—
For heaven's sake. This is my third attempt to write this, the first two tries full of stupid euphemisms and tortured attempts to avoid the subject. But there will be no censors reading this, and Robert has sworn he will not peep. And my hand is beginning to cramp. So to hell with it, I think you English say.
First of all, you must know that you are under no obligations whatsoever to me. I have the idea from someplace that the English have some odd notions of chivalry.

But what happened between us that night—oh God, more euphemisms. I refuse to rewrite this again.

But when we made love that night, when we had sex, I should say, it was all on me. I wanted you for two very good reasons. One of them you may realize was purely, what, mechanical (magical? technical? I don't know how to put it). But the other reason was for you, for being gallant and pretending you trusted my piloting, for being a handsome stranger, for being kind when you saw I was in difficulty, and for that first touch of your hand on mine in the canteen.

But if you have someone else, or if you don't and would just prefer to keep that night a happy memory, (it was happy, wasn't it? I know you enjoyed it too) then that is fine. Just tell me in the briefest note, and I swear I will not trouble you again.

However, if you want, if you really do want it too, then I would very much like to see you again. As soon as you come back from fairyland. I want to fly with you again. That's not a euphemism, it's the honest truth. I want to be in the air with you in a machine again. I can't tell you how frustrating it is to have to wait here while you fly in the skies of Faerie.

In the meantime, my dear, I will dream of you. Come back safely from fairyland.

Your amorous aviatrice,
Marie Moisan

P.S. Robert, if you read this, I hope you're blushing now. You deserve it.

There was yet another postscript scrawled in pencil in a different hand. It read:

If you break Marie's heart, I swear I will kill myself for the express purpose of coming back as a ghost and haunting you forever. Don't screw this up, boy, or you'll regret it.
Fondly,
Olwen Llewellyn

Though it was his second flight of the day, Harry couldn't help but feel a thrill as once more he felt the surge of power from the engine. His aeroplane seemed to be hurling itself off the ground, like a cat leaping towards a bird. Jernigan took the lead in a chevron formation as they formed up over the airfield, Powell to his left and slightly back and below, Murphy in the same position to his right, and Harry taking up a fourth spot to Murphy's right. They cruised due east at 10,000 feet, supercharged engines roaring, the blunt noses of the SEs punching through the air at 150 miles per hour.

Marie's note had given Harry an enormous lift. At the time of their encounter, he hadn't realized what his own feelings were, or perhaps they simply hadn't had time to form, but now he thought returning to Marie was so clearly his ultimate goal that any other consideration would have to be secondary. For a moment he felt a slight regret at having to go back for her as the idea of exploring this new world was still very appealing. But then he realized the two things weren't necessarily exclusive. Once all this was over, was there any reason the two of them couldn't return? They might be able to fly together through the glorious skies of fairyland.

Harry didn't have long to consider these possibilities. It seemed he'd fallen into another aerial reverie, something he knew he'd have to be careful of if he ever returned to a real combat situation, where enemies could materialize at any moment.

Now the formation was banking left, turning north just a couple of miles from the edge of the Shroud, taking a leisurely look at the results of A Flight's morning attack. There was a definite gap in the western edge of the dark mass. It was a good five miles long, and in the center of this gap the Shroud had thinned to the point that it was no denser than an ordinary morning haze.

B flight completed a circle, heading south again. Studying the first two pods southward past the gap A Flight had cleared, Harry saw a scattering of sparkles above them. As they drew closer to the enormous pods belching their curtains of smoke, Harry was able to see that this was a rather thin defensive screen, with no more than half a dozen or so of the tugs cruising above each of the nearest pods. The tugs didn't look like they would be interfering at all with the planned style of attack though there might have been some need to first clear them out of the way had they come in strafing over the top.

A red flare arced up from Jernigan's machine.

Jernigan and Powell bore slightly to the left, readying for an attack run on the first pod in line, while Murphy banked right to line up with the second, Harry following a moment later. Murphy fired a short burst from his Vickers gun, making sure it was ready to shoot and warming his barrel. Reminded of this bit of insurance, Harry yawed further right to take his leader completely out of his sights, and followed suit.

Harry thought that it might be just as well to double down on Murphy's plan. Notching the throttle down a tiny fraction, he drifted back and slipped to the right behind the lead SE, dropping down a hundred feet or so at the same time. Harry meant to direct his fire as nearly as possible at the same point on the target as Murphy—the extra space to the right and the difference in altitude being a hedge against an accidental collision.

Now they were lined up again, flying level towards the center of gravity of the target pod. Less than a thousand yards, now. Seven-hundred fifty... five hundred... four hundred... There! Murphy had opened up, the stream of his tracers almost unwavering as he bore in on the target. This was long range to start shooting in a dogfight, but with such a large target it was impossible to miss. Harry started firing as well, trying to angle his own line of tracers to converge with O'Meara's just at the point of impact.

A puff of flame! It was the same disappointingly small explosion Harry had seen the previous day, but even less impressive today as there was only the one, since their shots weren't traversing the surface of the pod.

Three hundred yards, two hundred, firing all the way. Were they even having any effect on the pod with their shots? Harry was wondering whether this had been a good idea at all, when he saw a sort of reddish luminosity shining through the gap their shots had torn in the pod's skin. A moment after that, the whole thing erupted in a colossal conflagration, a ball of flame a thousand feet in diameter and expanding. There was an enormous rolling boom a split second later. Murphy was already breaking left, and Harry threw his SE hard right. A hammer of wind hit just as he'd achieved a full vertical bank. The bulk of his aeroplane shielded Harry from the full impact of the blast, but still the air turned shockingly hot, and for a terrible moment he felt like he was being roasted.

There was a dizzying moment of extremely high acceleration. Harry's SE was flung about violently by the wind blast from the explosion. For a few seconds he lost his bearings completely and at last he realized he was diving straight down at well over two hundred miles an hour. Harry risked a quick glance to the sides at his wing planes and over his shoulder at his machine's tail. Everything looked to be intact. He eased back gently on the stick, not knowing if his rigging had been damaged, and—thank heavens—he could feel the resistance from the elevator cables. The SE slowly pulled out of its dive. He'd lost a good three thousand feet by the time he managed to right his scout and return to level flight. Finally, he was able to take a moment to look around again. There was nothing left of the pod except a vast cloud of smoke. Half a mile away, that little bug was Murphy. Like Harry he'd lost a lot of altitude, but he was climbing to regain position. Harry looked north. The other pod had been destroyed in the meantime, but he didn't know if it had gone up in so spectacular a fashion.

Five minutes later, they'd resumed formation. Harry flew close enough to Murphy to be able to exchange thumbs-up gestures with him. Both their machines looked to be intact, but he was shocked to see that the whole underside of Murphy's blue-and-white painted machine was now a smoky charcoal color. The explosion must have come very near to igniting their scouts. The fabric covering the aeroplane's skeleton of wooden spars was doped for strength with highly inflammable nitro-cellulose, and if it caught fire the whole frame would go up. It was a pretty close escape, Harry thought, but no harm seemed to be done.

Another red flare flew up from Jernigan's aeroplane. Harry thought that the flight commander had probably not come so close to disaster with his own attack run, and hadn't seen the immediate results of Harry and Murphy's attack, or he would have ordered them all back to the aerodrome. For a moment Harry considered shooting off his own green flare but some combination of bravado and reason constrained him. No damage had apparently been done to either of their machines and all they had to do was not get so close next time... right?

In any event he refrained from making any signal, as did Murphy, and again the two pairs of machines peeled off towards their separate targets. Harry observed Murphy carefully to see if the Irishman intended any different approach on this second run, but it looked as if he was going to do the same thing as before. Once again they lined up with the center of gravity of the target, Harry again drifting back in formation to observe his leader's line of fire. One thousand yards... Seven hundred fifty —and Murphy started firing again, this time at considerably longer range than the first attack run. Once again Harry tried to align his fire with Murphy's. This time there were several puffs of flame around the focus of their shots, as some of the bullets were diverging, but they were still able to hold to the line of flight well enough... and then he spotted that reddish interior glow from the pod shining through the gap their bullets had punched in the outer fabric.

Harry immediately broke hard right at around four hundred yards range, hoping O'Meara had the sense to do the same. This time the wind blast from the explosion was gentler, more like the swell of a big wave that had not yet crested as it approached the shore. The SE rocked and was lofted upwards and outwards by the blast, but Harry was able to keep control fairly easily, and the wash of hot air was much less intense. He even had the luxury of being able to flatten out his bank in time to catch sight of the terrible grandeur of the enormous fiery explosion. The fireball covered a good quarter of the sky from Harry's perspective, a shuddering gyrating sphere shading from crim-son to orange to yellow. The sphere at first expanded rapidly outward, as if to consume the entire sky, but then it abruptly collapsed in on itself, leaving behind myriad smaller fiery vortices spinning outwards and vanishing into nothing-ness. Harry was relieved to see that Murphy had likewise broken off in good time. A few seconds later, he saw a second explosion in the distance: Jernigan and Powell had destroyed their own target.

Once more the flight reformed, and again Jernigan shot off a red flare. On the third attack run, O'Meara and Harry followed exactly the same plan as before, and the pod's destruction came off as easily as it had the second time.

After once more experiencing the exhilarating sight of the enormous fireball burning itself out, Harry was now beginning to feel something like a sense of horror at his own power. He had done that, caused that vast destruction, by holding down the trigger button for a few seconds. It was almost a sense of transgression. Was it right and proper for a human to be able to do such a thing? Was he even human anymore? Perhaps he was a god, or even God. He had the wild idea that he could destroy anything by pressing down one finger for a few seconds. It wasn't incendiary bullets shot from a Vickers gun that had ignited a huge reservoir of hydrogen in the floating pod. It was a tiny movement of his own will deciding to destroy something and immediately being gratified. What if he angled his machine up, turned his sights on the Sun and pressed the trigger? What if later he climbed down from his machine at the aerodrome and looked at the Earth itself with the contempt it deserved, and allowed just the slightest twitch of his fingers? For just a fleeting moment, it seemed to Harry he might well be able to destroy *everything* if he wanted to, the entire world, all of creation itself, and he was afraid he wouldn't be able to resist the temptation.

But then the moment passed, the fireball burned itself out harmlessly again and Harry's sense of himself returned. There he was, Harry Tregeseal, Second Lieutenant, sitting in his cramped little cockpit, the control stick in his hand, his feet on the rudder bar, and the wash of the wind swirling around the SE's tiny windshield blowing against his goggled face. That grandiose sense of destructive power he'd suffered a moment ago was so embarrassing now he could hardly even bear to recall it, and so he put it completely out of his mind as he banked into a climb, returning to formation.

The green flare. Return to base.

The flight in company back to the aerodrome was pleasant enough. Harry didn't lose himself in thought again, but instead concentrated on paying attention to flying, keeping track of his surroundings and the positions of his comrades despite the lack of urgency in doing so. The Sun was still a shining golden orb blazing down on them from a deep azure sky as they flew west, but the quality of its light suggested the coming end of the afternoon.

They landed in formation, showing off a bit, but the wind was right, and the field was plenty wide enough to do it safely. Harry was paying careful attention to his speed and angle, not wanting to look clumsy in comparison to his more experienced comrades. He was aiming for a perfect three-point landing at the absolute minimum speed, and this care may have been what saved him.

As soon as he touched down, wheels and tail-skid contacting the grassy field at the same moment, he knew something was wrong with the undercarriage. There was a shriek of abused bearings from down below, easily audible past the engine noise, and something snapped down there giving off an explosive report. The aeroplane sagged downward to the left, and Harry lurched sharply forward, brought up short by his safety belt. The left wheel was off, and the SE skewed left across the field, out of control at fifty miles an hour, crossing the track of Murphy's machine only a dozen or so yards away. A moment later he felt the right wheel come off, and almost immediately the entire undercarriage collapsed, the aeroplane lurching forward off balance. For an instant the propeller was mowing the grass of the field, and then the remaining broken spars that had once held the wheels gave way and the fuselage fell completely to the ground, the lower wing planes scraping along the lawn, the fabric tearing and trailing along behind in long streamers. The SE's propeller radius extended a foot or so below the radiator frame that capped the aeroplane's nose, and so with the collapse of the undercarriage the blades slapped into the ground, shattering instantly, fortunately not spinning their fragments back into the cockpit. The SE had already lost some speed over the last several seconds of extended catastrophe, but it was still going at a moderate clip when the leading edge of the radiator shutters caught a bit of turf, and the whole aero-plane tipped up on its nose. For a moment Harry thought it was going to flip over completely, and he braced for the impact, but it swayed, and then flopped downward and back once more, smacking down into the earth with the sound of a few more breaking struts.

And then there was complete silence, except for a little pinging from the hot engine block cooling. At some point Harry had switched the engine off, though he didn't remember doing so. He sat there stunned for a few seconds, and finally managed with shaking hands to unclip his belt and leave the cockpit. With the undercarriage shaved off, he could step directly to the ground without having to climb down. It felt very odd.

Jernigan was already running up to him, while the other two B Flight pilots were still taxiing to a stop.

"You all right?"

"Yes." Harry was for the moment unable to say anything more. His wonderful aeroplane, broken in a moment. Was it his fault? He thought it had been a good landing. That first pod explosion must have done something to the wheel bearings, or weakened the spars holding the axle in place. His fault then. He felt a little sick.

Jernigan slapped Harry on the shoulder. "That was beautiful," he said.

"What?" Harry was taken aback.

"That was one of the prettiest crashes I've ever seen. No fire. I don't see any fuel or oil leaking. Even the lower plane is intact, more or less. It's not a total loss."

"But—"

"Come on, Tregeseal," said Jernigan. "I saw you coming in behind me. It was a lovely approach. Sometimes these things just happen, you know. Although I'm a little surprised. I would have expected the kobolds to do a better job. But perhaps they only care about the engines."

"No," said Harry, "it wasn't anything to do with mainten-ance. I got too close to the pod in the first attack run. The blast must have damaged the undercarriage."

"My fault, probably," said Murphy, who had run over with Powell after landing. "I should have started shooting from further back that time. I suppose I'm not much of a balloon buster—I'm in the habit of only shooting at close range."

"Come on boys," said Jernigan. "let's not compete for the blame, now. You're not hurt, and we've got plenty of spare SEs for you to fly until they fix this one up again." He paused. "Although... if you were knocked around on the first run, why the hell didn't you shoot off a flare? We're not in a race, you know."

Harry and Murphy looked at one another. "It didn't seem like anything at the time," he said. "The machine was working just fine. There was no way to know the wheels would seize up, or whatever it was that went wrong with the undercarriage."

Murphy said, "And anyway if we'd gone back home, he probably would have crashed just the same, but we would have gotten four fewer pods."

Powell grinned. "Mother is concerned for your safety, dears. Remember, always look both ways before crossing the street."

Jernigan turned on him. "I'd punch you for that, Mr. Middleweight Powell, but I don't think it would work out too well for me if I did. Lesson learned, all right? Don't get too close to the bloody things when you blow them up."

A crew of kobolds was coming up now, Bromley among them, and Harry saw Lambeth emerging from the ramp to the underground level and hastening across the field as well.

"I'm sorry to have to repay all your hard work with this sad scene, Bromley," said Harry.

"Don't worry yourself, sir," said the kobold corporal. "We'll soon have it in the air again. We've got plenty of spare every-thing." He turned to one of his crew. "Tell Mayfair we need two more full crews. And get some of those long steel poles out of stores. Three should do."

"I suppose you should oversee them getting the poor thing back to the hangar," said Jernigan. "And once they've reckoned all the damages, give me the bill, I'll have to submit the details for the records. Let's meet in the mess in half an hour. I want to talk over the job so I can write up a report. The Camel jockeys will want to hear about Murphy's brilliant idea."

The rest of B Flight went back to their aeroplanes. Lambeth

approached Harry then, followed by Lieutenant Moisan.

"I'm so glad you're safe, sir," said the kobold.

"Yes indeed," said Moisan, "you gave us quite the fright there for a moment."

"Thank you," said Harry. "but it seems no serious damage was done. We'll be meeting in half an hour in the mess hall, Robert, to review our attack on the Shroud. Apart from this"—he gestured at the wreck—"it went quite well."

"Ah, very good," said Moisan.

"Now then," said Harry to Lambeth, "how do you suppose they'll get this thing back into the hangar? I don't remember seeing even a flatbed cart about, much less a lorry with a crane."

"I imagine they'll just lift it, sir."

At this point a dozen kobolds trotted out onto the field from their underground quarters, joining Bromley's crew. Three of the mechanics carried long metal poles balanced precariously on their shoulders. It wasn't until they arrived at the wrecked SE and started working the poles under the nose, behind the wing planes, and under the tail skid that Harry realized what they were doing. It took just a few seconds. Eight kobolds squatted by the front pole, four on either side, another six set themselves by the center pole, and the remaining four stationed themselves at the tail.

"Up!" said Bromley and the kobolds lifted their poles as one, bringing the scout up to shoulder level in a single smooth motion. The pole under the nose had a sharp bow to it due to the weight of the engine, but it looked stable enough. "Forward!"—and they trooped off towards the north hangar as if it was a practiced maneuver.

"My word," said Moisan.

"It's only a ton and a half," said Lambeth. "Well under two hundredweight apiece."

♍   ♍   ♍

B Flight reconvened in the mess hall a few minutes later. Several of A Flight's pilots were already there, whiling away the time during patrol assignments. It was MacLeod's turn in the air.

Carstairs stood up first to greet him.

"Bit of bad luck, what?" Carstairs grinned, showing his teeth. Harry wasn't sure if he was being snide or not. "Lost your undercarriage, was it? You don't see that one every day."

Harry explained the circumstances of the crash.

"Oh well," said O'Meara. "It was only a matter of time till we had a crash or two. Good on you to take one for the team. No injury, right? So everything's good, and now we don't have to worry about it anymore."

"Brian," said Graham, "listening to you, one might almost believe you were superstitious."

"My dear fellow", said O'Meara, gesturing grandly, "you know you have my deepest respect. But look around you. We're in *fairyland*. We got here by *magic*. We're fighting *poisonous zeppelin monsters*. Now tell me where reason stops and superstition begins."

"Oh. Well. You may have something of a point."

"You chaps had better listen to this," said Jernigan, waving them over. "Our Aidan has come up with what seems to be a superior pod-shooting technique."

"Well, perhaps," said Murphy. "But it seems it's best used with care. I'm afraid I managed to muck up Harry's machine pretty badly with it."

He explained the approach they'd used.

"Makes sense," said O'Meara. "We had to waste some ammo clearing out those thread-tug things first before we could strafe the pods this morning. With your straight-in attack they wouldn't have been in the way. On the other hand, on our attack the things went down slowly, like they did yesterday, so there was no danger from the explosion."

"Yes," said Carstairs, "but look at this." He took a white silk scarf out of his uniform tunic pocket, handed it around. "The other fellows have been riding me a bit about this, but I think it's a serious concern." The scarf was smudged with two dark blots, rather different in appearance to the usual uniform stain caused by sprays of dirty castor oil.

"I wrapped it around my face before starting in," he said. "That Shroud stuff is supposed to be toxic, isn't it? That's where my mouth and nose was, against the fabric. We've been breathing in the bloody stuff."

"Hm," said Jernigan. "I must say that doesn't look good. On the one hand I gather it's only a serious problem in the long term. A brief exposure shouldn't be too bad. But on the other hand I'd rather not breathe any more of it than I have to. We might be flying a lot of these jobs."

"That's what I say too," said Carstairs. "With the strafing approach, the pod goes off while it's sinking into the Shroud, and the explosion blasts the whole top layer way up above its previous level. The stuff envelops us for a minute before we can fly out of it. Apart from the savings on ammo, Murphy's way sounds like it should minimize the exposure—the pod will explode above the Shroud, which should blow it downward if anything, and the attackers won't yet have entered the polluted area when they break off. Better safe than sorry, if you ask me."

"Sounds like another argument in favor," said Jernigan. "When Ryan and the major get back from their VIP dinner, we'll see if we can turn it into doctrine."

Discussion became more general after that. For Moisan's benefit, Harry started to recount the details of their recent attack job. In the middle of the account, he realized that Moisan wasn't their only new pilot.

"Say," he said, "is Buchanan recovered from making the trip yet? He might as well hear this too."

"Oh blast," said Carstairs. "MacLeod had him in hand during my patrol, but I didn't remember to look for him when it was MacLeod's turn to go up. I'll fetch him."

Carstairs came back a couple of minutes later, alone, a curious expression on his face.

"Well," asked Powell. "Did you find him?"

"Oh, yes," said Carstairs. "He was in the south hangar. Says he'll be along shortly. He was preaching, you see."

"Preaching?" Powell looked confused. "To whom?"

"Oh, to the kobolds, of course. He had a couple of work crews sitting cross-legged looking very interested while he read out gospel to them. He's an elder in the Church of Scotland."

"Carstairs," said Jernigan gently, "has anyone bothered to explain to him what they're like yet? Tregeseal, did you tell Buchanan when you ferried him over here this morning?"

"Uh, no," said Harry. He felt his face reddening. "It didn't come up. My batman was with us, you see. It would have been a little awkward."

Carstairs snorted. "Of course I told him. Had to give him fair warning, didn't I? He was shocked, too."

"Well, I suppose there's no harm done," said Jernigan. "I wonder what the kobolds are making of the lesson, though. Who knows, perhaps he'll start a mission."

Moisan looked rather confused at this exchange.

"Pardon me," he said, "but what are you talking about? What is it about the kobolds we should have been told? I did see a curious sort of notation on the major's information page."

There were a few snickers from the assembled pilots. Carstairs barked laughter for a moment, then cut it off. "Why," he said, "they're all queers, you see. Every one of them."

Moisan blinked. "Surely that's not possible. They wouldn't be able to reproduce—"

At this point Buchanan himself stepped into the mess hall. He was still holding a pocket Bible which he slipped into the lapel pocket of his uniform tunic as he entered.

"My apologies," he said, "No one informed me a meeting was scheduled. I hope I haven't missed too much." There was an edge to Buchanan's voice Harry thought sounded almost accusatory, as if he believed he'd been deliberately excluded.

"Oh, not too much," said Jernigan at the same time as Harry whispered to Moisan "I'll tell you about them later on."

Jernigan shot Harry an annoyed glance, then turned to Buchanan.

"Not too much," he said again. "But you'll want to hear our show and tell for today's job—this was our first real attack job, you understand—to get some idea what you'll be seeing in future. Harry? You were about to tell B Flight's story, I believe?"

Harry told the story over again, ending with another caution against getting too close to the pod during the attack run. Both Buchanan and Moisan asked a few questions, Moisan's tending more towards the philosophical and Buchanan's being more technical and military-minded.

"We've got some light left today," said Jernigan. "Since neither of you gentlemen has flown your aeroplane before, might as well get an hour in now, eh? I'll show Moisan here the rudiments of the SE, and perhaps one of you A Flight jockeys can give Buchanan some pointers on the Camel?"

"I'll do it," said Carstairs.

After this, the assembly broke up, and Powell approached Harry.

"You had some question about mythology," he said.

"Oh yes," said Harry. "About Rhiannon. I hardly know any-thing about her. Something to do with a white horse is about all of it really."

"Well, you've come to the right place," said Powell. "She's in the Four Branches, of course, and I also know a little about her other connections, as you might call them. Are you interested more in the stories from the Mabinogi, or the scholarly stuff like conflation with other deities?"

"Well, both, I suppose. But perhaps we can start with the stories?"

"All right," said Powell. "Come on, let's take a turn around the field, and we'll see how well I do on freehand translation from memory."

They left the mess hall and walked out across the airfield. Powell led Harry around the field to the northeast, and they stood silently for a moment on the edge of the meadow, which swept majestically eastward to the horizon from here. At ground level, the Shroud was too far away to be visible, and so the broad sweep of the flower-speckled grassland was un-interrupted as far as the eye could see.

"I love it out here," said Powell. "I have the sense I've been carrying a heavy weight around all my life, but walking on this grassy field, I feel I've been able to put it down for a while."

"It is beautiful," said Harry. "I'm sure it's worthwhile, what we're doing, defending the people who live here, but even if there was no one, I'd be willing to fly to stop the Shroud from polluting any more land."

"Just talking about the bloody thing makes me sick. Let's not speak of it for now." Powell shook his head, as if to banish the thought. "Tell me, Harry, why are you interested in Rhiannon, anyway? Do they tell stories of her in Cornwall?"

"Not so far as I know," said Harry. "But I was out on patrol today, you remember, before I asked you that question?"

Powell nodded.

"Well I saw something rather odd..." Harry explained his encounter with the herd of wild horses and the white mare. "And then that Mrs. Llewellyn had a white horse amulet. Have you met her, by the way, David?"

"Not I," said Powell, "though I've heard her name from a couple of the others. When I came over from Carnac, this Scottish girl was on hand to welcome me, and a French girl sent me through the passage. You say she gave you a blessing in Rhiannon's name?"

"Yes," said Harry, "and that's why I'm asking you about her. The connection with a white horse stuck in my mind. I might not have paid this incident today any special attention other-wise."

"All right," said Powell, "let me start by saying that until last week this was all just fairy stories to me too. I like the old tales and I've even memorized the Four Branches. But this was in service to art, nothing more than that, do you follow me?"

"Certainly," said Harry. "I should explain where I'm coming from, too. What I'm trying to do here is to get a grip on reality, I think you might call it. So magic is apparently a real thing. There's a world we're in now whose existence isn't even faintly comprehensible to science. I don't want to accept anything I

don't have to, though. I'm not going to start celebrating Lughnasadh or whatever you call it unless Lugh himself shakes my hand, and even then, well, say some magical being *does* shake my hand. Say Rhiannon is a real person. Does that make the old Celtic gods actually divine and worthy of worship? I'm not much of a churchgoer, but I'm pretty sure the answer to that has to
be a no."

Powell was silent for a moment. Then he said "You're getting in pretty deep, here, Harry. But for what it's worth, we haven't seen much evidence of religion here in this world. I think we can put the question of actual transcendent divinity aside for the moment. As you just suggested, it's possible for there to be an unusual white horse, maybe even a magical one, whatever that means, without having to buy the whole nine yards of all the ancient Celtic beliefs. But this line of talk gives me an idea, though—hang on, what's that?"

A distant hum could be heard, and turning toward the sound they saw a Sopwith Camel heading their way from the northeast.

"Ah, that's MacLeod finishing his patrol," said Powell.

As the aeroplane drew near, they waved, and MacLeod must have seen them because he executed a snap roll directly over their heads before flying over the aerodrome and pulling a wing-over to line up with the easterly breeze for a landing.

"Showoff," said Powell, and Harry laughed.

"Right, back to Rhiannon." Powell rubbed his finger over the bump in the bridge of his nose. "If I was a proper bard, I suppose I'd just sing you the whole first and third branches and let you puzzle it out for yourself—but I don't suppose you know Welsh, do you?"

Harry shook his head and Powell chuckled.

"I'll spare you, then. You'll just have to do with my lame prose synopsis. Let's see... Let me put it all in order."

They started walking around the perimeter of the aerodrome. Swinging around the field to the south, the prospect was of a moderate expanse of meadowland, and more of the low rolling hills further on.

"It seems to me," said Powell, "that there's two kinds of mention of people like Rhiannon in the Mabinogi. Often they're described as if they are just ordinary folks—nobles, maybe in the old Celtic sense—but still human. They eat and sleep, they have to walk or ride to get where they're going, they fight with ordinary weapons, and they love and marry too. They may sometimes have a magical trick or two, but nothing all that grand. But then there's another level, where they just go far and away beyond what you'd normally think of as magic tricks. Raising the dead, transforming into animals, speaking in oracles, that kind of thing. That's the god level. In the old stories, these characters slide from one of these states to another without any significant event taking place, and it's hard to tell sometimes what they can or can't do."

"How do you mean?" asked Harry.

"All right," said Powell, "when we meet Rhiannon in the first branch of the Mabinogi, she is very magical indeed. She appears to Pwyll the king of Dyfed almost like a dream vision, the most beautiful thing he's ever seen, and he pursues her for three days. But despite the fact her white horse never even breaks into a trot, he can't catch her. So you wouldn't be surprised if she turned out to be a goddess at that point.

"But then she finally appears before him after he rides up onto a portentous hill, and it seems she's just the daughter of some Welsh lord or other. She's bound to marry a man she despises, so she rode off on her own to find Pwyll to save her. It's love at first sight, naturally, though it's implied Rhiannon has already begun to love Pwyll despite the fact they've never met before.

"Now in this story Pwyll is just an ordinary king. But not all that many lines before Pwyll spends a year reigning over Annwn, the land of the dead, a kind of hell. Arawn, the lord of Annwn, chief god of the underworld, has traded places with Pwyll so that Pwyll can defeat Arawn's greatest enemy, which he does by striking him down with a single blow."

"So he doesn't just become a god, he becomes a man again afterward? Interesting."

"Yes, isn't it? Anyway, after some adventures, Pwyll and Rhiannon marry. They have a child, but she's weary from the childbirth, and while she sleeps her baby mysteriously vanishes before it can even be named. Rhiannon is falsely accused of infanticide and cannibalism by her ladies in waiting. Her dignity is too great to dispute with them, so she accepts as a penance the sentence of serving as a steed for anyone who visits the king's home in Dyfed. She has to carry visitors around on her back on all fours as a woman, mind you, not transformed or anything magical like that.

"Now at the same time another lord, a friend of Pwyll's, has a lovely white mare who foals every year, but every year the colt is stolen from the stable. So he brings the mare inside his house this year to give birth but the colt is stolen away anyhow by some kind of monster. The lord manages to cut the monster's arm off, but the colt is still lost. However, at his door the lord then finds a beautiful blond boy—Rhiannon is blond, you know—and the lord raises the child as his own. Eventually everyone is reunited properly, Rhiannon is vindicated, and the child, Pryderi, goes on to become king of Dyfed after Pwyll dies."

"Aha," said Harry. "I see why she's thought of as a mare. The story is very coy, though, isn't it? It doesn't say she transformed outright into a horse."

"I like it better that way," said Powell. "The story establishes this symbolic connection which is obvious to anyone who hears it being told, but it deliberately avoids the simplistic magic effect of a change in shape. This way, there's a lot more poetry and mystery to the story. Who knows? That might be what it actually means to be a god or a goddess in this world, to be able to assume a mythically appropriate role, not necessarily to perform miracles or do tricks."

They were walking now on the west side of the airfield. Two pairs of aeroplanes were being readied for flight, Camels and SEs, Buchanan and Moisan being escorted aloft for their maiden flights in fairyland. They watched as the two pairs of aeroplanes took to the air.

"So was that white mare I saw really Rhiannon?" asked Harry. "Assuming the role, as you say?"

"Not for me to say," said Powell. "But if this was a story from the Mabinogi there would be no doubt of it. Shall I continue with some of the scholarly lore about Rhiannon's connections with other gods and goddesses, like Epona, for instance?"

"To be honest," said Harry, "I'm feeling a little dazed right now as it is. You've been very helpful but it's a lot to digest. I still don't know what this means at all. If it means anything."

Powell shrugged. "Still to be seen, I suppose."

Overhead, the two Sopwith Camels buzzed around and around in a mock dogfight. Jernigan had led Moisan off to the north, perhaps to make sure they didn't get caught up in the game. Powell and Harry watched the flyers for a time in silence. They were locked into a circular path, each pilot cutting his turn as sharply as possible. If one of the aeroplanes managed to get behind the other the game would be over. It was a constant strain on the pilots, who had to balance the tightness of their turns against the danger of a stall which would also signal a defeat.

"I'm not sure which machine is which," said Powell, at last, "but it looks as if Buchanan is holding his own, at the very least. Bit of a prickly fellow, but he's a pilot, for sure."

"Yes. I'm not quite sure what to make of him yet."

Powell nodded. "Just as well he's not in our flight. Still, I don't think he's a bad sort. Troubled, I would say, wouldn't you?"

"Hm. Maybe so." The idea hadn't occurred to Harry, but it seemed plausible. "In any event I should thank you for today. I do appreciate all this lore you've provided."

Powell smiled. His craggy face was rather ugly and forbidding when at rest, possibly the result of taking too many punches, but when he smiled, there was a remarkable transformation.

"My pleasure," he said, "I don't get the chance to show off all that reading very often."

"I only wish there was something I could actually do with the information. I feel like one of the blind men with the elephant."

Now Powell laughed outright. "That's a good figure for our current case, I must say. But it's possible that we'll learn more as we make headway against the Shroud. Put me down as a subscriber to this chronicle of yours, by the way."

"Pardon me?"

"If it wasn't just a coincidence, and you really did encounter Rhiannon, I doubt that will be the end of it."

"What do you mean?"

"You can't just walk away from a goddess," said Powell. "That's not how the stories go. The gods do nothing casually. Now you've got at least two portents, it seems to me. That pretty much seals it. There will definitely be another chapter, and I have a professional interest in learning how it works out. Someone will have to write it all down, you see."

Harry groaned. "I don't know if I'm looking forward," he said.

The Camels had finished their mock duel and were lining up for landings. In the distance to the north Harry spotted a pair of bug-like specks that must be Jernigan and Moisan returning to the airfield. The luminous blue sky of day had by degrees darkened into a fairy twilight, the indigo and purple sky to the east shading into a liquid halo of yellows and pinks surrounding the flaming red orb of the sun just above the line of trees to the west. By silent accord Harry and Powell stood silently watching the slowly evolving colors of the sunset until the solar disk dropped fully below the horizon. By then Jernigan and Moisan had landed, the latter bouncing once before trundling to a halt but not doing a discreditable job.

"Dinner time," said Powell. "See you anon."

♍   ♍   ♍

The meal was a cheerful affair, as all the pilots were pleased with their performance that day. Quirk and Devlin were not present as they were dining with Prince Nuada.

With no resistance to their attacks seen so far, it was possible to project a successful conclusion to the squadron's mission in a few months. Of course, questions about the nature of the enemy, and prospects for some sort of counterattack were still up in the air—literally as well as figuratively—but in the absence of any serious opposition, the mood was upbeat. "Home by Christmas" was overly optimistic, considering the holiday was in two days' time, but an Easter date seemed possible, at least.

There was a sharpness audible in Buchanan's voice and choice of words over the course of the dinner, but his aerial performance that afternoon had clearly won Carstairs' respect, and indirectly, that of the other members of his flight. Moreover, as he said himself after the meal, Buchanan's first look at the Shroud from the air had blunted his skepticism. At this point, however, the mood turned darker.

"What a monstrous sight," Buchanan said, "and how terrifying a prospect it would be if the great powers in our own world adopted such methods. I suppose something along these lines may be inevitable, though, if something isn't done to stop it."

"How do you mean?" In the absence of the other senior officers, Jernigan was more of a cynosure than usual.

"The Germans started with those so-called strategic raids early in the war," said Buchanan. "First zeppelins, and now heavy bomber raids on Paris and London. Thank heaven they've not done that much damage, but whatever they may say, the Germans are deliberately directing these raids against civilians. Their intention is purely to damage national morale, and I suppose they don't have any notion at all how repugnant it is to attack noncombatants."

"Yes," said Jernigan, "I think we all agree with you there. But how does this relate to the Shroud?"

"Well, first of all I hear that we may soon be doing bombing raids on German cities ourselves, not just on military targets. And what will that accomplish except to kill civilians? It's escalation without restraint is what it is. Both sides have been using poison gas on the battlefield. Tactical, you might call that too, however ghastly the results. But what is the Shroud, really, but a strategic use of gas? Suppose the Germans—or us for that matter—suppose anyone started using wholesale gas attacks on civilian populations? That's what I mean by a horrifying prospect."

This observation put something of a damper on the tone of the evening, and the company broke up earlier than usual.

Moisan and Harry walked back to their cottage.

"I imagine you must still have plenty of questions about the situation here," said Harry, as they emerged from the mess hall. "I'll be happy to answer any I can."

"It's kind of you to offer," said Robert, then he paused, looking up. "My word, how beautiful the night sky is here!"

It was full dark now, and the stars had come out. The band of the milky way was clearly visible, and all the familiar constellations were in the sky. Yet another mystery. Was it even conceivable that the entire sidereal universe had been duplicated around this fairy world, or were their two worlds some-how superimposed in the same physical space, sharing the same sun, moon, and stars?

At last, Harry turned away from the starscape.

"I don't know that I can answer most of the big questions," he said, "but there may be a few things I've learned so far that I can help you with."

"That's very kind of you," said Moisan, "and I'm sure I can come up with something to ask you about this world and our enemy and so on, but to be honest I'm more interested in learning about the people here than anything else. Is it really possible that an entire race can be composed of homosexuals? It flies in the face of reason, I must say."

Harry explained what he'd learned about the kobolds.

"I see," said Moisan, "not homosexual so much as expressing sexuality differently towards their two genders. In one case for procreation, and in the other to cement social bonds."

"I'm not sure it's right to put it so clinically," said Harry, "but it's not a subject I've been very comfortable talking about. A few days ago, it would never have occurred to me that it was a topic that could be properly discussed at all, even privately."

"Oh yes," said Moisan, shaking his head, "I have to suppress my own ingrained reactions all the time even when thinking about topics that are not nearly so fraught with prejudice. I've almost come to despise culture now, because it—how would you say, it bakes into us as children these attitudes. Most of us don't ever realize we're going through life with blinders on, and then even if we do figure it out, they are terribly hard to remove. The really sad thing is that because they themselves are taught that homosexuals are weak, sick, or evil, people with that inclination sometimes wind up adopting the very qualities they are unfairly accused of."

"I see why the kobolds must be so interesting to you," said Harry. "They have no such inbred condemnation of their, er, proclivities."

"Exactly," said Moisan. "But that's just one reason. Of course, this bizarre gender imbalance must also have profound effects on their society, not to mention the fact of their distinct physical differences from us. But even if they were completely ordinary humans with no physical or sexual differences, they would still be fascinating subjects to study, just by virtue of living in this curious new world. Speaking of which, what about the fairy people who have brought us here? Les korrigans, we call them in Cornouaille."

The familiar-sounding place name distracted Harry from answering directly.

"Cornouaille? Where's that?" he asked.

"Oh," said Moisan, "didn't you know? There used to be a petty Breton kingdom of that name. Covering Morbihan and some adjacent départements, including my hometown of Carnac. They say settlers came from your English Cornwall to found a little country there sometime around Charlemagne's reign. We may be distant cousins, you know."

"I never knew. What an interesting coincidence."

"We do have an English branch of the family," said Moisan, "though they're in Devon now. Hence my fluency, you know. I used to spend my summers in England when I was a boy. I always wondered why my grandmother never let Marie come with me. Now I know. Training her, I suppose."

Moisan shook his head. "But about those people—what do you call them? From the Seelie Court?"

"I'd like to tell you more," said Harry, "but I haven't yet seen any of them up close except Hartshorn. Perhaps you can ask the major or Captain Devlin about Prince Nuada."

They reached the door to their shared cottage. A light showed from inside. Moisan put a hand on Harry's arm before they entered.

"Listen," he said, "I'd like to talk to our batman—Lambeth, isn't it?—I'd like to talk to him about kobold society and family life and so on. But I don't want to offend him, or you for that matter, Harry. If you think it would be, what did you say, uncomfortable, I won't."

"Not a problem," said Harry. "Last week, it might have been, for me. But I don't know if it's this world or something about the kobolds themselves—but the whole thing just seems not to bother me as much as I would have thought."

"Really? You think you've changed?"

"I don't know," said Harry. "So far I find that I quite like the kobolds. They seem, how shall I say it? Innocent is not the word. I don't believe they are a simple people, either, not in that fake condescending way you sometimes hear when people talk about primitive tribes. Perhaps what it is, they seem to be completely unmalicious. What they do in their spare time doesn't matter to me very much. If that's a negative at all, and for them I'm not sure it is, it's outweighed by their other qualities."

"Fascinating," said Moisan. "It sounds as if you're coming to admire them."

"Since you mention it, I suppose I do, at least to the extent that just a couple of days' acquaintance with them can mean anything."

"I'll be interested to see if I develop the same impression," said Moisan. "One more thing before we go inside, if you don't mind."

Harry nodded. Moisan's tone had changed, and he sounded quite serious now.

"I'm afraid there's no way to avoid an awkward note here," said Moisan, "but I am compelled to ask. That letter I gave you. Marie threatened me with the most dire consequences were I to read it. We haven't been as close as we once were, since the war started. I was away at school, and she was—well, however she managed it I have no idea, but she became a pilot somehow. She's a grown-up now, of course, but I can't help but think of her as a little girl, still. And, well..."

Moisan was having trouble completing his thought, but it was obvious to Harry where he was going.

"I understand," said Harry, "and the fact is, I do believe I'm falling for her. She flew me across France, you know, all the way from Pas-de-Calais to Carnac in a night flight. Not many pilots could do that. Then, after that..." Harry's willingness to be open about his feelings was one thing, but he couldn't quite force himself to admit their physical intimacy, not to her brother, not just then.

"Well, we only had a few hours together," he said after a pause, feeling a bit loutish for talking around the facts, "but she made an enormous impression on me. Frankly, I've been thinking about her quite a bit for the past few days. That letter was hugely gratifying. I wasn't sure how she remembered me, but it seems she did so fondly. I was thinking, before, how happy I was to have this new world to explore, and it's still a compelling prospect, but now I have a reason to return to our own world as well."

"I see." Moisan smiled warmly at Harry. "I'm pleased to hear it. I've been worried about—how shall I put it? About Marie's sentimental life for some time now."

Moisan held out his hand, and Harry took it.

"I hope the two of you are good for each other," said Moisan. "Good luck to you both."

Harry blushed and stammered out his thanks.

"I do hope, though, that she never has cause to complain to me of your behavior," said Moisan. "Because then I should be obliged to try and shoot you out of the sky at the first opportunity, and given the state of my aerial skills, well... I think it would be a shame if the Sorbonne were to be deprived of my talents, don't you think?"

Harry laughed, a little weakly. "Let's try to avoid that," he said. He thought that Moisan might really have meant what he said. Would he feel the same way about his own sister, should she ever complain to him in similar wise? A speculative thought materialized: Jennifer was 17 now, going on 18 in the spring. She had no particular attachments that he knew of, and Moisan seemed likewise unattached. Was it conceivable? Why not? There was no hurry, after all. Regardless, he would certainly mention Moisan in his next letter home...

When they entered the cottage, they found Lambeth within. He was reading a book in the dim candlelight—the cottages weren't wired for electricity—which he put down as he noticed the two pilots.

"Good evening sirs," he said. Harry tilted his head and read the book's title. *Handbook for the .303-in. Vickers Machine Gun* it was, by "a British Army Officer".

"Gun maintenance?"

The kobold nodded. "I was thinking about the problem of mounting a second Vickers gun. I think it's not impossible, after all. Tomorrow the crews will be taking apart your SE, so there will be an opportunity to install a second gun before they put it all back together. I wonder if you'd care to review the plans?"

The kobold produced a large roll of cyanotype paper. It was

a technically exact illustration of the S.E.5a dashboard layout, with views of front and back as well as the cable and wire runs for some of the instruments and controls.

Harry looked at Moisan. "Never mind," said the French pilot, "I can bother him some other time. I really should put in a little practice anyway. I wonder if passing between worlds has affected the timbre at all." He walked over to his dresser, and opened his violin case, removing the instrument, bow and a cake of rosin.

"Have no fear," he said, "I'll play it outside. Do you know I've never played by starlight before? I imagine it will be quite romantic."

"What is that, sir?" asked Lambeth. "Is it a musical instrument?"

Harry was struck by the implications of the question. From his fluency and his manner of speech, the kobold gave the impression of familiarity with every phase of modern British life, but of course his actual experience of British culture was meager at best.

"Why yes," said Moisan. "It is. I suppose you've never seen a violin before?"

"Oh! I've read about them, though. Is it like a harp? I've never seen one of those, either, but at least I know what they are. *Themselves* play them, I believe."

"Not the same thing," said Moisan. "You can pluck the strings like a harp, but usually you bow them. Do your people not have your own instruments?"

"No, sir."

"Really? No music of your own at all?" Moisan was surprised.

"Well, we do have work songs, for when a lot of crews have to coordinate their work. We sing them in the mines sometimes."

"But you've never heard instrumental music before?" Moisan was examining the violin. He plucked a soft note, and as the sound faded, he said "I will be fascinated to know what you think of my playing, in that case."

Lambeth looked uncertain. Harry realized with a small flash of insight that the kobold was torn between his interest in the instrument and his desire to work on the design changes required for the new machine-gun mount.

"Go on," he said to Moisan, "why not play something for us now? Apart from an ill-advised attempt by Jernigan on the harpsichord, I haven't heard any music at all since I was at the front, and that was just a tinny gramophone.”

“Very well. I won’t say I’m not very good, with the usual false humility, because I’ve been playing since I was six, but I’m definitely still an amateur. Are you familiar with Bach’s Chaconne? From his second partita for the violin?”

“To be honest, I didn’t even know Bach wrote violin music,” said Harry. “All I know are some of his keyboard pieces. I can’t play any instrument myself.”

“Ah. I’m sorry my playing will have to be your first hearing of the piece. In my opinion, this is the single greatest work composed for the violin, and possibly the greatest solo ever written for any instrument. It’s also very difficult, so much so that though I’ve been working on it for months I’ve never been able to play it to my satisfaction. Please bear with me if I have to play some passages more than once.”

Moisan spent a minute or so tuning the violin. After that he played a few quick runs up and down the scales—“to limber up my fingers,” he said.

“All right,” said Moisan. “Here we go.”

Harry sat down on his cot. He motioned Lambeth to a chair. The kobold had been staring at the movement of Moisan’s fingers on the strings with considerable fascination, and now he hesitated before taking a seat, as if it was an untoward assertion of privilege. And then Moisan began to play.

Harry was no connoisseur of music in any form and he knew little about the violin. Nevertheless, he was able to hear a tentative awkward quality in the opening notes, and he could see a grimace appear in the place of Moisan’s usually mild expression. Perhaps the piece really was too difficult for him. But then the pace and the rhythm of the music evened out and the rich sound swelled to fill the small room. Harry closed his eyes, the better to appreciate the music. Moisan’s playing had gotten much better in only a few bars.

After a short time listening, the power and emotion of the music was such that Harry felt himself disembodied, with no sense for anything but the music and the tremendous sadness he felt floating on the waves of sound. It seemed to Harry that the Chaconne moved from heartbreak to despair to rage and back again to the utmost depths of abject desolation. He had never heard music so expressive before, had never experienced first-hand any emotion so moving as this music conveyed.

At last the piece came to an end, its tragic conclusion resolving into a soft fading lament. The final note died away and Harry looked up. He realized he had no idea how much time had passed. His face was damp and it seemed he'd been crying. Now he could hardly recall the music itself, just the emotions it had induced. Across the room he saw tear tracks on Lambeth's face too, but the kobold was gazing up at Moisan now, his face seeming to shine with an eager passion. Harry looked to Moisan himself, and he saw to his surprise that tears were likewise running down Moisan's face. The bow dropped from his hand with a clatter and he staggered, almost dropping the violin as it slid from beneath his chin.

"My God," said Harry, his voice hoarse, "that was amazing."

"Sacré—I—I've never played that well before," said Moisan. He sat down heavily on his cot, looking at the violin as if he'd never seen one before. "Not a thousandth as well. I didn't know it was possible for anyone to play that well. I think, perhaps... I should break the instrument. What point is there in playing it more? It will never be that good again."

"Please don't!" Lambeth spoke up from his perch on the chair. He was wiping his cheek with one hand, but he looked as happy as Harry had ever seen anyone. "You mustn't, sir," he said, "you mustn't do that! It would be—I think it would be what you call a sin. Is that right?" He turned to Harry. "Is that what a sin is? Flight Lieutenant Buchanan spoke to some of us about sin earlier today. I think it would be a sin to stop playing."

"It might be at that," said Harry. "I agree with Lambeth. You must continue to play."

"Thank you," said Moisan, smiling a little. He reached down and picked up the bow, dusted it off. "I swear, though, that was nothing like I've ever played before. It felt like someone else was playing, using my body as an instrument, you know? And the feelings... Of course, it's a sad piece, everyone knows that, but I think I never understood what sadness was before tonight."

"Yes." Harry found that his nose was running. He snorted, wiped his nose, then laughed. "But I don't feel it now, do you? I feel happy, actually. Very light. As if I could fly without an aeroplane, almost."

"Oh yes," said Moisan, "that's right. I do feel it. I suppose it's like a catharsis. But I had no idea that music alone could produce such a powerful response."

It was clear to all three of them that something extraordinary had taken place. Moisan's description of his experience was particularly provocative. But none of them raised the subject. Harry thought perhaps the experience was still too raw to be easily talked about.

Harry arranged with Lambeth to look at the dashboard design the following morning, after his return from the dawn defensive patrol. He turned in early, and his dreams were of free bodiless flight—bodiless, but still somehow hand in hand with Marie—flying through luminous pink skies above a gorgeous tropical sea, with waves of a blue-green color so vivid that later, on waking, he thought no such hue could possibly exist in the real world.

CHAPTER 10
A SWARM OF WINGS

24 December 1917.

Harry was awoken the next morning by Lambeth's hand on his shoulder, the strange colors of his dream still glowing faintly behind his eyes. He dressed quietly in the near-darkness, not wanting to wake Moisan, but he needn't have bothered as it seemed his roommate was deeply asleep. *Not surprising*, Harry thought. If his own reaction to listening to that performance had been so intense, what must it have been like to play it? Moisan wasn't yet on the patrol rota, but would be accompanying B Flight on its scheduled afternoon attack run.

It looked to be another overcast morning as no stars were visible. This time Harry had the feeling that the cloud layer was more substantial than a mere morning haze, but it didn't have the feel of a low fog that would make it impossible to fly, and there was no smell of rain in the air either. He'd have to wait till later to be sure.

Harry walked through the pre-dawn darkness to the mess hall, flight suit and goggles rolled up under his arm, intending to promote a breakfast more filling than the hard-boiled egg he'd devoured on the way out of his cottage. There he found Major Quirk, up early as usual, filling in the lines in chalk on a large slate board that had been set up. It was a squadron roster.

"Morning, Tregeseal."

"Good morning, sir. I hope your dinner went well."

"Well enough," said Major Quirk. "Mixed results, not that it's the Prince's fault. But I did get one bit of good news. Our fuel convoy has come through, and *themselves* have agreed to escort it here. 200 tons, more or less. At least they know the route now, so I hope it will come timely. They've pressed more castor oil too. I was wondering at one point if we were going to get it at all."

"Really? Was the issue ever in doubt?"

Quirk shook his head. "You'd be surprised. There was some stiff resistance to the idea of bringing us over here in the first place. And no one on the pro side of the debate was told that periodic shipments of fuel would be required to support the effort. I gather that any number of lords whose lands lie along the route had to be placated."

"I thought they were all concerned about the prospect of the

Shroud's expansion?"

"They are indeed," said Quirk, "but even so it seems their internal divisions are such that hardly anything can get done without a fight of some kind. Rather like parliament, you might say, except without such clear dividing lines for the members. The notion of a temporary sacrifice for the common good is not a familiar one to most of *themselves*. They do have a more pragmatic and practical faction of which our friend Nuada is a member. It seems the High Queen is now more inclined to their point of view than before, so perhaps things will settle down on that front at least."

"Is there a party opposed to our presence here? Why would they not want our help?"

"That's where it gets complicated," said Quirk. "Nuada tried to explain it to me. They seem to be divided in many separate... axes, perhaps is the way to put it, rather than parties. There is a division between the border lords like Nuada and the more refined types in the interior. Then there's another division between those who favor our cultural trade goods—books, music, and so on—and those who prefer their own ways. Then there's the ones who see the Shroud as an immediate threat they have to deal with, and those who think it was a judgment of sorts on their enemies, and nothing to worry about, or else take the fatalistic view that there is nothing to be done about it."

"Sounds complicated."

"Yes," said Quirk, "and the really messy thing is that there are no clear lines of division, even among some of the families, except to the extent that Queen Medb herself has a loyal cadre who will do what she says no matter what."

"Just as happy not to have to worry about all that, myself."

"Yes, but it seems to have ended well for now, at any rate." Quirk smiled, "In the meantime, I understand our Aidan has come up with a new tactic, at the expense of two thousand pounds worth of aeroplane. Curious thing, isn't it? They weigh just about as much as they cost."

"I'm sorry, sir," said Harry. "I'm sure it was my fault for getting too close to the explosion."

"Not to worry," said Major Quirk. "So long as you're safe and have learned from the mistake, I really don't mind at all. Putting your machine back together will give the kobolds something to do. We have plenty of spare parts, but only eleven pilots."

Harry looked into the kitchen to see if anyone was there, and he found a kobold cook willing to fry him a couple of eggs with toasted barley-bread and goat's milk butter on the side.

Bringing it back into the mess hall, he saw Major Quirk contemplating the roster board.

"I was thinking about requesting permission to count pods as kills," said Quirk, "but on mature consideration, there seems little point. I doubt they will gazette any of our accomplishments here, and it will seem very strange to our peers if any of us come back to the front claiming more kills than Guynemer or Fonck."

"I'm sure you're right, sir," said Harry. "Frankly, just being here at all is reward enough as far as I'm concerned."

Quirk nodded. "I've been thinking much the same thing myself. But it's nice to have some acknowledgement of your work. Perhaps we can come up with some fictional justifications for medals, when all this is done."

"Since you mention it, sir," said Harry, "what do you think the government will decide to do about this whole thing once our work is over? Acknowledging the existence of this world will turn so many things upside down, I can hardly begin to imagine the uproar. I'm sure Whitehall would like to keep it a secret, but at this point there must be far too many people in the know to keep it under wraps for long. Especially when peace comes."

Quirk shook his head. "I haven't the foggiest idea what our masters will decide," he said. "I suppose we'll have to wait and see. But you know, every man in this squadron will be in demand as far as that goes. We'll be the only experts on the subject, the only ones who have actually lived in this world and know what it's like. Something to keep in mind, don't you think?"

♍   ♍   ♍

There was just enough light when he emerged from the mess hall for Harry to see that his guess about the weather was correct. There was a high overcast layer—Harry thought it might be altocumulus—somewhere around 15,000 feet which looked like it should present no obstacle at all to flying.

In the north hangar, Harry found that his damaged SE had already been stripped of its wing planes and all its fabric, leaving a skeleton of spars defining the fuselage. The machine had a rather forlorn look to it now. A kobold crew led by Bromley was working on his replacement machine, preparing it for its first patrol.

Harry went through his preflight inspection, noting somewhat to his dismay that the crew had put in the same meticulous cleaning effort on his new aeroplane.

"Good morning, Bromley," he said.

"Morning, sir. You'll be ready to go in five minutes."

"Thanks." Harry pointed to the stripped SE fuselage. "I've asked Lambeth to look into the possibility of a second Vickers coaxial gun. Would you tell whoever is in charge of working on it there's no point in putting it back together until we've made a decision about that?"

"Yes sir," said Bromley. "Your batman has already informed us. We'll wait for your... new design."

Harry noticed a certain coolness in Bromley's voice.

"Would you give me a minute, Bromley? I'd like to chat with you in private for a bit."

"Sir?" The kobold looked at him with flat red eyes. He was very hard to read at that moment. "Of course, sir."

The rest of the crew looked up as he walked away with Harry, then resumed their work on the new scout.

"Listen," Harry asked, "what do you think of him? Lambeth, I mean."

"I'm not sure what you're asking, sir," said Bromley.

"Do you have some sort of problem with him? I gather that supercharger of his caused a certain strain, is it? A strain in your community. Isn't that right?"

Bromley's impassivity broke, and he seemed astonished for a moment.

"You know about that? Sir?"

"Well, yes," said Harry. "Where I come from, turning a talented engineer into a personal servant is not considered a promotion."

"Oh." The kobold looked embarrassed now. "Well, sir, actually—"

Harry put up a hand. "You needn't explain why it's a desirable posting. I can't speak for the other pilots, but I'm afraid that in my case at least that particular outcome is not likely to happen. But I have to say that I find that I like Lambeth quite a bit, and I'd be sorry if his work on aeroplane design was somehow to set him back in your company."

"Oh, sir—" Bromley swallowed. He was obviously in the grip of some strong emotion. "I think you have the wrong idea. We have the greatest affection for Lambeth. It's true, what he was trying to do made it hard to work with him, but we know that really it was in service to the—to his people. How shall I say this? He was deliberately putting aside the feeling of working together in order to make a new way of working. We know it was… like a sacrifice for him."

"Does Lambeth know this is your opinion of him?"

"I hope so, sir," said Bromley. "But perhaps I should tell him directly. Most of us, me for one sir, most of us can't even imagine working that way. But we can see that's a limitation. It's one of the things we admire most about your people. You don't need direction. If Lambeth can show us how to be… more free, I suppose, that would be a huge benefit for us all. It would be worth some discomfort to us to learn how to do that, so long as we can keep our, our togetherness. But I hope you don't think we are making any difficulties for him in any other respect."

Bromley looked embarrassed. "The fact is, sir, we are very much enjoying what he has told us about the talks you have had with him. We like hearing about what all the batmen have to say, but him, and you, and now Lieutenant Moisan—"

The kobold shook his head.

"I'm sorry, sir," he said, "I think I'm getting lost in what I'm trying to say. Lambeth's way of working may have made us uncomfortable, to the point we did have to remove him from his work crew, but we don't hold it against him at all. And I'm sure his old crewmates treat him with the same—the same fondness as ever when he sees them at the end of the day."

"Well," said Harry, "you've completely answered my question. Lambeth told me something about your people's mutuality ideal, and I saw it for myself in the workshop the other day. I didn't want to encourage him to act in some sort of divisive or invidious way. I suppose it's time for my patrol now."

"Sir!" The kobold called out, so Harry turned back to Bromley.

"Sir, may I just say that in all the time we've spent in service to the Unseelie Court, none of our masters have ever shown us a hundredth part of the consideration we've had from you pilots in the last ten days. And you, sir, more than anyone…"

Bromley trailed off. Harry wanted to say that he wasn't one of the kobolds' masters in any event, but then he considered Bromley's stripes. What else was an officer to an enlisted man, anyway?

"Sir," said Bromley in a low voice, "I know you said you have no interest in—sir, I'm sorry, but I have to say—if you should ever, well, change your mind…"

Oh my god, Harry thought. He was about to say something, but Bromley spoke in a rush.

"Sir, I'm sorry, sir. It's just… You're so very kind, and if it's just, just—if it's just not being used to the idea, I thought it would be a pity not to—" He cut himself off. "I'm sorry, sir. I shouldn't have said anything."

Harry had imagined his capacity for really profound embarrassment had been burned out by Mrs. Llewellyn's casual exposure of him and Marie a few days before, but it seemed he'd been overly optimistic. But he supposed he'd brought it on himself.

"Thank you," he said, cheeks burning. What was he supposed to say? "I'm sorry to have to demur, but I do appreciate the thought."

He walked back to the SE with the idea his face was probably as red as a kobold's, and indeed Bromley had turned away, blushing himself.

♍   ♍   ♍

Climbing into the cockpit, Harry found it difficult to go through the takeoff sequence with anything like equanimity. Bromley had excused himself, leaving puzzled looks on his crew's faces. It wasn't until the propeller started spinning up that he managed to refocus on the task at hand. It wouldn't do to total another SE on takeoff just because of a silly thing like this.

The strange clarity of dawn showed the cloud layer as a mosaic of faintly luminescent blue-violet scallop shapes floating below a dark indigo sky. It was mildly cooler today, but still much more like late spring than the early winter he'd left behind in France.

Harry managed to get off the ground in good order, and was up to 5,000 feet on the first leg of his patrol circuit before his thoughts reverted to his exchange with Bromley. Was it possible, he wondered, that he'd been somehow asking for that offer without realizing it? Somewhat despite himself, Harry found himself wondering what it would be like to actually sleep with one of the kobolds. In the past, he realized, such a thought would never have arisen in the first place, or if it did somehow, it would have sparked revulsion. The idea of submitting to another man had always been repugnant to Harry, and neither man nor boy had ever prompted that instant arousal that a woman's presence—real or imagined—could so easily provoke in him. And now, Harry thought with a touch of relief, he felt no great interest in Bromley's offer. Perhaps the lack of a revolted response to the idea was simply a sign of maturity, a kind of mental growth even.

Still it was rather odd to receive two such curious bits of flattery on two successive days, after a lifetime without. Harry thought he was under no illusions regarding his appearance. He was sure he looked well enough, nothing grossly out of place in his physiognomy, but nothing remarkable, either. And indeed, outside of his mother, no one had ever told him he was handsome before, and certainly no one had ever told him he was sexually attractive. But to receive that letter from Marie... Harry lost a full minute to an erotic reverie: had some German somehow dived down on him out of the fairyland upper layer, he would have been easy pickings. Well, his erection, somewhat painful in his flight suit, seemed to be reinforcing his sense of his heterosexuality, anyway.

With the sunrise, the scalloped cloud layer 10,000 feet above Harry's head went through a marvelous color shift. The whole eastern half of the sky turned from purple to gold with the diffused sunlight radiating in a network of shimmering shafts piercing the gaps between the cloud plates, and elsewhere the indigo background lightened to cerulean, while the violet clouds turned pristine white. This would not be a good flying position at the front, as patrols made a practice of flying just above a layer like this one, dipping down occasionally to look for victims to ambush. But here in fairyland, the layer was merely a visual distraction.

It wasn't until the final leg of his first patrol circuit that Harry noticed anything at all of interest. At first he thought he'd found the herd of wild horses he'd seen the day before, but then he realized he was looking at a cavalry troop. Resisting the urge to buzz and scatter them he descended to take a look. At the moderate height of 500 feet, low enough to see them clearly, but high enough not to be very threatening, he saw a dozen riders standing in their saddles looking up at him. They were armed with lances and bows. He waggled his wings as he passed overhead, but flew by too quickly to be sure if the troop leader's raised-hand gesture was a salute or an insult. Oh well, at least they were up early.

Harry completed his patrol without incident and reported sighting the cavalry troop to Jernigan, mentioning it to Powell as well, who was taking over responsibility for the next patrol.

Harry found Lambeth working in the north hangar. He'd partially dismounted the stripped SE's dashboard, revealing the cabling and fuel hoses in between the panel and the engine firewall, and had set up an adjacent drafting table with a plan sketching the layout there.

"How are you making on with the guns?" asked Harry.

"Well, sir," said Lambeth, "now I understand why the SE only has one Vickers gun. If I'd been on one of the flight crews I'd have already known the answer. With this narrow nose, there's only room for one ammunition box."

Harry peered at the space, visible because the fabric had been stripped from the fuselage. The area between the engine firewall and dashboard was almost entirely taken up with a single ammunition box for the existing Vickers gun, along with the metal frame of an ammunition feed designed to get the belt up to the breech of the gun without snagging. It didn't look like there was any room at all for the ammunition box for a second gun.

"Do you want help with the design?"

"Oh yes, thank you, sir!" Lambeth was eager, smiling, but then he took himself in hand. "Or rather, I thank you very much, sir, but I wonder if you would permit me to work on it myself?"

"Ah," said Harry. "I understand. You want to do it all yourself, is that right? To prove you can."

Lambeth nodded. "Yes, sir."

"Really, Lambeth, that supercharger qualifies you in every respect as an engineer, developed from someone else's design as it may be. You must have overcome all kinds of problems to get that to work. Probably there were half a dozen innovations along the way."

Lambeth looked embarrassed. "You're right, there were some... issues. I didn't mention them the other day, because I was too ashamed at the time to admit it. I had to come up with a connection between the Wolseley Viper direct drive shaft and Mr. Ellor's supercharger, which was originally designed for a geared engine system. Looking at it the first time I had no idea what to do. I almost gave up the first day in despair."

"So how did you solve the problem?"

"Well, sir... there's a thing we do sometimes. I'm not sure you'd approve..."

"You may as well tell me," said Harry. He was prepared at this point to hear some account of the use of sodomy to solve engineering problems.

"It's just that I think you must be a Christian. I don't want to offend."

Harry laughed. That was a relief, he realized. So much for maturity and growth and all that. "I'm not devout. Perhaps you shouldn't tell Mr. Buchanan, but your beliefs are not going to offend me. And Robert would probably be fascinated to hear them, for that matter."

"It's not something we ourselves really believe in," said Lambeth. "It's just a story we tell. To be honest, I'd be embarrassed admitting what I did, even to my workmates."

"You needn't go into it if it makes you uncomfortable."

"No, sir, you've been so open with me, and it's really not a problem. I think it would be wrong if you said the name to one of *themselves*, you know, the fairy lords, but for you, sir... The story goes that our people were created by a lady named—in English it would be 'she who makes the red earth'. In our language, it's Sandraudiga."

Lambeth pronounced the name with a tone and inflection quite different from his usual English. It sounded distinctly German to Harry's ears.

"The red earth," said Harry, "would that be hematite or some other kind of iron ore? Or does it refer to the bloody earth after a battle?"

"We like to think the former," said Lambeth. "But she is said to be pleased by blood as well as iron. Though there is iron in blood, isn't there?"

"Yes," said Harry, wondering how Lambeth knew that. It wasn't the sort of thing you were likely to read in Dickens, or even in a RAF engineering manual.

"Well sir, it's something I would have said was childish if someone else had told me they'd done it."

Lambeth paused here, looking uncomfortable. Then he said in a rush, "So I took the main rotor out and cut myself with the turbine blade."

"You did *what*?"

"I let the blood flow out of my forearm onto the blade and down to the earth and said a few words, asking Sandraudiga for help. I... well... I begged her for help with the supercharger. Then I bandaged up my arm, feeling like a complete fool, and went to bed. When I got up the next morning, the design for the power coupling was in my head, and all I had to do was build it out. Of course, the rotor blade got all rusty."

"Are you sure it was Sandraudiga who aided you? Do you think it's possible that given the chance to sleep on the problem, you were able to come up with something on your own overnight?"

"I'd like to believe it was all my own work," said Lambeth, "but I can't. I don't think I'd ever seen the kind of mechanism that came into my head before. That's why I wasn't thinking of myself as a designer when you told me that's what I was. Remember, the first time we talked."

"Huh," said Harry. "Well, one way or another, with or without divine assistance, you're a designer now."

"Thank you, sir."

Harry left his batman to the work and went back to his quarters. He was feeling like he couldn't escape a sort of constant encroachment of mythological divinity into the situation here. Good luck charms, white horses, conceivably some kind of afflatus coming over Moisan the day before, and now even the kobolds with their own set of superstitions. But they weren't superstitions if they worked, were they? Was it even possible for there to be some sort of consistent explanation for all this?

Harry put these thoughts aside for the moment to write a letter back to Marie. He considered writing something similarly explicit to match the tone she had set in her note, but then thrust the notion aside. It just wasn't in him to write that way. Perhaps in private, he'd be able to be more forthright. Anyway, there was no way for Harry to guarantee that Marie would be the first or only reader of any letter he sent, so he would have to be somewhat circumspect in any event.

> 24 December 1917
>
> Ma chérie Marie,
>
> Please forgive me for not writing this reply properly in French. I have no Mrs. Llewellyn to assist my translation and I am too shy to ask your brother for help. I'm afraid my fluency is too poor to communicate my thoughts properly to you except in my native tongue, and even then this will probably sound rather clumsy. Perhaps Robert will be able to help me a little with your language over the time that we remain at this posting—he is my room-mate now, by the way.
>
> I was deeply moved by your note. I don't believe I have ever felt quite so happy as I did after reading it when I put your letter back into my jacket and flew off through these astonishingly beautiful skies on my first solo patrol here.
>
> Marie, you should know that you have occupied my thoughts and dreams ever since our last meeting, and the prospect of seeing you again has given me more motivation to succeed with my mission than any other

possible spur I can imagine. I wish I could write my feelings here with the same inspiring directness and warmth as in your own letter, but I cannot be sure what officious censors may read this along the way, and I would not wish to embarrass you (again!) for all the world. But I do know the difference between ma chère and ma chérie, and I hope the latter is right and proper between us. You mentioned a certain sweetness fondly in your letter. I too have a sweet tooth, and one might even say a craving.

(By the way, Mrs. Llewellyn, if you should happen to read this please be sure I would never think of *you* as officious, and indeed I promise to do my best to obey your instructions.)

If you will permit me, Marie, I will say a few elliptical words about the situation here. I hope that someday soon you will be able to come and explore it with me. It seems most unfair that you should have to remain in France, hearing so much about this land without ever being able to visit. I should have said confidently a week ago that the war in the air was no place for a woman; but that was before I found out how good a pilot you are. I still feel that war is no place for a woman, but only because it is also no place for a man.

The country is remarkable and unexpected in many ways, but most of all it is beautiful. Every time I look at the sky I see a new vista of surpassing loveliness. And the beauty is doubled and redoubled from the air. I wish you could be here with me now to fly in formation and see these sights, just as you wrote in your letter. The land is pristine and unspoiled—flowers everywhere in the meadow in which our aerodrome is set, lushly verdant growth in the forested area nearby—and as one of our English hymns goes "every prospect pleases". That hymn continues "and only man is vile", but I've never much liked that notion myself. On the other hand, the people acting as our mechanics and servants here—I believe you know who I mean?—despite certain very curious ways really seem to be a superior type. At times I find it almost embarrassing that we are set above them as officers in this situation.

As regards our actual work here, again I must be careful what I write to avoid the censor's wrath, but while there are still many profound mysteries to unravel, so far at least we seem to be having some success, with less danger so far than at the front.

If only I knew for sure when this assignment was to come to an end, I would be counting the hours until we might meet again. As of now, though, I remain,

Your impatient aviator,

Harry Tregeseal

A Flight returned from their morning attack job shortly before noon. Harry and all of B Flight (except for Murphy who was on patrol) gathered with them in the mess hall for lunch. They had accounted for another eight downed pods. Captain Devlin had required Buchanan to hang back to observe their first attack run, and had allowed him to participate on the second.

"Quite the bonny show it was," said MacLeod, smiling widely. "Barbaric in their beauty, those fireballs, you might say. Ran oot of ammo or else we'd hae shot down the entire front."

"Caw canny now, my friend," said Jernigan, slapping him on the shoulder. "You'll want to leave a few for us if you please."

"Och aye," said MacLeod absently, lifting a tankard of the brown fairy ale and starting to drink before whipping his head back around to look suspiciously at Jernigan. "Caw canny, is it noo? Leave the Scots to the Scotsman, why don't you, and I'll leave a few pods to you southrons."

"Och aye," said Jernigan.

"We did see something unusual, though," said Devlin, "or at least Buchanan did. Off to the east, he said one of the pods looked to be out of place."

"Out of place?" Jernigan asked, "What do you mean by that?"

"It was up at 15,000 feet, a mile above all the others, just below the cloud layer, and it wasn't belching smoke at all. Ten miles or more to the east of the line, though. Buchanan, is that right? Did you notice anything else?"

Buchanan nodded. "Yes. It was just at the limit of visibility due to the clouds and haze. I wasn't sure if it was something unusual or not, since this was my first time out there. I could be wrong because there was nothing else nearby to compare it with, but I think it may have been larger than the pods down at 10,000 feet."

"I wish I'd seen it myself," said Devlin. "I'd have led us over there to take a look. Next time shoot off a flare or something and lead the way yourself."

"Yes, sir. Sorry I didn't do it back there."

"No harm done," said Devlin. "As you said, you couldn't have known it was something special. Still, you boys in B Flight might look out for it on your own job later on."

♍   ♍   ♍

The five pilots of B Flight gathered in front of the north hangar, their biplanes pegged outside, ready to fly.

"All right, Mr. Moisan," said Jernigan, "for your first job, I want you to stay up above us and watch what we do. You'll be able to see the size of the pod explosions for yourself so you'll know what to expect next time. Don't want you ending up like Harry, after all."

"Yes, sir."

"As for the rest of you, just two pods apiece this time. I want to save some ammo in case Mr. Buchanan's rogue pod shows up. As before, red flare to attack, green flare to go home. Now if that strange pod is right there on the line when we arrive, we'll go after it first. Otherwise, if it's still back in the interior of the Shroud someplace, after we shoot down 4 pods, another red flare will mean to fly over and take a recce, and when we get there a red flare will mean to shoot it down. Harry, you're with David this time. Aidan, with me. Is that clear?"

"As glass," said Powell, and the pilots dispersed to their aeroplanes.

The flight took off one at a time, flying in echelon with Moisan on the end of the diagonal line. Moisan had a little difficulty slotting himself into the formation at first, and Harry couldn't help feeling a little superior until he recalled how recently he'd had similar problems. He realized that his own flying skills had improved markedly over the last few days. The hesitancy and confusion he'd sometimes felt trying to keep up with his flight over Ypres was gone now, replaced by an easy confidence in his own ability as well as in the capabilities of the machine he was piloting.

The scalloped clouds of the morning had merged now to form a uniform overcast layer that looked to be a little below 15,000 feet. The sky had none of the darkness that portended bad weather, however, and the sun's location was obvious due to a bright glow around thirty degrees southwest of the zenith. As they closed on the Shroud, it seemed like they were approaching some kind of celestial architecture, the dark smoke below forming a floor, and the white clouds overhead a ceiling. Though there was a mile between the two layers it still looked to Harry like a narrow space to have to fly through.

There was no sign of Buchanan's rogue pod as they circled at 12,000 feet, a mile away from the edge of the Shroud. Either the pod had descended to join the others at 10,000 feet, or else perhaps it was somewhere above the cloud layer. The thought made Harry uneasy. But even if was just above them, what could the pod do, after all, but launch some of those slow and ineffective thread tugs. Despite this consideration, Harry wasn't entirely sure what Jernigan would decide to do until he saw the red flare. He peeled off to join Powell for the first attack run.

The destruction of the first pair of pods came off as usual. B Flight formed up and separated once more to target the next two. Harry was concentrating on aligning his scout with Powell's just before opening fire on their second pod when he was distracted by a flash off to his left. What was that? For a moment he was confused, and then he realized it was a white flare drifting down from above. A white flare? What was that supposed to mean? Powell hadn't noticed the flare—he was firing now—but Harry thought he should break off to see what was going on. He turned hard right, and at that moment something big rocketed right in front of him from above, missing a collision by just a few yards, diving by too fast for Harry to see what it was before it was out of sight.

Harry continued his turn, Powell now out of sight behind him. Looking up he saw half a dozen small aeroplanes diving down towards either him or Powell. From the angle and distance, he wasn't sure who was the target, though clearly at least one had just tried to ram him.

Harry's first thought was to go after Powell, who might still not be aware of the situation if he was shooting at a pod. He continued his hard turn through 270 degrees, and just as he was about to level out another attacker roared by him. This time he had a good view of it and—that wasn't an aeroplane at all! It was a giant insect, at least twelve feet long, somewhat resembling an elongated hornet with enormous dragonfly wings. One of the wing pairs was greatly enlarged and held stiffly out like the lower wing plane of a biplane, while the other wings flapped rapidly, though not with the blurring speed of an ordinary insect.

And there was Powell, five hundred yards away. He'd failed to shoot down the pod on his own and had broken left to avoid ramming into it. Fortunately, none of the diving insects had smashed into him either, but now Powell was caught between a pair of hornets that had moderated their dives rather than shooting past him. Harry saw that the insects that had missed him in their dives were hundreds of yards below. They were performing zoom climbs to recover from their dives as if they were biplanes, but their performance on the climb was poor, and it looked to be a while before they rejoined the fray. So Harry felt free to target the insects swarming around Powell, who was now cutting sharply left, evidently meaning to fight them.

As he roared towards Powell, Harry saw that the insects were highly maneuverable in level flight, able to cut corners and turn more sharply than Powell; the hornets he had been trying to get on the tail of had almost caught up with the Welsh pilot around the curve of the turn he was performing. But now Harry was able to shoot without fear of hitting Powell, and he pressed the trigger button on the control stick. The stream of tracers reached out, cut through one of the giant insect's lower wings, and it fell off to the left, tumbling into a spin. The rest of the little dogfight was in front of him, and so without stopping firing he was able to direct the stream of tracers into the tail of a second hornet. The results this time weren't as immediate. At first the insect ignored the bullets, and even though Harry could see bits of its tail and abdomen shattering and falling away, the insect didn't veer off or change its course. Then his shots by chance punched through the base of the upper wing pair, and the hornet lost most of its mobility, now able only to curve gently around like a glider.

Powell continued his hard left for a moment, but then he realized he was no longer engaged and banked back to the right to hunt down the injured hornet, soaring past him in a gentle arc which it was unable to break from with only its lower wings working. Harry bore slightly to the right, intended to make up the two hundred yards gap to Powell for a brief thumbs-up gesture before turning to hunt down the remaining hornets.

Just as he nudged the stick to begin the maneuver, he felt a massive shock communicated through the body of the fuselage, and the nose of his aeroplane rocked violently towards the vertical. Looking back over his shoulder Harry was horrified to see one of the hornets had latched onto his machine's fuselage. It must be a new one he hadn't seen, diving down from above. The shock of the impact combined with the hornet's weight on the tail knocked the SE into what was almost a vertical stall. He had some airspeed still, but the aeroplane's nose-up attitude would lose it in just a few seconds, and then he would be completely out of control, assuming the hornet didn't finish him off first. Harry pushed his control stick hard over, but there was no effect. The insect's unbalancing weight and enormous wings were having much more effect on their combined aerodynamics than the little control surfaces of rudder and ailerons.

For an instant Harry was simply frozen, unable to act. What was he supposed to do now? They hadn't covered this sort of situation in flight school. He looked over his shoulder at the giant reddish hornet, seeing its bulbous black eyes just five feet away, antennae waving slowly above its head. It didn't look monstrous at all, oddly enough. Harry had the absurd notion that if he'd seen the creature flying by at the usual size, he might have put his hand out for it to land on.

Very deliberately the hornet raised its head slightly and then smashed its mandibles into the top of the fuselage, breaking a spar and tearing at the fabric. Another few seconds and the SE would fall out of the sky, regardless of what the hornet did to the spars. And then a row of holes appeared in the fuselage cutting across the body of the SE, and at the same time small explosions erupted from the thorax of the hornet. Harry was dumbfounded for a moment, completely uncomprehending, but then he realized someone was shooting at him, or rather at the insect. But the bullets had no immediate effect, and now Harry felt that hesitating shudder that would normally precede a stall. If he'd stalled out in the usual way the weight of the engine would force the nose down and he'd be able to fly out of it eventually, but with this huge insect on the tail Harry thought he might be pulled down backwards.

It was then that another diving aeroplane roared by in a near-collision. Its undercarriage smashed into the hornet, tearing its body in half and carrying most of it away. The shock was tremendous, as was the sheer unexpected impact of the other machine flying by so close to his head. When Harry recovered his senses a couple of seconds later, he found that the SE had at last fallen into its inevitable stall and tailspin. It took all of his remaining self-possession to keep from sawing at the stick until he'd gathered enough speed to fly again, and then he was able to hammer the rudder bar with his heel to end the spin. Agonizing seconds later, he managed to pull back up into level flight and at last he was able to take a moment to see what was going on. The hornet's head was the only part of it still attached to Harry's SE, its mandibles buried a foot deep in the body of the aeroplane. Deep gouges had been cut in the fabric along the length of the fuselage by the thing's claws, but apart from that his machine seemed to be intact. Harry had no idea where Powell was now or any of the remaining hornets, but below him, almost lost in the murk of the Shroud, he saw his rescuer still spiralling downwards in his own spin.

Oh my God, Harry thought, *that must be Robert*. Was his SE damaged? Did he even know how to recover from a spin? Harry watched in horror as Moisan's aeroplane disappeared completely into the dirty black smoke. There was nothing he could do but watch and hope—but he should really be looking out for Powell. What was going on with the hornets? Harry pointed his nose back up, and he saw three aeroplanes flying together now, all of them pursuing one remaining hornet. Jernigan and Murphy had either not been attacked or had dealt with their attackers and rejoined Powell. Then Harry turned back, meaning to circle over the point in the Shroud that Moisan had disappeared but he saw that the Frenchman's machine was emerging from the smoky depths, wings and fuselage now covered with a layer of charcoal-black sooty stuff. On breaching the surface, Moisan's machine left behind it a trail of the Shroud's material like a rocket and for a moment Harry thought his engine might be on fire, but after a few seconds the stream of smoke faded away. Two minutes later they were all back in formation with no hornets left to be seen in the sky.

They were close enough together now that Harry could see Jernigan's gesture upwards before he fired his flare gun. A red flare. They flew upwards to the white overcast layer, which proved to be fairly thin, only a couple of hundred feet. They were through it in a few seconds. Now a fluffy white floor just beneath them was stretching out to infinity, and the brilliance of the afternoon sun blazing down was almost blindingly bright at first, a dramatic change from the dreary gray skies below the clouds.

And there it was, Buchanan's rogue pod, a vast grayish blot just above the cloud layer. The thing was gigantic even compared to the other pods, easily a thousand yards in diameter, and instead of belching black smoke from below it had a dome-like structure emerging from its underside, probably a hundred yards across. The dome looked to be faceted, and its appearance seemed familiar to Harry, though for a moment he couldn't say what it reminded him of. Then he saw a black speck emerge from one of the facets, followed by half a dozen more and then another dozen of the things. It was obvious now. The pod was a flying hive.

For a moment Harry had the urge to fly straight toward the pod, to engage the hornets and shoot the whole thing down himself, but he realized how crazy that was. Then he saw Jernigan shooting a green flare, and so the flight turned back to the west. The hornets did not pursue.

♍   ♍   ♍

Back at the aerodrome, Jernigan shot off his last red flare before landing to warn the squadron of an emergency, but they all landed safely, even Moisan in his Shroud-blackened scout. Major Quirk and the pilots of A Flight met them outside the north hangar, except for Carstairs who was on patrol.

"Well, we've been waiting for the other shoe to drop," said Jernigan. "And here it is. Mr. Buchanan was right on the money."

He delivered a quick report about the attack of the giant hornets and the subsequent reconnaissance of the aerial hive.

"Harry saved me," said Powell. "Shot the ones on my tail out of the sky, he did. I didn't see them coming till it was too late. They're more maneuverable even than the Camels, I think."

"And Robert saved me," said Harry, nodding to Moisan. "That was incredible, what you did up there. I thought you were done for, too, when you spun down into the Shroud. What happened? I was having to pull out of my own spin, so I didn't see it."

"Ah, I'm not quite sure," said Moisan. "I was trying to shoot the one on your machine. I used my Lewis gun because I was afraid of setting you on fire with my incendiaries. I'm afraid I must have holed you pretty badly, too. I was just trying to stay on target because the bullets didn't seem to be doing all that much. Then I flew by, just missing you, too, and my whole aeroplane just flipped over. I suppose I must have clipped you?"

"Your landing gear cut the thing in half," said Harry.

"Oh. That explains it. I blacked out, I think, and when I woke up I was whirling around in that black stuff. I was lucky to pull out of it. I tried all kinds of things until I finally stepped on the rudder in desperation."

"What?" Jernigan was outraged. "No one ever taught you how to pull out of a spin?"

"Ah, no," said Moisan. "My training, was, how should I say? Abbreviated."

"Ha," said Jernigan. "You're not supposed to have to figure it out for yourself. What you do is, you put the stick back to neutral and stamp on the rudder, the way it's resisting the most. While you're spinning, the rudder is the only thing that will have any consistent effect to stop the spin. Then if that doesn't work, you panic."

"I see. I'm afraid I did it the other way around. I panicked first."

After the laughter died down, Murphy said, "Well, anyway, the good news is the bugs are slow as hell when they're not diving. And the wings are a weak spot. Their bodies are tough, but a few shots through the wings will knock them right out of the sky. I think we should have no problems with them next time. Just don't try to dogfight them. They don't have guns, after all, so you don't want to give up speed and let them get close. Fly past them, and you'll have plenty of speed to get away and come back. The captain and I had no trouble with the hornets ourselves, since they ambushed only Tregeseal and Powell."

"All right," said Major Quirk, "but be that as it may, we can't have the damn things diving at us in future. We can't let this go till tomorrow. No telling where the hive will be by then. Robert, Harry, are you both all right? Good for a third flight?"

Harry considered the question. It had been a very close call, and being ambushed by these monstrous insects should have been a horrifying experience. But he felt fine. Eager to return to the air, even.

"No problem at all, sir," said Harry, and Moisan echoed the reply. "My machine needs maintenance, though, and I think so does Robert's. Oh, you'll want to see the creature up close. Part of it, anyway. Come on into the hangar."

"Jesus Christ," said Devlin. Bromley had just given him the detached hornet head to hold. He could barely work his arms around it. "This must weigh a hundred pounds by itself." He set it down on a bench, tried to brush away the ichor that had leaked out of the severed neck onto his flight suit.

"It's 3:30," said Major Quirk. "Carstairs should be back in 20 minutes or so. Bromley, can your people prepare all our machines for takeoff by 4:00? Replacements for Harry and Robert, if these two aeroplanes won't be ready by then."

"Yes sir," said Bromley. "I'll just send a runner to the sergeant-major, and get everyone out to the hangar to work on your aeroplanes. I believe Mr. Moisan's machine is all right to fly again, but Mr. Tregeseal will require another replacement."

"Good. Sunset is at 4:30," said the major. "We should have the best part of an hour of twilight after that, enough time for a run at that hive pod and a safe return. Just in case, Bromley, dig a trench by the aerodrome, and get ready to pump some petrol down it to provide a landing guide if it gets dark by the time we come back. We'll have A Flight engage any hornets that come out, and B Flight will shoot down the pod."

♍   ♍   ♍

The sun was on the western horizon as Elfshot Squadron closed on the hive pod. They were coming in at 16,000 feet, the highest Harry had ever flown before. The extended flight at this altitude had not quite made Harry light-headed, but he was conscious of a certain sharp-edged quality to his perceptions, his heart was beating faster than usual, and the cold thin air filtering through his scarf seemed exceptionally pure and heady, the atmospheric equivalent of champagne, perhaps. It had taken them half an hour to make the flight, as the Sopwith Camels of A Flight didn't have the power needed to achieve this height all that quickly, and their speed was reduced without superchargers to compress the thin air for the engine intakes. To the east the sky was darkening, not yet the midnight blue of night-time but a rich ultramarine on the eastern horizon shading towards a royal blue closer to the zenith. Behind them the sun was just kissing the cloud layer to the west, the yellow disk surrounded by an orange-red halo.

Against the soft white background of the cloud layer, the hive pod was clearly visible a very long way off. The initial approach was uneventful, and as they circled in their twin formations at a two mile range no hornets were visible. Either the insects were soaring in or below the clouds somewhere, or else they had returned to the hive. Major Quirk was flying with the squadron for this raid. He fired off his red flare, and the Camels of A Flight formed an extended echelon and peeled off towards the hive protruding from the underside of the pod, just a few hundred feet above the cloud layer. After waiting thirty seconds or so, B Flight split into two pairs separated laterally by a hundred yards, Harry leading Moisan this time, and Powell and Murphy off to the left. All four pilots were intending to target more or less the same section of the pod. Jernigan was following above and somewhat behind in case of trouble, and Major Quirk was circling even further back to observe the whole situation from a high vantage.

The idea was for A Flight to draw off any hornets that might emerge to defend the pod, to distance them, and to turn and shoot them down at leisure while B Flight was thus freed to destroy the pod. No one was sure just how the hornets would react and so the flight leaders had been given considerable flexibility in interpreting their orders.

The delay between the motions of the two flights allowed the Camels of A Flight a good mile of distance to the fore. Harry was able to watch their approach while the pod steadily swelled in front of him. The first hornets emerged when Devlin, at the head of the echelon, was still half a mile away from the hive. The half-dozen hornets that had emerged by the time A Flight engaged them were moving less than half as fast as the Camels, no more than 50 miles an hour.

The first engagement came off just as expected. Opening fire at long range, A Flight quickly sent four of the first six hornets spiraling or tumbling down into the clouds. As A Flight passed on, the remaining two hornets turned to pursue. Meanwhile another dozen hornets were emerging from the hive, and the Camels raced on past them as well, following the plan.

At this point even though B Flight was still over a thousand yards away the pod's bulk interposed and Harry lost track of the action. It was time to concentrate on his own job anyway. They opened fire at around 750 yards, the long range due to their concern over the size of the explosion such a gargantuan pod might release.

Harry held his thumb steadily down on the trigger button for a good ten seconds, hearing the rattle of the gun over the roar of the engine. Four lines of tracers reached out from the two pairs of SEs, and the focal point of their fire erupted in a burst of small gas explosions. Harry and his wingman Moisan broke right at 350 yards, and the other two pilots broke left. As they bore steadily around to reverse directions back to the west, Jernigan roared in down the middle, pouring his own fire into the pod and pulling up into an Immelman at the end of his attack run. It took several minutes for them to form up once more at about the point they had started, two miles west of the pod.

At this point, A Flight was no longer in sight, having long since flown past the pod to the far side, but the fact that Major Quirk was still circling patiently in the same position as before suggested that nothing too disastrous had taken place. Meanwhile, the fires they had started on the surface of the pod had burned themselves out, and a gaping black hole could be seen where the surface skin had been blasted or burned away. Wisps of smoke were leaking out, but evidently no mortal damage had yet been done.

Another attack run. This pod obviously had a much thicker skin structure than the others forming the Shroud. They started a few more fires, but again failed to cause any serious internal damage. On forming up again, Harry was able to spot a group of six dark flecks several miles to the southeast, A Flight flying in formation towards a larger cloud of dots that must be the hornets they had drawn off.

But then it was time for a third pass, and once again they split into pairs. Harry was growing concerned about ammunition. They'd burned through well over half their incendiary ammo, and they might not have enough for a fourth pass—there was no way to be sure how many rounds were remaining in the box behind the dashboard.

1,000 yards... 750 and opening fire... 600, still nothing—and there, six giant hornets coming over the top of the pod! They must have crawled up somehow from below, and now they were launching themselves down directly at him and Moisan of to his side and a little behind. He'd have to turn away from his attack run in a moment to avoid running into the pod. Breaking hard right as he'd done on the previous two attack runs would give up his precious airspeed, and surely the hornets would be able to take the opportunity to strike. Harry pushed the control stick sharply down, wondering if he had time and space to get below the huge bulk of the pod before ramming into it. His last sight of the ruptured front of the pod, a mere two hundred yards away before it slipped out of sight overhead, showed an ominous red glow radiating from somewhere deep in the interior.

The sensation diving straight down from level flight without first inverting was sickening. Harry felt he'd left his stomach somewhere far above, and the rush of the translucent gray fabric of the pod seemingly close enough to touch made things worse. Blood rushed to his head and his vision turned red, but still he held the stick down until he felt he was about to pass out. And then the wall of the pod he was racing past abruptly vanished. He was diving beneath it now, and as he pulled up just a bit on the stick to relieve the horrible sensation, he risked a look at the airspeed gauge. It was pegged, hard up against the end of the dial; he was doing over 250 miles an hour. He hadn't had time to ease back on the throttle. Harry looked up. A flash of the hive on the underside of the pod, a dome composed of hexagonal units, some showing dark passages to the interior of the structure. Here and there on the surface he saw hornets crawling about on it, but Harry had no time to study the view, as he was rocketing past faster than he'd ever travelled before and he needed to focus on flying. The fabric on the wing planes was rippling with an almost sickening effect considering how tightly it was supposed to be attached to the spars. And where was Moisan? He risked a glance over his shoulder. There, behind him, Moisan had made it too. But Harry had had to keep going, had to keep diving down, the white clouds rushing by now, because the pod was about to—

The world turned red. The clouds were shining with the light of the erupting pod above. For a frozen moment Harry regretted being so far down in the clouds. If he was going to be blown to hell, he at least wanted to see the explosion as it came for him. And then the clouds broke apart around him as the SE breached the bottom surface of the overcast layer. A moment after, still diving, Harry looked up to see the red clouds blown apart by the force of the explosion hundreds of yards above, his wish granted. The fireball up above was gigantic, covering the entire breadth of the sky. For a frozen moment, nothing more than that, and then he heard the shattering thunder of the explosion and he felt the hot blast of the wind from behind, chasing him down despite the speed of his dive. His machine felt oddly unstable, the control stick suddenly loose in his hands, and he saw the airspeed needle bouncing back towards zero. He'd been caught in a blast of wind moving even faster than his machine, and for a moment he lost all lift and all control. But then the turbulence hit, and the SE spun crazily around, tossed about by some vortex of hot air calved off from the explosion high above.

Harry was in another spin, spiralling violently towards the charcoal surface of the Shroud below him, down at 10,000 feet. For a short while he lost all orientation, couldn't even say which way he was spinning, but then he remembered the rule Jernigan had repeated for Moisan's benefit, and he pushed his foot hard against the rudder bar on the side that gave the most resistance. For a nauseous few seconds nothing happened at all, and then at last the spin slowed, stopped, and the only question was whether he was inverted or not; for another sickening moment he couldn't be sure. At last he was able to ease back on the stick, pulling out level just before entering the Shroud itself. Amazingly, everything about his machine seemed intact. And there was Moisan just a few hundred feet away. He'd either pulled out of his spin even more adeptly than before or he'd been more fortunate in evading the force of the blast, but either way they were able to climb together back to the scene of the action.

Harry was relieved to discover the rest of A and B Flights

waiting for them a mile up. They returned to the aerodrome in company, the fading after-sunset glow on the western horizon turning a flat cobalt blue and then darkening towards indigo as they flew home. There was just enough light left that petrol fires were unnecessary, but when he finally bounced to his third landing of the day Harry found that it was almost completely dark, the remaining skyglow having been cut off at ground level by the forested hills to the west.

♍   ♍   ♍

"I hope they don't have too many more of those damn things," said O'Meara.

Dinner had come and gone, and the loyal toast, and the pilots of Elfshot Squadron were sitting in the mess hall with tankards of ale, discussing the day's events.

"My guess is they don't," said Murphy. "For what my guess is worth anyway. If they had more, why hold them back? I'd say that hive pod must have been working its way slowly up to the western edge of the Shroud for days now, probably ever since we first started shooting the regular pods down."

"Makes sense," said Carstairs.

"But on the other hand, they may be building more, or growing them, or whatever," said Devlin. "We'll have to watch out from now on whenever there's a cloud one of these things might be hiding behind. And it's not impossible some bugs might be accompanying even the regular pods."

"Good on you to remind us," said Jernigan, "but I'll tell you one thing. Close as those calls were today, I'd rather fight those poor slow bugs than German Dreideckers. Now we know what they're like, honestly I don't think all that much of them."

"All right, gentlemen," said Major Quirk. "I'm going to leave you now and try to figure out how to write all this up in my report. I can only imagine the reaction today's work will provoke when the brass get around to reading it."

MacLeod laughed, as did several other officers.

"The high heids'll say you're havering for sure," he said. "But there's an idea! Why do you nae send along that bluidy great hornet head of Harry's, then? Physical evidence, isn't it noo?"

"You don't mind, Tregeseal?"

"Oh, no," said Harry. "As trophies go, it's something else, all right, but I don't think I'd like to have to cart it around for the whole war. Probably it will start to smell soon, anyway."

"Well, that solves one problem," said Major Quirk. "Before I go, though, I'd like to congratulate all you gentlemen on several jobs well done today, from Mr. Buchanan's spotting of that pod to begin with down to all of your performances in shooting it down this afternoon. I'm particularly pleased you remembered my instructions not to die, too."

♍   ♍   ♍

Harry and Moisan walked back to their cottage from the mess hall.

"Listen, Robert," said Harry, as they paused outside the door, "I still don't think I'm really feeling it, but I was a dead man flying up there. If you hadn't smashed that bug off my SE, I'd never have been able to recover."

Moisan smiled. "Happy to be of service," he said, "but isn't that what's supposed to happen? I mean, in combat at the front? You saved Powell and I was able to save you, though I have to tell you it really was just luck. Tomorrow maybe you'll save me, right?"

"I suppose so," said Harry, "I won't forget it." He held out his hand, and Moisan took it.

♍   ♍   ♍

When they entered their cottage, Harry and Moisan found Lambeth waiting for them. He had a rolled up cyanotype scroll under his arm.

"I take it you've had some success?", Harry asked. "Did you come up with space for a second ammo box somehow?"

"Well, sir, not yet," said Lambeth. "Though I do have an idea I'm working on. I wanted to show you the cable runs I installed for the sync gear for the second gun, and the revised dashboard layout, first. Will you accompany me?"

"Certainly," said Harry, "let's take a look."

They walked over to the north hangar. Harry's stripped-down SE showed its internals very clearly from the outside, with the fabric taken off the spars and the dashboard removed. There was a sort of pathetic nakedness about the fuselage now. Harry imagined a cadaver opened for dissection by a medical student might have a similarly sad appearance. He still could see no room whatsoever for a second ammunition box, but on reflection he decided not to say anything about it to Lambeth.

"The changes look good," said Harry. "Very speedy work on the dashboard and gunmount, for sure."

185

"Thank you, sir." Lambeth was clearly pleased, but then he said after a pause, "I'm sorry to trouble you, sir, but do you have a moment to talk?"

"Yes, Lambeth," said Harry, "what is it?"

"It's about Bromley, sir. We all regret extremely what he said to you this morning. I have been directed to ask you what punishment you think is appropriate for his offense, and to ask you if you think the matter should be referred to the major instead."

"Oh." Harry was taken aback. He recalled Graham's remarks from two days before. No doubt a homosexual advance was some kind of court-martial offense. "But, um, surely what he did is not, ah, unique? I have the impression that others have made similar offers?"

"Yes, sir," said Lambeth, "but I had made it clear that you were not to be disturbed by such offers. Your discomfort with, ah, relations of our sort was obvious to me as soon as our first conversation. We have at last come to understand that some of your people regard our behavior as outrageous and indeed as sinful. Mr. Carstairs, for example, was very clear on the subject, as was Mr. Buchanan."

Harry felt a surge of anger, and he wondered why; then he realized that being lumped together with Carstairs and Buchanan was the reason.

"Listen, Lambeth," he said, "it's true that I have no interest in sleeping with Bromley, but I really cannot take offense at your people's normal behavior. I suppose it should be taken as a compliment, not as an outrage. And I'm rather fond of Bromley, too. As far as I'm concerned, the matter is over and done with. Is that all right?"

"Oh, yes sir," said Lambeth. "I will be overjoyed to report as much, and I'm sure everyone else will be pleased to hear it."

When they returned to the cottage, Moisan was putting his violin back in the case.

"Oh, sir," said Lambeth, "were you playing?"

"Yes," said Moisan, "but with no unusual effects this time. I do think my playing has improved a great deal, though, and I'm not sure how to explain it. I hardly like to take credit for it myself."

Neither Harry nor Lambeth had any reply to this, though Lambeth asked, "Sir, I wonder—I've told some of the others about your playing. Some of us are very interested to hear it. Do you think it would be possible to, ah..." he trailed off.

"To give a performance?" Moisan smiled. "Until recently I

should have said I wasn't good enough for anyone to want to listen, but I suppose under the circumstances... Well, I'll work something up. Something lighter than the Chaconne, just in case whatever that was happens again. I'll let you know when."

"Thank you, sir."

"Now then," said Moisan, "do you have a few minutes, Lambeth? If you do, I'd like to ask a few questions about your people, and how you live."

"Of course, sir."

"And you, Harry? Is this a bother for you? We can go outside, or to the hangar if you prefer."

"Oh no," said Harry. "Go right ahead. I'd just as soon take my mind off those hornets. What a day! Say, Lambeth, wasn't there something you wanted to ask us, too?"

"Oh yes, sir," said Lambeth, "if you don't mind."

"Well, let's hear your questions first," said Moisan. "It seems only fair. Come sit down and talk more comfortably."

Harry and Moisan sat down on their cots, and Lambeth pulled up a chair.

"I hope this doesn't seem silly," he said, "but we've been reading and enjoying many of your books. Novels mostly. There's a number of things we don't understand in the stories, but we have worked out that certain things are well, how shall I put it... Conventions of fiction. Things that are put in that the reader understands aren't real."

"Oh," said Harry, "you mean like how characters in books will often speak in these long paragraphs with complete sentences. No one talks that way normally, but it makes dialog easier to read."

"Well, there *is* Graham," said Moisan. "He talks that way all the time."

"Er, yes," said Harry, "I suppose. But anyway, it's not nearly as common in real life as in books. A fictional convention, correct?"

"Yes, sir," said Lambeth, "but really I meant something else."

"Oh. Sorry."

"In many of your stories there is at least one romance. Usually a young man falls in love with a young woman, and the story is about how they overcome all obstacles to be together."

Moisan smiled. "Does that seem strange to you?"

"Well, a little," said Lambeth, "though we really like that kind of story. But that's the question. The idea of such a thing happening is wonderful, but is that a convention too? Or does it really happen?"

"Do you mean the adventures, the rivals, the tragic coincidences, that sort of thing?"

"Oh no," said Lambeth, "all that is fun to read about, but it's obviously just invented. I mean the falling in love part. Do your people actually fall in love? And do they stay in love? Is that a real thing at all, or is it just something in your stories?"

"I see," said Moisan. "I think it really does happen. Perhaps not with the same frequency or intensity you read about, but people do fall in love. Sometimes it doesn't last. But then, sometimes it does. You meet mature and older couples who obviously love each other deeply. Just, well, not as many as you might hope for, is all."

"Thank you, sir," said Lambeth. "It's good to hear that it does happen. But..." He trailed off.

"Yes?"

"Well, you said 'you think'. Have you never experienced it yourself, sir?"

Moisan blushed. "Well, ah, no," he said. "Affection, yes, and what you might call physical longing, but not the kind of love you read about in books."

Lambeth turned to Harry. "Sir, may I ask? Have you?"

"I would have to say no," said Harry, "but I think I'm very close to it."

He nodded to Moisan. "There's a woman I just met before I came over here, and to be honest, she's been in my thoughts almost constantly since then. You might even say she was haunting my dreams, if it wasn't so pleasant."

Moisan and Lambeth both smiled. Harry wondered if it was for the same or different reasons.

"But the fact is," said Harry, "that even now, it wouldn't be fair to say I'm in love with her. If we'd had just a little more time... But it was only a few hours, most of which I spent sitting in the gunner's seat of a bomber while she flew me across France, so we might as well have been miles apart. But I have high hopes for my return. If you ask me again after that, perhaps I'll be able to give you a better answer."

"Oh sir," said Lambeth, "I do hope it works out for you."

"As do I," said Moisan, chuckling. "He's talking about my sister, you understand."

"Your sister! But of course, you grew up in a family, like *themselves* do. I knew that," said Lambeth, "but I never really thought about it."

Moisan said, "Your question leads to one of my own."

"Yes, sir?"

"I suppose from the way you framed the question that your people don't have that kind of relationship themselves."

"No, sir."

"But you say you find the idea appealing? And so do many of your friends?"

"Yes indeed."

"May I ask why, then, your people don't actually love in that manner?"

"Oh," said Lambeth, "it would be so unfair. It would never work out for everyone, not all at once. And we'd lose our mutuality. But that's not why, I think, or not the main reason."

"Pardon me?"

"What it is, I think, sir—I've been thinking about this lately, trying to compare ourselves to you, I mean, and I don't know enough about you, not for sure, so I may not be right..."

"That's all right," said Moisan, "neither of us knows enough yet."

"Yes, sir, well, I mean no offense, but I think there's two things we do that you don't. I mean, that have to do with this question."

"Yes?"

"Well, the first thing is, with each other, we can tell that someone wants to be, well, loved, I suppose you would say. And we all want that."

"I suppose we all want to be loved too," said Moisan.

"Yes, sir, but the thing is, we can *tell*. We can sense it. And we can't bear not to love in return. It would be so unkind not to. So that's why—" Lambeth cut himself off.

"No," said Moisan, "you're not being offensive. I think this is important for me to understand your people. Please finish your thought."

"Well sir, what it is, we all love each other. We just have to. But it's—it's a mild sort of love compared to the romances in your books. We want to be loved that way. We want to love that way ourselves. But then someone else wouldn't be loved, or someone would be torn between two people—"

"That has been known to happen among us."

"Yes," said Lambeth, "and to us that would be unbearable, sir. To cause that kind of unhappiness. So we don't do it. But when we read your books, we think how nice it would be."

Harry listened to all this, at first with some discomfort he hoped wasn't obvious, but then with growing curiosity and even admiration. The idea of a people who couldn't bear even the thought of allowing someone in their community to go unloved was remarkable. But he remembered how Lambeth had cut himself off, and a thought occurred to him and he spoke up.

"Lambeth, you were going to say something before. I gather this sense of what others are feeling, it doesn't work from your people to ours, does it?"

"No sir, you're right. Only among ourselves."

"So then, that's why..."

Moisan completed the thought. "That's why there have been these, ah, incidents the major told me about. You see that we are not engaging, in, ah, relationships amongst ourselves, and you put yourselves in our places. You think we want to be loved, and so you feel the obligation to, to, ah connect with us as well."

"Yes, sir. There's more to it than that, of course. We admire you in many ways. Then there's the novelty of course, the question what it would be like, the fun it would be to explore the differences between us, the fun of making love to new people. You're so different and exciting, you see." Lambeth paled, shook his head violently. "Ah! I mean, not you yourself, sir, I mean your people. Not that I wouldn't want—" He looked down at his feet. "I'm sorry, sir."

Moisan coughed. "Never mind," he said, "I understand what you mean. But putting aside those other considerations, your people imagine we are, well, in need of affection, and your way is to offer it where it is desired. Is that right?"

"Yes, sir. That's it."

"That's wonderful," said Moisan, and Lambeth looked up at him curiously. "What I mean is, among our people, kindness is supposed to be a virtue. But I'm afraid our notion of kindness is much inferior to yours. This sense of the invidious, of the unfairness of binding an affection—it's not really something we feel ourselves, I'm sorry to say." He shook his head. "But I suppose this must have been a source of considerable consternation among your people, all these rebuffed and rejected offers that must have been made in your first few days with us."

"Sir," said Lambeth, "you're right. But then we were told that you only approve of male-female relationships and that made a little sense, though why you have no women here—" He cut himself off again. "But at the same time, we know that's not really true. So even now, we're confused about what you think and believe."

"I don't understand," said Moisan. "What's not true?"

"Well sir, at various times, every one of you pilots, except you yourself, sir, Mr. Carstairs, and Mr. Buchanan, has been, ah, asked if he would like to make love with one of us. And all of you have declined."

Moisan looked confused. "Yes," he said, "but how is that confusing?"

"Sir," said Lambeth, "I should say that all of you have declined *the first time.*"

"Oh," said Moisan, blushing.

Harry couldn't help it. He started to laugh. What made it funnier was that just days before it would have been shocking, but now it seemed hilarious.

"You mean to say," Harry managed to get the words out, "that some of us have in fact been sleeping with you kobolds?"

"Yes, sir," said Lambeth. "Three of the nine of you we've asked so far, in fact. So when Clerkenwell asked—"

"Please don't," said Moisan, interrupting. "The individuals in question would be horrified to learn we were told their names. I daresay you all talk freely amongst yourselves as regards, ah, these relationships?"

"Yes, sir. Of course. We share everything."

"Of course. Naturally, you do. Listen, though, Lambeth, this is serious. Please don't tell any of us the names of any of—of those of us who have these relationships. They are supposed to be forbidden."

"I'm sorry, sir," said Lambeth, "I didn't understand. I thought you asked me to speak freely."

"Oh yes," said Moisan, "about anything but the names of one of our people who are, ah, engaging in this kind of relationship. They would be terribly embarrassed if it were to come out."

"Why, sir? I understand intellectually, about sin and so on, but not, not really. It doesn't make really sense to me."

"I don't think I can even begin to explain the attitude," said Moisan, "because I don't think there's much logic to it myself, even if I nevertheless feel some of it myself. Please just take my word for it, though. You agree, Harry, do you not?"

"Oh yes," said Harry, who had recovered from his fit of hilarity. "Very much so. Even if none of us objected at all—I don't myself, and from what I gather we're rather a more tolerant group than most—well, the people involved would be terribly embarrassed. Best just not to talk about particulars. Nothing that would even hint at anyone's name."

"Very well, sir. Thank you for explaining this. We certainly wouldn't want anyone to suffer in any way for this."

"Of course," said Moisan, "and if you had told us, I'm sure

neither of us would have ever mentioned it anyway. It's just better to be safe in this sort of situation, because some of us have very strong views, very much opposed to any hint of homosexuality whatsoever."

"Yes, sir. That we understand, even if, well, we don't understand how some of you—"

"Never mind," said Moisan. "The whole thing embarrasses me to speak of it, not because of what your people do or what these other officers do, but because of our own people's attitudes on this subject. Perhaps we can move on?"

"Of course, sir."

Moisan produced a notebook and a pencil. "Well, then," he said, "if you don't mind, I have a few questions about what life was like for you as a child. How far back can you remember?"

Harry sat and listened for a while as Moisan asked questions of Lambeth. At first they both seemed a little hesitant, formal and self-conscious in their questions and answers. However, Moisan was clearly fascinated by Lambeth's account of his childhood, and after giving an account of his own experience growing up in Brittany and Devon, the conversation became quite free and easy. It seemed a kobold childhood resembled what Harry imagined a benevolently run orphanage would be like, one that provided vocational training in mining and metal-lurgy.

♍   ♍   ♍

25 December 1917.

Harry woke to a pattering sound—a light rain was coming down. A little gray light was filtering through the shutters— evidently his scheduled patrol had been negated by the weather, and Lambeth had allowed him to remain asleep past dawn.

Faint rag-tag bits of a dream remained in his consciousness. He had been flying through a dense fog in his SE, but he was unable to maneuver properly as his stick and rudder bar seem- ed to be locked in place. Then he noticed he was actually flying in company with Marie, who was somehow sitting next to him as if on the bench seat of an automobile. She had her own set of controls, as in a trainer, and they'd been fighting over them wordlessly. In the dream he'd been unable to speak; the possibility never even occurred to him, so he could only communicate through the controls. At last it had occurred to Harry to stop fighting with her, to completely relax his grip. As soon as he let go, Marie was able to bank and turn, and they emerged from the clouds to see a beautiful lush meadow off in the distance, the one with Harry's airstrip, in fact. She smiled at him then, as if to say, "See, I was right all along," and he felt a surge of mixed tenderness and desire. In the dream, he was already anticipating their landing with the intention of making a bed together with Marie in the wildflowers and clover behind the aerodrome, but he woke up before they had even lined up their descent.

Sitting up in bed, Harry gave voice to an inarticulate noise, a sound that mixed frustration, shame, and resentment. The fading images of his dream seemed almost taunting. Perhaps if he hadn't been so obstinate at first with the controls—But he realized at that point in the dream he had been flying solo, and it was only Marie's appearance beside him that had brought about the emergence from the clouds.

Moisan awoke then, grumbling something incoherent in French from his cot across the room.

"Sorry," said Harry, "go back to sleep if you like. Looks like it's a rainy Christmas in Fairyland."

The Frenchman turned over and muttered words that could have been "Joyeux Noël" rose from his pillow.

♍   ♍   ♍

When Harry ventured out into the morning, he was prepared to make a run for the mess hall through the rain. But it was a fine prickling drizzle, and the delicate fall of the tiny droplets was almost like a massage on Harry's face, so he slowed his pace and relaxed his hunched-over posture. Though the cloud cover was locally quite thick over the aerodrome, and a ground fog had merged with the low clouds to smear the horizon out into a vague blur, other parts of the sky were much brighter. Here and there in the distance Harry could see diffuse shafts of light piercing the overcast, lending a soft radiance to the sky just at the limits of visibility and making it seem as if radiant pillars were supporting the dome of the heavens. Even close by, the gray of the clouds and the green of the meadowland blended into a soft pastel effect, very different from the bleak appearance of a rainy day at the front.

By the time Harry got to the mess hall, his hair and shoulders a bit damp but not really wet, he found O'Meara standing in the open doorway looking out over the airfield.

"Now this is what we call a foin soft marnin'", he said, for a moment putting on an exaggerated brogue.

"Is it ever like this in Ireland?"

"Well, sometimes," said O'Meara, "though it's not quite this warm in December, usually, nor do you get such an ostentatious heavenly display most of the time," he gestured at the pillars of light, "but the green and the gray, the mist, the wet, the smell of the moist earth and all that, there is a homely side to it."

"Come on in," he said then, stepping out of the doorway. "Unless you'd rather go to the prayer meeting over in the south hangar."

"I think not," said Harry. "I'm more interested in breakfast myself. Have you eaten?"

"Not yet, but it's an idea," said O'Meara, and they went inside.

This morning the cooks provided buttered griddle cakes, mutton sausages, and some dried apple slices, along with fried eggs. Harry and O'Meara were the only pilots present at the moment, and they sat down across from one another at one of the mess hall tables. Harry took a mug of coffee, made from beans that had been sent across with the shipment of squadron supplies, and O'Meara drank tea, also supplied from England.

"Pity they've no swine about," said O'Meara, "could do with some bacon, too."

"Yes. I suppose we could have some sent through. What a strange idea, though."

"Oh?" It was more of a grunt, as O'Meara already had his mouth full.

"Go from one world to another, and send back for breakfast supplies. Funny, don't you think?"

"Makes all the sense in the world to me."

They ate in companionable silence for a while. Then Harry asked, "What is this prayer meeting you mentioned?".

"Oh, it was after you and Moisan left last night. Someone mentioned it was Christmas tomorrow with no chaplain in the squadron, and Buchanan offered to lead a prayer meeting. Christians only, he said, by which he meant no Catholics. And I'm just as happy not to attend, I must say."

"I'm not sorry to have missed it," said Harry. "Would you be at mass today if you were home, Brian?"

"Probably," said O'Meara. "Doubt I could get out of it. I'm not what you'd call religious, but you know, family and solidarity and all of that. But for me an Englishman saying 'Catholic' is pretty much a code word for 'bloody Irish', so if you want to get a rise out of me, you know how to do it. I've almost gotten used to that kind of thing from the English, but I would have thought a Scotsman... well, never mind. I'm blithering on. Bloody proddy. Begging your pardon, Harry; I don't mean you."

Harry smiled. "No offense taken. But since you mention it, I suppose I'm the closest thing to an Englishman in the whole squadron, so if you'll take my apology for a thousand years of the bloody English, I'll be glad to offer it."

O'Meara laughed. "Go on," he said, "you're no more what I mean when I say 'proddy' than Devlin is. He may be a unionist and a Church of Ireland man, but if they were all like him, there'd be no Troubles in the first place. Now then, since we've got some time to kill, I might as well give you an introduction to the game of kings."

Hours later, Harry emerged from the mess hall, L-shaped patterns of white and dark squares—knight moves—flickering in the forefront of his consciousness. He'd known the basics of chess since childhood, but had never seriously tried to play the game. Something about the knight seemed alien to him, at odds with his idea of what a knight was supposed to be. The ability to shift from the white to the black squares, to jump over intervening pieces, to show such threatening and bewildering behavior down through myriad potential moves vaguely sensed in possible futures of the game...

"Aye," said O'Meara when he'd suggested something along these lines, "without the knight, chess would be child's play, wouldn't you say? But that special power it has, that remote control you might call it, that's the key, isn't it?"

"Key?", Harry had asked, "Key to what?"

"Ah, and if I knew that," said O'Meara, "well..." He trailed off.

♍   ♍   ♍

Later, Harry stopped by the hangar, finding Lambeth hard at work at his drafting table.

"Working on the guns?"

"Yes, sir." Lambeth was meticulously drawing circles with a compass on a cyanotype representation of the S.E.5a dashboard. The mounting of the second gun would require part of the existing panel to be cut away, and several instruments had to be adjusted a few inches to make room for the gun breech.

"This looks very fine, but have you solved the ammunition problem?"

"Not yet," said Lambeth. "But these little details have to get done. Sir, I feel confident about it, though."

"You're sure there's an answer?"

"Yes, sir. I don't know why I feel that way. But I think there has to be a solution. It's there. I can almost reach out for it."

"And you didn't feel this way about the supercharger?"

"Oh no, sir. That was like wandering through a huge dark forest, completely lost. Here it's like I'm in a neat little closet, and I know the answer is in there someplace."

The kobold seemed so eager to do the work, so excited by the prospect of success that Harry wanted to slap him on the back by way of support, but he hesitated, not sure how it would be taken. Was it possible Lambeth felt the same way about him as Bromley, but was just a bit more discreet?

The hell with it, he thought, and put his hand on the kobold's shoulder. "I'm sure you can do it," he said. "At least if the closet isn't that big. I'll be interested to see your solution when it's ready."

Lambeth flinched a little at the contact but looked up at him cheerfully enough. He smiled, showing his slightly-too-sharp teeth and said, "Thank you, sir! I'm sure it won't be long till I've got something to show you."

♍   ♍   ♍

Christmas dinner turned out to be exceptionally mannered and polite, and during the meal conversation was restricted for the most part to the food. The kobold cooks had gone to some extra effort preparing the traditional dishes, which here included goose, joints of lamb in the place of gammon, parsnips, bread sauce, turnips in place of potatoes, redcurrant jelly, and an exceptionally good chestnut stuffing. For dessert a colossal pudding was brought out, flaming in Major Quirk's private brandy stock.

At length the last plates were removed, and the men of the squadron sat back in their seats, empty glasses in front of them. A feeling of benevolent lassitude spread around the table with the ending of the feast, and conversation came to a pause.

"Gentlemen," said Major Quirk, raising his voice just enough to gain everyone's attention, "It's come to my attention that Monsieur Moisan here is something of a violinist, so I thought it might be pleasant to hear a little Christmas music. With your indulgence, Robert..."

"Of course," said Moisan, rising to his feet and retrieving his violin from a sideboard. "I don't propose anything very tedious, but I think it would be in the spirit of the day to play some carols."

The pilots turned to face Moisan, who settled the violin under his chin.

"Perhaps someone can suggest something?"

"How about Silent Night?" asked Powell. I can give you the words, if you like."

Powell's speaking voice was an ordinary baritone, but in song he proved to have a remarkably pure tenor. About halfway through Harry realized that something akin to the Chaconne phenomenon was recurring. But not quite the same thing. The music was lovely, conveying an otherworldly feeling of calmness and grace, but at no point did Harry completely lose his sense of time and place. Where Bach's Chaconne had unleashed a torrent of feelings that had carried Harry beyond himself into a realm of pure emotion, this version of Silent Night seemed more sedate, more controlled, more of a work of artifice than of nature.

Moisan lowered his bow, unlimbered the violin from the crook of his neck. Harry looked around the room. Many of the pilots had closed their eyes, and a few looked now to be waking as if from a trance. Buchanan's eyes jerked open, and with a start his arm twitched, knocking over his empty wine glass. He flushed, seemed about to speak, and restrained himself.

"Bravo," said Devlin. "That was superb. I've never heard the like." He started applauding, and the other pilots followed suit. Harry saw Powell looking surprised, almost shocked now that the song was over, but he noticed Moisan was smiling. That was the difference, Harry realized. The previous night Moisan had been overcome by his own music, and by whatever afflatus or unaccustomed zenith of performance he'd achieved. This time, though, he'd remained in control.

"Thank you," said Moisan. "You sang beautifully, David. I was stupid not to have asked in advance for a singer to accompany."

"That was something," said Powell. "I've never done so well before. It was... well, I don't know what it was."

"Perhaps we should try something a little lighter for the next tune," said Moisan. "Silent Night is German, so let's choose an English carol instead. How about Deck the Halls?"

Powell laughed. "That's not English."

"What? It isn't?"

"No indeed," said Powell. "It's Welsh. Very old, too. The English words are a recent innovation. Strike it up and I'll show you."

He turned to the company. "Perhaps you gentlemen can help

us out with the fa-la-la bits."

This time Harry heard the power even in the opening notes. He had always thought of the song as being rather insipid and annoying with its dull jangling chorus, but it sounded very different this evening.

"O mor gynnes mynwes meinwen"

Powell gestured and the company responded with a fa-la-la line. Harry was surprised to recall a flash of his encounter with Marie. He remembered the softness of her breasts against his cheek.

"O mor fwyn yw llwya meillionen"

More fa-la-las, heartily delivered, but in a harmonious chorus. And now, though he was perfectly aware of his seat on the mess-hall bench, between Murphy and Jernigan, at the same time he seemed to be in company with Marie, holding hands and smiling into each others' eyes.

"O mor felus yw'r cusanau"

No fa-la-las this time, but a lovely flourish from Moisan's violin, and not a single uncertain note sung by any of the pilots, as if they'd all known the third line required no refrain. But in the usual English version there was one, Harry was sure. And now Harry recalled the moment Marie had lowered her body over his on that cot in Carnac, the moment of entry, the sweetness of the sensation, the warmth of her body...

"Gyda serch a mwynion eiriau"

Another round of fa-la-las, and the song went on. Powell fell silent, and Moisan finished with a solo verse, developing an instrumental variation on the spur of the moment. Harry was left with Marie's remembered scent in his nostrils and the feeling of her lips on his mouth.

A round of applause began, but was interrupted when Buchanan got up abruptly from his seat, pushed past Carstairs, and hurried out of the room, his face flushed. No one commented, however. Harry looked around the room, and noticed some color rising in the cheeks of several of the pilots. He wondered if anyone else had recalled similar memories just then. It occurred to him that three of their number, at least, might have experienced rather more recent memories of love.

Jernigan chuckled. "That wasn't what I would call a Christmas carol, was it now, David?"

"Well, not exactly," said Powell. "More of a new-years sort of thing, I'd say. Did you catch the words?"

"A few of them. I'm not really fluent. But even so, gynnes m-ynwes, a warm bosom, that I know. Doesn't seem quite like

Christmastime material."

"Oh," said Moisan, "Were those lyrics risqué? I hope we didn't offend anyone."

"I think the only one of us who might possibly have been offended has already left the room," said Major Quirk, "and I doubt he speaks Welsh."

Powell bowed his head. "I'm sorry sir," he said. "It was meant in fun. And those really were the original lyrics. Nothing too scandalous."

"I'll take your word for it," said Quirk. "But though I don't speak a word of your barbarous Brythonic tongue, I must say the music seems to have carried my thoughts in a most unexpected direction... That aside, I wonder if someone would mind checking on Buchanan? He didn't look well."

"I'll go," said Devlin. He returned a minute later. "James sends his apologies," he said. "Apparently he's eaten something that disagreed with him."

"Too bad," said Quirk. "But no doubt he'll feel better tomorrow."

"Speaking of tomorrow," said Devlin, "it looks like the clouds are breaking up. We may have flying weather for Boxing Day."

"Ha," said O'Meara, "just as well. I was wondering if I could stand two days off in a row."

Devlin smiled. "Keen, aren't you? But I must say, I feel the same way. The sooner we clear the skies to the east the better."

After the dinner broke up, Harry left the mess hall in company with Moisan and Powell. As Devlin had mentioned, the overcast had broken up into patches of clouds. It was a little cooler than usual in the aftermath of the rain, but otherwise the humidity had been washed out of the air, and it was another pleasant evening in fairyland.

"Right," said Powell as soon as they got outside, "what was that, then? Don't even try to tell me you don't know what I'm talking about."

Moisan bowed his head. "I thought I had it under control," he said, "but it seems not so much. Likely it was your contribution that pushed it over the top."

"It? It? What do you mean?"

"I'm sorry," said Moisan. "I don't know for sure, but at present I believe it to be a species of glamour, somehow connected to music. Was this the first time you've done any singing? I mean, while you were over here?"

"Yes, since you mention it. Are you trying to tell me that will happen whenever we play any music?"

"No," said Moisan, "it's been somewhat unpredictable. Though I think if I knew what lyrics you were singing I might have guessed. But if you don't mind, can you say how it felt, for you?"

"What?" Powell shook his head. "I'm not really sure right now. I think... it was like I was flying, but without an aeroplane. For that Silent Night, towards the end... have you ever been out at night when it was snowing, but there was still plenty of light?"

"Yes."

"All right. Well, imagine it's like that, but you're flying. The Moon's out somehow, and the snowflakes are glittering in the light. Now you turn off the engine, you're gliding silently, and all you see is this field of a million sparkles of light rushing by. I thought it was just a daydream of some kind. It didn't interfere with me singing, and at the same time, I could see everyone in the room perfectly well. It was like a kind of double vision."

"I didn't see that," said Harry, "but I think I felt it."

"Yes well, that was all very pretty. But then after that I had the foolish idea of singing Nos Galan—"

"Pardon me?"

"Sorry, the original Welsh lyrics to Deck the Halls."

"Of course. Go on."

"Right," said Powell, "so now I'm standing up there and I swear Caruso himself had nothing on me, never sung like that in my life, and meanwhile Robert here is playing the fiddle like an angel, and I'm back to flying again."

Here he coughed. "But this time," he said, "in company, if you know what I mean."

Moisan blushed. "I think so. I hope the others don't blame us for that."

Powell laughed. "Don't worry about it. Except maybe for Buchanan, I think you're in the clear there. But if you could bottle it, you'd make millions, for sure."

Harry said, "You can say better what it was like this time than I can, Robert, but compared to last time, I had the feeling you had the effect under control."

"Last time? What was that?" Powell wanted to know.

Moisan explained the circumstances of his playing of Bach's Chaconne.

"I see," said Powell. "And then it didn't happen in practice afterwards? Maybe it requires an audience."

"Oh," said Moisan, "that makes sense. A nice insight."

"Perhaps it also has something to do with the passions

aroused by the music," said Powell. "Silent Night has that sweet lullaby quality to it, and of course Nos Galan..."

"What do the words actually mean?"

"Oh," said Powell, "nothing very strong. The Song of Songs in the Bible is much hotter stuff. But even so, it's a bit warmer than your average Christmas carol. Let's see, I'd put it like this, line by line:

Oh, how warm my fair girl's bosom,
Oh, the lovely fields of clover,
Oh, how sweet the kisses,
With pleasured words of love.

"Of course, a proper translation would be more poetic, but you get the idea. Not risqué at all, except perhaps if you were expecting something completely tame like the English lyrics."

"Certainly," said Moisan. "Very sedate compared to the Folies Bergère or the Moulin Rouge. But I must admit the effect was, well, remarkably aphrodisiac."

"Yes. I imagine most everyone has figured it out for themselves by now, but I suppose I should say something to the major, just for form's sake."

"I agree," said Moisan. "Shall I go with you?"

"Never mind, I'll do it myself," said Powell. "It was my lyrics after all."

Returning to their cottage, Harry and Moisan found Lambeth waiting for them, a rolled-up blueprint under his arm.

"Good evening, sirs. I hope your dinner went well."

"Not too bad," said Harry while Moisan put his violin away.

"Sir," said Lambeth, "with respect to the matter of the two Vickers guns..."

"Yes?" asked Harry, "Have you solved the ammunition problem?"

"I took the liberty of drawing up a plan," said the kobold.

Harry scanned the blueprint. There was still only one ammunition box, but it had expanded a few inches to both sides using the entire available space of the narrow SE hull, and was now split down the middle to accommodate two separate belts. Moreover the ammunition feed, a metal framework on top of the box meant to guide the belt to the breech of the gun, had been eliminated, the box extended another few inches in height, and two angled feeds incorporated into the box design itself.

"Why this is very clever," he said. "I suppose it's not quite two boxes worth of ammunition, though."

"No, sir," said Lambeth, looking crestfallen. "600 rounds in two compartments. I'm sorry I couldn't manage to find space for 800. I'm very sorry, sir."

"Never fear," said Harry. "It's still superior to the 400 in the existing box plus the 97 in the Lewis gun drum. Not to mention the fact that two parallel Vickers guns will focus fire on a target much better than the current arrangement. This is really excellent work."

"Thank you, sir." Lambeth was beaming now.

"I suppose all that's left is the right-hand gun fairing, but it's just the mirror image of the existing fairing on the left side."

"Shall we work on it tomorrow, then, sir?"

"Certainly," said Harry. "By the way, did you have much trouble coming up with the idea of that split box as a solution to the ammunition problem?"

"No, sir," said Lambeth. "I tried for a while to find room for a second box, but when it became clear that was impossible, the idea of splitting a single enlarged box just, well, it just dawned on me."

"No need for Sandraudiga this time, eh?"

"No, sir."

"Well," said Harry, "no disrespect to the goddess, but I think it's just as well. Honestly, we should send this design back to Farnham for the RAF to consider. Let's make a prototype and see how it works. Will you need me to sign off on the design? I mean, to avoid any, ah, unpleasantness with the work crews?"

"No, sir, thank you sir." Lambeth bowed. "I've already talked over the matter with Bromley and Kensington."

"Very good," said Harry. "I'm grateful for your work."

CHAPTER 11
DAYS AND NIGHTS

26 December 1917.

Boxing day provided some lovely flying weather. A few huge cottony tufts of cumulus left over from the previous day's overcast were floating around 9,000 feet, but for the most part the sky was clear with no haze at all, and a brilliant sun shone down on the prairie land between the aerodrome and the Shroud.

Harry's morning patrol was uneventful in the vicinity of the Shroud, though he was on edge the whole time, looking out for the possibility of hornets in the sky, perhaps hiding in the clouds. There was no sign of any hive pods, however, nor any individual hornets to be seen either.

Once more Harry spotted a cavalry squadron not far from Prince Nuada's fort. The troop was heading east, presumably on their own patrol of the area. He gave them a snap roll at 500 feet as a salute and passed on. Again there was no sign of a wild horse herd.

Later that morning A Flight conducted another successful raid on the Shroud, downing another 9 pods without incident, and B Flight managed 7 in the afternoon before running out of ammunition. This time the floating tugs were more widely deployed around the pods, but not in sufficient numbers to be able to interfere with the attack—many more of the slow-moving tugs would have had to appear to have any significant effect. The day off on Christmas due to the bad weather had allowed pods from the interior of the Shroud to replace those that had been shot down over the previous two days.

♍   ♍   ♍

At dinner that night, Major Quirk outfitted himself in white gloves and served food to his batman, Hammersmith. It was traditional in the Army for officers and enlisted men to swap roles on Boxing Day, but it seemed no one had told Hammersmith about it until the last minute, and the kobold's astonishment was by turns touching and hilarious.

After the loyal toast, Major Quirk nodded to Moisan, who stood up from the table to address the company.

"Gentlemen," he said, "I'd like to apologize for any untowardness you may have experienced last night during that little recital. It seems that musical performances in this world sometimes have a little more power than we are used to. Mr. Powell is certainly not to blame as he had no idea what might transpire, but I must admit I should have known better as something of the sort happened two days before."

"Come on, man," said O'Meara, "that playing wasn't untoward, it was delightful. If that's what you can do with Christmas carols, I for one would like to hear some real music next time."

"That is very kind of you to say. But even so, I fear that some of you may feel as if a certain liberty was taken in the playing of that music last night."

Here Moisan paused, but no one else answered. Harry noticed some of the pilots glancing at Buchanan at that moment, and Buchanan himself seemed aware of the attention, because he shifted uncomfortably and spoke up.

"Well for my own part," he said, "I consider all music more or less frivolous, but it would really be quite ridiculous for me to object to it. I'm sure I am guilty of worse offenses in ordinary conversation than inadvertently stirring a few... emotions... with some old melodies."

Moisan bowed his head briefly and seemed about to speak, but Buchanan continued.

"Still, I do think it might be well not to play without giving a little warning first. Just in case."

"Of course," said Moisan. "I would not want to inflict even the best playing in the world on an unappreciative audience. For that reason, I think in future I will play outside, well away from any of the cottages."

"You will let us know when, though?" Powell asked. "I'm with Brian on this one. I want to hear what your playing sounds like when it's not just some hackneyed old carol. I'm interested professionally, if you understand."

"Certainly," said Moisan. "It will be a pleasure. I should practice some pieces first, but perhaps in a couple of days we can have some music after dinner."

♍   ♍   ♍

27 December 1917.

A lovely day: golden sunshine and a high haze. No aerial encounters in the morning, and a routine day of pod-busting in the afternoon, if the fiery destruction of seven more of the smog-spewing behemoths could be called routine. Still no signs of additional hornets or hive pods.

After B Flight's return from the Shroud, Harry spent some time looking over the shoulders of the kobold crew crafting the bifurcated ammunition box. The speed with which the kobolds milled and assembled the metal sheets that made up the case was no longer surprising, but even so watching the team at work was almost mesmerizing. Not only was the process itself fascinating, but Harry felt an unexpected pleasure in watching Lambeth's design come together.

On his return from the workshop, Harry heard the call for the post, and hurried to the mess hall, hoping for another letter from Marie. All the officers were gathered, hoping for something from home.

"And here's something for you, Tregeseal," said Captain Devlin, sorting through the mail and parcels. Harry was surprised to receive a substantial package, not just an envelope. After looking at the addressing his surprise was redoubled: this had been sent from his home in St. Just.

"Something the matter?" asked Murphy, who was standing next to him at the trestle table.

"No," said Harry, "I'm just amazed to receive anything at all from home. It's been less than a week since I sent my first letter home, and only two weeks since I left England. Even with magic intervening, I can't imagine how the post could be so fast. Surely anything sent to the front would still be in transit."

He unwrapped the parcel. It contained several letters, two books, and a large tin.

"Ah! Peppermint creams, and the books I asked for. That means it's been less than a week."

He carried everything back to his hut, and opened the first letter, from his mother, finding a solution to the puzzle in the first paragraph.

> 24 December 1917
>
> My Dearest Harry,
>
> Happy Christmas! You must be shocked to hear from us so quickly, but not half so shocked as we were to have your post delivered to us by hand and par avion at one and the same time. I daresay we are now the talk of all Penwith—not every family gets their mail delivered by a French bomber! And of those few aeroplanes that the locals may ever have seen, I am sure none were flown by such a charming pilot as Marie Moisan, or for that matter carried a passenger as memorable as Olwen

Llewellyn. Apparently it was *convenient* for them to stop off in St. Just on their way back to France from Uffington, on some errand of great importance. Can you imagine a world in which such things are *convenient*? Perhaps there is something to all this aviation business after all!

Now, Harry, I must tell you that however amazed we all may have been to receive such unexpected guests, that surprise paled in comparison to my reaction to the news Mrs. Llewellyn told me, in private, regarding the nature of your new assignment. If it wasn't for a certain proof she offered (in combination with her surprisingly deep knowledge of our family tree), I would say she was mad, but that proof was, if I may say so, almost *magically* convincing. And now, as you may well imagine, my world has turned quite upside down, but despite everything I'd rather have you where you are now than at the western front.

You will perceive, no doubt, that I am writing rather elliptically about the whole subject, despite Mrs. Llewellyn's assurance she will send this directly on to you without it having to go through the regular army post system. This is partly because writing anything down about your current location and work seems to make the whole thing impossible to believe, and partly because I am not entirely confident a certain sibling of yours might not contrive to accidentally on purpose sneak a peek at this somehow, and she has not yet been told what is going on.

Now then, Harry, time is short. Mr. Roscrow has brought the coach round to carry our aviatrices back to their vehicle, and I must finish this without further ado. I cannot say how much I look forward to your safe return, and to your stories of what "over there" was like. Mrs. Llewellyn has promised to return some time when she has the leisure to tell me more.

With all my love,
Your Mother,

Next, a brief note from his father:

Dear Harry,
I understand now why a French dictionary is needful. Evidently the field of aviation has advantages of which I

have heretofore been unaware. I admit in the past I have been rather skeptical about your prospects as a pilot and an engineer, but at last my eyes have been opened. Indeed, were I twenty years younger and unattached, I could even see myself entering the field—with some language training as preparation, of course.

That Mrs. Llewellyn stayed closeted with your mother for over an hour, and she emerged looking as befuddled as ever I have known her. During that time I enjoyed a little conversation with this Mlle. Moisan with whom I am told you have flown. A very pleasant young woman, I must say.

Now then, Harry, I am well aware, and not just from your letter, that there are things I am not being told about your current situation, but I am content to wait for your safe return to learn the details. In the meantime you should know we are all very proud of you indeed, and are eagerly awaiting your next correspondence. Your aerial post-mistresses are almost done with their preparations for departure, and so I must close this,

In haste,

Dr. Mark Tregeseal

Finally, a scrawl from his sister:

Harry!!!

This is the most amazing thing ever! We shall all be talking about it for months. Two women have landed a bomber in Mr. Roscrow's field, apparently just to bring us your mail! I suppose you know who they are. The funny old Welsh lady Mrs. Llewellyn is one, and this French girl Marie is the other. I had no idea they let girls fly aeroplanes! Why didn't you tell me? Now I am going to have to learn to fly myself.

But Harry, when I asked her if she knew you, the way she smiled! If you're not already aware, and I know how oblivious you can be sometimes, I'm telling you now that you must make sure to sure to look Marie up when you are done with whatever it is you are doing. And really, Harry! A secret mission! Could anything be more romantic than that? I can hardly believe it of you, Mr. Mildness himself. But perhaps now you are in the army you are Lieutenant Daring? But everyone refuses to tell me what is going on and I am quite overcome with frustration not to know.

Anyway, I hope you are happy with the mints. I had to rush down to town on my bicycle to get them while everyone else was having tea, and you are lucky that Mr. Hammett had any left at his shop. And now they are getting ready to take off, and I have no time to write anything more.

Love, Jennifer

28 December 1917.

Another day of good flying weather, another 16 pods destroyed in gorgeous fiery explosions, no hornets sighted at all, and once again the squadron was making substantial inroads into the number of pods on the edge of the Shroud. No enemy activity was reported at all.

Late in the afternoon, a fuel convoy arrived from the north, a train of large drays pulled by teams of workhorses. Each dray carried a thousand-gallon zinc tank which had to be pumped into the permanent tanks buried beneath the hangars. Not including the troop of knights who had escorted the convoy, a good hundred drovers were required to manage the wagons and their teams. They camped out with their horses on the far side of the airfield during a night in which kobold crews working in shifts managed the pumping. Major Quirk thought the teamsters and their escorts deserved some kind of visible return for their work, so the next morning he had Jernigan and Buchanan—by general acclaim, the squadron's two most skilled pilots—put on a little air show by way of thanks.

Harry stood in front of the north hangar, watching the aeroplanes looping, diving, and hurtling low overhead. He wondered what the fairy teamsters made of the display. Were they impressed? Fearful? Pleased with the results of their hard work?

One of the tanks had sprung a leak during pumping out. Rather than repairing it, the major had designated it as a target for a demonstration strafing run. Just enough petrol was left in the tank to produce a good vapor pressure, and it blew up quite prettily when Buchanan roared down from the sky at it, opening fire just 50 feet above the ground. Harry could see the impact of the twin rows of bullets a hundred yards out in front of Buchanan's Camel tearing up the earth on their way towards the tank. And then came the explosion, an enormous swirling ball of burning gas rising up from the ground, Buchanan pulling up and breaking hard right to avoid the blast, and Jernigan following a hundred yards behind in his SE, rocketing through the roiling cloud of smoke left behind.

"A most impressive display."

Harry turned, surprised. A stranger, a native he realized, had come up beside him while he was engrossed in the aerobatics. The man was tall and lean, dressed in a red cloak pinned over the shoulder with a silver brooch, atop a leather jerkin made of overlapping tabs reinforced with leaf-shaped bronze plates—armor. He wore a twisted gold rod around his neck. A scabbarded sword hung from his belt. His trousers were ordinary enough, tucked incongruously into a pair of English cavalry officer's boots. The man's face was long and thin, framed by straight reddish blond hair down to his shoulders. His face was lined with pain, it seemed.

"Sir?" Harry was taken aback.

"Pardon my interruption. I'm Nuada." The man's accent was hard to pin down; not a brogue or a burr, but carrying with it a sort of softness that Harry thought he might have associated with Portuguese if he'd heard it elsewhere.

"Oh! Your highness!" Harry had never met a nobleman before, even in England, and had no reflexive understanding how to react. He considered a bow, and then decided a salute was more in order, and started it at the same moment Nuada extended his hand. At last Harry managed to grasp the extended hand.

"Honored, sir," he said, "Second Lieutenant Harry Tregeseal at your service, Your Highness."

Nuada laughed without much humor. "A pleasure. We're not at court, though: please use my name."

"Yes, sir." Harry couldn't quite bring himself to address the prince informally.

"I suppose that's not very much of a show compared to one of the pods exploding," said Nuada.

"Imagine a quarter of the sky going up like that tank," said Harry. "That's what it's like. I've never seen anything close to it back in my own world."

"I'd like to see it. A pity your flying machines are so weighted with iron. Otherwise I'd want to learn to fly one myself. I can't imagine anything more delightful than to fly."

"Well, sir," said Harry, hearing the yearning in the man's voice, "I've only been flying for a couple of months now, but I have to say it is very fine, indeed, glorious even."

Harry thought about the squadron's Avro two-seater, which he still hadn't seen wheeled out of the hangar. Was there steel even in the fittings of the cockpit? Yes, he supposed there must be. But perhaps the kobolds could do something about that?

"Yes, sir," he said. "I beg your pardon, but may I ask how severe your, ah, sensitivity to iron is? Is it only a matter of contact?"

Nuada grimaced. "It's worse than that," he said. "I can feel it now, just the closeness of the masses of iron and steel in the hangar over there. There's no mistaking it. But even a touch can be fatal to—to those of my blood."

"I'm sorry," said Harry, "I've been told something about this, but I didn't know how serious a problem it was for you."

"Yes," said Nuada, "I don't know how you bear it. You and those kobolds. You really can't feel it?"

"Feel what, sir? What is it you feel?"

"It's, well, you know how an oven or a big fire feels when you get close, the blast of heat?"

"Yes. Is it like that?"

Nuada shook his head. "Different and worse, but that's the closest thing I can think of. It's not heat but cold, a horrible coldness. A *seeking* coldness, is more like it. An oven will burn you if you touch it, but that's all. You take one step away and there's no blast of heat anymore. No one fears fire just because it can burn you. But iron... I can sense it from a hundred yards away. I feel like it's alive, seeking me out."

"I'm sorry," said Harry. "I had no idea it was that bad for you. Shouldn't we move away, then?"

Nuada shook his head. "No," he said. "That's how it feels, but I know it's a lie. Just like a fire, all I have to do is not touch it. It's not really a—a malign thing. It's a weakness to overcome. That's all."

Harry realized now where the lines of pain on Nuada's face were coming from. He wanted to say that he was impressed by the fairy lord's determination and fortitude, but he couldn't think how to word it without condescension.

"If I may ask, sir, how far do your cavalry patrols range?"

"We ride sometimes almost all the way up to the curtain of smoky stuff," said Nuada. "It's a bit of a trek, so usually we don't go that far, but I like to make sure all my lancers get a chance to see it up close from time to time."

"Well, I don't know if I can offer you a ride in the sky, sir, but perhaps we can at least schedule an attack for you to view from the ground?"

"Not a bad idea," said Nuada. "It might be good politically, too."

"Sir?"

"Most of the men in my command are, ah, not really my own men, you understand? I have my own household knights, and men of the border service, but also several squadrons of lancers contributed by other lords in response to the Queen's orders. I'm ashamed to say that not all of us are of one mind regarding the Shroud's threat and your presence here."

"Oh," said Harry, "I think I see."

"It would be useful for them to see you and your machines in action, I think."

"That makes sense to me," said Harry. "I'm happy you think it's a good idea, but perhaps you should talk to Major Quirk about the scheduling?"

"Of course," said Nuada. "But I must thank you for the suggestion. I should have thought of something like that myself."

They turned back to the field. Jernigan and Buchanan had just landed and come to a halt out in the middle of the field, apparently to allow the drovers to observe their machines more closely, though neither the fairy teamsters nor their escorting horsemen showed any inclination to approach. *Not surprising,* Harry thought, *if they all have the same reaction to iron as Nuada.*

"Well, sir," he said, "it looks like the show is over. Would you like to greet the pilots? Captain Jernigan is in the SE, and Flight Lieutenant Buchanan is piloting the Camel."

"What? Oh yes, if you please, introduce me. I've met Captain Jernigan, but not yet Lieutenant Buchanan."

Even though they were walking toward aeroplanes laden with close to two tons of steel, Harry could see Nuada relaxing a little as they put a little distance between themselves and the hangar, in which a great deal more was stored. And yet as they approached the scouts Nuada put his head down and seemed to be bulling his way forward.

"Careful sir," Harry put his hand on Nuada's arm to hold him back. "The props are still spinning down. They're only wood, but they'll kill you just as dead as iron if you walk into them."

"Oh. Thank you."

They moved toward Jernigan's SE. Harry could see Nuada's gaze was fixed on the gun mounts and exhaust pipes, the most obvious pieces of exposed steel from where they were standing. Nevertheless, he walked with Harry right up to the cockpit.

"Captain," said Harry, "Prince Nuada is here and would like

a word with you.”

“Of course!” Jernigan unstrapped his belt and hoisted himself out of the cockpit, stepping down to the grass of the field. Harry noticed Nuada flinching as Jernigan casually brushed his arm past one of the rigging wires holding the wing planes together. Steel cables, of course. Harry hadn't even thought about them as he led Nuada up to the cockpit. The two took a few steps away from the biplane and Harry relaxed a little. He realized he'd been holding his breath.

Harry turned to walk over to Buchanan's Camel. The Scottish pilot was still sitting in the cockpit.

“Lieutenant? Do you want something?” Buchanan's voice was a little tense, Harry thought.

“Just thought you might want to meet Prince Nuada. That's him over there talking to Jernigan.”

“Oh. Well, I suppose I should. Thank you.”

Harry waited for Buchanan to climb down.

“I take it that, ah, gentleman represents the Seelie Court?” Buchanan spoke in a low voice. He sounded a bit nervous now.

“Yes,” said Harry. “He seems to be a decent sort. I gather that in addition to being a Prince he's a sort of cavalry commander. It's taking a lot out of him to be so close to all this steel, though.”

“Really? I read the major's notes, of course, but it's hard to believe that iron is really a problem for these people, not just some sort of superstition.”

“I don't understand it myself, but it's real, all right. He's game though, trying to ignore the effects. Still, when he's done talking to Jernigan, let's take a few steps away from the machines.”

At that point, Jernigan and Nuada turned from their private conversation, and Harry led Buchanan forward, moving slowly enough that it was natural for Nuada and Jernigan to meet them halfway, which brought them at least ten yards away from the engines.

“Your Highness,” said Jernigan, “please allow me to introduce a recent addition to our ranks, Flight Lieutenant Buchanan of the Royal Navy. Quite possibly our most skilled pilot. After myself, of course.”

“A pleasure,” said Nuada, extending his hand.

Buchanan was taken left-footed by the gesture, just as Harry had been; he had snapped a reflexive salute.

“I'm honored,” he said, but whatever else he was going to say, he cut off. Harry saw the color draining from his face, and wondered what the problem was.

"You're—" Buchanan swallowed, shook his head, managed to push his hand out before the lapse became grossly offensive.

Nuada recognized that Buchanan was suffering some kind of difficulty or distress. After the briefest contact of their hands for form's sake, he said "Keep up the good work, Lieutenant," let go, and turned back to Jernigan.

"I'm sure Major Quirk will want to pay his respects," said Jernigan. "Shall I escort you to his office?"

"What? Oh, certainly," said Nuada. "It's been a pleasure, gentlemen. A wonderful display of aeronautic prowess. Perhaps I will be able to stay longer on my next visit, but for now I will stop by to greet the major and then I have to see to all these wagoneers."

"Harry," said Jernigan, just taxi my SE to the hangar, would you?" He gave Harry a meaningful glance toward Buchanan, who still seemed somewhat dazed.

"Yes, sir."

It was only after Jernigan and Nuada had walked some distance towards Major Quirk's office that Buchanan seemed to recover himself. Harry hesitated to ask him if he was all right.

"Will you need a hand to turn your prop?" He decided to confine himself to a purely technical matter.

"What?" Buchanan shook his head, not in negation, but apparently trying to regain his composure. "Oh. Tregeseal. The engine's warm, so I expect it will start on its own. But if you would be so kind as to stand ready, just in case—"

"Certainly," said Harry.

Buchanan moved to walk back to his Camel, but then he stopped and turned back to Harry.

"Listen," he said, "did I just make a complete ass of myself?"

Harry laughed. "You came pretty close. Fortunately, I don't think Nuada cares too much for ceremony, though you must have puzzled him. What was the problem?"

Buchanan stiffened, but after a moment he sighed and relaxed a little.

"He just reminded me of someone. Someone who died."

"Oh," said Harry, speaking carefully. "I can see how that might be a bit of a shock."

Buchanan was obviously suffering. Harry didn't think interrogating him further on the subject would be helpful, so he left it at that. He couldn't help wondering though. On first meeting the Prince Harry had noticed a certain resemblance between Buchanan and Nuada. Could it have been a family member, a brother perhaps, who had died?

Both the SE and the Camel started up with no difficulty, and Harry and Buchanan taxied back to their respective hangars.

In the north hangar, Harry walked over to his own damaged scout, which was taking shape once more. The fuselage was decently covered with fabric, the dashboard was back in place, and a new undercarriage had been mounted. The Lewis gun and its mount were gone, and the fairing for the new Vickers gun was in place now. It only remained to complete the new ammunition box and calibrate the synchronization gear before installing the second Vickers gun.

Later that day, the afternoon attack run was another successful job. Eight more pods destroyed before running out of ammunition. On this occasion they'd returned to the scene of their attacks of the previous week to shoot down pods that had replaced some of their early targets.

"These jobs are becoming routine," said Powell.

The pilots of B Flight had gathered around a mess-room table to discuss their observations, but nothing had changed in the behavior of the pods and their ineffective thread-tug defenders, and still there were no more hornets sighted at all.

"I have to say I'm growing a little nervous," said Powell. "Even if the enemy really had just that one hive, I would at least expect some sort of redeployment of the pods, not this sort of herd-like behavior. And I'd expect them to start moving west, too. I don't know if we could destroy the entire front before they got here. But they just float there waiting to be shot down. And why have there been no more thread-tug attacks like the one ten days ago?"

"I was thinking about this," said Murphy. "Suppose the pods are in fact living things, unmanned, rather stupid, and not very easy for the enemy to direct. Perhaps the hive was more amenable to some kind of direct control or orders. It's hard to imagine how, but perhaps the pods were bred specifically for this one function, occupying a region and forming the Shroud. I don't doubt something is being planned, but if I'm right the enemy has some rather severe limitations on what they can do."

"Well that's a heartening thought, anyway," said Jernigan. "Any other observations? Insights?"

"Nothing from me," said Harry, "but I think my twin-gun SE should be finished soon. The extra firepower might give us a bit of our own back against A Flight. They're shooting down more pods than we are with all that extra ammo they can bring to bear on target."

"Splendid," said Jernigan. "What about you, Robert? Any thoughts?"

"I'm afraid I have nothing to add," said Moisan, "but I have to agree with Mr. Powell. I feel uneasy about the current situation. It can't go on this way for long. The enemy has to do *something*. I can't imagine they like losing this much matériel, even if the pods really are bred instead of built."

♍   ♍   ♍

The night of the 28th Harry attended a recital given by Moisan out on the field between the two hangars, where the acoustics allowed for a reasonable concentration of sound without echoes. Among the officers, O'Meara, Murphy, Powell, and Major Quirk were in attendance, as well as Buchanan, somewhat to Harry's surprise. In addition, several dozen kobolds had assembled, including Lambeth.

Moisan arranged his music on the drafting table that he had co-opted for use as a music-stand. He coughed once and addressed the company.

"A few nights ago I played the Chaconne from Bach's Partita number two. It was an amazing experience, but also so moving, so exhausting, that I could not wish it on an audience. With your permission, I will play the Sarabande from the same work tonight. It's also an emotional piece, but not nearly so tragic in tone."

From the first notes, Harry once again felt that strange transition, a sort of liberation from the constraints of time and space, a distancing from the airfield and the canvas-walled hangars, and an entrance into a world composed only of music.

But there was a difference, apart from the different emotive content of the music. The Sarabande was a calmer and more contemplative movement of the partita, to be sure, but tonight Harry felt like he was riding as a passenger in an aeroplane under someone else's masterful control. While listening to the Chaconne, he'd felt more like a balloonist flying through a storm, buffeted about by the gusts of tragic emotion inherent in the piece.

When Harry came to himself again, he felt as if an age of the world had come and gone, though afterwards Moisan told him it had been only around five minutes. He felt at peace with himself. Looking around the audience, who for the moment were completely silent, Harry saw that the assemblage of kobolds, which had started out in neat rows, had coalesced into clusters of five or six, seated together on the lawn. Here and there among the company he could see a hand resting on another's shoulder or some other casual contact.

After a brief pause, Major Quirk began clapping, followed by Harry and the other officers, and then the kobolds. It occurred to Harry that they might never have applauded before.

"I'd call for an encore," said Major Quirk when the clapping died away, "but you said you had another piece ready."

"Yes," said Moisan. "This next one is something of a show-off piece or a tour-de-force. It's extremely hard to play, and I've never attempted it back home without getting my fingers knotted up somehow. I hope the kobolds here will not take offense at the name. This is Bazzini's Scherzo Fantastique, also called La Ronde Des Lutins, which in English works out to The Dance of the Goblins. Just the violin part, as it is usually accompanied on the piano. Anyway, it's a strong contrast with the Bach partita, and since I never could play it properly before, I'm wondering how it will come out this time."

In fact, he played it perfectly. Bazzini's piece was cheerfully frenetic, alternating extremely fast delicate movements of the bow with equally quick changes of fingering and pizzicati. At first, Harry noticed no unusual effects, but after a while, he realized that his visual focus had come to exclude everything except Moisan's hands and instrument. Soon he could almost hear the piano accompaniment, a rolling bass line contrasting with the dancing frolic of the violin, this despite never having heard the piece performed before.

The applause this time was enthusiastic and sustained, now that the kobolds knew what to do. When at last it died away, Moisan bowed.

"Thank you," he said. "I had one or two other small things planned, since I didn't expect this one to come off very well. Frankly, I'm amazed. I realize I've just been playing for ten minutes or so, but I wonder if you will forgive me for not going on? Sustaining this level of performance is more fatiguing than I expected."

♍   ♍   ♍

29 December 1917.

Another day of routine, at least insofar as flying through the fairyland skies looking for giant hornets and flying jellyfish was routine. More pods shot down, and though replacements were steadily moving up from the interior, a strip of more or less clean air nearly 50 miles long and three or four miles deep had now been cut out of the Shroud.

The latest fuel shipment was on its way, and news from the western front, relayed between worlds with the post, continued to be positive. It seemed both sides were getting ready to settle in for the winter, and the arrival of American troops in the Spring was thought to herald the beginning of the end for the Triple Alliance.

For a day, at least, all was quiet.

CHAPTER 12
STURM UND DRANG

30 December 1917.

Harry was shaving in the cottage they used as a bath-house when Lambeth interrupted.

"Your aeroplane is ready for your inspection, sir."

"Repairs complete? Already?"

"Yes, sir. Ready for your patrol this morning. Would you care to take a look?"

He wiped off the blade, folded the razor and put it in his pocket before hurrying off to the hangar.

Bromley and Kensington were present, along with their crews, forming a sort of honor guard as Lambeth led Harry to his repaired S.E.5a, its twin Vickers guns mounted and zeroed in.

"A lovely piece of work," said Harry, looking over the guns while standing on the lower wing plane. "When the chaps at the RAF see this, I wouldn't be surprised if all new SEs came out this way."

Harry climbed down, now looking at the undercarriage, rigging, and control surfaces. As usual everything had been brought to a point of perfection so exquisite as to be embarrassing. Going through the motions of inspecting such a vehicle almost seemed an insult. At last he emerged from beneath the wing planes to address the crews again.

"I think I understand a bit of how you must have felt when you found that our machine-work wasn't anywhere close to your expectations. I felt some of the same surprise on first sight of that ungainly Lewis gun mounted on an otherwise lovely flying machine. The whole aeroplane just seems to make more sense to me this way."

"You might see a mile or two per hour more speed, too," said Bromley. "No drag up top from the wing gun now."

Harry laughed. "In the DH.5 I was flying a couple of weeks ago, that would be noticeable. But in this monster, I'm not sure I could tell the difference. Thanks again, though. I suppose we can wheel the machine out to the field now."

As Harry prepared to take off, the sky still dark to the west and a reddish glow rising in the east, Major Quirk came trotting out of his office hut, waving his hand.

"Good morning, sir. Is anything the matter?"

"Not at all," said Major Quirk, standing beside the cockpit, "but I gather it was you who suggested to the Prince he should come and watch us shooting down some pods?"

"Oh yes, that was me. Sorry, I forgot to follow up with you about it. I hope there's no problem?"

"Not at all," said Quirk. "A fine idea. But seeing as he will be viewing your flight's afternoon job today, you might be able to spot him on your patrol this morning. He'd have to be on his way at dawn to get there in time, I think, at least if he's sparing his horses. I suppose they'll likely camp out on the prairie tonight. Might as well keep an eye out for him, eh? I'm sure he's taking the right path to get a good view of the action, but it wouldn't hurt to confirm it."

"Certainly, sir," said Harry, "I'll look out for him. I've spotted cavalry patrols a few times now."

"Excellent. Well, don't let me keep you."

And so aloft into the blue haze of a fairy dawn, a crow's raucous call sounding from somewhere just before the engine start. At present there were no clouds in the sky, but a red glow rising in the east suggested the possibility of unsettled weather to come. Hopefully it wouldn't interfere with the afternoon show for the Prince.

Once into the air Harry spent a few minutes working the SE through a series of increasingly difficult maneuvers. It was less like a shake-down than a reunion with an old friend. The machine felt alive around him, as the feedback from the ailerons and stabilizers vibrating through the control stick and the resistance of the rudder bar under his feet together gave the sense of a living mount bearing him through the air. He ended with a falling leaf, a forced stall in which control was applied with a delicate touch to keep the aeroplane stable while falling straight down. If not executed properly you could tumble into a spin. It was a maneuver Harry had never attempted with more than moderate success. But this time he had the sense of the wings as his arms, the control surfaces as his hands and fingers, and the rudder as an extension of his legs and feet. And so, he descended several thousand feet with no airspeed at all, almost as smoothly as if riding downward on a lift. Then, letting the nose drop to pull out of the stall, he opened up the throttle, engaged the supercharger, and regained the lost height in no more than a minute or two, the engine's growl suggesting a beast eager for a race.

Resuming a level course, Harry engaged the CC synchronizing gears and cocked both guns. Then he pressed the trigger buttons on his stick. A medium burst, 5 seconds or so, no more than 40 or 50 rounds from each gun—both guns firing, the two belts moving as one, cartridges ejecting to either side—it worked! Of course, it did, but he'd been holding his breath, hoping the guns wouldn't jam, the belts wouldn't tear, that there'd be no defect in the synchronization. But yes, his propeller was still spinning: he hadn't shot it off.

The first time around on his patrol circuit, the ground was still too dark for Harry to spot much of anything down there from the usual 8,000-foot altitude of his patrol. The sun rose shortly after Harry passed over the aerodrome on the beginning of his second patrol circuit. There was nothing to see on the first leg heading off to the southeast, but then he unlimbered the binoculars after the turn north along the face of the Shroud. As he casually swept the optics across the horizon above the wall of smoke, he saw nothing unusual, but since the sun had risen and the ground was now well illuminated, it occurred to him that something might be visible down there. Prince Nuada could hardly have made it anywhere near the Shroud as yet, but Harry wasn't far from the spot he'd seen that herd of wild horses some days before, and he thought perhaps he might be able to spot them with the glasses.

Harry banked the SE into a circular course, the angle giving him a good view of the ground below. Satisfied that the course was stable, he looked down at the ground, his field of view through the binoculars rushing dizzily with the turning path of the aeroplane. Nothing. No horses, no movement at all on the ground. But—was that a flash of light? It was hard to keep anything in particular in view on the ground with the movement of the SE. Removing the binoculars he saw nothing, but then, putting them back—yes, another flash. A sparkle, really. He had the impression it wasn't on the ground, but in the air below him someplace. Could it be?

Harry put his binoculars away and inverted into a dive heading away to the west. When he had lost a mile in altitude and got down to 4,000 feet he resumed level flight and looked back to the east. No need for binoculars now; the angle of the sun was such that every one of the thousands of crystalline bombs dangling on the cables of the thread-tugs was glittering. It looked to be an all-out attack. All the pods up and down the length of the Shroud must have launched their tugs, probably at just about the same time that Harry had taken off on his patrol. It had taken them this long to descend and move west through the Shroud, and now the nearest were perhaps thirty miles from the aerodrome.

Harry fought the urge to turn to the east and shoot down as many of the tugs as possible. His duty was obviously to report back immediately so he checked his compass and set a course straight back to the aerodrome. With full throttle and the supercharger engaged, this close to the ground he was up past 170 miles an hour, a speed that would have seemed ridiculous just two weeks before. It should be only a little more than ten minutes till his return. But then it occurred to Harry he might well be passing directly over Nuada's troop in a couple of minutes. It would do no harm to try at least to signal him, since the afternoon attack job would certainly not go off as scheduled. So he dropped down to 1,000 feet, feeling this gave the best balance of a long-distance view and a chance to spot cavalry moving through the tall grass.

There—what was that? Figures moving down below? Harry pulled up and turned to get a better view. Not cavalry: no horses. Infantry perhaps. Could Nuada have regular ground troops here too for the afternoon attack? That didn't make sense. It would take them far too long to walk to the Shroud, even at double-time, and anyway, Harry hadn't even heard that the fairy lord had infantry available. Besides they were heading west, not east. Was it possible they were enemy ground forces? Refugees, perhaps? He had no way to find out, short of landing and asking them.

Over the next minute or so, Harry thought he'd flown over perhaps a thousand heads, loosely spread out over several miles of ground. They weren't marching in close order like soldiers, but that proved nothing. He slowed and then dipped down to 50 feet to try and take a better look. A blur of figures, half-hidden by the prairie grass. None of them seemed to be in uniform, but would fairy troops even have uniforms in the first place? He didn't know. They didn't give Harry the sense of being soldiers, though he was too moving too fast to study them closely. A mystery, he thought, and perhaps a threat, but not an immediate one as it would take them the rest of the day to come anywhere close to the aerodrome if that was indeed where they were headed.

Moving back up to a thousand feet, Harry thought he spotted more people on the ground to the north and south, but he didn't feel he had the luxury of time to investigate. He couldn't help but wonder about them, though. Surely refugees wouldn't cover such a broad and diffuse front, but would form more of a column? But troops, even skirmishers, wouldn't be so spread out and so lacking in organization either. And whether troops or refugees, surely they should show more interest in an aeroplane flying right over their heads?

Harry almost overlooked the riders entirely, caught up as he was in a mix of anxious speculation and the urge to return to the aerodrome as quickly as possible. But there they were a mile or so up ahead, horses and riders, unmistakable when at last he noticed them. The troop of around two dozen lancers was facing a much larger number of the same walkers he'd been flying over for the past few minutes. What were they doing? It wasn't until he was almost overhead that Harry realized. *Jesus,* he thought, *that must be the enemy after all.* The riders were loosing arrows. And now they were forming up and lowering their lances. They were charging!

Even though he banked hard right as soon as he realized what was happening, Harry nevertheless overshot the melee by almost a mile before he was able to turn around. He throttled down, disengaging the supercharger to give him more time to see what was going on. By the time he was back at the scene of the fight, he was down to a relatively sedate 75 miles an hour.

It seemed that the troop had been victorious in this particular action as they had reformed—but no, two horses were down. And more of the infantry was approaching off to the flank, the troop now wheeling around in formation to face them. Did the lancers realize how outnumbered they were in the large scale? Were they going to try to break out? Harry had no way to communicate with them. But he knew he had well over 500 rounds left. A few minutes spent here wouldn't materially affect the squadron's chances against the tugs, but if he could help save the troop here—perhaps he could at least give them some breathing room, and maybe his action would help them to realize how outnumbered they really were.

Except for a couple of hours in flight school shooting at straw targets, Harry had never done any strafing. But he knew how difficult it could be to aim at the ground and stay on target, so out of fear of his shots coming too close to the friendly horsemen he decided to avoid the actual melee. But there were plenty of other targets to choose from nearby. Many more of the scattered infantry were headed toward the fight, dark blots moving through the fields of yellow grass.

Harry pulled up to 500 feet, slowing almost to stall speed, then angled his aeroplane's nose down towards the nearest group of the enemy. His thumb hovered over the trigger buttons on the control stick for a moment. Could he shoot? Just then he felt he'd be damned if he let anything happen to Nuada if it was within his power to stop it. There was no hesitation, no revulsion. He pressed the buttons, the guns rattled, and the distant figures fell down as if scythed, erased by his shots.

One pass, two, and Harry thought he might have burned through half his ammo. The enemies moving on the ground didn't react at all to his attack. They didn't run, didn't even look up, just kept moving towards the lancers until his bullets brought them down. He turned back to the fight. *Damn.* It looked like half the horsemen were down—dismounted or killed, he didn't know which. More infantry had gathered around them, and it seemed there was no path to freedom for them now. The troop was surrounded, fighting with sabers in the midst of an enemy throng. Still, Harry thought he had cleared a considerable swath of territory on one side of the fight. Perhaps there was still some hope if the riders could win free of their immediate foes. He had to press the attack more closely, even at the risk of shooting his allies.

Flying now at the bare minimum speed possible, Harry felt like he was walking a tightrope, with the control surfaces on the wings and tail as his balancing pole. There, that delicate hitch that meant a stall was coming, dip the nose, get a good line on the mass of enemy troops trying to enter the fight—shooting now, and the enemy infantry fell before him, two rows of bullets plowing up the ground—thumb off the triggers for a moment to spare a riderless horse rearing up in the midst of the action— shooting again, more enemies down... and he was past the fight. Pulling up, not enough airspeed for a wingover, goosing the throttle, banking hard right, and back again, into the melee.

More horses were down, now, but few infantry were left in the immediate area around the melee—Harry had cut many of them down, and the others were now in the midst of the fighting. One more pass, a few stragglers went down—and the breeches of his guns clacked one last time. Out of ammo.

Harry circled back again. More infantry off in the distance, but none within a mile that Harry could see. The fight, though: it looked like a complete shambles. Dead and dying horses scattered here and there around the field, men lying on the ground, no way to tell from the air from which side of the fight they were. There were no obvious victors at all. Was Nuada down there? If so, he might be dead now. But perhaps there were still survivors? It was hard to tell from the air.

Later, Harry couldn't say what had motivated him to risk it. Nuada had seemed a decent enough fellow, and Harry had sympathized with his private struggle against the influence of the squadron's steel machines. But even so he couldn't say for sure why he was throttling down now for a landing on the bloody torn-up field. What could he do, after all, if there were enemy survivors still on the field? He wasn't even carrying a pistol. Sidearms had seemed pointless here in fairyland. And the grassy field might be concealing ditches, boulders—who knew what obstacles might prevent him taking off again. The one thing he didn't have to worry about was a manual prop start. The twin magnetos and the superb tuning of the engine gave him that much confidence, anyway. But in the end he faced the SE into the light breeze and bounced to a stop not far from the carcass of a horse.

He climbed down from the biplane and walked over to the scene of the slaughter. The smell hit him first, a hammer-blow of the combined odors of blood and excrement overlaid with something worse, a sort of toxic aroma, like a failed chemistry experiment.

Then the sights. Corpses were everywhere. First, he saw the ragged forms of the people he'd been thinking of as enemy infantry. But they were obviously not soldiers, not even militia. Some were naked, others wore scraps of clothes. Women and children were among them, and most of these were unarmed. But here and there one or another of these pathetic forms had fallen clutching a knife, an axe, or a club. Dead horses were scattered about too. Some had been almost torn apart, disembowelled and even dismembered, and many showed bite marks. It was possible there were survivors still in the carnage, and so he walked amongst the bodies, bending over from time to time to check for a wound or a breath. Most of the horsemen had fallen fairly close to one another, but a few were further off in the midst of another gathering of bodies.

He walked numbly through the charnel field for what seemed an eternity and then he saw them. Two survivors of the cavalry troop—or was it just one? One figure was trapped under his horse, and might be dead, and the other was lying beside him, tugging vainly at the horse's limbs covering the downed man, but clearly severely wounded himself. The whole area was splashed with blood, and Harry wondered for a moment how either of them could still be alive, but then he realized it was mostly the horse's blood—its throat had been cut.

"Are you all right?" As he spoke these words, Harry realized how stupid they were, but this was no time to worry about it.

The wounded man looked up at Harry, said something incomprehensible in Gaelic. Harry shook his head, and the man gestured urgently at the body trapped beneath the horse's hind-quarters. The body was only partially covered, lying prone on the ground, and it might be possible to drag him out.

Harry knelt in the bloody grass, grasped the rider's arms, and as the wounded man made an ineffectual attempt to budge one of the horse's hind legs, Harry pulled. Fortunately, the blood-slick grass beneath the horse's carcass was thick and had a little give to it, and after heaving with all his strength Harry was able to pull the man out from the slight arch formed by the horse's twisted torso. It was only after Harry spent a moment untangling the rider's spur from one of the stirrups that it occurred to him to look to see if he was still alive. Ignoring some more Gaelic from the wounded man, he turned the body over, put a hand in front of his face—a breath! It was then he looked at the man, and perhaps the knowledge that he was alive resolved the image in Harry's vision from a vaguely humanoid shape into an actual person. Nuada.

Harry tried for a moment to rouse the unconscious prince, not very roughly, as he was worried about the extent of Nuada's injuries. He was interrupted by an urgent statement from the wounded man, who Harry now had a moment to look at. He was in bad shape. It looked like he had suffered a deep wound to the side, and one of his arms was obviously broken. It seem-ed some injury was preventing him from rising to his feet or even attempting to do so. But still, with his good arm, the man was fumbling with a pouch at his belt. Harry bent over the man and tried to help him but was ignored. At last the man managed to come up with his pouch, handed it to Harry, and gestured toward Nuada.

The pouch held several small items including some silver coins, a small medallion, a cloisonné brooch, and several colored twists of cloth. Harry produced each in turn, and the man said "Dim" as he did so, which he decided was a Gaelic "no". At last he came to a twist of red cloth, and the man gasped out "Ta" and something else Harry couldn't make out. He unwrapped the twist of cloth and found a few greasy purple leaves. He brought them experimentally to his nose, and the pungent smell cut through the horrible reek of the battlefield. Something like smelling salts, he decided, and he rubbed the leaves between his fingers, placing them beneath Nuada's nose, even as the wounded man fell back.

After a moment or two Nuada's eyes opened, and his leather gauntlet batted Harry's hand away. He said something in Gaelic, tried to get up, but then paused and almost collapsed to the ground, drawing a sharp breath.

"Are you hurt?"

More Gaelic, then: "What? Oh, it would be you." Harry wasn't sure what to make of that.

"Tregeseal. Please get me up. My leg seems to be broken. What has happened?"

Harry struggled for a moment to get Nuada back upright. As he pulled the prince up on his good leg, Nuada gasped. He leaned for a moment against Harry, who had his arm under Nuada's shoulder.

"Your leg, sir?"

"Ah! No. You have iron on you."

"What? Oh!" Harry remembered he was still carrying the kobold razor around. "I'm sorry, sir."

"Never mind. There are more important things to worry about."

He looked around the field. It was stained with blood and littered with bodies. Not far away, a horse screamed, tried to get to its feet, and fell back again.

"I think—" Harry staggered for a moment, and they both almost went down. The enormity of the situation was only now affecting him. "Sorry," he said, "I think everyone is dead here. Except you and this man. He's in a bad way."

"What? Oh, Conal." More Gaelic, and then Nuada stifled a sob. "Please, help me back down. I must see to him."

Harry lowered Nuada beside the wounded man as gently as possible, but he still elicited a sharp gasp from Nuada on the way down. They wound up sitting next to the injured man, half propped up on the corpse of Nuada's hose.

"Ah, Conal," said Nuada, and then more Gaelic. Harry saw tears streaming down Nuada's face. He reached out, touched the man's cheek, and Conal's eyes fluttered open. For a moment he said nothing, then he smiled, said something to Nuada. Nuada replied, and Conal laughed briefly, then coughed. He closed his eyes, gasping, and Nuada bent forward, kissed him on the forehead, and leaned back. Conal seemed now to have lapsed into unconsciousness, but he was still breathing, a rasping sound coming from deep in his chest.

Nuada said a few more words in Gaelic, sounding very formal to Harry's ears, and then he produced a small leaf-shaped bronze blade from his belt. At first Harry didn't understand what Nuada intended, but then he did, and he knew he could have intervened. But in the end, he held back.

Nuada said a few more words in Gaelic, then bent over and

kissed Conal on the lips. After a moment, he thrust hard and fast with the blade. Conal jerked once, and fell back. Nuada looked at Harry, tears still flowing. "Up, please," he said.

The two men stood in the midst of the battlefield. Harry thought something close to two hundred people lay dead around them. How many had he killed? Fifty? More, even? He recalled the decision to fight, even the beginning of his first strafing run, but after that everything was a blur until he climbed down out of the cockpit.

"Is your aeroplane in working order? Can you take off?" Nuada's voice brought Harry back to the here and now.

"Oh. Yes. I landed after the battle was over. I should be able to fly back."

"Very good," said Nuada. "I will trouble you to fly back to my fort. You must tell my man Idwal what has happened here. He has enough English to understand you. He must muster the men and help defend your airfield."

"Yes, sir," said Harry. "But what about you? There are no horses left."

Nuada laughed harshly. He offered Harry the bronze dagger, which was still wet with Conal's blood.

"Can you do me this service?"

"If I had to, maybe. I don't know. But sir, we can still escape!"

"Really?" Nuada pointed, and Harry followed his gesture. In the distance he saw figures moving through the tall grass, perhaps two or three minutes away.

"Well, I suppose I can probably kill a few of them," said Nuada. "It's our duty after all. Would you find me a sword?"

"Prince Nuada," said Harry, "I have an aeroplane. I can take you with me, I think."

"What? I've seen your machine. There's room only for one. I couldn't possibly fit in your cockpit along with you."

"No sir," said Harry, "but there's a stunt I've seen done. You could ride the wing."

"Ride the wing?" Nuada was taken aback.

"Yes sir. It will be very hard but it's a chance. Will you try it?"

"Up in the air? With all that iron and steel? Me weak after all this fighting, with a broken leg? Death a false move away?"

Harry was going to reply but Nuada laughed. He sounded happy, almost giddy even.

"Of course I'll try it. Even if I fall it will be a famous death. Come on, let's go before I lose my nerve."

They staggered together through the fields. It was only 50

yards back to the SE, but it seemed to take forever to get there.

At last, Harry let Nuada slump down against the fuselage.

"Look." He pointed at the lower wing, near the fuselage. "There's a gap there between the cables and the strut. If you lie flat there, head down, holding on as hard as you can, it might be possible. Will you try it?"

"Yes. But you'll have to help me up. I'm sorry." It was a struggle, but Harry managed to hoist Nuada up on the lower wing plane.

Nuada grunted, swore in Gaelic. "Ah! It's so cold!"

"What?" Harry realized that Nuada had brushed a shoulder against one of the steel rigging cables. Even through his leather armor he must have felt the effects of the contact.

"There," said Harry, "you're in place. Are you all right?"

"Not even a little," said Nuada, "but that doesn't matter. Hurry, please."

Harry took off his belt, looped it through Nuada's and around one of the struts. "This might help a little. The wind will be very strong. You must remember to lie flat and hold on tight."

"I'll try," said Nuada.

"All right," said Harry, "here we go."

He climbed back into the cockpit, strapped in. There were more thralls approaching now, only a few hundred yards away. And already crows were gathering. One black and grey bird almost the size of a raven settled on the corpse of the horse near the SE and cawed twice before it dug its beak into the bloody wound in the horse's neck.

Harry cranked the magneto handle and switched on, saying a private prayer, and the engine caught. The propeller spun up as smoothly as if he'd been in the hangar. Now to take off through tall grass and uncertain ground. Adjust the mixture, open up the throttle, hold the nose down…

And they were off. He had to keep a foot on the rudder and the stick off center to balance Nuada's weight, almost as if he was flying a rotary machine again. He glanced to his right. Nuada was there still, face down on the wing, one arm wrapped around a strut with the cable an inch or two away, the other over the edge of the wing. He seemed to be hanging on all right, for now at least.

The transition from the bloody stinking battlefield to the pristine air and the clean blue skies of fairyland was at first shocking, then delightful. It was like being reborn or escaping from hell into heaven. Harry had to resist the urge to open up to full throttle, but the wind at 170 miles an hour would blast Nuada off the wing, belt or no belt, and so he kept his speed down to just above stalling.

How long had it been since he first noticed Nuada's troop down there? Surely it had only been fifteen minutes or so strafing and on the ground, all told. And now, perhaps another fifteen at this crawl back to the aerodrome.

The time in the air passed in a blur. Visions of the battlefield kept intruding on Harry's consciousness. The pathetic broken bodies, the blood, the awful stillness... Worse than the memory was the terrible knowledge he'd been responsible for it all—it had been his suggestion that sent Nuada out there in the first place, and then he'd killed so many of those pitiful creatures himself.

Approaching the aerodrome an eternity later, Harry had a moment of dismay when he couldn't find the Very pistol in its clamp on the right wall of the cockpit, but then he remembered it still in his pocket. He loaded a red flare and fired it when first he thought he was in visual range of the airfield, loaded another and fired it while lining up for landing. Nuada was still there on the wing, in what shape he didn't know, as his head was down and there was no way for Harry to call out to him over the roar of the engine and the blast of the wind.

This would be a touchy landing. Harry had to balance the unaccustomed weight on the wing while trying to land as delicately as possible. It wouldn't do to jounce Nuada into the cables, and not even considering the steel, there was his broken leg to worry about. In the event he thought he brought it off well enough, with a bit of jarring but nothing too gross. Harry pulled the SE to a stop in front of the hangar, where Major Quirk, several other pilots, and a crew of kobolds awaited him, along with Lambeth. Evidently someone had spotted his flares.

Harry vaulted out of the cockpit, finding his legs would support him, barely. He'd rehearsed what he needed to say while in the air, but found now that his voice was little more than a croak. Captain Devlin was already trying to tend to Nuada, who had a death-grip on the wing strut he was holding onto.

"Prince Nuada," he said, "he's in a bad way. Broken leg, maybe other wounds. Possibly iron poisoning as well, whatever that means for these people. There's a fleet of thread-tugs on the way, probably be here in two or three hours. I think every pod up and down the line must have launched their tugs. I spotted the leaders around eight to ten miles west of the

Shroud line. They're coming in a broad front at around 3,000 feet, should be impossible to miss. There are also many enemies on the ground. Hundreds, maybe thousands. They seem to be something like refugees from the Unseelie court region, but they are hostile. Overwhelmed Nuada's lancers with numbers. Poorly armed and disorganized, moving slowly on foot, so they are probably at least half a day away."

"Jesus, man," said Major Quirk. "You've got blood all over. Are you all right?"

"Yes. I had to land to pick up Nuada. It's other people's blood. Sir, I have to get to Nuada's fort, to tell his man to muster their cavalry. I think I need to refuel."

"No, I'll do that myself. Hold on a moment," said Quirk. He paused, looked down, calculating, then looked up again.

"Devlin."

The captain turned from where he was unstrapping Harry's belt from Nuada, who was still lying prone on the wing. Harry saw a few feeble movements from the fairy prince now.

"Find a kobold medic for Nuada, then take A Flight and locate those ground forces. Just reconnoiter for now, I want to know exactly where they are and how many. We'll have to coordinate on the ground with Nuada's captain. Depending what Jernigan finds, you'll either shoot tugs with B Flight or you may wind up running ground support jobs later on."

"Sir, will do."

"Jernigan. You take B Flight and find those tugs, start shooting them down. I'll need to know after your first job if you think you can get them all on your own, or if you'll need A Flight as well."

"Yes, sir." Jernigan saluted, the first time Harry could recall him ever doing that, and hustled off to the north hangar, waving the other SE pilots to follow him. Harry was about to go as well when Quirk waved him back. "Hold up, Tregeseal, I need to talk to you a little more. You can miss your flight's first sortie." Quirk turned to the kobold corporal.

"Dagenham, get my aeroplane ready. I'll fly out to Nuada's fort and get his man to muster his troops. Send runners out to the squads to the east and pull them back, have them set up their guns on the perimeter of the airfield. Set up any spare guns we have in storage, too. Then make sure there are enough crews ready to refuel and rearm all our machines—we're going to be flying for the rest of the day, I'm sure. I'll try to be back in half an hour."

Men and kobolds scattered, obeying orders.

"Listen, Harry," said Major Quirk, "I'll want to hear your full report later on. For now though, just tell me two things."

"Yes, sir." Harry had recovered some of his strength now, but he was still feeling numb, cut off from the world.

"First, is there anything more I urgently need to know about these two threats? In the air or on the ground?"

"In the air," said Harry, "I don't think so. I wanted to return as quickly as possible to give word, so I didn't try to fly the length of the Shroud to get a better count of the tugs. Jernigan will be able to tell you more when he gets back." Harry paused, took a breath. How could he say what it had been like on the ground?

"The enemy on the ground..." Harry shook his head. "Those people—I think they're just peasants, many of them unarmed. They weren't organized at all. And they weren't behaving naturally. Not like refugees, not like fighters. They were just sort of straggling across the fields. They ignored me completely while I was in the air. Sir, I must have killed fifty of them, maybe more than that, strafing in support of Nuada's troop. But they didn't even try to get out of my way. They just went for the horsemen."

"How did Nuada get caught, then? He must have had time to escape."

"You'll have to ask him, sir. By the time I got there they were engaged. The enemy—if you can call them that—they went for the horses first, I think. They're slow and disorganized, but completely fearless. Perhaps Nuada didn't have a good view of their numbers. It might have seemed at first contact that there wasn't that many of them. He had two dozen riders. They probably could have slaughtered five times their number of the enemy on their own, but it turned out there was more than that."

"I see," said Major Quirk. "Nuada told me something about thralls living under the Shroud a couple of weeks ago when I first arrived, but I didn't know what he meant. He didn't think them much of a threat."

"Perhaps they're not," said Harry, "compared to real soldiers. Still, there are a lot of them. I just wish there was something we could do besides killing them. I don't think they are in their right minds at all."

"Yes," said the major, "I understand. I'm serious when I say tell me if you have any better ideas. But I'm afraid we have to think about our own safety and also about the people we're supposed to be protecting. If we fail, the Shroud may expand to cover more ground. I think we're going to have to fight these people if they come anywhere near the airfield, and also if the fairy troops need our help in defending their own territory."

"Yes, sir. I wish I could think of something, myself. Was there anything else, sir?"

"Harry. I know what you did back there. Evacuating Nuada like that was quite a trick. Even without hearing the details... I can't take the time to acknowledge it properly right now. Still, I have to ask: are you good for more time in the air? I can't spare a single pilot."

"I'll be all right, sir."

"Good," said Quirk. "Anyone would have their wind up at least a little bit after an exploit like that. Thank God there's no one trying to shoot us down. Not yet, anyway. After today is over, I'll need your full report. For now, though, take a rest for as long as it takes Jernigan to fly one job. Have a drink or something. I'll be back as soon as I can."

Crews were beginning to wheel aeroplanes out from both hangars. Harry turned to watch Major Quirk trotting off to his Sopwith Camel. He felt drained. Not tired, but enervated somehow. Perhaps it was the result of being left alone while everyone else went off on their urgent tasks.

"Is there anything I can do, sir?"

Harry turned. Not alone after all: Lambeth was there. It was hard to judge the kobold's expression, but Harry thought he looked worried. For a moment he wondered why, then he realized: *He's worried about me. But I'm fine, aren't I?*

"If you'll take off your flight suit, sir, I can give it a quick going-over," said Lambeth. "Or if you like, I could draw you a bath."

Harry laughed. He must look frightful. "I don't think a bath is in order just now, Lambeth. But I suppose it would be good to get some of this blood off. Oh, and I should check on Nuada." He looked around, couldn't find the prince. Someone must have carried him off already. "Is he down below?"

"I believe they've taken him to one of the unused cottages," said Lambeth. "*Themselves* don't like it much, being underground. And there's all of our iron and steel down there, too."

"Oh yes, of course." Harry began to struggle out of his flight suit. "I'll just stop by to see how he is, then I'll find you back at my own cottage." Lambeth helped him off with the suit, and Harry handed him his goggles, gloves, and scarf as well. "Thanks," he said, and as the kobold turned to leave, he said "Oh, Lambeth, I nearly forgot. The guns worked out quite well.

Quite possibly they saved Prince Nuada's life today."

Lambeth brought up short, and turned around. "I'm very pleased they gave satisfaction," he said slowly, "but I'm sorry they had to be used that way."

"So am I," said Harry, his voice cracking. And then he seemed to be back in the cockpit, thumb on the trigger buttons, hearing the guns rattling, seeing tiny dark figures falling before his bullets, and he was trying to line them up for the most efficient use of his shots. And now he was on the ground, walking among the corpses. The twisted bloody figures of these starveling peasants, discarded like garbage, destroyed wantonly... They were all around him, holes blasted through their bodies by his bullets...

"Sir! Sir, are you all right?"

"What?"

Harry realized he was down on one knee, one hand against the ground to hold him up. His face was wet, so he reached up with his other hand to wipe away the moisture. Was he crying? Somehow, he didn't remember the transition between standing and finding himself down on the ground. Lambeth was beside him, now, an arm around his shoulder.

"Sir! Please say something."

"Oh. Lambeth. I'm all right, I think. Let me up."

"I was worried, sir! You almost fell over. And then you wouldn't speak, but I could see you were crying."

This spell, or fit of weakness, whatever—it was terribly embarrassing, but perhaps because Lambeth wasn't human Harry didn't feel as ashamed of it as he might have if someone else had been present. Yes, that must be why. Lambeth let go of his shoulder, and he stood up. He felt perfectly fine, now.

"How long? I don't remember what happened after I said 'so am I'."

"I don't know," Lambeth shook his head, "a minute, I think."

"Oh. I was—I was back on the battlefield, it seemed. I killed a lot of them with those guns. I thought they were enemies, but they were... just people."

"I'm so sorry, sir. Is there anything I can do?"

"I think... not." Harry patted the kobold on the shoulder. "Thank you, Lambeth," he said, "but I'll be all right now. Let me go check on Nuada, and I'll meet you in a few minutes."

Aeroplanes from both flights were beginning to take off now as Harry dodged across the field toward the cottage Lambeth had indicated. He found a kobold he didn't recognize inside, engaged in tying a splint to Nuada's shin. The Prince had been stripped down to his underclothes and was lying prone on the cot, pillows propped up around his chest and head. He appeared to be unconscious.

"Sir?" The kobold looked up as Harry approached the cot on which Nuada had been laid out.

"Checking on Prince Nuada," said Harry. "How is he doing?"

"I believe he'll pull through," said the kobold. "Apart from a mild concussion, simple fracture of the tibia, separated fracture of the fibula, and moderate disruption of the ankle joint, he has contusions over much of his torso. But the worst of his injuries is an iron burn. Here."

The kobold peeled back a length silk cloth that had been draped over Nuada's back. It was slathered with some kind of highly aromatic ointment.

"Jesus!" Harry was appalled. A deep red channel about half an inch across ran from the top of Nuada's left shoulder blade diagonally down his lower back. The channel was surrounded by an inch or so of dark bruising on either side and the skin all around it was inflamed and puffy. "But he didn't touch any iron," said Harry, "not directly, anyway. He was wearing his armor the whole time."

"Yes, sir. That's what saved him. Otherwise it probably would have cut through his spine. I suppose he must have fetched up against one of the rigging cables on your scout. In *themselves*, the close presence of iron tends to damage any tissue it comes near, even without actually touching. If he had touched it with bare skin, the damage would have been much worse, and he would have been poisoned by the contact as well. He has another minor burn on his hip, but it's nothing much in comparison."

Perhaps that one had come from brushing too close by the razor in Harry's pocket.

"I see... But he'll recover?"

"I think so, sir," said the kobold. "We know a lot about iron burns. He'll be sick for a day or so. I think probably that comes from something having to do with the tissue damage. There will be plenty of scarring, and then he'll be laid up while his back heals. But so long as he didn't touch the metal with his bare skin, he should pull through."

"What about infection? Gangrene?"

"Sir," said the kobold, shaking his head, "I read about that in your medical field manuals. It doesn't happen here. I don't know why, though."

"Oh. Well, that's good," said Harry. Could it be those germs didn't exist at all here? He didn't know enough about medicine to say. "But I see he's unconscious. Is that from the shock, or some injury?"

"Morphine, sir, delivered orally in a tincture. Our hypodermmic needles are all steel, of course. He'd be in very great pain without the draught, and it also made it easier to reduce the fracture." The kobold paused. "I had to insist he drink it. Assuming he responds like one of your people, he'll probably wake up in a few hours."

"Ah, that makes sense. Will you stay with Nuada? I'll have to go back to flying soon, I think."

"Yes, sir. We'll take good care of him. Private Whitefoot is making up plaster bandages for a cast now, and I'll apply them when they're ready. Then I'll stay with him so long as no one else is severely injured, but even if I'm called away there will be someone with him at all times."

"Very good," said Harry. "I think we haven't met, by the way. I'm Tregeseal."

"Yes, sir," said the kobold. "I'm Private Hoxton. Actually, we have met, though. I'm usually in Corporal Bromley's crew."

"Oh! I'm sorry," said Harry, "I didn't realize. I'm just used to medics always being medics, I suppose. You impress me as knowing what you're talking about, medically speaking I mean. How did you manage to cram that kind of studying in while also learning your mechanic skills?"

"Perhaps I am not as skilled as you think, sir," said Hoxton. "We've always known something about bone-setting and the treatment of burns, and I was trained as a mine medic. But all your pharmacopeia is new to us. We haven't had time to learn nearly as much about chemistry as we'd like to, and we've never done dissections or anything like that either, so I only know the basics of gross anatomy as I was taught in the mines. I would never be able to serve as a nurse in one of your hospitals without a great deal more training."

"Hm. I wonder. Well, you certainly are convincing enough as a corpsman, at any rate. I'm sure Nuada is in good hands."

"Thank you, sir. It's mostly just from reading your field manual."

Harry returned to his cottage, where he found Lambeth industriously scouring the worst of the blood stains off his flight suit with a bristle brush and some kind of cleaning powder.

Lambeth looked up as he entered. "I found you a new scarf and gloves, sir," said the kobold, gesturing at the dresser with his brush.

"Thanks," said Harry. "Nuada seems to be doing all right. I'm told he'll recover."

"That's good to hear, sir. I understand he's not so bad, not for one of *themselves*."

"Yes, I think so. So far of the three of his sort I've met, two have been rather unpleasant. I hope that's not the expected ratio."

"I wouldn't know, sir," said Lambeth. Harry thought he was being carefully political. He would have replied, but at that moment he heard a faint drone in the distance—an aeroplane returning. He went out onto the field and spotted a single machine returning from the north, presumably Major Quirk's.

The Camel jounced to a halt near the south hangar, and Harry met the major as he climbed out of the cockpit.

"No one else has returned yet, sir," he said.

"I imagine both flights are still on the job," said Major Quirk. "How is Nuada doing?"

"I spoke to the medic, Hoxton. He put Nuada to sleep with some morphine, but says he'll be up in a few hours. I think he reduced the fractures without too much trouble. The broken leg is probably going into a cast right now. Nuada also has an ugly wound on his back, caused by pressing up against one of the steel cables in my rigging. Hoxton says it will heal in time, though."

"I see," said Major Quirk. "Well, good to hear he's going to recover. I had time to think about it on the way over. Frankly, I don't know if we could have continued without the Prince. All this ridiculous politics on their side. You might have just saved the entire operation by rescuing Nuada."

A crew of mechanics was coming out now to service Major Quirk's Sopwith Camel.

"No need to refuel her," said the major to the corporal in charge of the crew. "I don't expect I'll be going up again today."

He turned back to Harry.

"Well, I suppose we just wait for one or the other flight to get back. Might as well take a turn with me around the field."

They walked out to the east side of the aerodrome. Several additional Vickers and Lewis guns had already been set up on tripods along the perimeter, in advance of the return of the squads from the outlying posts.

"How did it go at the fort, sir?"

"I had a fine time getting past some of Nuada's junior officers who pretended they couldn't understand me, but when I finally got to Nuada's lieutenant, a chap called Idwal, we had a meeting of minds you might say.”

“They are mustering their troops?”

“Yes,” said Major Quirk. “Idwal is clearly devoted to his lord. When he heard that Nuada was injured and at the aerodrome, he made no bones about calling for his regiment. There are half a dozen forts on a line stretching north around a hundred miles or so. North and west are where the more populated parts of the Seelie Court lands can be found, so most of their forces are up that way. Idwal’s sending riders up that way for reinforcements, and is taking his local troops to us right away. He reckons that troops from the next fort to the north should get to us in a few hours’ time, and the remainder should be available in the next day or two.”

“How many will that be?”

“A hundred lancers from the nearby fort, another hundred from the next fort to the north. Perhaps another thousand all told from the entire frontier.”

“Hm,” said Harry. “I don’t know if 200 of these horsemen will be enough to face thousands of those thralls.”

“I’m not so worried about them, at least not as a threat. You haven’t seen one of the ground assaults at the front yet, have you?”

“No, sir.”

“Just as well, I suppose, but I have. Might as well tell you the story while we wait.”

Major Quirk knelt by one of the guns, working the action as if he was preparing to fire. Several large ammunition transport cases were stacked neatly next to the weapon, along with two spare barrels. The Vickers gun had an unfamiliar metal sleeve around the barrel, connected by a hose to a small tank. Liquid cooled. It looked like a good 10,000 belted rounds were available in boxes set aside just for this weapon.

“My squadron was patrolling at Arras this summer,” he said, “with another offensive in store, part of the big push by Nivelle. We were flying Nieuports back then, and were being outclassed by the latest Albatros models. Camels hadn’t yet made it out of production, you see, and only the navy had the Sopwith triplanes. Still, we had numbers, and we’d almost cleared the skies when Von Richthofen and JG-1 was called up there to meet our threat. One of those bloody red bastards shot up my machine badly enough I had to take a forced landing after I lost all my oil and the engine seized. Fortunately, I just made it past no-mans-land back to our lines. A few infantrymen collected me, brought me to some kind of field headquarters where an infantry captain was preparing his company for the assault. He gave me a drink, congratulated me on surviving, and placed a call back to my aerodrome for me. Nice fellow. Because the ground attack was about to begin I was going to be stuck there for a while until someone found a car for me, and just then everyone back at Brigade was far too busy with ground support to help some stranded RFC man get back to his aerodrome."

The major fiddled with the iron sight of the gun for a moment before continuing his story.

"Listen, said the captain to me, we're going in behind the barrage in a few minutes. You may as well call HQ when you see what happens to us. And he handed me a letter. I'd appreciate it, he said, if you send this on if it looks like we didn't make it. So I shook his hand, and wished him luck."

Major Quirk cocked the Vickers gun: a single quiet clack. He sighted down the barrel, as if looking for an enemy to shoot.

"Of course, at this late date the brass had the benefit of all these failed offensives on both sides. This time was going to be different. We had new tactics—the creeping barrage with a new kind of fused shell, counter-battery fire, machine-gun platoons on the offense, tanks, the whole nine yards. Everything was in our favor, supposedly. So I watched from a bunker as the barrage began."

Major Quirk shook his head. He pulled the trigger on the gun and the hammer fell with a sharp click, but of course with no ammo belt threaded, that was all there was to it.

"It was the most terrific thing I'd ever seen or felt before. When one of those pods goes up, it makes a pretty show, for sure. But you need a massed artillery strike coming down close by to really get the feel of hell on earth. I tell you it was like a wave of destruction moving broadside down the field. Nothing could possibly live in the path of those shells coming down, so it seemed to me. And our platoons were running as close behind it as they dared. The idea of course was to get to the enemy lines while they were still hunkered down in their trenches, but it seemed to me there would be no point in racing forward. Even in the deepest trench, I thought no one could survive that wave of shells coming down."

Quirk got up from the gun. He sighed, shook his head again.

"I imagine our generals felt the same way every time they saw an artillery demonstration, every time they called for a fresh offensive in this war. And they've been wrong every time. I had a good vantage on the progress being made by my new friend the captain and his men, and I could see other companies up and down the line moving at the same time. It really was a well-orchestrated assault, none of the screw-ups and botches you may have heard about, at least not where I was watching. The timing on the barrage was right, and at least in this sector they'd silenced the enemy artillery, too. But what they hadn't done is taken out the enemy machine guns. These things"—he gestured at the Vickers gun—"are deadly half a mile off, or even further if you've got a lot of targets and you're not fussy about which ones you hit. So say you've got people running over broken muddy ground at you from trenches a thousand yards away. They're probably making no more than ten miles an hour, so you've got a good two or three minutes to shoot at them before they get to you. That's well over a thousand bullets fired from a single gun during that time. And a single defensive machine-gun section probably has four guns, while a full company might have a couple of dozen—the Germans really like their machine guns.

"So try and picture this. My friend the captain has four platoons, each with around 50 men, running across the battlefield in a sort of diamond pattern. Three rifle platoons and a support platoon. Other assault companies up and down the line are doing much the same thing. That wave of artillery strikes is smashing its way forward, tearing up the ground, blasts of smoke and dust like a black squall line rolling just in front of them. I'm thinking I'm watching the first breakthrough of the war, when all at once the men start falling. I can't even see where the bullets are coming from through all the dust and smoke, but whoever it was had some good aim, probably with zeroed in lines of fire prepared well in advance. The lead platoon is just about cut down all at once, and the left and right flank platoons start falling too. Some of the men go to earth of course, but now they're pinned down, and there's not much they can do with just rifles. The rear platoon, the support platoon, some of them try to set up their own guns, but they're too exposed, they can't do it. In less than a minute, a hundred men killed, and for the next few hours, I'm watching while some of our troops are trying to crawl back to where they came from, and some of them, bloody fools, are still trying to move forward. By nightfall, twenty men made it back to my bunker, and the highest ranking survivor was a corporal. I had to send the letter off to the captain's wife. Writing the note enclosing it wasn't easy."

"But you said this was the Nivelle offensive?" Quirk nodded. "Wasn't that a success? Didn't we win at Arras?"

"That we did," said Major Quirk. "As these things go it was a famous victory, and if the French had won at the Aisne it might have made some kind of strategic difference or other. But since they didn't it turned out not to matter very much either way. I think the final butcher's bill was 150,000 casualties just on our side, for a few miles movement of the front."

"Jesus Christ," said Harry. "What a waste."

"That's what I'm telling you. So I called in to Battalion HQ, had a hell of a time explaining who I was. Finally, I got through to the lieutenant colonel, who by the way had not actually participated in the attack himself and wasn't even in position to observe the assault. He wanted to know where the captain of B Company was so he could give him a piece of his mind for not reporting in, and it took me a good five minutes to get him to understand that there was no more B Company, and indeed all that was probably left of his battalion was his HQ. Anyway, the next day my car arrived, at about the same time as the next battalion in line moved up for a new assault."

Harry couldn't think of anything to say at this point that wasn't either trite or actively treasonous, so he just shook his head.

"Anyway," said Major Quirk, "that's why I'm not too worried about our safety here, not now that I have a better idea what the enemy is like. No ranged weapons, no organization, is what you said. When we get fully set up here, when the squads come back, we can easily man two dozen guns. That's 10,000 bullets shot in a single minute, and we've got all the ammo in the world. This is open meadowland, no cover at all. If they come this way, we will absolutely destroy them, even without strafing and bombing."

"Poor bastards."

"Yes indeed," said Major Quirk, "but better them than us."

Harry rubbed his eyes. They were burning now, and rubbing just made it worse. "I just wish there was some way we could head them off without having to slaughter them."

"Listen, Tregeseal." The major's voice was harsh. "Don't think I want to shed even a single drop of blood here. But I'll be damned if I lose any of my men in a fight if I can avoid it. If any of the enemy are capable of surrendering, I'll gladly grant them quarter. But from what you say, and from what Nuada told me before, they're just like animals. Worse than animals, really. Animals would never attack like that. Even the poor bloody infantry will try to stay alive if they can."

"Yes, sir," said Harry. "I have to agree with you. I don't have any clever ideas myself. I'm just happy I don't have to give the order to open fire."

"For pity's sake, man," said Quirk wearily, "don't rub it in."

"Oh." Harry was abashed. "Sorry, sir. I didn't mean it that way."

"I know."

They spent a few minutes in companionable if somewhat solemn silence before Major Quirk looked up and pointed.

"Flight's coming back. Jernigan, I believe."

Harry peered off into the distance. He could just make out four black specks above the horizon. In another minute they could hear the drone of the engines, and the specks had resolved themselves into recognizable aeroplanes.

CHAPTER 13
DEFENSIVE ACTION

Harry and Major Quirk met the returning pilots at the north hangar. Four kobold crews were ready to wheel the aeroplanes into the hangar for refueling and rearming, while Harry's SE was already set up on the grass.

Jernigan pulled his goggles up on his forehead to address Major Quirk, the rest of B Flight standing at his side.

"All the floaters in the world," he said, "just as Harry said. Estimate about 2,000 or so, but it's hard to say for sure. They're 25 miles off, the lead elements, but the rest are further away, strung out to 50 miles or so. Bearing straight for us, up and down the line, all heading our way."

Quirk asked "How long do we have?"

"They have a bit of a headwind to deal with. Say three hours for the leaders if we don't do anything about it."

"So let us say there's time for six sorties, minimum. Maybe more as they get close and the flying time goes down, maybe a lot more if we shoot down all the leaders and the others are still coming up. How many did you get?"

"I think we got over a dozen each before running out," said Jernigan. "Possibly a few more. Boys, is that right?"

"Yes sir," said Murphy, "I'd say fifteen or so. I lost count at some point."

"All right," said the major. Say 75 per flight, just to be safe. Both flights shooting down tugs. We'll let the threat on the ground wait till they actually get here. That's around a thousand downed during your three hours. Should be enough to clear the lead elements, wouldn't you say? Then we'll have more time for the ones further off."

"I think so," said Jernigan. It might be a near-run thing though."

"I'm not too worried," said the major. "We'll have plenty of guns set up on the ground here to take care of any stragglers. If there are no surprises, it sounds like we should make it. I just hate to waste so much fuel."

"Well, we could always wait for them here," said Jernigan, "I daresay we could camp out in the fields after they burn our cottages. Or maybe we could bunk with the kobolds."

Major Quirk snorted. "You're lucky I'm not a stuffed shirt," he said. "Also, I need every pilot, even the Welsh."

Jernigan laughed. "This from the only Manxman pilot on the

entire front."

"Just keep in mind I'm the only Manxman officer commanding on the entire front, too."

"Yes, sir."

"Right then," said Quirk, "just to keep things simple, why don't you take B Flight out after thread-tugs to east and south, and I'll send A Flight after the ones to east and north. You'll just have to keep going out as soon as you're refueled and re-armed each time, but if things are going well, maybe there will be time for a break a little later, when we can have a council of war."

"All right. Looks like our machines are already coming back from the hangar. Tregeseal"—turning to Harry—"are you ready to go?"

"Yes, sir. Are they still at 3,000 feet?"

"Yes," said Jernigan. "They're so many, you want to come in from on top, like strafing almost, so as not to get tangled up in all the cables. But with no archie and no hornets either, it's just target practice. The big thing is to avoid running into your friends. Or shooting them down. I'm looking at you, Powell."

"I was lining up on that one," said Powell. "How was I to know you'd get in the way?"

"Yes, well, if we collide up there, the Manxmen would be outnumbering the Welsh, and we wouldn't want that, would we?"

"Anyway, it's good to have you back with us, Harry," said Jernigan through the general laughter, as they began to walk back toward their machines.

"Thanks. I'm just as happy to get back in the air," said Harry.

"I won't ask," said Jernigan. "Not now. We can talk about it after this is over."

B Flight took off in formation, and Harry found his spirits rising with the altimeter. Clear blue skies over green and golden fields, and for a brief span it was possible to forget about the bloody events of the morning, and to put off thinking about the grim prospects of the afternoon. They flew east at 5,000 feet, and for ten minutes Harry was able to enjoy the ride.

Jernigan, up ahead, banked slightly right, and following the maneuver on the trailing end of the diagonal echelon formation, Harry caught sight of the distant sparkle marking a thread tug 2,000 feet below. Over the next minute or so, as the distance narrowed and the sun's angle became better for refractions, hundreds and then thousands more sparkling glints became visible over a vast arc sweeping out north and south. As they approached the wave of enemy vehicles, Harry had the impression of an enormous gossamer tapestry strung with diamonds, a vast matrix of brilliant rainbow lights gently bobbing through the air as the tugs made their way westwards against a moderate breeze. Perhaps a thousand of the dark, gently undulating tugs could be seen in array, spaced about a hundred yards apart from one another. In the distance, more tugs could be seen, a second wave, spanning a wide arc stretching from northeast to southeast. B Flight nosed downward to just a couple of hundred feet above the tugs and began their attack runs.

Following their prearranged plan, each aeroplane in the flight peeled off along a different vector so as to avoid the chance of coming into each other's line of fire. Harry was conscious of Murphy's machine slightly below him to his left, and he banked another five degrees to carve his own path further south of east through the tugs. At 200 yards distance to the nearest tug Harry fired a short burst. There was a puff of flame and when the flaring cloud of smoke dissipated, Harry saw nothing left of the tug, the detached cables with their payloads of crystalline bombs now falling freely toward the ground. Another tug was already passing by underneath him. He'd taken so long ad-miring the results of his first shots it was too late to fire at the next in line. But there were plenty more left to shoot at without having to turn around

Harry soon developed a rhythm to the job. Line up on a tug, shoot a very short burst at 200 yards range. Then, trusting the shots would be effective without even looking at the result, immediately pull up to clear the smoke, and dip down again for the next tug in line.

After destroying eight tugs on a southeastern course, Harry found himself far enough into the midst of the things that he pulled up and took a new line back to the northwest.

Then southeast, and northwest again. When his guns finally ran out of ammo, both breeches clacking open in the same moment, he realized the rest of B Flight was circling a couple of miles off waiting for him. He'd been deep in a reverie of concentration, and hadn't been paying attention to the rest of the flight at all. Hastily he resumed formation, and the flight wore away west back to the airfield.

Back on the ground, the pilots of B Flight gathered outside of the north hangar, waiting for their machines to be refueled and rearmed.

“What the hell was that?” Powell was the first of the pilots to reach Harry as he watched Bromley’s crew wheeling his machine into the hangar.

“I’m sorry,” said Harry, “I didn’t mean to keep you all waiting. I must have lost track of the rest of the flight.”

“You don’t understand what I’m asking, do you?”

“Um, no. Did I do something wrong?”

“Harry, how many tugs did you shoot down?”

“What?” Harry was taken aback. “Uh, I don’t know. I wasn’t counting. Should I have been?”

Jernigan had come up by now and had caught the tail end of this exchange, “Harry, while we were waiting for you, you shot down ten, maybe twelve of those goddamn things. Murphy. How many did you get?”

“Eighteen. I used my Lewis gun on the last two.”

“Eighteen for me too. Powell? Moisan?”

“Sixteen,” said Powell, “I think. I forgot about the Lewis gun.”

“Fifteen for me,” said Moisan, “and I did use my Lewis gun, though I didn’t try to reload it in the air.”

“Right,” said Jernigan, “so we were all out of ammo while you were still shooting. If you had the same rate of kills while we were flying, you must have downed, what, thirty? Thirty-five maybe? Even more?”

“Hence, what the hell,” said Powell.

“Oh,” said Harry. “Well, I do have the two Vickers guns. That’s double the rate of fire and fifty percent more bullets.”

“Sure,” said Jernigan, “but you’ll run out of bullets faster, won’t you? I can buy the idea your shots might be more efficient, coming two at a time, but even so you should have been done before the rest of us, or at least at the same time.”

“I see what you mean,” said Harry slowly. “I’m sorry, but I was concentrating too much on what I was doing, so I can’t compare my approach to yours. Here’s how I went about it, though.” He recounted his way of flying, lining up a sequence of targets to attack one after another.

“Yes,” said Murphy, “I think we all were doing the same thing. With so many slow targets in a sort of marching array like that, it’s the obvious thing to do.”

“Well I’m sorry then,” said Harry, “but I can’t explain it.”

“You said you were concentrating too much to notice the rest of us?” Moisan asked. Jernigan and the others looked at him curiously.

"Yes. I'm afraid I didn't notice you all circling, waiting for me."

"Interesting."

Harry wasn't sure what Moisan was driving at. "Perhaps. Does it matter? I'll try not to let it happen again."

"On the contrary," said Moisan, "maybe you should try to repeat it."

"What?"

"You say you were concentrating on flying and shooting, to the point that you forgot everything around you until you ran out of ammo. When my violin playing produced those, ah, strange effects, I too was lost in concentration."

Harry tried to recall what it had actually been like during the recent flight. It was all a blur. He vaguely recalled snippets of his time in the air, lining up a tug, tapping the triggers, nudging the stick down or back for the next target... a blur of gas explosions all running together.

"What now?", asked Powell. "You're saying it's some kind of magic? Harry here is a wizard or something?"

Moisan shook his head. "I don't know what magic is," he said, "but I doubt it. I'm just saying there's some strange phenomena cropping up here and there around us in this place, and it seems to have something to do with concentration. You must have felt it yourself, Christmas night, when you were singing along with my playing."

"Oh." Powell paused for a moment, lost in thought or reminiscence. "Well, perhaps..." He was about to say something more, but Jernigan cut him off.

"This is all very interesting, gentlemen, but our machines are ready. Powell, you pay attention to Harry's first few runs, and then do your own shooting. I'll pick him up when I'm out of ammo, and we'll see whether he's come up with something clever, or if he's just got magic guns."

On the squadron's return to the thread-tug fleet, Harry noticed a layer of dark haze down near the ground, and a few columns of black smoke scattered around the landscape. At first he wondered if the Shroud had somehow appeared here with no pods to generate it, but then he realized the smoke and haze was the result of fires started by the bombs of the downed thread-tugs. Fortunately, the land hereabouts was fairly well irrigated by small streams and little ponds. Though the incendiary crystal bombs could burn out patches of landscape and start the occasional small fire, there was as yet no general conflagration.

Harry felt self-conscious as he began his first attack run, knowing Powell was above and behind him, watching his motions. But soon the engrossing routine of trying to target each tug in line without overflying them took hold. Each time he finished shooting down a line of tugs he was able to recall himself enough to look up while making his turn towards the next line of targets, and after his second turn, he realized Powell had peeled off to hunt his own targets. After the fourth pass he noticed that Jernigan was taking up a station above him, as he had promised, and after the fifth, he realized the rest of the flight was circling, waiting for him. Half-way through the sixth set of targets his gun breeches clacked open, and he pulled up to re-join the flight.

♍   ♍   ♍

Once again the pilots stood by the north hangar, waiting for their machines to be readied for another sortie.

"Forty-two," said Harry. "I kept count this time."

"Yes," said Powell. "I was watching his first run. I could barely see the tracers at all. Must have just touched the trigger each time."

Harry nodded. "I think that's right. I was shooting the smallest burst I could manage, just a tap on the trigger buttons. Maybe not even a full second."

"Jesus," said Murphy, "no wonder. How many bullets do you shoot in half a second? Five, maybe?"

"More like seven or eight from two guns," said Harry. "My ammo box holds 600 rounds. How long are you shooting?"

"I tried reducing the length of my bursts," said Murphy, "and that helped a bit, but I'm finding if I shoot for less than three seconds or so, the tug might not go down. A synchronized Vickers gun fires 500 rounds a minute, right? So for me that was something like thirty shots per kill. No wonder your score is so much higher. I got all of twenty this time, and I knew you'd be taking some extra time so I reloaded the Lewis gun once, too."

"I suppose there must be some benefit to delivering two bullets at a time. Double the firepower."

Jernigan shook his head. "Maybe, but I don't think that's the whole answer. Fifteen shots from a single gun will only take a second and a half to shoot. All of those bullets will be passing through the gasbag or whatever it is at pretty much the same time. And yet we're using twice as many bullets and shooting down half as many tugs."

"What can I say?" Harry shrugged. "Is it really possible that just concentrating on shooting makes the bullets more effective? I suppose we could prove it out next time. What happens if you try it?"

"I already did," said Powell, "but all that happened was I didn't fly so well because I was paying too much attention to my gunsight."

"Hm. I suppose I could try *not* concentrating."

"Don't be silly," said Jernigan. "If you try to do badly, I'm sure you'll succeed, but we need to shoot the goddamn things down before they get here. There will be plenty of time for experiments another day."

"Oh. Of course." Harry was embarrassed. "Sorry, that was a stupid idea."

"Not to worry," said Jernigan. "Thanks to your guns or magic or whatever it is, and to our own improved practice, I think we're shooting down closer to 120 of the things now than the 75 the major guessed at. At that rate we ought to be all right."

Another job, another round of shooting down thread-tugs, and then another after that. Harry had never flown nearly this much in a single day before, though Marie's night flight had covered twice the miles. The effort of flying for so long, the roar of the engine, the vibration, the blast of the wind, it wore on him after a while, numbed his senses and the rest of his mind too.

♍   ♍   ♍

Back at the aerodrome. It was now 11:30 AM. Harry had only been awake for a little more than four hours and yet he felt like he'd been hard at work for a full day. How many more sorties were left to do? He had no idea. He was already anticipating being back in the air. The rhythm of combat seemed to be baked into his nerves now. If he closed his eyes, he could see the array of tugs once more, their deadly burdens sparkling beneath them. He could feel the engine vibration hammering his spine, the living play of the control stick in his hand, the trigger buttons under his thumb—

"Harry!"

"What?" He looked up. Jernigan had just said something, but he'd missed it. "Are our machines refueled already?"

Jernigan peered into his eyes. "Are you all right, Tregeseal?"

"Yes," he said, "more or less. Ready to fly, anyway."

"That's fine," said Jernigan, "but we're taking a break, so come back to earth. The major has decided things are going well enough in the air, so we're going to grab a bite to eat. A Flight's coming in now, and we'll be able to talk things over a little."

Eleven weary pilots sat together on the trestle benches of the mess hall. Major Quirk was outside with Idwal, who had recently arrived on his own in advance of the main body of his lancers. They were looking in on Nuada, who was still sleeping.

Mutton sandwiches had been prepared, and Graham shared out a bottle of H.P. sauce from his private stock. The smell of the meat triggered a ravenous hunger in everyone, and for a time the only sound was mastication. At length Harry swallowed a last bite of his sandwich and looked up from his plate. Around the table other pilots were also finishing their food, MacLeod waving one of the cooks over to ask for a second helping.

"I suppose we have another few hours of flying left to do," said Captain Devlin, "but it looks as if we have the upper hand now. That seem right to you, Jernigan?"

"Yes. We're about ready to start on the second wave, I think. Thank God they don't shoot back."

Powell rapped a knuckle against the table, and both Murphy and Graham opened their mouths to speak. After a moment, Murphy nodded to Graham.

"Never mind," said the older pilot, smiling a little. "I won't bore you with any obvious comment. Did you have something, Aidan?"

"Not much," said Murphy. "I was just going to say, if each of these things counts as a kill, imagine the lines in the Gazette." He pretended to read from an invisible broadsheet. "'Lieutenant Murphy recorded 187 kills on the 30th, ultimo, bringing his total to 203 in December alone.' Take that, von Richthofen!"

"Victoria Crosses all around," said MacLeod around a mouthful. "Aye right, just play the daft laddie. Everyone else in the entire army would say we cheated somehow."

When the laughter died down, Harry spoke up. "I don't want to put a damper on things, but I don't suppose anyone has any clever ideas what to do about these people on the ground."

There was a brief silence.

"We've taken a look at them," said Devlin, at last. "A pretty close look, at that, though I suppose not as close as you, Tregeseal. They're not anything like soldiers, that's for sure. The thing that really seemed strange is they paid us no attention at all, even flying right over their heads."

"Yes," said Harry. "They've lost their minds. I believe they are Unseelie Court peasants who've survived somehow under the Shroud. It seemed like they were following orders, almost, and the orders had nothing to do with me." He paused, looked down, hoping not to cry in front of the other pilots. "I killed a lot of—of those people, early this morning. I didn't realize they were even worse than slaves, then. I was thinking about them just as enemies, and I was trying to save Prince Nuada. It might even have been the right thing to do. I don't know. But I think I would do anything not to have to kill any more of them."

Harry wiped his eyes, and saw Carstairs opening his mouth. He felt a surge of anger, and at that moment he thought if he heard something patronizing, even something slightly snide, he'd be over the table and at the man, but then the other shook his head and looked down.

It was Buchanan who spoke up.

"I concur," he said. "The idea of killing these people sickens me. I found myself wondering just a few minutes ago if we might not be able to lure them under the tugs, use their own weapons against them. A truly demonic notion, though, a sickening thought."

O'Meara shot a glance at Buchanan, and then he spoke. "I agree completely. Killing these people would be monstrous. Almost any course is better than that."

"And yet," said Devlin, "it must be said: if they come against us... Well, we can't abandon the aerodrome. Too much is at stake here."

Another pause.

"Is there no way to free these people?" Moisan asked.

"I don't know," said Harry. "From what Nuada told the major, it seems more like a condition of living under the Shroud than one of the fairy spells. If the poison has destroyed their minds somehow, then I suppose there's nothing to be done."

"I don't know about that. There's something a bit odd here, it seems to me." Graham spoke even more slowly than usual.

"What do you mean?"

"Needless to say, I know almost nothing about magic outside of fairy tales. But as regards poison or drugs, well..."

"Well, what?"

"There are chemicals in our world that can damage the taker's mind over time. I can just barely credit the idea of a drug that completely destroys higher brain function. But that's not what we seem to have here."

Graham paused here, seemed to be working something out in his mind, but no one interrupted him. After a moment, he continued.

"Tregeseal, you said before you had the impression they were following orders. Can you explain that a little more clearly, please?"

"Well, I'm not sure," said Harry, "but when I rescued Nuada, they were converging on his troop from all directions. They had no order or organization at all, but they attacked the horses and Nuada's lancers with their bare hands or whatever crude weapons they were carrying. They completely ignored me in the air. It wasn't just that they were intent on their victims. When I was strafing them, they ignored the bullets, and I killed—I killed a lot of them. It was as if I didn't even exist. Even animals would have fled from my aeroplane, or at least taken some notice of it. So I got the notion that someone had told them 'destroy any men and horses you find'—and hadn't bothered to tell them anything more, like 'try to save your own lives' or 'get out of the way of attacks'. It's pure speculation on my part, but I had the feeling they were obeying orders to the letter and not doing anything more than that."

"I see," said Graham. "That's what I thought you meant. That seems to me to be rather more severe than any sort of hypnosis I've ever heard of. More like the result of a geas than a narcotic, wouldn't you say?"

"What does that mean?"

"Possibly nothing," said Graham. "But first of all, if they can obey orders, their minds have *not* been destroyed. Suppressed, perhaps, but not destroyed. Moreover, if we suppose that drugs or poison alone could not produce such a narrow and rigid mental slavery, and if magic is somehow involved, well..."

Harry picked up the thread. "The effect could be dispelled, you mean?"

"Perhaps," said Graham. "It seems that the glamour magic used by the fairy people here is temporary and reversible. Why not this as well?"

"But how?" Powell asked. "The touch of iron?"

"No good," said Harry. "It's poisonous to them, just to begin with. But maybe the risk of death would be worth it. Still, even if worked, there's no way to deliver the cure without being attacked. They'd swarm anyone who came near them. In a way they're worse than beasts."

"Oh!" Moisan looked excited. "Congreve!"

"Rockets, you mean?" Jernigan shook his head. "We only have signal flares."

"Don't you English know your own playwrights?" Moisan laughed, then shook his head. "Not the rocket man. William Congreve. 'Music has charms to soothe a savage breast.' But everyone says beast not breast, you know."

"What?" Carstairs was incredulous. "Are you serious? You're going to put them all to sleep with a lullaby? That's crazy!"

"I don't know about that," said Powell. "In this world—well, it's the kind of thing you'd expect from a fairy story. It may not be impossible."

"Come on," said Carstairs. "Magic is one thing, but this is just silly. Moisan is no Merlin."

"And I'm no Taliesin myself," said Powell, "but without even trying, I think that Silent Night a few days ago almost put you all to sleep. Perhaps it would work better with some kind of intention behind it."

"But—" Harry paused as he considered the implications of the idea. "How could we be sure it will work?"

Moisan shrugged. "I have no idea. Probably it won't. But we do have evidence that music has, well, extraordinary effects here. Magical effects, maybe. If it does work, it will work over a moderate distance anyway. Even if it doesn't actually break the spell these people are under, perhaps at least it might pacify them? That would be better than nothing. Then we could try the cold iron idea."

"I'm skeptical too," said Devlin. "We have a brigade's worth of these people approaching the aerodrome. And you walk out there with a violin? Suppose it doesn't work? They'd tear you apart."

"It's problematic," said Moisan. "But maybe we could try it out after all. Harry, you said they're spread out and disorganized?"

"Yes, they're scattered all over a wide front."

"Couldn't some of Nuada's men forcibly abduct one or two of them from the edges of the group? Some must be straggling or separated from the others. We could test out both the music and the iron cure."

"I—well, I think it's possible," said Devlin. "Listen, Robert, let's find Major Quirk and sell him your idea. The rest of you in A Flight—I'll see you at the south hangar in 10 minutes. We still have 500 of these goddamn tugs to shoot down."

"Right," said Jernigan. "Robert, we'll wait for you at the north hangar. There's plenty of work to do first."

CHAPTER 14
FORLORN HOPE

2:30 PM. The last sortie of the day for B Flight. Harry had burned through close to 6,000 rounds with his dual guns without a misfire or a jam. And at last the skies were clear of tugs. A ten-mile wide strip of prairie that extended more than fifty miles to the north and south had been devastated by incendiaries, and the view to the east was dark with the smoky haze of burning grass. Despite Buchanan's disavowal of the idea of deliberately using the tug incendiaries against the army of thralls marching their way, Harry was afraid that some of them must have been caught up in the swathe of destruction. However even now there still was no great wave of wildfire covering the region. The many small chemical fires had mostly burned themselves out without merging to form a general conflagration.

On the return leg of their last sortie, the pilots separated, hunting for stragglers on the way back to the aerodrome. Not seeing any tugs along his flight path, Harry dropped down to the deck, looking for the thralls who must be headed their way. He spotted the leaders little more than five miles from the aerodrome. Minor variations in their walking speed had spread them out over a very wide east-west band covering miles of ground. Now though, as the thralls to north and south converged on the aerodrome, their scattered numbers were beginning to bunch up again. It looked like the first of them would be approaching the aerodrome in two hours or so, and they would continue to come, in their hundreds and thousands, over the next few hours after that.

On landing, Harry learned that he was the last member of B Flight to return. After reporting what he'd seen to Jernigan, he hurried back to his cottage where he found Moisan applying rosin to his bow.

"Massenet or Debussy?" Moisan was muttering to himself. He put down the bow, and picked up a scorebook, the rosin still in his other hand.

"Sorry?"

Moisan flipped through the pages distractedly.

"Idwal's riders captured one of the thralls," he said, without looking up. "Now I'm trying to decide what to play for him. Both those composers have very serene and contemplative pieces. I think that Bach partita is too emotional, even just the

Sarabande. Listen, Harry—" here, Moisan turned toward him, but he interrupted himself, turning back to the score.

"What is it?"

"I—well, what if it doesn't work?"

"Come on, Robert, don't think that way. It's got to."

Moisan put the scorebook down, seemed surprised to find the rosin still in his other hand and put the cake down too.

"It's ridiculous, isn't it? I should never have volunteered for this. As if music could really turn aside an army."

Harry felt a burning in his chest now. What if Robert was right? He realized he'd been pinning his hopes on the notion that this would actually work.

"Please, Robert! You've got to at least try it. They'll be here in two hours. If you can't break the enchantment or whatever it is, we'll be machine-gunning them. Two thousand. Maybe more. It'll be like the front, except they're not even soldiers, they won't even know what's happening to them. My hands are bloody enough already. For God's sake, man, I don't know if I could live with myself if we wind up killing them."

Moisan looked up, paying full attention to Harry for the first time since he'd entered the room.

"Jesus, Harry, I know! I'll try it. I will. I just feel like—I can't believe it will work. It was hubris to think it would."

"Robert, remember the Chaconne. Your other pieces. Didn't they go beyond what you thought you could do, and what you thought music could ever do? Whether it's coming from within you, or it's something from outside, it was real then, wasn't it? Let it be real now."

"If it wasn't me—" Moisan shook his head. "I hadn't seriously considered that. I think—I think that makes me feel a bit better about the whole thing. It won't hurt to try it anyway. I just wish—Never mind. But I have still to decide which one to play. The question has me practically paralyzed."

"Just choose one," said Harry. "Whichever you know better, right? If it doesn't work, try the other."

"All right, all right. I'll try the Massenet. It's supposed to be accompanied, though. But the Debussy piece is orchestral too. No difference. Both the solos can stand alone anyway. Come on, Harry. If I dither here any longer I'll lose my nerve again."

They went out into a typically beautiful fairyland afternoon, a brilliant sun set in deep cerulean skies, a few innocuous puffs of fluffy white clouds drifting about in the west. And yet on the eastern horizon a line of brownish haze could be seen—not the Shroud but drifting smoke from the incendiaries.

A hundred fairy horsemen had arrived in the interim. They were camped out on the south end of the aerodrome, their horses grazing in an impromptu pasture that had been set up with ropes and stakes, more of a notional enclosure than an actual fenced-off area. Kobolds had rolled out a few barrels of ale to serve as refreshments for the visitors, who were keeping to themselves. The other pilots of B Flight were already present when Harry and Moisan arrived, along with Major Quirk. A Flight was still in the air, on their last sortie against the thread tugs.

"Are you ready?" Jernigan asked. "That's Idwal over there talking to the major. They've got a prisoner or victim or what-you-may-call-him for you to practice on."

Idwal was a tall lanky man cut out of the same mold as Nuada, with dark auburn hair and what looked like a saber scar along his jaw. His red cloak was hemmed with silver thread, and instead of a torc he wore a flat crescent-shaped silver collar over his tunic.

"Ah," said Major Quirk, "Lord Idwal, these are the officers I was telling you of. This is Lieutenant Moisan, who will be trying to break the enchantment, and this is Lieutenant Tregeseal—"

He was interrupted by Idwal stepping forward to wrap Harry up in a fierce embrace, almost crushing the wind out of him. The gesture was too unexpected for Harry to react to, but it only lasted a moment before Idwal released him and stepped back.

"The Prince is a great man," said Idwal. He had a thick accent, neither a brogue nor a burr, but something in between mixed with a soft delivery reminiscent of Portuguese. "Only a hero could save him."

"I was lucky to be in the right place at the right time," said Harry, gasping a little from the effects of the hug. He didn't say that in retrospect he might not have saved the Prince at all had he understood what he was doing with his guns.

"No. Not luck. Luck is for backgammon and piquet," said Idwal. "Luck is not for the deeds of the mighty. Fate is. Do you understand?"

"Yes, sir," said Harry, though he didn't agree, neither about the roles of luck and fate, nor about his rescue of Nuada. The burden of further conversation along these lines was lifted by the distant drone of engines. The party turned to scan the horizon. Several specks were visible to the northeast, scattered across twenty or so degrees of arc.

"A Flight is coming home," said Major Quirk. "That should put paid to the aerial threat, anyway."

Over the next minute or two nothing was said, as it quickly became obvious that only five aeroplanes were visible, not the flight's full complement of six. Idwal must have been aware of a certain tension amongst the watchers as he didn't say anything more himself, either.

The five returning machines had resolved themselves into aeroplanes clearly recognizable as Sopwith Camels when Jernigan called out "There!" and pointed off to the east. A last speck was now visible over the horizon. The sighs of relief from the company were audible, but no one said anything for a moment. Harry supposed it was desirable to pretend one hadn't been worrying.

"Well," said Moisan at last, "where is this prisoner? I suppose there's no point to putting off the trial any longer."

"Oh yes," said Idwal, "we have him over here."

Harry hadn't noticed anyone resembling one of the thralls he had seen earlier in the day, and had been wondering where the prisoner was being held. When a group of horsemen made way for their approach, he realized that there was a figure lying supine, spread-eagled out on the lawn.

"Staked out? I never thought I'd see anyone laid out like this." Jernigan shook his head. The captive was a wasted-looking man wearing only a few filthy scraps of clothes. He was terribly thin, and his torso was heavily bruised and scratched up. His mouth and nose were bloody, and with his black eyes it looked like someone had recently smashed him in the face with a blunt object. Ropes had been attached to his wrists and ankles and pegged into the earth leaving him no room to move, and yet even as they approached, Harry could see the man was straining at his bonds. His back was arched, and his eyes were bulging with the effort. The man's breathing was harsh, but he uttered no sounds at all, not even grunting as he struggled.

Two horsemen remained standing guard over the staked figure as they approached. One of them had his arm in a sling, and the other had a bandage tied around his forehead. The bandaged lancer exchanged a few words with Idwal as the party approached.

"He says he hopes it was worth the trouble. This thrall put up a good fight when they tried to take him."

"I don't suppose he can be untied," said Moisan.

"Oh no," said Idwal. "He would fight us. We'd have to kill him or knock him out, then. When these two men brought him in, they had him wrapped up in so much rope he looked like a-a—" Here he lapsed into Gaelic.

"A caterpillar," said Major Quirk.

"Yes. They can't stand to be bound for long, though. If you can't break the enchantment, he'll find a way to kill himself soon enough."

"How horrible." Moisan was shaking his head.

"Best just to kill them," said Idwal. "More mercy that way. Months ago, our own wise men failed in doing what you yourself are trying now. The thralls, they used to raid often, but in smaller numbers. We never imagined they would come in such numbers as today. We thought they had all died out by now. No raids last month. No farmers working in Unseelie lands anymore, so we thought they starved. But perhaps they eat one another."

Moisan paled, and Harry thought he was on the verge of being sick. But he shook his head again, and visibly regained control of himself.

"I guarantee nothing," he said. "In fact, I am not sanguine at all about this. But as was just pointed out to me," he nodded at Harry, "there is no harm in making the attempt, and not trying to free these people would be criminal in itself."

Moisan unlimbered his violin case, then looked up. "But I suppose we should wait for our comrades to land." And indeed, the first five Camels of A Flight were almost over their heads now, overflying the airfield to set up their landings. Their engines were loud enough to silence conversation.

Idwal watched the aircraft with fascination. As was not uncommon two of the Camels bounced on landing, one of them lurching the better part of fifty yards in the air before finally settling down.

"Prince Nuada rode on one of those?"

"He rode on my wing," said Harry, not bothering to make the distinction between a Sopwith Camel and a S.E.5a. "There was no room in the cockpit."

"Ha!" Idwal barked his laughter. "I think, myself, I would rather be killed. But it was a notable deed. The Prince will not escape promotion this time."

Harry wanted to ask Idwal what he meant, but now the first five members of A Flight were making their way over to the group, and the final aeroplane was lining up for a landing. It seemed that Buchanan was the straggler.

During this period Harry found it hard to take his eyes off the prisoner. The man was making a determined if futile attempt to pull himself free, but apart from that struggle he showed no signs of awareness of his situation, as his eyes didn't settle on anyone or anything around him. And yet not that long ago this man and thousands of others like him had been living their lives as ordinary folk. How had they come to deserve such a fate? Harry realized his hands were clenched into fists. Killing was bad enough, he thought. He felt he'd be carrying the guilt of this morning's deeds for the rest of his life. But what had been done to these people was worse even than murder. *Someone would pay for this.* He'd make sure of it.

Then he realized what he'd been thinking, and Harry almost laughed out loud at himself. Someone would pay, would they? And how was he going to make sure of that? For a minute there, he'd felt like a king or a general, about to command some horrible punishment be delivered to his foes. No, really the attitude was of a god readying a thunderbolt to smite some offending mortal. But come to think of it his twin .303 guns were more destructive than any lightning-stroke...

"There," said Moisan, "he's down."

Harry looked up to see Buchanan had brought his machine down to earth in a perfect three-point landing and was taxiing back to the hangar. The other five pilots of A Flight were now joining the group.

Devlin saluted Major Quirk. "The skies are clear, sir."

"Excellent. You're just in time. We're about to see if Moisan can do anything to calm this poor fellow's savage breast."

Major Quirk performed a round of introductions between Idwal and the newly arrived pilots, and this allowed Buchanan time to make his own way over from the hangar. He whispered something in Devlin's ear, and the captain nodded.

"Sir," said Devlin, "Buchanan has discovered something interesting, possibly urgent, too. Perhaps we should hear it before Mr. Moisan begins to play?"

"Yes?" Quirk seemed a bit put out, but if anything, Moisan looked relieved.

"Sorry to interrupt," said Buchanan, "but I was slow to return on this sortie because I spotted something unusual on the ground. This time I followed up on it. I saw a group of fifty or so, marching in what looked like close order, escorting a person on horseback."

Major Quirk's look of annoyance vanished. "What? An actual enemy? Where was this?"

"Approximately 10 miles off, I should say, somewhat behind the rest of the thralls. There was only one rider. I noticed them because of the grouping. The others looked like an honor guard."

Quirk turned to Idwal, "Have your men ever encountered horsemen with the thralls?"

"No. No riders at all in the Unseelie Courts. Major, this must be our true enemy. I think I will take my men and see who this rider may be."

Quirk paused, then shook his head.

"Buchanan, this rider, he's headed our way along with the rest of them?"

"Yes, sir, at least, that's the way it looked. Should be here in two or three hours, I'd say."

Quirk turned back to Idwal.

"I know this must be frustrating, Lord Idwal, but if you can hold back I think it would be better to wait for them. On the one hand you'd have to fight your way through miles of these thralls to get to this rider, whoever it is. On the other, if Lieutenant Moisan's music does the trick, we might be able to embarrass this rider, perhaps even capture him when he gets closer. If he sees you fighting your way toward him, he might possibly flee. You'll agree it would be a good idea to finally find out who our enemy is, I'm sure."

"Yes!" Idwal was definite. And then he asked, "But will the music work?"

Quirk smiled. "Let's find out. Robert, are you ready?"

Moisan nodded jerkily, and removed his violin from the case. Harry thought he looked pale, and very ill at ease.

"I don't think there's any other excuses I can come up with to put this off," he said, "so let me just say a few words about the piece first, and then I'll begin."

"The Massenet?" Harry asked.

"Yes. This piece was written a little over 20 years ago as the entr'acte of an opera called Thais. The opera is about a monk in the early days of the church who tries to convince the courtesan Thais to convert and to abandon her life of pleasure for one of contemplation and prayer. It doesn't end very well for the hermit, as he loses his faith even as Thais gains her own, but this piece is covering the period of meditation that the courtesan has reluctantly decides to undertake before making up her mind. At the end, Thais agrees to renounce her material life and accompany the monk through the desert to a convent. Along with the musical serenity of the piece, this idea of the quiet renunciation of the material world is why I thought it might serve to break the enchantment or at least provide a little peace for the listener."

Moisan raised his bow, nestled the violin under his chin and quickly ran through a set of scales. Frowning, he adjusted a tuning peg and tried again. At last he took a deep breath, exhaled, and then said formally, "Massenet's Meditation from Thais."

From the first few notes, Harry knew something was wrong. It was a pretty enough piece, but that's all it was, and it obviously was begging for accompaniment. Even to Harry's untrained ears he had the idea it was being played by only a moderately skilled amateur, with noticeable flaws in the performance. For a full minute, and then for another, Harry waited for that curious otherworldly transition he'd experienced on past occasions when Moisan had played, but now there was nothing. It was just music, and it had no emotion behind it at all, except perhaps the growing frustration that was obvious enough to see on Moisan's face.

Midway through Harry glanced at the thrall pegged out on the ground. The music was having no effect on him at all, and indeed the struggling man showed no signs even of noticing it. It was then that Moisan abruptly stopped playing in the middle of a measure.

"Nothing," he said. "I knew it wouldn't work. I'm sorry to have wasted everyone's time."

He turned away from the company then, head bent, and started putting his violin back in the case.

Harry thought he should say something then, but he felt paralyzed, unable to think of anything comforting or heartening to offer. He had the sense of an opportunity in the process of being lost, a door closing that should have been wide open, but there was nothing he could do about it. Behind him he heard Major Quirk clearing his throat, and he knew that in another moment when the major said whatever he was going to say, the chance would be irretrievably squandered—

"Please sir. Please try again."

Harry looked up. It was Lambeth, putting his hand on Moisan's shoulder. Harry hadn't even realized the kobold was present.

Moisan turned, eyes widening.

"Qu'est-ce—"

"You mustn't give up, sir. It would be too sad if you did. There's still time, sir. Please try again."

"But it won't work."

"How do you know that, sir? What makes you think that? I heard you play the Chaconne, and just a few days ago the Sarabande and that funny piece you said was about us. There was power in your music then, sir. Why shouldn't it be here, now?"

"I don't know, but—"

"Then, please, sir, do try again. We all want you to succeed. No one here can do anything but you, sir."

Moisan took a deep breath that was almost a sob.

"Very well," he said after a moment. "You're right. I owe it to all of you to make the effort." He wiped his eyes on his sleeve. "This piece is by Debussy, it's—ah, merde. To hell with it. I'll just play it." He refitted the violin under his chin and raised his bow.

The first few notes seemed just as artless, just as powerless as before, but this time Harry could at least hear some emotion in the playing. It was a lyrical piece and it gave the impression of a pastoral scene. Harry could almost see a rolling green hillside now, a stream trickling off to the side. Butterflies were dancing here, from somewhere nearby arose the faint friendly humming of bees, and in the distance small birds were singing. Was that a rider on a horse slowly pacing down from the hillside? A woman, yes, tall and slender in the saddle, her white mare graceful as she placidly made her way along the stream. The woman's hair was straw-blond, Harry was sure of that, but he couldn't quite see her face.

And now a part of him realized that Moisan's playing had indeed had its effect. Though the violin was the only sound he really heard, at the same time it seemed there was an entire string section harmonizing in the background, with a harp delicately accompanying the violin.

At length Harry came back to himself, the last notes still sounding in his ears. His eyes were closed, so he opened them. He saw that most of the company were likewise stirring, rousing themselves. Moisan was standing there, bow slack in one hand, violin dangling from the other. His head was bowed, but he looked to be at peace. Lambeth was gazing at Moisan in admiration, and the light of affection and wonder naked on his face would have been almost embarrassing to see so clearly, if it wasn't so innocent in its candor.

At last it occurred to Harry to look at the prisoner. The man had stopped struggling and was lying flat on the earth, eyes closed. But now he raised his head, opened his eyes, and looked at his body splayed out on the ground in obvious astonishment. He opened his mouth and said something plaintive in Gaelic before starting to cough, a weak and feeble sound.

Harry thought to go to the man's side, but Idwal was there first, a bronze knife in his hand. Harry recalled in a flash that terrible moment with Nuada and Conal earlier in the day (was it really that same day? It seemed like ages ago) but Idwal was using his knife on the ropes, not the man. Now he had the man's head cradled, and was offering him a drink from a silver flask he'd produced from his hip.

"Well done," said Major Quirk.

Moisan came back to himself with a start.

"I never thought it would work," he said.

"Certainly you did," said Powell, slapping him on the back, "or you wouldn't have suggested it in the first place. You just doubted it afterwards. But now—"

"Now I don't quite grasp what happened, but, no, I don't doubt it anymore."

"Come, gentlemen," said Major Quirk, "I hate to derail the congratulations, but we have to consider how we're going to work this. We have a little over an hour to prepare for our, ah, guests."

"Oh," said Moisan. "I hadn't even thought that far ahead."

Major Quirk walked over to Idwal and the prisoner, who was now sitting up and looking dazedly around him.

"How is he?"

"This man is a hunter named Menyn, of a border village in the lands of the Unseelie court. He himself is very confused, he does not know where he is or how he got here, but he is a man again. I did not think it could be done, but your—but the officer, Lieutenant, ah—"

"Moisan."

"Yes. Lieutenant Moisan. His playing broke the geas. His playing and perhaps—perhaps." He shook his head. "No," he said, "she is no more. But—" and he trailed off.

Major Quirk let these remarks pass by, but Powell looked sharply at Idwal, clearly suppressing the urge to ask what he was talking about.

"Please tell this man Menyn he has nothing to fear," said Major Quirk, "and we will take care of him as best we can. But Lord Idwal, I think we have need of your men now, not so much for fighting, but as messengers."

"What?" The fairy lord looked up. "What do you mean?"

"We may have as many as 2,000 of these people to take care of tonight if all goes well. We don't have enough supplies for so many for more than a day or two, not to mention medics and so on. Can you send couriers to the lords and villages within a few days travel? I'm afraid we'll need everything they can send our way. Food especially, but also clothes, blankets, and anyone who can be spared to help out here."

"I see," said Idwal. "Yes. This will be hard. Much food is already going to you and to the kobolds. I think it is possible, but there may be... difficulties. I will try."

"Not just to try, Idwal. To accomplish." The voice was forceful but strained. Harry turned to see Nuada, barechested except for a long bandage wrapped around his torso, one leg in a cast, supported partly on a crutch and partly by the kobold medic Hoxton standing by his side.

Idwal said something heated in Gaelic then, while Hoxton turned his head to Major Quirk. "I'm sorry, sir," said the kobold, "but the Prince insisted on leaving his bed. He said he'd crawl if I didn't help him to walk."

Nuada smiled and tried to stand completely upright. His plaster-clad foot just touched the ground and he winced, but then he recovered his composure.

"Thank you, Hoxton," he said, and nodded at Idwal and Major Quirk. "But is it true? You've found a way to break the spell on these poor creatures?"

"Yes, Your Highness," said Major Quirk. "We think so. Lieutenant Moisan has managed it, somehow. I may be looking too far ahead, but if he can repeat the feat in an hour or so when the first of these people arrive, we may have a great many refugees on our hands we'll have to take care of somehow."

"I see," said Nuada. He rummaged in his belt pouch and would have lost his balance if Hoxton wasn't there to support him. At last he managed to extract a golden brooch-pin, a crescent-shaped item holding a large red gem like a ruby or a garnet.

"An croí fola!" Idwal was shocked.

"Just have your courier carry this to the local lords and village chiefs. I'll write something giving the command in the High-Queen's name. I think the required supplies will be forthcoming."

Idwal replied with a flow of Gaelic.

"Yes, my dear brave fellow," said Nuada, "but one does have to keep these things secret until they're used. Ready a troop and I'll have some copies of my note ready for them in a few minutes."

He handed over the brooch-pin, and Idwal received it with every appearance of reverence, taking what looked like a lace handkerchief out of his own belt-pouch to wrap it in, then bowing and returning to the assembly of horsemen to issue orders. The hunter Menyn was left sitting on the ground, looking at the gathering with a mixture of confusion and awe.

"An croí fola is the high-queen's bauble," said Nuada. "She gave it to me in case I needed to pull rank for something. When I heard about this attempt to break the Shroud's curse, I couldn't wait in bed to hear the result. I'm only sorry I didn't have a chance to hear the playing itself."

"I imagine you'll have the opportunity in an hour and a half or so," said Major Quirk. "This will help us a great deal, your highness, but shouldn't you return to your bed for now? No doubt we can work out a stretcher or a portable chaise or something when the time comes."

"I suppose so," said Nuada, but before I do, I must shake the hands of your two gallant lieutenants here. Mr. Tregeseal?"

Harry approached the Prince. He felt an urge to bow, but wasn't sure what the proper protocol would be, and so instead he saluted before holding out his hand.

"Quite apart from saving my life, you've given me the ride of a lifetime. I am deeply in your debt." Nuada grasped Harry's hands with both of his.

"Thank you, sir," said Harry. "I'm happy I was able to be of service. Any of us would have done the same."

"Perhaps," said Nuada, "but you were the one who did. It will not be forgotten. And some day, I swear it, I will return to the air."

He released Harry's hand, and turned to face Moisan.

"Mr. Moisan, I believe?"

"Yes, ah, your highness." Moisan was stammering a little, but he managed a salute of his own.

"We have been killing these men and women for months now, because we couldn't find any better means of dealing with them. We thought we were doing them a favor, but it seems you have found a better way. I am also in your debt for that, but if you are successful tonight, the entire kingdom will be as well."

Nuada grasped Moisan's hand the same way he had Harry's. Moisan stammered out his thanks, and Nuada smiled and slapped him on the back, nearly losing his balance in the process, but Hoxton saved him from falling.

"What do you say," asked the Prince, "when you wish for a good performance? I know you players are sometimes super-stitious."

"Ah, I think on the French stage the players and dancers wish merde to one another before a show."

"Oh? Merde to you then."

Major Quirk barked out a laugh. "You may say that in France, but in England we say 'break a leg.' And I think the Prince has managed that for us already. Let's get him back indoors before he breaks another one. Robert, you have an hour to prepare. Relax, have a drink or two, and get yourself ready for the big event. We'll make sure you're summoned in good time, never fear."

The major issued a flurry of orders then, but none went Harry's way, so he and Lambeth accompanied Moisan back to the dormitory cottage.

"I hope you both understand," said Moisan, as soon as they had made some space away from the other officers, "that you're both as responsible for freeing that man as I am."

"Don't be silly," said Harry. "Neither of us can even carry a tune."

"You know very well I was on the verge of quitting without even making the attempt before you found me. And if Lambeth hadn't spoken up, I would never have tried a second time."

Harry was embarrassed. "Yes, well, if you insist, we can share a bit of the credit, but even if the idea had occurred to any of us, we wouldn't have been able to actually work it. Success or failure, it's really all yours, I think."

"I don't know..."

They reached the cottage. Lambeth spoke up as they got to the door.

"Is there anything I can bring you, sir? Drinks or something to eat, perhaps? There won't be much time for it, later on."

"Oh, yes, please. Thank you very much."

Lambeth left for the mess hall, and before Moisan entered Harry asked, "Would you rather relax on your own for a while?"

"Oh no," said Moisan, "I'd only grow anxious. It's bad enough already. If the playing even works again next time, I'm imagining this colossal crowd of people falling over one another. I guess I'll have to walk around while I play. I've never done that before. And supposing it does work again, what if the range isn't that great? There might be some of them taken peacefully by the music while others are still trying to fight. What if I can't save them all?"

Harry followed Moisan inside.

"Listen, Robert," he said, "I'm sure Major Quirk is working through some of these questions now. There's no way to be sure what's going to happen. It may be not all those people will be saved. But that won't be your fault. Without your playing, they're all going to die. The machine guns are waiting for them. Even saving that one man, Menyn, is a victory. However, many you can rescue, that's more to your credit."

Moisan sighed, put his violin-case down on the dresser, and sat down on his cot.

"I know that intellectually," he said, "but not here." He patted his heart.

"All right," said Harry, "I think I'd feel the same way in your place. But keep in mind, everyone here will be cheering you on, hoping for your success. You have no idea how unhappy it makes me not to be able to do anything more than that myself."

"I suppose it would be silly for me to use the same argument on you that you just used with me? But I take your point."

There was a knock on the door, and it opened. Lambeth entered carrying a platter of food, and Powell entered immediately behind him with a magnum bottle under one arm and a cluster of wine-glasses splayed in his other hand.

"Major's compliments," he said, setting down the bottle, and fishing for a corkscrew in his pocket. After taking a minute to remove the cork and pour a few glasses of fairy wine, Powell offered the first glass to Moisan, then poured out another for Harry.

"Mind if I stay awhile? Not just for the wine, I've been wanting to ask about that piece you played. Is that all right?"

"But of course," said Moisan. "What did you want to know?"

"I, ah, while I was listening to your playing, I had a vision, I think."

Harry asked, "A blond woman riding a white horse?"

Powell's eyes widened, and he cut off what he was about to say, poured out another glass for himself. Then he nodded.

"You too? Might have been a scene right out of the first branch of the Mabinogi, just like I told you a few days ago. I was wondering if it was just me. The other fellows I asked didn't remember any such thing."

"Blond, you say?" Moisan smiled. "I'm afraid I don't remember any vision, myself. When I play like that the whole experience is a sort of a blur. But since you mention it..."

"What?"

"That Debussy piece, I never had a chance to give an introduction to it, to say anything about it. I was a little too anxious at the time, I suppose."

"Come on, Robert, what is it?"

"Oh well, it's called the Girl with the Flaxen Hair, in English, you know. It's a sort of musical poem."

Powell gulped down a glass of the fairy wine, and paused in involuntary appreciation of it. At last he put down the glass and said, "I think it's you who's the bard, or maybe the ollam, Robert, not me. You do understand what you just did?"

"I'm getting an idea, but I'd rather have you say it plainly. It's not the sort of thing I think I can even say out loud for myself."

"Very well," said Powell, "I'll tell you. By luck, wisdom, or by dint of *someone's* intervention, I think you just invoked the power or presence of Rhiannon herself to free that man from the Shroud's tynged."

"David," asked Harry, "didn't you tell me you don't believe in the old myths?"

"I'm not saying I do now, either," said Powell, "not the way you mean, anyway. But I think I have to believe there is something there. It may be she's a goddess, it may be she's something else, it may be she doesn't even exist as a person, and it's just that the music and the imagery is just *right* somehow, fitting and proper within the system, as it were. But with these visions, now..."

"Couldn't it be some sort of autosuggestion?"

Powell shook his head. "That was what I was trying to find out," he said. "If it was only me, maybe so. I could convince myself it was something at least halfway natural, something coming from my own mind. But not now that Harry says he saw her too. That's not a reasonable coincidence at all. And not with his sighting of a mysterious white mare, either. It's all lining up too neatly, almost like someone is sending us a message."

"Hm," said Moisan, pausing to sip from his own glass. "I'm not sure how I think about this now. On the one hand, I think I was secretly fond of the idea that I myself had this magical power, that I had it all along. But on the other, it certainly is a weight off my mind to think it's not my success or failure really, but someone else's."

"It's still your playing that invokes it," said Powell. "You know, I tried a little test, singing those two pieces we did at Christmas a capella to my roommate Aidan the other day. No effect. It's not just anyone's playing or singing that works the charm. It's yours."

"I see. But why me?"

"No idea," said Powell. "Perhaps she just chose you. You were the first of us to play any real music here, if you don't count Major Quirk and Rhys plunking out a few notes on the harpsichord. Perhaps you caught her attention with your playing."

"But why music? Is Rhiannon supposed to be a goddess of music?"

Powell shrugged. "No, actually she has no special connection to music at all that I know of," he said. "That, I can't explain except to point out that in the old days bards were practically priests, druids, you understand, so perhaps all the gods liked music. But one way or another your music has its effect here. Maybe you just invoked Rhiannon for the first time today, and you always had the potential, but it could only be expressed here in this world. Or maybe it's someone *else* who touched you with that power, and that gave you the ability to summon the goddess. Or I could be totally wrong about everything, and there's some other explanation. I'm just pretty sure at this point there's no coincidence about it."

Conversation subsided at this point, and they finished off their meal in silence—cold chicken sandwiches with coleslaw, and some leftover slices of Christmas pudding.

CHAPTER 15
THE THRALLS' MARCH

The sun was low on the western horizon when Harry, Moisan, and Powell returned to the line of machine guns set up on the east side of the aerodrome. Things had changed in the last hour. Kobold crews were manning the guns now. Most of the horsemen had departed, presumably sent off to act as messengers, but a troop was standing by, their horses still grazing in the cordoned-off pasture. A small group of unhappy-looking villagers had gathered, standing near a line of the mess-hall's trestle tables laden with food and drink. Stacks of tarpaulins and blankets were laid out here as well.

The hunter Menyn stood well apart from the other villagers, his rags now replaced by army fatigues. He was gazing east toward the darkening horizon, and Harry wondered what he was thinking. The man had likely lost everyone and everything he'd ever known. Apart from the horror of it, the shock, and the sadness, there must be a strange feeling of having come adrift from the world. Harry wished they shared a language, but then what would he be able to say to the man, anyway? He felt a sickening twist in his stomach at the thought it was possible he himself had killed some of the man's friends or family this morning. Telling himself that others might yet be saved didn't do much to help.

"Reporting for duty, sir," said Moisan, approaching Major Quirk. Quirk had himself been peering east at the horizon, along with Captain Devlin who had the benefit of a pair of binoculars. The rest of the squadron officers were standing by.

"Right," said Major Quirk. "This is the plan. Lieutenant Moisan, when the enemy is sighted, you will take up position a little to the east of the line here, still well within range of the machine guns. You will be accompanied by a squad of kobold volunteers, who will strive to protect you should that be necessary. I should say that every kobold present at the aerodrome volunteered for this duty.

"Depending on the practical range of the effect of your playing, and the speed at which the thralls come forward, you may find it necessary to move up and down the line, or else-where on the field. You will be reminded, forcibly if necessary, to retreat behind the line if your playing does not appear to be affecting the enemy. A platoon will be standing by, ready to respond if any need arises. If all goes well, they will retrieve sleeping or recovering thralls from the field, while our medics will attempt to treat those who require urgent aid, and these villagers will take care of the rest. Is that all clear?"

"Yes sir," said Moisan. "I'll do my best."

"I'm sure of that," said Major Quirk. "But I used the word 'enemy' deliberately just now. Until they are, ah, pacified and the spell is broken, that's what they are. If necessary to protect you or anyone else here, I won't—well, I won't say I won't hesitate to open fire, but I'll give the command if it's necessary."

"Understood, sir."

"Good man. I wish you the best of luck. I'm sure everyone here thinks the same way."

There was a general murmur of assent from the assembled pilots.

"If all goes well, and for that matter even if it doesn't, I'm afraid most of the rest of you won't have much to do," said Major Quirk. "Lieutenant Buchanan and Captain Jernigan have a little night-flying experience, so they'll be standing by their machines, in case there's some use for ground support."

Murphy raised his hand. "What about that organized group that Buchanan found?"

"We'll see if they deign to approach our position here," said Quirk. "Frankly, I doubt they will, whether or not Moisan's playing has its effect. However, Lord Idwal will have a squadron of horsemen camped out behind the hill over there waiting for an opportunity. Once we've dealt with the thralls, if the enemy group hasn't approached, we might be able to fly reconnaissance to find them since the moon will be up soon after sunset. But if the enemy does show up here—well, we'll have to play it by ear... Sorry about that, Robert. It's possible they too will be affected by the playing, but if not, the horsemen should be able to chase them down if they try to flee. And if they come against us..." Major Quirk glanced at the line of machine guns. "Well, that will be too bad for them," he said.

After a pause, Harry asked, "Sir, may I accompany Robert as he plays? There may not be that much I can do to help, but after this morning—" he cut himself off, not knowing how to explain himself without seeming too self-pitying.

Major Quirk looked sharply at Harry, reminding him of the way Captain Fish had looked him in the face after his return from his first combat against those German pilots. After a moment he nodded.

"Very well," he said, and held up his hand as more voices were about to be added to Harry's. "The rest of you, though, I don't think so. Harry is Robert's roommate, after all. Too many would just get in the way. The rest of you can act as observers, watch for any stragglers coming in from the odd direction, and if an emergency arises you might be needed as pilots, night-flying experience or not."

"Sir, I think I see something." Devlin handed the binoculars over to Major Quirk and pointed a little to the north of east.

"Ah, yes," said the major after a few moments. "I'd say they're around a mile and half away. I think we may expect the first of our guests in twenty minutes or so. Ryan, if you would be so kind as to take a turn around the hill to let Idwal know, I'll inform Prince Nuada myself."

The next few minutes seemed at once to rush by and to take forever to pass. The brilliant red eye of the setting sun lit fiery outlines in a cloud bank on the western horizon. Long ghostly fingers of pink and purple stretched high over the dome of the sky until the last crimson glint of the solar disk disappeared into the west. It was that curious transition from day to dusk, during which from one moment to the next the quality of the light changes, the sky growing visibly darker, especially in the east.

Harry was waiting with Moisan, along with Lambeth and ten other kobolds looking very military with their tin hats and Lee-Enfields. To the east, the first of the thralls were clearly visible now only a thousand yards away, walking faster now than Harry had seen earlier that day. Perhaps fifty of them were within a mile, but hundreds could be seen in the distance, and no doubt many more were on their way. All of them seemed to be converging in straight lines on the airfield, with no attempt being made to maneuver or encircle the base.

"All right, gentlemen," said Major Quirk, "I believe you can take up your position. Far enough past our line to attract their attention, not so far as to make it hard to return. Lieutenant Moisan, you are in charge of your detachment. You may begin playing at will. I expect you to retreat at once to our lines if you feel yourself to be in danger."

"Yes, sir."

"Tregeseal, I understand that while he's playing Robert may not be able to do much else. If he's absorbed in the music and anything goes wrong, you must make the decision for him. Try not to get distracted."

"Yes, sir," said Harry. "Understood."

"Very good."

They exchanged salutes and then they moved out past the

line of machine guns. Moisan walked in the center of a half-circle of kobolds, Harry to his left and Lambeth to his right. Their batman had joined the kobold squad without saying a word, but Harry was strongly conscious of his presence. The other kobolds were led by a corporal Harry hadn't met before. It seemed Lambeth was accompanying them independently, not as a member of the squad, but the corporal showed no hesitation in accepting him into their company.

The patch of meadowland at which they stopped was a trifle higher than the surrounding terrain, just enough to be prominent on the mostly flat lawn. The ground was tufted with grass and the occasional spray of clover, and the yellow heads of buttercups stood out against the dark background of the field which was turning from green to grey in the slowly dying twilight. There was a lone alder tree not far off to the right, but aside from that there was nothing to block their view east all the way to the horizon. Turning back for a moment, Harry could see the machine gun crews silhouetted against the brighter light to the west, and now he heard engines starting up. Buchanan and Jernigan, no doubt, preparing to take off.

"Well," said Moisan, "here we go. How far would you say they are, now?"

"Four hundred yards," said Harry. "Say they walk a hundred in a minute. Perhaps you should start playing when the leader is a hundred yards off?"

"Yes," said Moisan. "That sounds right. The whole piece lasts only three minutes, so when I finish that may be time to move."

"Good."

"Corporal," said Moisan, turning to the rifleman with two stripes on his sleeve, "I think we haven't met before."

"Yes, sir," said the kobold. "Corporal Wandsworth, at your service."

"Thank you for accompanying me. I hope you won't need to use your rifles."

"We hope so too, sir. And if I may say so, sir, it's an honor to guard you, sir."

"And you, Lambeth," said Moisan, "I very much appreciate you coming with me as well."

"I won't let anything happen to you, sir. I promise you that." The kobold's eyes were fixed on Moisan's, and Harry wondered if the Frenchman was aware of the depth of Lambeth's regard. A slight stammer suggested that perhaps he did.

"W-well, thank you all. I'll try to calm down for a minute, and then I'll begin."

Moisan unlimbered his violin and handed the case to Lambeth, who slung it over his shoulder. He stood with head bowed and eyes closed for a minute, taking deep breaths. The first of the thralls walked closer, inexorably, and now Harry could see their faces clearly, even in the darkening twilight.

Christ, he thought, *that one's just a little girl.* The leader, or rather the closest of the walkers, looked to be no more than ten or eleven years old. Tatters of a smock on her wasted thin body, naked legs scratched and stained with dried blood, she was gazing straight at him, face devoid of emotion or expression. Someone's daughter she was, perhaps someone's sister—and he thought of his own sister Jennifer, how he would feel if anything happened to her. The cold rage he'd felt before flared hot and bright now. *Someone will pay*, he thought. *For sure.*

A hundred yards away, now, and Harry thought to say something to Moisan, but before he could the French pilot slid the violin under his chin and without further preparation began to play.

From the first few notes, Harry could hear the power in the music. Even after the successful trial, that had been a question he hadn't dared seriously consider: *would it work a second time*? And though Moisan's playing had obviously achieved that supreme plateau of skill and emotion that meant he was successful in whatever it was he was doing—invocation, evocation, or who knew what—even so, the thralls were still coming closer. *We should have done more tests*, he thought, *determined the effective range.* Harry felt calmer than he should rightfully be, perhaps an effect of the music, but he wasn't allowing himself to fall into the sort of reverie he'd felt on previous occasions. It was too important that he remain alert and able to act, and so he felt the music was washing around him, like a river current flowing around an island.

Eighty yards away. And still they came. Sixty. Through the music, Harry heard distinctly a series of ratcheting clacks from behind him. Machine gun crews cocking their guns. Wandsworth and the kobold guards showed no signs of concern, however, and Harry managed to restrain himself as well. No sense in jarring Moisan out of his trance, if that's what it was. The little girl was still out in front. Harry resolved that if all else failed, he'd at least try to overpower her, and forcibly bring her back to their lines.

Fifty yards, and closer. Time seemed to stand still. When she was around forty yards off, the little girl staggered. For a moment an odd look seemed to come over her face, and then she yawned hugely and sank to the ground. Those behind her were affected similarly as they approached. Some stood swaying for a while, and others fell, tried to get up, and fell again. But one way or another after a few moments' exposure to the playing each of the approaching thralls fell completely asleep.

Moisan continued his playing for another two minutes, long enough for fifty thralls to be affected by the music. At last he brought the piece to its conclusion, and looked up, swaying a little unsteadily himself for a moment.

"Dieu merci! It worked again."

Harry looked around. More thralls were converging on their position from a broad arc to the east. They were indeed attracting the thralls' attention, which was a good thing considering the limited range of the musical effect. He'd been concerned that some would slip by them to the sides, but it seemed this was not going to be a problem, at least not yet. Still, if they didn't move at all, the sleeping bodies would pile up on the perimeter, and soon it would become difficult to manage the situation.

"Let's move a little distance," said Harry, "and give the rescue squads a chance to recover some of these sleeping beauties. Quick, before they get too close."

They ran a hundred feet to the north, and if the situation wasn't so dangerous it would have been funny to see Moisan sprinting, bow in one hand and violin in the other, accompanied by a squad of riflemen. But it was unnerving to see the whole formation of nearby thralls changing their path to follow them. The nearest of the newcomers was only twenty-five yards away now, and some seemed to be wavering, perhaps undecided between following Moisan or heading past the little group to the line of guns.

"All right. Let's stop here. We can't let any of them get by."

"Yes," said Moisan, "and here I go again."

Again the music swelled forth, and this time it had immediate effect on the nearest thralls. Harry was gratified to see that the thralls who had been wavering in their path headed straight for the music now; apparently the sound was attracting them, not just the physical presence of the musician and his guards. Meanwhile Harry could see groups of kobolds sprinting out toward the fallen bodies, loading them into stretchers. It looked to be risky work, as other thralls were still active nearby, but for the moment at least they were ignoring the stretcher-bearers and making for the source of the music.

Another three minutes of Debussy, and another sprint to a new location. The number of thralls was increasing. They'd put almost 200 of them to sleep, and now the main body was coming closer. The rescue squads were struggling to keep up with the pace, and they had to abandon many of the sleepers temporarily as too many other thralls were coming close. But fortunately, most of the thralls' attention was still focused on Moisan and his playing.

Another run to a new position. This time Moisan tripped and almost fell, but Lambeth caught him easily, holding him upright with just one hand. From seeing them so easily lifting and moving his damaged scout around, Harry had understood that the kobolds were strong, but this was brought home now with Lambeth hoisting Moisan back to his feet almost effortlessly.

"Th-thank you," said Moisan. He was breathing hard, and looked rather pale. Harry wanted to ask if he was all right, but dared not. Hundreds more thralls were approaching now, and Moisan had no time or breath to spare. He brought the violin back up to his chin and began once more to play.

Once more the music welled up, and as before it was clear that Moisan had brought forth whatever power it was that was having its effect on the thralls. But this time the music seemed perceptibly weaker, the circle of its influence was narrower, just twenty-five yards or so across, not the forty it had been.

Jesus, he's running out of strength, Harry thought. The crews had been able to save perhaps fifty of the thralls so far, with well over a hundred still asleep on the ground, but a thousand more were all around them, and who knew how many were coming behind them. He looked on in frustration at Moisan standing there just a few feet away, his playing as exquisite as ever, but its effect diminishing, the sound be-coming weaker by the second. What could he do? There was nothing he could think of. Lambeth looked at him then, almost beseechingly, but without saying anything, and Harry knew he was thinking the same thing. Harry shook his head. The radius of the music's effect was barely twenty yards now, and more thralls than ever were converging on them. In another minute, they'd have to break off and run for their lives, and then... the machine guns would open fire.

Harry wouldn't have done it if it wasn't a dire moment, and afterwards he couldn't say what had motivated the gesture. To physically interfere with Moisan's playing seemed like a foolish thing to do. But it would only be a few moments and he'd have to interrupt him anyway. He wanted to put a hand on Moisan's shoulder just as a comforting gesture, but the Frenchman's bowing was too active, and he'd mess up the playing for sure. So Harry wound up putting a hand on Moisan's back, on his spine below the neck. It was an awkward gesture, but he felt a strange connection, and as he made contact, he could almost sense Moisan's ebbing strength.

"Robert…" But Moisan hadn't noticed him, was still wrapped up in his playing. Harry tried to will the music to grow stronger, but nothing happened. He looked up. The nearest thralls were just ten yards away now, staggering, sinking to their knees, falling asleep, but others were coming behind, pressing forward relentlessly.

Harry bowed his head. In another moment, he'd give the word, and they'd have to run back to the guns. But for that one last moment it was nice to listen to the music, the flowing run of it, and again he could hear an entire spectral orchestra backing Moisan up, the string section harmonizing, the harp running glissandos and arpeggios up and down the scale behind Moisan's melodic line. And once again, he saw that dreamlike scene, the hillside, the blond rider on a white horse. He couldn't see her clearly, couldn't make out her face at all, but nevertheless, Harry had the sense the rider was smiling at him, and he felt a sort of warmth, as if the sun had emerged from the clouds and was shining down on him.

He looked up with a start. Time had passed. The music had stopped. He'd taken his hand from Moisan's back. Moisan himself was still standing there, swaying slightly, head bowed. The violin was dangling loosely from his left hand, while his right arm was slack, the bow fallen to the ground.

"What the hell?"

Harry looked around. They stood at the center of an array of hundreds upon hundreds of sleeping thralls, laid out on the ground over an enormous fan-shaped area that extended far to the east, for a mile or more. The kobold guards were half-asleep on their feet, just now rousing from the effects of the music. Only Lambeth seemed to be reasonably alert, and now he stepped forward to support Moisan, who was in danger of falling over.

"Mince alors! Quoi?" Moisan returned to his senses with a start of his own. "What was that?"

"I'm not sure," said Harry, "but it seems to have worked in our favor, anyway. Lambeth, were you awake the whole time? How long was it?"

"I'm not sure, sir. I remember... I remember I was about to do something. Mr. Moisan's playing was losing its effect, I think, and the thralls were getting too close. Then... Then you reached out and put your hand on his back, and, well, that's where I'm not sure what happened next. Oh, but I do recall Mr. Moisan finished his piece, and then I realized I'd been standing here all that time not doing anything at all. That was just a moment ago. So if he was half-way through, it must have only been a minute or so."

Moisan bent over to pick up his bow. He shook his head, looked at it like he'd never seen it before.

"I don't know," he said. "I had the feeling I was in a small dark room, with the walls closing in on me. The playing was holding them back, I think, but it was terribly exhausting to keep it up. And then, all of a sudden, it was if the walls just collapsed outwards, and I was standing playing in a sunlit field, and she—and someone was smiling at me. I remember being so happy, but at the same time I knew I had to finish the piece. And now, here we are, and..." he gestured vaguely at the fallen thralls.

"I think they're all asleep," said Harry.

"I'm amazed. I mean to say I was amazed that the playing worked at all at first, but now—Listen, Harry, was it you who helped me? From what I recall, and what Lambeth said... I think I was on my last legs. And now this... Did you do something?"

"I wanted to, for sure," said Harry, "but I don't know if I actually did. All I did was put my hand on your back. Why should that have done anything? But I saw that vision again. The hillside, the golden-haired woman on the white horse. I almost hate to say it, but I think Powell might be right. Perhaps... perhaps if Rhiannon was somehow involved, then I might have helped you evoke her, or her power, or whatever it is..." He trailed off, not sure if he was even making sense.

"It could be. Either way, it looks like we've earned a bit of a rest anyway. If there are more of them out there, they're too far away to see. It's gotten quite dark, hasn't it?"

Indeed, the dusk had given way to evening. It was still some ways off from full darkness, but a few stars could now be seen in the sky to the east, and to the west Harry saw Venus riding a few degrees above the guttering purple glow that was all that was left of the sunset.

"I suppose we might as well go back and report. If there any more of them out there, it will be quite some time before they arrive. Come on, Wandsworth. Let's go."

They turned to start walking. Harry felt light-headed, almost dizzy, and at one point he almost tripped and fell over nothing in particular.

"Take care, sir. Are you all right?" Lambeth was there to take his arm.

"Yes," said Harry. "Just tired. I think this back-touching-in-support-of-the-goddess business must really take it out of you."

Moisan laughed. "I feel rather like a hot-air balloon, myself," he said, "as if I might come unmoored and float off at any moment. It's not a bad feeling, though. Rather like one imagines getting drunk on champagne must be before one ever tries the stuff. If only it was really that nice..."

As they made their way back towards the machine guns, stretcher-bearers were filtering out to the fallen thralls. Among them, some other figures were darting, rushing about, looking around in confusion. A few of the thralls who had already recovered their senses were back on the field now, searching frantically for friends and family. Harry's joy in the situation was tempered by the sight of them. Perhaps few if any of would find anyone they were looking for. Of all the maybe hundreds of thousands or more who must have lived under the Shroud, so few were left on this stretch of meadowland...

But then he saw it. The hunter Menyn on his knees, in his arms the little girl Harry had seen at the head of the first group of thralls. The man was crying, sobbing, but the girl was smiling, happy, looking a little puzzled as she hugged him. A daughter, perhaps? Or a younger sister?

"Sir? Are you all right?"

What was it you were supposed to say at a time like this? Oh, yes. "Just something in my eye," said Harry, and laughed out loud.

♍   ♍   ♍

"That was astonishing," said Major Quirk. "It appeared you were having some sort of difficulties out there, and then they all just fell over. It was a sort of a wave, and they all went down like bowling pins. I don't think the ones further away could even have heard you playing."

"I can't really explain it," said Moisan. "We have a sort of an idea, but... well I hardly even like to say just now. It wasn't anything very deliberate, though, or we would have done it to begin with."

"I see," said Quirk. "Do you think you've put them all to sleep?"

"I'm not sure. It's gotten too dark to see very far. There may be more coming. We might have to go back out there."

"Oh well, as to that we may be able to shed some light on the matter."

Major Quirk produced a Very pistol and shot a white flare into the sky. The flare shone brilliantly for a few seconds before arcing back to earth where it lay sparking and smoking on the ground, but it didn't cast much light on the field.

"Pardon me?"

"Just wait a minute," said the major.

After a brief pause, they heard the faint drone of engines overhead. The sound grew steadily louder.

"I had them go up high enough that the noise wouldn't be a distraction to your playing," said Quirk. "They're having to dive to get low enough to be helpful."

Then they saw two white lights appear high overhead, each vastly brighter than the flare Major Quirk had shot off. The lights very slowly drifted downward over the field, casting a stark illumination a wide area. While the first two lights were still in the air, another pair appeared high in the sky, further to the east.

"Star shells," said Major Quirk. "We rigged bombing cables on Buchanan's and Jernigan's machines. They've each got two pairs of parachute shells. White flare if we need illumination, and red's if we need support. Now then, Ryan, d'you see anything?"

Devlin was scanning the field with his binoculars.

"Just a whole lot of sleeping thralls," he said. "A few of them are getting back up now, but they seem confused. I think the spell's been broken for good. We'd better get more people out there before they get themselves into trouble, though. Don't want them thinking we're going to hurt them."

"Right," said Quirk. "Hammersmith!"

"Yes sir." The kobold batman was at the major's side.

"Tell Dagenham to belay the stretcher duty for the moment. Have his squads go talk to those folk out there, try to get them to understand we're trying to help, see if any of them are in good enough shape to help with the others. Oh, yes. Where's that hunter from before? Menyn, was it?"

"He's with some of the others, sir," said Hammersmith. "Shall I fetch him?"

"If you please."

A minute, and the former thrall appeared. He was escorted by a kobold, the little girl at his side. The kobold said something to Menyn, and the hunter rushed forward, obviously surprising Major Quirk. He came to a stop in front of the major and sank to his knees, shuffling forward with his head bowed to embrace the major's thighs.

Quirk looked terribly embarrassed, but after a moment he put a hand on Menyn's shoulder, and when the man looked up, he helped him back to his feet. Menyn said something then, a rapid stream of Gaelic.

"I'm sorry," said Quirk, "I didn't catch all that. What did he say?"

The kobold translated. "Ah, he says he is your man forever, everything he has is yours, and he thanks you for rescuing his people and especially for saving his daughter."

"Oh."

The major attempted some Gaelic of his own, and Menyn bowed and retreated.

"I told him we need all the assistance we can get taking care of his people out there, and I asked to him to find those who can help from those who are recovering. At least they can reassure those people they needn't run away. Hammersmith, would you find a squad to go around with him, in case they need something we can easily provide?"

"Yes, sir."

"Oh hell," said Devlin, still scanning the horizon with his binoculars."

"What?"

"I think... Yes. It's that group Buchanan spotted back in the afternoon. They're coming."

He handed the binoculars once more to Quirk, pointed out the bearing. Harry peered in that direction, but even with the star shell illumination it was too far in the distance for him to see anything unaided.

"Damn it," said Major Quirk, "not now, with all this still unsettled. Right then. Send a runner to Idwal, tell him to get ready in case pursuit is needed. How long till they get here, do you make it? Ten minutes?"

"I'd say so," said Captain Devlin. "They're coming pretty fast. I think the escorts are running to keep up with the rider."

"Try to get these people clear of the field in time if it's possible. I have to go tell Nuada. He insisted on being informed if an actual enemy showed up."

"Sir, if you please!" Harry spoke up. "What did you see?"

"Fifty men, maybe, and a rider too, coming this way," said Quirk. "You agree, Ryan?"

"Yes. I wonder what they're thinking. Even if we didn't have our guns, they wouldn't be much of a threat."

Another hiatus.

Squads of kobolds were circulating once more among the fallen thralls, carrying them back behind the line of guns, aided by those who had managed to recover to the point of understanding where they were and what had happened to them. Many of the awakened victims were in such a state of confusion or extremity they were unable to do much of anything at all, but even so a growing number were helping to minister to their compatriots.

The star shells guttered out before the enemy group came close enough to be visible to unaided eyes. The last vestiges of the sunset were gone now, but it was a clear night and starlight alone was enough to give moderate illumination to the field.

Harry and Moisan were standing near the guns, watching all this. Harry felt like he should be doing something, but he didn't think one more hand out in the field with the thralls would do all that much good, especially considering he didn't speak the language. Anyway, Moisan was clearly exhausted, and Harry thought it best to stay with him, in case any more playing would be required. Lambeth had promoted a few mugs of ale from the spread of food and drinks and for the last few minutes they'd been looking out over the field, drinking in silence.

"Congratulations." Powell walked up to them. "I think we've all been wondering what to say, but that's about it from me, anyway. The others will probably be over shortly. A little nervous, I expect they are."

"Nervous?" Moisan asked. "How do you mean?"

"You do understand that just by playing a violin solo you've put an entire battalion worth of people to sleep, don't you, Robert? You've preempted a battlefield, and saved probably a couple of thousand lives. And you've done it with what we have to say is magic, if not something more."

"Y-yes," said Moisan, "I hadn't thought about it that way until now. I'm still trying to accept the reality of it myself, I suppose."

"Right," said Powell, "so I think we're rather awed by it, is what I'm trying to say."

"But surely, not by me," said Moisan, embarrassed.

"By extension, yes, I'm afraid so. At least for the moment. Hopefully we all get over it soon. But I'm feeling that way myself right now."

"Oh."

After a pause Harry asked, "What did you mean when you said something more than magic?"

"Magic is just a thing people do," said Powell. "It's strange, frightening even, for people like us who aren't used to it. But in a sense it's not any more awesome than a locomotive or an aeroplane. I think it's not too hard to accept magic, once we learn the rules. But this time... I saw *her* again out there at the end. When you put them all to sleep at once."

"Rhiannon," said Harry. "We saw her too, or I did, anyway. Another vision."

"I wonder if the others did this time. It almost seemed to me she was out there in the distance, riding among the thralls, I mean."

"It wasn't so clear to me," said Harry. "Perhaps because we were out there ourselves. Did you actually see her on the field?"

Powell shook his head. "I suppose not really, not seen with my own eyes. I just well, *had that impression*, if you understand me. Like the memory of a dream, maybe."

"I'm sorry," said Moisan. "I did have a sense of, well, her presence, you might say, but I didn't really see anything myself until the end. I was too caught up in the playing."

"Well anyway," said Powell, "it seems to me that Rhiannon's presence, however it's perceived, whatever she is, it's more awesome and world-shaking than magic by itself. That's what I meant."

"Rhiannon is dead. She passed into Annwn long ago."

They all turned to see Nuada in a wheelchair, one with no back and a sort of shelf in front for him to lean on. He was being wheeled around by a kobold attendant, and Major Quirk was accompanying him.

Powell was taken aback. "Pardon me, sir? Your Highness?"

"I overheard the tail end of what you gentlemen were saying," said the Prince. "Is it true, Mr. Moisan? Do you believe your playing was inspired by Rhiannon?"

Moisan looked up. "Frankly your Highness, I can't say." He paused, then continued carefully. "But we have experienced some, ah, phenomena that seem to suggest something along those lines."

"I see."

"Sir," said Harry, "if I may ask. For us Rhiannon is a name out of old stories, out of myth. Who is she to you? What was she?"

"She was a goddess," said Nuada.

"Yes sir. I don't mean to be impertinent, but we don't know what that means."

"Do you not? But—Oh, yes." Nuada's puzzled look vanished, and he smiled. "I beg your pardon," he said, "I had forgotten that your womenfolk have been keeping all this a secret from you. I suppose I could ask you much the same thing about how your Christ can at the same time be a man and the universal God."

"I've never understood that myself, to be honest," said Harry. "But I imagine Lieutenant Buchanan can explain it."

"Gentlemen," said Major Quirk, "interesting as this philosophical discussion may be, I think we are out of time for it at present." He pointed east, past the line of machine guns. Just on the horizon, a flash of silvery light could be seen.

"What? Oh, the moonrise." Harry had been at the point of attributing the unexpected illumination to something magical, but it was just after the full and this was the proper time for a moonrise, dramatic as it may have been.

"No," said Major Quirk. "Not the moon. Nearer than that."

Harry blinked and lowered his gaze a little. Sure enough, he saw movement rather closer at hand, a group of men approaching perhaps half a mile away, silhouetted in the light of the rising moon.

Perhaps Major Quirk's presence had broken the hesitation that had prevented the other squadron officers from approaching them during this brief span, or perhaps it was just the urgency of the situation, but Captain Devlin came hustling towards them now followed by the other pilots.

"Sir," said Devlin, "they're coming."

CHAPTER 16
A STORM OF WINGS

"I see them," said Major Quirk. "Give me another flare, would you? This may be a parley of sorts."

"At last," said Devlin, fumbling in a pocket for a Very pistol and a flare. "Maybe now we'll finally find out what this is really all about."

He fired a white flare, and moments later the signal was answered by another pair of star shells from high above the aerodrome.

Harry looked out over the field. The shells were casting a harsh light which made every landscape feature stand out in stark relief. Many of the former thralls had been evacuated or had retreated under their own power, but hundreds were left on the flanks, some receiving aid from kobolds and their own people, while others were scattered here and there on the ground, still asleep or unconscious. The central approach to the aerodrome was clear, however, and it was on this path that the newcomers were approaching.

This was obviously no random collection of peasants. These fifty men were all dressed uniformly in ornate leather armor chased in gold. They wore identical black cloaks and their faces were concealed by polished bronze helmets with nasals and flaring cheek-guards that recalled some artifacts Harry had once seen in a collection from ancient Greece. They trotted stride for stride in close order, almost a phalanx, but instead of long spears and hoplite shields they wore bucklers and carried javelins in each hand, swords strapped to baldrics over their shoulders. In their midst a rider on a black horse, caparisoned in tattered black silk embroidered with gold thread.

Harry heard a sharp intake of breath from behind him and heard Nuada muttering something in Gaelic.

"The royal bodyguard of the Unseelie Court," said Nuada. "Or they used to be."

Powell asked, "They're not cavalry?"

"The Unseelie Court took pride in rejecting all our ways," said Nuada. "Among us only those of high birth ride. So for them horses were a symbol of something they wanted to be rid of."

"But then, who is that—"

"I don't know. But I think—I think I fear to learn."

This seemed to Harry to be so uncharacteristic of the forthright fairy lord that he turned to study Nuada. To his surprise, he saw the Prince had his head bowed and turned to the side, as if he was trying to avoid even looking at the scene.

Meanwhile the Unseelie warriors and their escort marched closer, paying no heed to the star shells drifting above them or to the thralls and kobolds to their left and right.

Harry saw Major Quirk whispering a few words to the kobold sergeant in charge of the machine guns, and then he stepped forward, apparently with the intention of crossing the line of guns to approach the oncoming troop. Devlin, not far away, had raised his hand and was saying something to the other pilots, several of whom had started forward as if to go with Quirk. And now Hammersmith, Quirk's batman, rushed forward grabbing his arm, and Harry could hear him say, "Sir, please, they have javelins! They haven't called for a parley yet. There's no herald on the field!"

"Thank you," said Quirk, "but I really must address them when they come. This whole campaign may hinge on what is said here. Stay back, now. I'm afraid this is no place for you." He patted the kobold's shoulder, and Hammersmith bowed his head and reluctantly let go of the major's arm. The major walked out past the guns—not far, just ten yards or so, but far enough to obviously represent a gesture at a parley.

The Unseelie troop was much closer now, only a hundred yards away, and Harry strained his eyes to study the rider. Despite the stark illumination from the star shells burning brightly overhead, the rider was hard to make out. He was cloaked not in embroidered black silk like the horse, but in some billowing stuff, particolored in black and gray, that made it impossible to pick out any fine details.

At fifty yards distance from the major's position, the entire troop came to an abrupt halt without any obvious orders being given, a perfect parade-ground maneuver. As one, they raised their javelins, and for a heart-stopping moment Harry thought they were going to throw them. But they merely clashed the metal spearheads together, making a brassy clanging sound that echoed throughout the field. In the silence that followed, the warriors stepped aside to left and right to allow the rider to move forward.

The horseman approached and as he neared, it became clear he was holding a long staff or branch, not a weapon.

Moisan let out a deep breath and at the same time Powell said quietly, "A staff, not a sword or a spear—this must be a parley after all."

"Halt!" The major's voice was as loud and clear as any that Harry had ever heard. He repeated the command in Gaelic. The rider came to a stop, but so smoothly the maneuver might have been planned, not executed in response to the instruction.

"You are brave, soldier of Man." The rider's voice was mellifluous, almost bell-like in its clarity, and carried as well as Quirk's.

"Does he mean the Isle of Man?" Powell whispered in his ear, "But how would he know?"

From behind him, Harry heard Nuada muttering something in Gaelic. It sounded like a prayer, and a desperate one at that. Glancing back for a moment, Harry saw that Nuada's eyes were clenched shut, his face was pale and strained, and he was shaking his head.

"No," he said then, "it can't be..."

But Major Quirk was speaking again, and Harry had no opportunity to ask Nuada what he meant.

"You know who I am? Perhaps you will be so kind as to reciprocate. But sir, you are the brave one." Quirk's voice was projected without effort or strain, and yet its volume was undiminished. "Indeed, you have delivered yourself into my hands," he said. "Have you come to parley, or to surrender?"

The rider laughed. The sound was beautiful and inhuman, and so loud as almost to be painful even at a distance. He whirled back his cloak and vaulted to the ground in an improbably graceful and acrobatic motion, landing more lightly than any ballet dancer. In that moment the cloak parted enough for Harry to see that the figure was female, wearing some kind of metallic corselet contoured to her figure.

"Jesus," said Powell, almost whispering, "a woman warrior in black and grey..."

"Oh no." Lambeth's voice was urgent. He'd been silent for some time, assuming a deferential and almost obsequious pose in Nuada's presence, but now he was speaking quickly, a hand on Harry's arm. "She's never been one to respect a peace. She could do anything. The major is in danger!"

"She? Who is she?"

Powell hissed, his voice as tense as Lambeth's. "The Morrígan. Or the Babd. One or the other of them, or both together maybe in one person. The goddess of war. The battle-crow. The bloody-handed nightmare queen herself."

From twenty yards away, the cloaked figure's head snapped around to point directly at their little group.

"I do declare," she said, her voice belling out, "someone has called my name." She held out her arm and extended her staff like a baton, pointing it straight at Powell. "Come forth, fili."

Powell stiffened, then he raised his head and strode forward.

"Sir," said Lambeth, "Please don't go. It's not safe!"

"I must," said Powell, and he walked on.

Harry made to follow him or to call him back, he wasn't sure which, but Moisan put a hand on his shoulder. "No," he said, "let him go. He may have immunity. She called him fili. It might mean she respects his status as a bard. Though how she knows who he is I don't know."

"*Might mean?*"

"I don't know for sure," said Moisan, "but if one tenth the stories about her are true, anyone else would be a fool to go out there now, even under our guns."

"But the major!"

"He's out there already. Going out after him won't help. Let's see what she says. We need to find out what's going on, after all."

Harry relaxed. What was he going to do out there, anyway? Even now it was unclear for what purpose these people had come, or if they were associated with the Shroud at all.

Major Quirk waited for Powell to join him, and the Morrígan seemed content to wait as well. When at last Powell stepped up beside the major, it was she who addressed him.

"So, fili, tell me how your people remember me."

Powell paused a moment, and when he replied, his voice too carried throughout the field, though he should have been barely audible at this distance. He gave no bow or salute, but addressed her directly.

"Madam, I do not merit that title. I am a mere student, and moreover I am a man of Gwynedd where tales of the Morrígan are not told. But I can relate what meager knowledge I have of the lore of Éire."

She curtsied, a surprisingly modern gesture.

"The tales are confused and contradictory in many respects," he said, "and they were all written down in Christian times, so their accuracy is dubious at best, if indeed they are not simply fabrications and fantasies. But all agree that the Morrígan is the goddess of war. Many sources tell that there are three such goddesses, sisters as may be, but others say there is only one. When three are named, one is always the Badb, the battle-crow. Other names are Nemain, and Macha, and Anann. It seems the chroniclers may perhaps have given a single person many names, or else to many people they gave a single name.

"Indeed," she said, "and what of my deeds?"

"The Morrigan is well known as Cuchulainn's doom," said Powell, "though in the Ulster cycle it is written that he bested her three times and defeated his enemies in battle despite her opposition. But in the end, it is said she wrought his death. They say she is never good luck to any man but always a bane of some sort, her appearance either foretelling a death in battle or something worse yet. In no story are her deeds entirely pure, and often they are vile."

He paused, but she didn't respond so he continued, "It is also said that in times long before Ulster, when the Tuatha de Danaan waged their war against the Fomorians, it was the Morrigan who won the day, either through deeds on the battlefield or by directing the course of the battle through prophecy. Before the war, the tale is that she took the Dagda himself as a lover and promised him the blood of the Fomorian king."

Here she laughed, softly it seemed, and yet as before her voice echoed throughout the field.

"As for her heritage," said Powell, "though many tales say the Morrigan is one of the Tuatha de Danaan, to the extent my limited mastery of the Irish lore permits me to express an opinion I have always doubted this account."

"Say on then, apprentice. Whence do I come?"

"I speak of mythology," he said, "not of real persons, such as you yourself must be."

She snorted but didn't otherwise interrupt, so he continued.

"In considering that old story of the war against the Fomorians, it occurred to me that the title Morrigan bears a certain similarity to the name of her ancient foes. Some scholars say the name means Sea-Queen, but they refer to the Brythonic word mor meaning the sea. And yet the name is Irish, and in the Goidelic tongues I believe the word mor is related to monster, or to nightmare. Hence the Fomorians are always depicted as monsters. And for this reason most scholars call the Morrigan the Nightmare Queen or the Phantom Queen. So I thought to doubt that the Morrigan was in fact of the line of Danu. Instead it seems to me most likely she was of the same blood as those she fought. Betrayal is said to be an attribute of the Morrigan, after all, as well as bloodlust and spite."

"An interesting speculation," she said. "And not entirely incorrect. Yet you are mistaken in one important particular, among many."

"Madam?"

"The word mor originally meant neither monster nor night-mare, but merely mare. And so my name is rightly Mare-Queen."

"What?" Powell was surprised. "But what about—" He shut his mouth.

"Perhaps you were about to say, poet of Gwynedd, what about Rhiannon? Rhiannon of the songbirds? Of the golden hair? Rhiannon the kind, the beautiful, the merciful?"

Powell said nothing.

"There, there," she said, reaching out a hand toward his face. Powell flinched, but didn't turn away. She touched his cheek. "It's all right. You can't offend me, little bard, with the name of a vanquished rival. I sent her down to Annwn with my own hands, you know. Her beating heart I plucked out of her soft-bosomed chest, and I bit into it like an apple and swallowed it down. I devoured her, Dafydd ap Powell! Even now, part of her is still within me! What do you say to that?"

Powell paled, but he answered strongly.

"First of all," he said, her hand still against his cheek, "my name is not Dafydd but David, and my father's name was Dylan. Whatever your sources of information, you are behind the times as regards the styles of our names, I'm afraid."

"It seems so, *David.*" Her voice was cold, disinterested.

"But if indeed you are telling the truth, Morrígan," said Powell, "and this is not, as it appears, the fantasy of a dis-ordered mind, then you are worse even than the tales made you out to be, and I will have no dealings with you."

He raised his hand to dislodge hers, but before he could act, she moved her hand down to his chin, holding onto his jaw, and this gesture seemed to paralyze the Welsh poet.

"Ha!" she said, "At last I am not in the third person any more. No more talk of the Morrígan and *her* and *she.* I wonder-ed for a while who it was you thought you were speaking to."

"Enough!" Major Quirk struck her hand away. "Get back, David," he said in an aside, "I'll deal with her now."

Harry heard a hissing intake of breath from Nuada, almost a gasp, and at the same time Lambeth cried out "No!" in a horrified voice.

The Morrígan, if indeed that was her true identity, whirled in a violent motion. Harry was sure that a deadly attack had been aimed at the major. But in mid-action she somehow arrested her movement, stopping still as a statue, her hand an out-stretched claw, her staff raised. And then she relaxed.

"No," she muttered, head bowed and turned slightly, as if

speaking in an aside to someone else, though her words still carried over an unnatural distance. "No, I must not—Yes, yes, I understand. Premature. There's still a chance..."

Her voice tailed off, and she turned to face Major Quirk, lowering her hands. Before she could speak again, though, he advanced on her, leaving Powell a few paces behind. To Harry, it seemed that Major Quirk was towering over the woman who called herself the Morrigan, though at the same time he was aware that nothing had really changed.

"I have no time for mythology," said the major, his voice as cold, cutting and full of authority as any Harry had ever heard. "Call yourself Morrigan or Marigold, it's all the same to me. Now is the time to explain your presence here. Are you of the Shroud? Why have you come?"

The woman spread her arms wide, almost as if to embrace him. "No time for mythology?" Her voice was full of affected wonder. "You say this here and now? Gazing so sternly down at me with Arthur's cold eyes? Speaking so harshly in his very voice of command? Don't you know where you are, soldier of Man? Don't you know what you are becoming?"

"Answer my questions," he said. "You are in deadly peril if you do not."

"Oh oh, deadly peril! I am all aquiver now. It's been long and long since I was spoken to that way. The last time may well have been by your namesake. It would be well to remember what happened to *him*. But of course, I have come to answer your questions. What other reason could there be?"

Major Quirk said nothing.

"To address your first question," she said, "I am not of the Shroud; the Shroud is of me. You gallant pilots have been shooting down my poisonous children for a sennight and more, and my pretty little hornets as well. That was a well-aimed stroke, I must say. I had hoped for better of those insects. But I'm afraid the period of grace is about to come to an end."

"For what reason—"

"Hush," she said, and for all the power in his voice a moment before, the woman spoke over Major Quirk and silenced him. "And as for the second question, I have come to repair a grievous error. A mistake we have jointly shared."

She turned away from Major Quirk, toward the line of machine guns and the other listeners.

"Listen, men of the six nations," she said, "the gods love you, even as they despise the weaklings and the failures of this shadow world. A sacrifice was required of these pathetic creatures, one which would have spared the lives of a myriad of myriads in your own world. A trifling price to be paid by mere thousands of worthless thralls. And yet you have foolishly interfered with our plan, and thus condemned millions in your own world."

"We've grown beyond the need for human sacrifice," said Major Quirk.

"Have you now, indeed? What do you call the dead of the Marne, of Verdun, of the Somme, and of Ypres? What will you call the dead who fall in the coming year, and in the years to come?"

Major Quirk was silent for a moment. Then he said, "I'm surprised to hear the Morrígan speaking of the futility of battle."

"And who better? I, who perched on a rafter in the Roman Curia when Cato called for war, and who soared on the hot winds rising above Carthage as it burned. I who drank mare's milk mixed with blood fresh from the teat at Baghdad as mighty Temujin piled up a mountain of skulls. I who plucked the eyes from the corpses of the Light Brigade at Balaclava. Come now, soldier of Man, who better than I?"

"So what is your remedy?" he asked.

"As I said, a trifling price to pay. These thralls here, whom you have foolishly freed from their servitude. The mere act of freeing them has diminished their value as scapegoats, reduced the burdens of malice they carry. But even so, their deaths will still serve to save many lives in your own world."

"You ask us to kill innocent people on the strength of your word?" Major Quirk shook his head. "Don't be ridiculous."

The woman calling herself the Morrígan laughed.

"Oh no," she said at last, "you are mistaken, my darling man. I know you wouldn't do it, not even if you believed my words. You are far too noble, are you not, *Arthur*? So noble as to plunge your world into decades of darkness, terror and chaos for the sake of keeping your hands clean."

Quirk tried to speak then, but she rode over him again.

"No," she said, "it won't be your problem. But my hands are ever red with blood, and as another of your bards once pointed out, the stain will never be washed away. After so many millions, another few thousand is of no particular account. There would have been more value in their deaths if you'd cut these thralls down when you had the chance, but it's too late now. So rest easy, soldier of Man. We shall kill them for you."

And then she raised her staff, and shook it gently. To Harry's vast surprise it *chimed* as if it was a glass bell or perhaps a tuning fork.

"Mon Dieu," said Moisan, beside him, "it's the bell branch!"

Harry wanted to ask what he meant, but in that moment, he found he could no longer move. Everyone on the field was motionless as if frozen in time, men, kobolds, and fairies alike. Or almost everyone.

"Ha," said the Morrígan, "the Dagda was worthless as a cocksman, but his little wand has power still."

She thrust the staff in the earth, where it flowered, bringing forth twigs and leaves even as Harry watched.

"So," she said, "if there are no further objections…"

She paused, and appeared to be savoring the moment.

"Let the killing begin!"

Ever since the Morrígan had advanced to parley with Major Quirk, her guardsmen had maintained their salute, holding as still as statues. But now that everyone else was frozen in place, they began to move, dropping their javelins and drawing leaf-shaped bronze swords from their baldrics. They broke their ranks and some began stalking towards the thralls on the flanks who had not yet been removed beyond the lines of machine guns, while others moved toward the guns themselves. What-ever this magic was, it seemed that the touch of iron had no power to break the spell as even the kobolds manning the mac-hine guns in their steel helmets were paralyzed.

Out of the corner of his eye, Harry could just make out Moisan, frozen beside him. To the right and a step in front of him was Lambeth, also unable to move. The whole field was trapped in amber except for the Morrígan and her men.

Harry tried to move, to act, to take a step, but all he achieved was a palsied trembling in his limbs. He couldn't even close his eyes to block out the sight of what was about to happen. It would only be half a minute until the first of the swordsmen had reached a thrall. He tried again to move, failed.

Then he saw it. Lambeth's hand had jerked forward a spasmodic inch before stopping. Harry could sense the kobold's straining effort to free himself. He'd managed to overcome the spell or whatever it was, at least for an instant. Harry wished he could help somehow, and then he remembered the moment when he'd somehow aided Moisan's playing not long before. He'd placed a hand on his back. And Lambeth was right there a yard away—but he couldn't move. He made another desperate attempt, but still with no success. Lambeth was frozen, too, unable to do anything more on his own. And the swordsmen were nearing the thralls. Harry was desperate, and at last he recalled the kobold razor, still in his pocket.

It was a feeble hope, as steel wasn't helping the kobolds themselves with their steel helmets and their hands on their steel machine guns. But Lambeth had broken the paralysis, just for a moment. Perhaps the combination of steel and effort—

And what the hell. *Rhiannon,* he thought, *you, your power, whatever, you aided us before. Please...* And he remembered how Moisan's playing had sounded, recalled the image of the hillside, the rider on the white horse, the feeling of warmth... So slowly, as if moving through gelatin, he saw his hand moving toward his pocket... And he touched the folded blade through the fabric.

With the contact, he lurched forward. He pulled the razor out, slapped the hand holding the folded blade up against the kobold's back. Lambeth took a convulsive, staggering step, and Harry too almost fell, but then they both recovered themselves. Everyone else on the field was still frozen. Harry realized the ringing in his ears was gone now. The resonance of the bell branch had faded, and all he heard was a faint drone—engines from the aeroplanes circling high above.

"Sir! What should we do?"

Harry thought fast. Even if they both manned one of the machine guns, the Unseelie Court swordsmen had dispersed too far to shoot them all, and in moments they would be in amongst the thralls. The Morrígan was still standing close by Major Quirk and Powell. Perhaps it would be possible to take a shot. But the danger... Was there some way to distract her?

"Take the razor," said Harry. "It seems to have helped, somehow. Try to break the spell on the machine gunners," he said, "but don't shoot unless the way is clear or there's no other choice. I have one thing to try, first."

"Yes, sir!"

Harry raced the few steps forward to Captain Devlin's side, and he was aware Lambeth was trying to free one of the machine gunners from his paralysis. He slapped his hand down on Devlin's shoulder, but there was no effect; the man stayed as rigidly frozen as before. He started digging frantically into the captain's pockets. There was the flare gun. Would the damn thing not come out? He ripped at Devlin's pocket lining, pulled the pistol out, scattering several flares to the ground. Christ! Which one was red? There!

Harry looked up, fumbling to load a flare into the Very pistol. The Morrígan had as yet paid them no attention; she seemed to be engrossed in directing the swordsmen. One had his sword raised over the body of a sleeping thrall...

"Sandraudiga!" At Lambeth's shout the Morrígan's head whipped around and swordsmen all across the field froze in place. Harry turned to look. Lambeth had been unable to rouse any of the other kobolds. But his sleeve was peeled back, and now he cut his bare left arm with the razor. Immediately a flow of blood came forth, and he held his hand down so that it would drip to the ground.

"Sandraudiga," he called out again.

"Who calls on Sandraudiga?" asked the Morrígan, stalking forward a little ways. Good, she had separated from the major and Powell.

Lambeth recited something first in what must be his native tongue, something like German, and then he repeated it in English. "Lady of the red earth, lady of the black iron, aid us now!"

The Morrígan turned now to face Lambeth directly. "Sandraudiga? *You* call on *her*?" She laughed.

Lambeth was obviously petrified with fear, but he managed to speak.

"Y-yes," he said, "our mother, our creator. Please..."

"You pathetic failure!" she said, "You weak, stupid little queer. You *idiot*! Who do you think Sandraudiga is?"

"What?" Lambeth was shocked.

"Oh, this is too much," she said, laughing again. "Have you not the faintest clue, even now? I suppose I should make things clear for you worthless creatures, too."

The Morrígan flung back her black and grey cloak over her shoulders, where it seemed to vanish completely. And now she looked quite different from before. She had been a lithe young woman in burnished mail, but now she was gaunt and tall, grey-haired, and completely nude. It seemed she was standing on a patch of blood-soaked ground, visibly red even in the light of the star shell. She was holding an iron sickle in one hand and her other hand was dripping blood, just as was Lambeth's.

"With these bloody hands," she said, "I plucked your forebears from my own womb. With this sickle I cut the cords. My greatest failure, it galls me to say. You were supposed to be mighty warriors, wielding iron to reap the ranks of the pawns of this wretched shadow world. But you never did like the sight of blood, did you? Wayland's seed was weak, and his children perverse. I wanted you to slaughter your way through the ranks of the Courts, but no, you'd rather spend your time buggering one another instead. I would have eliminated the lot of you, long ago, but for—Well, a use was found for you in the end, wasn't it?"

"No!" Lambeth was horrified. He paled, and fell to his knees.

"Oh yes," said the ghastly woman. And somehow she reached back and swirled her vanished cloak around her again, and once more she was the Morrígan, clad in mail.

Harry fired the Very pistol. A red flare arced up over the field, settling not far from the Morrígan's feet, smoking and giving off a harsh red light that made the earth around her once more look as if it had been drenched with blood.

"What now," she said irritably, turning toward Harry. "You too? And how did *you* break free of the Dagda's spell?" She reached out a finger and tapped the planted staff.

Once more a bell sounded (though Harry thought it was weaker than before), and again he and Lambeth were frozen in place like everyone else. This time he had no razor in his hand, and the steel flare gun didn't help at all.

"I smell that blonde bitch's work here," said the Morrígan, "but no matter. The little that's left of her in the world will work no more mischief. I'll make sure of that. But first to our business."

The Morrígan raised her hand, and once more the Unseelie Court swordsmen moved forward, lifting their swords. But then she paused, a look of annoyance on her face. Yet again the swordsmen halted their motion.

"What is that noise?"

The droning sound was growing louder. The Morrígan looked wildly around for a few seconds, then at last looked up.

"Ridiculous," she said, and the line of bullets from Jernigan's diving S.E.5a punched into her body, hammering her into the earth. The tracers walked forward inexorably, just missing Major Quirk and moving onwards. The aeroplane had been invisible in the darkness above the guttering star shell flares during its descent but now its presence was obvious, a great roaring winged shape pulling up barely in time to avoid hitting the ground.

Harry was still frozen in place, unable to move. He wanted to cheer, but then he saw the Morrígan pick herself up and struggle to her feet. Several bloody holes had been punched through her corselet but she was still able to laugh, despite the injuries.

"Very nice," she said, pausing to cough and spit out a gout of blood, "but not good enough." She grinned, started once more to laugh, and now a double line of tracers appeared from above, Buchanan's Sopwith Camel following Jernigan's diving path. Once again bullets plowed into the Morrígan's body, and this time the double line of tracers continued onwards, smashing into the planted staff, shattering it into splinters. The Camel zoomed upwards in turn, also barely avoiding a collision, and once again the Morrígan struggled back to her feet. Her left arm had been shot off at the elbow, and her head was missing a big chunk above the right eye, but still she was laughing.

At that moment the paralysis that had seized Harry broke, and he lurched forward. Everyone on the field staggered at once. Lambeth fell prone to the ground from his frozen kneeling position, and Harry saw Moisan rushing toward him.

"Well struck," said the Morrígan, "but still—"

"Fire," said Major Quirk, and grabbed Powell's arm. The two of them dove for cover.

A dozen machine guns opened up, and twelve streams of tracers converged on their target. The Morrígan was smashed down a third time to the earth, but the firing didn't stop; the gunners lowered their aim and their bullets ploughed up the ground, raising a cloud of pulverized earth that obscured the scene. Nothing more could be seen of the Morrígan, but after a moment her laughter resumed, though it sounded now more like cawing and shrieking. The sound wasn't coming from her location anymore but had arisen from a number of positions all around the field. At first Harry thought the laughter was coming from the throats of the still-motionless swordsmen, but then he realized many of the voices were from coming from too far away and from the wrong direction entirely.

"Oh, well struck, you fools," called out the Morrígan's voice, coming in a monstrous chorus from dozens of throats all at the same time. "But there are still sacrifices left to make. What the Unseelie Court failed to offer up, the Seelie Court may yet provide. I would have spared them before, but now the Shroud will take them too. And you as well. Soon I will rise again from the cauldron, but all of you will sink into Annwn forever!"

Over the hammering of the guns, Harry heard a storm of wings beating, and all around he saw dark forms flying up into the night sky. A murder of crows. Now he understood where the voices had been coming from. At that moment the fifty Unseelie Court swordsmen all collapsed to the ground at once, like puppets with their strings cut.

The next few minutes were chaotic. Major Quirk's first orders were to secure the fallen swordsmen, but it was soon discovered that all were dead, with no obvious wounds. Lacking any other gainful employment, Harry shooed peasants away from the shallow trench along the side of the airfield into which petrol was being pumped to guide the returning pilots. This didn't take long, and when it was done, the trench ignited, and a green flare shot off to summon the fliers for landing, he rejoined the other officers finding Moisan at the center of a group of men.

"There you are, Harry," said Powell, slapping him on the back. "I saw you shoot off that flare when the rest of us were paralyzed. Saved the day, I think."

"Oh, well. I was lucky to break free of that, what was it you called it, Robert?"

"The bell branch," said Moisan, "out of Irish mythology, I believe. Do you know the story, David?"

"Yes," said Powell, "just as *she* said, a gift of the Dagda in the old story of Cormac. Had the power to put people to sleep, but I guess that wasn't quite right."

"Close enough," said O'Meara, "but Jesus, man, that's a lot to digest. All she said, I mean. And what happened. Magic is one thing, but this—no one would believe it. What are we going to do about this, now?"

"First thing, gentleman, will be to write up detailed reports." Major Quirk had just joined the group. "She told us a lot, and a lot happened, just as Brian said. And I don't want to lose a word of it. Assuming nothing else earth-shaking happens overnight, we'll fly patrols as usual tomorrow, but there will be a council of war at noon. I expect to have your reports well before then. God knows what my own report back to headquarters will look like."

Amid the chorus of yessirs, Powell spoke up.

"Major," he said, "if you don't mind my saying so, I'm amazed at the way you stood up to the Morrigan. You faced down a goddess. I don't think I've ever been so relieved as when you knocked her hand away from me like that. I was completely helpless out there."

"Not so," said Major Quirk. "You told her off yourself, as I recall."

The major addressed the other pilots. "But there's plenty of praise to go around, I'm sure. Ryan, I'm afraid it's going to be a late night for both of us, but the rest of you might as well take off until morning. Well, wait for Jernigan and Buchanan, anyway. I'm sure they'll want to hear the story, since they probably have no idea what just happened."

The major turned away to the half dozen kobold NCOs who

were waiting for orders. In the lull that followed, Harry approached Moisan.

"How are you feeling, Robert?"

"I don't even know," said Moisan. "Dizzy, I suppose. Very tired, too. So much has happened, and half of it I can barely comprehend, much less explain. Perhaps it will make sense tomorrow."

"I hope so," said Harry. "But this is all so crazy... Hey, what happened to Lambeth? Is he all right?"

"Merde! I lost track of him. I helped him bandage his arm, but then, I forget—Oh, yes, I had to report to Major Quirk, and —I don't know where he is. Poor fellow, it can't be easy to learn your goddess is a monster. Let's see if we can find him."

The first few kobolds they asked didn't know where he was, but then Harry spotted the major's batman, Hammersmith, re-turning from an errand. When asked, he turned his head and looked east past the line of guns, now no longer manned. "Out there, I expect," he said.

"Oh hell," said Harry, "that can't be good."

"Agreed."

They walked out onto the field. With the star-shells gone and full dark come, the moon was the main source of illumination. The meadowland by moonlight would ordinarily have been a beautiful scene, but tonight the flowers were trampled and there was debris everywhere, rags and scraps left over from the passage of almost 2,000 former thralls who were now in the process of establishing a tent city on the far side of the aerodrome.

"There he is."

It was the scene of the confrontation, and of the Morrígan's ignominious defeat. The ground was torn up and the lawn was gone in a five yard circle, chewed up by bullets. There was no sign of the Morrígan's remains whatsoever except for a reddish stain perfusing the muddy ground. This impossibility would have stood out for Harry except that tonight it was lost in a sea of even less likely phenomena.

Lambeth was there, sitting on the ground. His left sleeve had been torn up to use as a bandage for his arm, and with the hand that had been dripping blood only a few minutes before, he was dabbling idly at the red earth. Periodically another kobold would appear, pause and look at Lambeth, tentatively approach the circle of blood-stained earth, and bend over to touch it before retreating, all without saying a word.

"Hey, Lambeth." Harry was a little dismayed at how his voice sounded in his own ears. Stupidly hearty and jocose, he thought.

"Sir." The kobold's voice was flat and distant.

"I know this can't be easy—" He stopped. "Oh, hell. What can I say at all?"

Harry sat down beside his batman. There was an unpleasant metallic smell coming from the blood-soaked earth in the circle. After a moment, Moisan sat down on the kobold's other side.

"Sir—Sirs, what are you doing?" There was some animation in his voice now.

"We've been looking for you, Lambeth," said Harry. "You were a hero out there, you know."

"I was?"

"Putting aside the fact you convinced Robert to go on with his playing before, and saved a couple of thousand lives that way. Out there with the Morrígan. We were all paralyzed. Those Unseelie Court swordsmen were going to start killing the thralls. They might have gone on to kill us too. I felt like there was nothing I could do about it at all. And then I saw you move, just an inch, and I realized it was stupid to stop fighting."

"Oh. I remember now. There was a—a woman, I think, and she was holding out her hand. Her fingers touched me, and I could move again."

"Yes, and then you distracted the Morrígan for a few crucial seconds. There wouldn't have been enough time for the aeroplanes otherwise before the swordsmen started killing. And even if there had been, they probably would have shot down Powell and Major Quirk as well, except you drew her away."

"Did I do that?"

"Indeed you did," said Moisan. "You have no idea how happy I was there, when I saw you and Harry break free from that bell branch spell. Somehow, I knew things would work out, then. It would have been too horrible for us to succeed with the thralls and then have that monster kill them anyway."

"But—that monster, you call her, she's—"

"Oh hell," said Harry, "I can't even pretend to imagine how that must feel. But remember she said she created your people to be warriors?"

"Yes. I suppose this is the true red earth right here. The red of blood, not iron ore at all. Just as you said the other day, sir."

"Damn it, that's not the point," said Harry. "I mean, the Unseelie Court wanted you to fight for them. You all could have done so enthusiastically, like *she* wanted, too. But you chose not to, didn't you? You rejected that path for yourselves."

"Y-yes. I suppose we did."

"She said it was weakness, but it sounds like strength to me. But let's say the Morrigan was telling the truth about everything, even though there's no way to be sure about any of it. So what? Your life is your own, after all."

"Sir, sirs, I mean—You're being very kind. Why are you going to such trouble?"

"For heaven's sake," said Moisan, "why do you think?"

"Uh—" The kobold looked down, embarrassed.

"Come on," said Harry, "before this gets too sentimental. Between the three of us, we've shed too much blood and tears already today. Probably best to put an end to it for now, don't you think?"

They got to their feet, and walked back to the aerodrome, pausing at the point where their paths diverged, towards the cottage and the underground level.

"Is there anything else I can do for you tonight, sirs?"

"Not aside from getting some sleep," said Moisan. "We'll talk more about what this all means tomorrow."

"Oh," said the kobold, "I almost forgot. Your razor, sir."

Harry took the razor, and grasped the kobold's hand. "Thank you, Lambeth," he said.

♍   ♍   ♍

Back in their cottage.

"Lambeth really was a hero, though, wasn't he?"

"Yes, he was," said Moisan, "as were you, and I too, I suppose."

"Jesus yes," said Harry, "you especially. Jernigan and Buchanan, of course. No idea how they knew what to do from just that flare, or how they did it. And Powell for standing up to her like that. And the major. He was like a god out there, wasn't he?"

"Yes. I want to think about that some more, though."

"What? What do you mean?"

"Never mind for now. Tomorrow."

"Right. Tomorrow."